"A passionate love too long denied drives the action in this multifaceted, emotionally rich reunion story that overflows with breathtaking sexual chemistry."
—*Library Journal* on *McKettricks of Texas: Tate*

"This is a delightful story of two people who should be together, but whom circumstances have pulled apart. Watching them find their way back to each other is both heartwrenching and satisfying, because Miller crafts amazing, deep characters who tug at readers' heartstrings. Thoroughly entertaining!"
—*RT Book Reviews* on *McKettricks of Texas: Tate*

"Miller's fast-moving, emotional contemporary romance continues the McKettricks series' plotlines, with more installments to come."
—*Booklist* on *McKettricks of Texas: Garrett*

"[Miller's] subtle blend of sensuality, chivalry, and the clear roles of her men and women create charming romances. The McKettrick brothers are sexy gentleman with Stetsons. Whether they're from 1810 or 2010, Linda Lael Miller's cowboys are timeless."
—*JoyfullyReviewed.com* on *McKettricks of Texas: Garrett*

"*McKettricks of Texas: Garrett* is a fitting addition to the... well-written McKettrick novels from Miller. This one will not disappoint either old fans or new."
—*The Romance Reader*

"The tale of Austin McKettrick...is completely wonderful. Austin's interactions with Paige are fun and lively and the mystery that began in Tate's story ends with Austin's love story and adds quite a suspenseful punch."
—*RT Book Reviews* on *McKettricks of Texas: Austin*

LINDA LAEL MILLER

McKettricks of Texas:
GARRETT

CANARY STREET PRESS

CANARY
STREET
PRESS™

Recycling programs
for this product may
not exist in your area.

ISBN-13: 978-1-335-99947-4

McKettricks of Texas: Garrett

First published in 2010. This edition published in 2024.

For questions and comments about the quality of this book, please contact us at CustomerService@Harlequin.com.

TM is a trademark of Harlequin Enterprises ULC.

Canary Street Press
22 Adelaide St. West, 41st Floor
Toronto, Ontario M5H 4E3, Canada
CanaryStPress.com

Printed in U.S.A.

Dear Reader,

Welcome back to Blue River, Texas—home of the McKettricks!

Garrett is the second brother, and the second book, in this trilogy about modern-day McKettrick men. These three Texas-bred brothers—Tate, Garrett and Austin— meet their matches in the Remington sisters. Political troubleshooter Garrett and drama teacher Julie are as different as two people can be, but opposites have a way of attracting!

These stories give me a chance to bring together some of my favorite things: Western settings, cowboys and ranches, romance… Not to mention kids and animals!

Speaking of animals, I want to make my usual plug for them. My cats, dogs and horses have always been an important part of my life, and I'm sure the same is true for you. Let's make sure every pet is a wanted pet; spay and neuter—and encourage others to be equally responsible. Animals bring so much love into our world, and we owe them the best care we can give them in return.

Please visit my website, lindalaelmiller.com, for information on upcoming books, contests, my (almost) daily blog and more. And please feel free to leave your own comments!

Now, saddle up, and let's head out to Blue River, where the sky is endless and the land seems to go on forever. The people in this friendly town invite you to join them for a visit…

With love,

For Jeremy Hargis
with love

CHAPTER ONE

GARRETT MCKETTRICK WANTED a horse under him—a fleet cow pony like the ones bred to work the herds on the Silver Spur Ranch. But for now, anyway, the Porsche would have to do.

Because of the hour—it was a little after 3:00 a.m.—Garrett had that particular stretch of Texas highway all to himself. The moon and stars cast silvery shadows through the open sunroof and shimmered on the rolled-up sleeves of his white dress shirt, while a country oldie, with lots of twang, pounded from the sound system. Everything in him—from the nuclei of his cells outward—vibrated to the beat.

He'd left the tuxedo jacket, the cummerbund, the tie, the fancy cuff links, back in Austin—right along with one or two of his most cherished illusions.

The party was definitely over—for him, anyhow.

He should have seen it coming—or at least listened to people who *did* see it coming, specifically his brothers, Tate and Austin. They'd done their best to warn him.

Senator Morgan Cox, they'd said, in so many words and in their different ways, wasn't what he seemed.

Against his will, Garrett's mind looped back a few hours, and even as he sped along that straight, dark ribbon of road, another part of him relived the shock in excruciating detail.

Cox had always presented himself as a family man, in public and private. A corner of each of his hand-carved antique desks in both the Austin and Washington offices supported a small forest of framed photos—himself and Nan on their wedding day, himself and Nan and the first crop of kids, himself and Nan and *more* kids, some of whom were adopted and had special needs. Altogether, there were nine Cox offspring.

The dogs—several generations of golden retrievers, all rescued, of course—were pictured as well.

That night, with no warning at all, Garrett's longtime boss and mentor had arrived at an important fundraiser, held in a glittering hotel ballroom, but not with Nan on his arm—elegant, articulate, wholesome Nan, with her own pedigree as a former Texas governor's daughter. Oh, no. This powerful U.S. senator, a war hero, a man with what many people considered a straight shot at the White House, had instead escorted a classic bimbo, later identified as a twenty-two-year-old pole dancer who went by the unlikely name of Mandy Chante.

Before God, his amazed supporters, the press and, worst of all, Nan, the senator proceeded to announce that he and Mandy were soul mates. Kindred spirits. They'd been lovers in a dozen other lifetimes, he rhapsodized. In short, Cox explained from the microphone on the dais—his lover hovering earnestly beside him in a long, form-fitting dress rippling with ice-blue sequins, which gave her the look of a mermaid with feet—he hoped everyone would understand.

He had to follow his heart.

If only the senator's *heart* were the organ he was following, Garrett lamented silently.

One of those freeze-frame silences followed, vast

and uncomfortable, turning the whole assembly into a garden of stone statues while several hundred people tried to process what they'd just heard Cox say.

Who *was* this guy, they were probably asking themselves, and what had he done with the Morgan Cox they all knew? Where, Garrett himself wondered, was the man who had given that stirring eulogy at the double funeral after Jim and Sally McKettrick, his folks, were killed a decade before?

The mass paralysis following Morgan's proclamation lasted only a few seconds, and Garrett was quick to shake it off. Automatically, he scanned the room for Nan Cox—his late mother's college roommate—and found her standing near the grand piano, alone.

Most likely, Nan, a veteran political wife, had been in transit between one conversational cluster and another when her husband dropped the bombshell. She was still smiling, in fact, and the effect was eerie, even surreal.

Like the true lady she was, however, Nan immediately drew herself up, made her way through friends and strangers, enemies and intimate confidants to step up to Garrett's side, link her arm with his and whisper, "Get him out of here, Garrett. Get Morgan out of here *now*, before this gets any worse."

Garrett glanced at the senator, who ignored his wife of more than three decades, the mother of his children, the flesh-and-blood, hurting woman he had just humiliated in a very public way, to gaze lovingly into the upturned face of his mistress. The mermaid's plump, glistening lower lip jutted out in a pout.

Cox patted the young woman's hand reassuringly then, acting as though *she*, not Nan, might have been traumatized.

The cameras came out, amateur and professional; a blinding dazzle surrounded the happy couple. Within a couple of minutes, some of that attention would surely shift to Nan.

"I'm getting *you* away first," Garrett told Nan, using his right arm to lock her against his side and starting for the nearest way out. As the senator's aide, Garrett had a lot of experience at running interference, and he always scoped out every exit in every venue in advance, just in case. Even the familiar ones, like that hotel, which happened to be the senator's favorite.

Nan didn't argue—not then, anyway. She kept up with Garrett, offered no protest when he hustled her through a corridor crowded with carts and waitstaff, then into a service elevator.

Garrett flipped open his cell phone and speed-dialed a number as they descended, Nan leaning against the elevator wall now, looking down at her feet, stricken to silence. Her beautifully coiffed silver hair gleamed in the fluorescent light.

The senator's personal driver, Troy, answered on the first ring, his tone cheerful. "Garrett? What's up, man?"

"Bring the car around to the back of the hotel," Garrett said. "And hurry."

Nan looked up, met Garrett's gaze. She was pale, and her eyes looked haunted, but the smile resting on her mouth was real, if slight. "You're probably scaring poor Troy to death," she scolded, putting a hand out for the cell phone.

Garrett handed it over just as they reached the ground floor, and Nan spoke efficiently into the mouthpiece.

"Troy? This is Mrs. Cox. Just so you know, there's no fire, and nobody's been shot or had a heart attack.

But it probably *is* a good idea for me to leave the building, so be a dear and pick me up behind the hotel." A pause. "Oh, you are? Perfect. I'll explain in the car. Meanwhile, here's Garrett again."

With that, she handed the phone back to Garrett.

When he put it to his ear, he heard Troy suck in a nervous breath. "I'm outside the kitchen door, buddy," he said. "I'll take Mrs. Cox home and come straight back, in case you need some help."

"Excellent idea," Garrett said, as the elevator doors opened into the institution-sized kitchen.

The senator's wife smiled and nodded to a bevy of surprised kitchen workers as she and Garrett headed for the outside door.

True to his word, Troy was waiting in back, the rear passenger-side door of the sedan already open for Mrs. Cox.

He and Garrett exchanged glances as Nan slipped into the backseat, but neither of them spoke.

Troy closed her door, but she immediately lowered the window.

"My husband needs your help," she told Garrett quietly but firmly. "This is no time to judge him—there will be enough of that in the media."

"Yes, ma'am," Garrett answered.

Troy climbed behind the wheel again, and Garrett was already heading back through the kitchen door when they pulled away.

He strode to the service elevator, pushed the button and waited until it lumbered down from some upper floor.

When the doors slid open, there were the senator and the bimbo.

The senator blinked when he saw Garrett. He looked older somehow, and he was wearing his glasses. *"There* you are," he said. "I was wondering where you'd gotten to, young McKettrick. Nan, too. Have you seen my wife?"

Nan's remark, spoken only a minute or two before, echoed in Garrett's mind.

My husband needs your help.

And juxtaposed to that, the senator's oddly solicitous, *Have you seen my wife?*

Garrett made an attempt at a smile, but it felt like a grimace instead. He narrowed his eyes slightly, shot a glance at the mermaid and then faced the senator again. "Mrs. Cox is on her way home, sir," he said.

"I imagine she was upset," Cox replied, looking both regretful and detached.

"She's a lady, sir," Garrett answered evenly. "And she's behaving like one."

Cox gave a fond chuckle and nodded. "First, last and always, Nan is a lady," he agreed.

Beside him, the mermaid seethed, clinging a little more tightly to the senator's arm and glaring at Garrett.

Garrett glared right back. This woman, he decided, was no mermaid, and no lady, either. She was a barracuda.

"It would seem I haven't chosen the best time to break our news to the world, my dear," the senator said, patting his beloved's bejeweled and manicured hand in the same devoted way he'd done upstairs. "I probably should have told Nan in private."

Ya think? Garrett asked silently.

"You work for Senator Cox," said the barracuda, turning to Garrett, "*not* his wife. Why did you just go off and leave us—him—*stranded* like that? The reporters—"

Garrett folded his arms and waited.

"It was awful!" blurted the barracuda.

What had the woman expected? Champagne all around? Congratulatory kisses and handshakes? A romantic waltz with the senator while the orchestra played "Moon River"?

"Luckily," the senator told Garrett affably, as though there had been no outburst from the sequined contingent, "I remembered how often you and I had discussed security measures, and Mandy and I were able to slip away and find the nearest service elevator."

The corridor seemed to be closing in on Garrett. He undid his string tie and opened the top three buttons of his shirt. "Mandy?" he asked.

The senator laughed warmly. "Mandy Chante," he said, "meet Garrett McKettrick, my right-hand man."

"Mandy Chante," Garrett repeated, with no inflection at all.

Mandy's eyes blazed. "What are we supposed to do now?" she demanded.

"I guess that depends on the senator's wishes," Garrett said mildly. "Will you be going home to the ranch tonight, sir, or staying in town?"

Or maybe I could just drop you off at the nearest E.R. for psychiatric evaluation.

"I'm sure Nan will be at the condo," the senator mused. "Our showing up there could be awkward."

Awkward. Yes, indeed, Senator, that would be awkward.

Garrett cleared his throat. "Could I speak to you alone for a moment, sir?" he asked.

Mandy, with one arm already resting in the crook of the senator's elbow, intertwined the fingers of both hands to get a double grip. "Pooky and I have no secrets from each other," she said.

Pooky?

Garrett's stomach did a slow roll.

"Now, now, dear," Cox told Mandy, gently freeing himself from her physical hold, at least. "Garrett means well, and you mustn't feel threatened." Addressing Garrett next, the older man added, "This is not a good time for a discussion. I'd rather not leave Mandy standing alone in this corridor."

"Sir—"

"Tomorrow, Garrett," the senator said. "You and I will discuss this tomorrow, in my office."

Garrett merely nodded, clamping his back teeth together.

"It's weird down here," Mandy complained, looking around. "Weird and spooky. Couldn't we get a suite or something?"

"That's a fine idea," Cox replied ebulliently. There was more hand-patting, and then the senator turned to face Garrett again. "You'll take care of that for us, won't you, Garrett? Book a suite upstairs, I mean? Under your own name, of course, and not mine."

"Sure," Garrett answered wearily, thinking of Nan and the many kids and the faithful golden retrievers. Pointing out to his employer that nobody would be fooled by the suite-booking gambit would probably be futile.

"Good," the senator said, satisfied.

"Do we have to wait here while he gets us a room, Pooky?" Mandy whined. "I don't like this place. It's like a cellar or something."

Cox smiled at her, and his tone was soothing. "The press will be watching the lobby for us," he said reasonably. "And we won't have to wait long, because Garrett will be quick. Won't you, Garrett?"

Bile scalded the back of Garrett's throat. "I'll be quick," he answered.

That was when he started wanting the horse under him. He wanted to hear hooves pounding over hard ground and breathe the clean, uncomplicated air of home.

Duty first.

He went upstairs, arranged for comfortable quarters at the reception desk, and called the senator's personal cell phone when he had a room number to give him.

"Here's Troy, back again," the senator said on the other end of the call, sounding pleased. "I'm sure he wouldn't mind escorting us up there. If you'd just get us some ice before you leave, Garrett—"

Garrett closed his eyes, refrained from pointing out that he wasn't a bellman, or a room service waiter. "Yes, sir," he said.

Fifteen minutes later, he and Troy descended together, in yet another service elevator. For a black man, Troy looked pale.

"Is he *serious*?" Troy asked.

Garrett sighed deeply, looking up and watching the digital numbers over the doors as they plunged. His tie was dangling; he tugged it loose from his shirt collar and stuffed it into the pocket of his tuxedo jacket. "It would seem so," he said.

"Mrs. Cox says the senator is having a mental breakdown, and we all have to stick by him," Troy said glumly, shaking his head. "She's sure he'll come to his senses and everything will be fine."

"Right," Garrett said, grimly distracted. He'd sprint around to the side parking lot once he and Troy were outside, climb into his Porsche, and head for home. In two hours, he could be back on the Silver Spur.

They were standing in the alley again when Troy asked, "Why do I get the feeling that this comes as a surprise to you?"

The question threw Garrett, at least momentarily, and he didn't answer.

Troy thumbed the fob on his key ring, and the sedan started up. "Get in, and I'll give you a lift to your car," he told Garrett, with a sigh.

Garrett got into the sedan. "You knew about Mandy and the senator?" he asked.

Troy shook his head again and gave a raspy chuckle. "Hell, Garrett," he said, "I drive the man's car. He's been seeing her for months."

Garrett closed his eyes. Tate had accused him once of having his head up his ass, as far as the senator's true nature was concerned. And he'd defended Morgan Cox, been ready to fight his own brother to defend the bastard's honor.

"What about Nan? Did she know, too?" Remembering the expression on her face earlier, in the ballroom, Garrett didn't think so.

"Maybe," Troy said. "She didn't hear it from me, though."

He drew the sedan to a stop behind Garrett's Porsche. News vans were pulling out on the other end of the lot, along with a stream of ordinary cars.

Film clips and sound bites were probably already running on the local channels.

Turn out the lights, Garrett thought dismally. The party's over.

The senator not only wouldn't be getting the presidential nomination, he'd be lucky if he wasn't forced to resign before he'd finished his current term in office.

All of which left Garrett himself up Shit's Creek, without a paddle.

He got out of the sedan and said good-night to Troy.

After his friend had driven away, Garrett climbed into the Porsche.

He made a brief stop at his town house, swapping the formal duds for jeans, a Western shirt and old boots. Once he'd changed, he could breathe a little better.

Returning to the kitchen, he turned on the countertop TV, flipping between the networks, watching in despair as one station after another showed Senator Cox and Mandy slipping out of the ballroom, arm in arm.

Deciding he'd seen enough, Garrett turned off the set.

Now, NEARLY TWO hours later, only about a mile outside of Blue River, Garrett sped on toward home, the word *fool* drumming in his brain. He was stone sober, though a part of him wished he were otherwise, when the dazzle of red and blue lights splashed across his rearview mirror.

Garrett swore under his breath, downshifted—Fifth to Fourth to Third to Second, finally rolling to a stop at the side of the road. There, without shutting off the ignition, he waited.

He buzzed down the passenger-side window just as Brent Brogan, chief of police, was about to rap on the glass with his knuckles.

"Are out of your freakin' *mind*?" his brother's best friend demanded, bending to peer through the opening. Brogan's badge caught a flash of moonlight. "I clocked you at almost one-twenty back there!"

Garrett tensed his hands on the steering wheel, relaxed them without releasing his hold. "Sorry," he said, gazing straight ahead, through the bug-splattered windshield, instead of meeting Brogan's gaze. Tate had dubbed the chief "Denzel," since he resembled the actor's younger self, and used the nickname freely, especially when the moment called for a little lightening up—but Garrett wasn't on such easy terms with Brent Brogan as his brother was.

"You're sorry?" Brogan asked, in a mocking drawl. "Well, that's another matter, then. Garrett McKettrick is *sorry*. That just makes all the difference in the world, and pardon me for pulling you over before you killed yourself or somebody else."

Garrett thrust out a sigh. "Write the ticket," he said.

"I ought to arrest you," Brogan said, and he sounded like he was musing on the possibility, giving it real consideration. "That's what I ought to do. Throw your ass in jail."

"Fine," Garrett said, resigned. "Throw me in jail."

Brent opened the passenger door and folded himself into the seat, keeping his right leg outside the car. He was a big man, taller than Garrett and broader through the shoulders, and that made the quarters feel a mite too close. "There's no elbow room in this rig," Brogan remarked. "Why don't you get yourself a truck?"

Garrett gave a harsh guffaw, with no humor in it. Shoved his right hand through his hair and waited, too stubborn to answer.

It was the chief's turn to sigh. "Look, Garrett," he said, "I know you—you're not drinking and you're not high. Of all the people I might have pulled over tonight, shooting along this road like a bullet headed for the bull's-eye, you've got more reason to know better than most."

The old ache rose inside Garrett, lodged in his throat.

He closed his eyes, trying to block the images, but he couldn't. He heard the screech of tires grabbing at asphalt, the grinding crash of metal careening into metal, even the ludicrously musical splintering of glass. He hadn't been there the night his mom and dad were killed in a horrendous collision with an out-of-control semi, but the sounds and the pictures in his mind were so vivid, he might as well have been.

For the millionth time since the accident, a full decade in the past now, Garrett tried to come to terms with the loss of his parents. For the millionth time, it didn't happen.

What would he have given to have them both waiting at the ranch house, just like in the old days?

Just about anything.

"You fixing to tell me what's the matter?" Brogan asked, when a long time had passed. "I'm on duty until eight o'clock tomorrow morning, when Deputy Osburt relieves me. I can sit here and wait till hell freezes over *and* till the cows come home, if that's what I have to do."

Garrett assessed the situation. Dawn was hours away. The September darkness was weighted with heat, and with Brogan holding the Porsche's door open like that, the air-conditioning system was of negligible value. He tightened his fingers around the steering wheel again, hard enough to make his knuckles ache.

"I had a bad day, that's all," he said. *And a worse night.*

Brogan laid a hand on his shoulder. "You headed for the Silver Spur?"

Garrett nodded, swallowed. He could feel the pull of home, deep inside; he was drawn to it.

"I'm going to follow you as far as the main gate," Brogan said, after more pondering. "Make sure you get home in one piece."

Garrett looked at him. "Thanks," he said, without much inflection.

Brogan got out of the Porsche, shut the door, bent to look through the open window again. "Meantime, keep your foot light on the pedal," he warned. "About the last thing on this earth I want to do right now is roust your big brother from his bed and break the news that you just wrapped yourself around a telephone pole."

Tate was only a year older than he was, Garrett reflected, and they were about the same height and weight. So why did "big" have to preface "brother"? He was pretty sure nobody referred to him as *Austin's* "big brother," though he had a year on the youngest member of the family, along with a couple of inches and a good twenty pounds.

Garrett waited until Brogan was back in his cruiser before pulling back out onto the highway. The town of Blue River slept just up ahead; the streetlights tripped on, one by one, as he passed beneath them.

At this time of night, even the bars were closed.

As Garrett drove, with his one-man police escort trailing behind him, he thought about Tate, probably spooned up with his pretty fiancée, Libby Remington, in the modest house by the bend in the creek, and felt a brief but bitter stab of envy.

They were happy, those two. So crazy in love that the air around them seemed to buzz with pheromones. Tate and Libby were planning the mother of all weddings for New Year's Eve, following that up with a honeymoon cruise in the Greek Islands. The sooner they could give Tate's six-year-old twin daughters, Audrey and Ava, a baby brother or sister, they figured, the better.

Garrett calculated he'd be an uncle again about nine months and five minutes after the wedding ceremony was over.

The thought made him smile, in spite of everything.

The countryside slipped by.

At the main gates opening onto the Silver Spur, Brogan flashed his headlights once, turned the cruiser back toward town and drove off.

Pushing a button on his dashboard, Garrett watched as the tall iron gates, emblazoned with the name *McKettrick*, swung open to admit him.

Home, he reflected, as he drove through and up the long driveway leading toward the house. The place where they have to take you in.

How did anybody manage to sleep in this huge place? Julie Remington wondered, as she flipped on the lights in the daunting kitchen of the main ranch house on the Silver Spur Ranch. She and her four-going-on-five-year-old son, Calvin, along with their beagle, Harry, had been staying in the first-floor guest suite for nearly a week because there were termites at their rented cottage in town and the whole structure was under a tent.

Taking her private stash of herbal tea bags from a cupboard, along with a mug one of her high school drama students had given her for Christmas the year before, Julie set about brewing herself a cup of chamomile tea.

Coffee would probably have made more sense, she thought, pumping hot water from the special spigot by the largest of several sinks, since it would be morning soon, but she still had hopes of catching a few winks before the day began in earnest.

She had just turned, cup in hand, planning to head back to bed, when the door leading into the garage suddenly opened.

Julie nearly spilled the tea down the front of her ratty purple quilted bathrobe, she was so startled.

Garrett McKettrick paused just over the threshold, and she knew by the pensive look in his eyes that he was wondering what she was doing in his kitchen.

She was unprepared for the grin breaking over his handsome face, dispelling the strain she'd glimpsed there only a moment before.

"Hey," he said, shutting the door behind him, tossing a set of keys onto a granite countertop.

"Hey," Julie said back, wondering if he'd remembered her yet. She crossed the room, put out her free hand for him to shake. "Julie Remington," she reminded him.

He laughed. "I *know* who you are," he replied. "We grew up together, remember? Not to mention a more recent encounter at Pablo Ruiz's funeral."

A trained actress, Julie was playing the part of a woman who didn't feel self-conscious standing in someone else's kitchen in the middle of the night, drinking tea and wearing an old bathrobe. Or *trying* to play the part, anyhow.

It was proving difficult to carry off. Especially after

she blew her next line. "I just thought—with all the people you must know—"

All the women you must know...

Garrett's eyes were that legendary shade of McKettrick blue, a combination of summer sky, new denim and cornflower, and solemn as they regarded her.

Julie's heart took up a thrumming rhythm. "I suppose you're wondering what I'm doing here," she prattled on.

What was *wrong* with her? It wasn't as if she'd been caught breaking and entering, after all. Tate had practically insisted that she and Calvin move into the mansion, instead of taking a motel room or making some other arrangement, while the cottage was being pumped full of noxious chemicals.

One corner of Garrett's mouth tilted up in a grin, and he walked over to the first of a row of built-in refrigerators, pulled open the door and assessed the contents.

"Actually," he said, without turning around, "I wasn't wondering that at all."

Julie, who was not easily rattled, blushed. "Oh."

He plundered the refrigerator for a while.

"Well," Julie said, too brightly, "good night, then."

Holding a storage container full of Julie's special chicken lasagna, left over from supper, Garrett faced her, shouldering the refrigerator door shut in the same motion. "Or good morning," he said, "depending on your viewpoint."

"It's barely four," Julie remarked.

Garrett stuck the container into the microwave, pushed a few buttons.

"Don't!" Julie cried, rushing past him to rescue the dish. "This kind of plastic melts if you nuke it—"

He arched an eyebrow. "I'll be damned," he said.

Then, while Julie busied herself transferring the contents of the container onto a microwave-safe plate, he added, "Are your eyes really lavender, or am I seeing things?"

The question flustered Julie. "It's the bathrobe," she said, as the microwave whirred away, heating up the lasagna.

"The bathrobe?" Garrett asked, sounding confused. He was standing in Julie's space; she knew that even though she couldn't bring herself to look directly at him again, which was stupid, because just as he'd said, Blue River was home to both of them. They'd gone to the same schools and the same church growing up. And with their siblings engaged, they were practically family.

Julie, who never blushed, blushed again, and so hard that her cheeks burned. She was really losing it, she decided.

"My—my eyes are actually hazel," she said, "and they take on the color of whatever I'm wearing. And since the bathrobe is purple—"

As soon as the words were out of her mouth, Julie bit down on her lower lip. Why couldn't she just *shut up*?

Mercifully, Garrett didn't comment. He just stood there at the counter, waiting for the microwave to finish warming up the leftover lasagna.

"Mom?" Calvin padded into the kitchen, blinking owlishly behind the lenses of his glasses. He wore cotton pajamas and his feet were bare. "Is it time to get up? It's still dark outside, isn't it?"

Julie felt the usual rush of motherly love, and an undercurrent of fear as well. Recently, Calvin's biological father had been making overtures about "reconnecting" with their son and, although he'd paid child support all along, Gordon Pruett was a total stranger to the boy.

"Go back to bed, sweetheart," she said gently. "You don't have to get up yet."

The dog, Harry, appeared at Calvin's side. The adopted beagle was surprisingly nimble, although he'd been born one leg short of the requisite four.

Calvin's attention shifted to Garrett, who was just sitting down at the table, the plate of lasagna in front of him.

"Hello," Calvin said.

Harry began to wag his tail, though Julie figured the dog was at least as interested in the Italian casserole as he was in Garrett, if not more so.

"Hey," Garrett responded.

"You're Audrey and Ava's uncle, aren't you?" Calvin asked. "The one who gave them a real castle for their birthday?"

Garrett chuckled. Jabbed a fork into the food. "Yep, that's me."

"It's at the community center now," Calvin said, drawing a little closer, not to his mother, but to Garrett. "The castle, I mean."

"Probably a good place for it," Garrett said. "You want some of this pasta stuff? It's pretty good."

Unaccountably, Julie bristled. *Pasta stuff? Pretty good?* It was an original recipe, and she'd won a prize for it at the state fair the year before.

Calvin reached the table, hauled back a chair and scrambled into it. With a jab of his right index finger, he pushed his glasses back up his nose. His blond hair stuck out in myriad directions, and his expression was so earnest as he studied Garrett that Julie's heart ached a little. "No, thanks," the little boy said solemnly. "We had it for supper and, anyway, Mom makes it all the time."

Garrett looked up at Julie, smiled slightly and turned his full attention back to Calvin. "Your mom's a good cook," he said.

Harry advanced and brushed up against Garrett, leaving white beagle hairs all over the leg of his jeans. Garrett chuckled and greeted Harry with a pat on the head and a quiet "Hey, dog."

"Calvin," Julie interceded, "we should get back to bed and leave Mr. McKettrick to enjoy his...breakfast."

Garrett's eyes, though weary, seemed to dance when he looked up at Julie. "'Mr. McKettrick'?" he echoed. His gaze swung back to Calvin. "Do you call my brother Tate 'Mr. McKettrick'?" he asked.

Calvin shook his head. "I call him Tate. He's going to marry my aunt Libby on New Year's Eve, and he'll be my uncle after that."

A nod from Garrett. "I guess he will. I will be, too, sort of. So maybe you ought to call me Garrett."

The child beamed. "I'm Calvin," he said, "and this is my dog, Harry."

And he put out his little hand, much as Julie had done earlier.

They shook on the introduction, man and boy.

"Mighty glad to meet the both of you," Garrett said.

CHAPTER TWO

THE COMBINATION OF a fiercely blue autumn sky, oak leaves turning to bright yellow in the trees edging the sun-dappled creek and the heart-piercing love she felt for her little boy made Julie ache over the bittersweet perfection of the present moment.

She turned the pink Cadillac onto the winding dirt road leading to the old Ruiz house, where Tate and Libby and Tate's twin daughters were living, and glanced into the rearview mirror.

Calvin sat stoically in his car seat in back, staring out the window.

Since Julie had to be at work at Blue River High School a full hour before Calvin's kindergarten class began, she'd been dropping him off at Libby's on her way to town over the week they'd been staying on the Silver Spur. He adored his aunt, and Tate, and Tate's girls, Audrey and Ava, who were two years older than Calvin and thus, in his opinion, sophisticated women of the world. Today, though, he was just too quiet.

"Everything okay, buddy?" Julie asked, tooting the Caddie's horn in greeting as her sister Libby appeared on the front porch of the house she and Tate were renovating and started down the steps.

"I guess we'll have to move back to town when the bugs are gone from our cottage and they take down the tent," he said. "We won't get to live in the country anymore."

"That was always the plan," Julie reminded her son gently. "That we'd go back to the cottage when it's safe." Recently, she'd considered offering to buy the small but charming house she'd been renting from month to month since Calvin was a baby and making it their permanent home. Thanks to a windfall, she had the means, but this morning the idea lacked its usual appeal.

Calvin suffered from intermittent asthma attacks, though he hadn't had an incident for a long time. Suppose some vestige of the toxins used to eliminate termites lingered after the tenting process was finished, and damaged his health—or her own—in some insidious way?

While Julie was trying to shake off *that* semiparanoid idea, Libby started across the grassy lawn toward the car, grinning and waving one hand in welcome. She wore jeans and a navy blue sweatshirt and white sneakers, and she'd clipped her shiny light brown hair up on top of her head.

A year older than Julie, Libby had always been strikingly pretty, but since she and Tate McKettrick, her one-time high school sweetheart, had rediscovered each other just that summer, she'd been downright beautiful. Libby glowed, incandescent with love and from being thoroughly loved in return.

Julie pushed the button to lower the back window on the other side of the car, smiling with genuine affection for her sister even as she felt a brief but poignant stab of stark jealousy.

What would it be like to be loved—no, cherished— by a full-grown, committed man like Tate? It was an experience Julie had long-since given up on, for herself, anyway. She was independent and capable, and of course she had no desire to be otherwise, but it would have been nice, once in a while, not to have to be strong every minute of every day and night, not to blaze *all* the trails and fight *all* the dragons.

Libby gave Julie a glance before she leaned through the back window to plant a smacking welcome kiss on Calvin's forehead.

"Good morning, Aunt Libby," she coached cheerfully, when Calvin didn't speak to her to right away.

"'Good morning, Aunt Libby,'" Calvin repeated, with a reluctant giggle.

"He's a little moody this morning," Julie said.

"I'm *not* moody," Calvin argued, climbing out of the car to stand beside Libby on the gravel driveway, then reaching inside for his backpack. "I just want to live on a ranch, that's all. I want to have my very own horse, like Audrey and Ava do. Is that too much to ask?"

Julie sighed. "Well, *yeah*, Calvin, it kind of *is* too much to ask."

Calvin didn't say anything more; he merely shook his head and, lugging his backpack, headed off toward the house, his small shoulders stooped.

"What was that all about?" Libby asked, moving around to Julie's side of the car and bending to look in at her.

Julie genuinely didn't have time for a long discussion, but she had always confided in Libby, and now it was virtually automatic, especially when she was upset.

"Maybe I shouldn't have let you and Tate talk me into staying on the Silver Spur," she fretted. "It's only been a week, but Calvin's already too used to living like a

McKettrick—riding horses, swimming in that indoor pool, watching movies in a *media room*, for heaven's sake. I can't give him that kind of life, Libby. I'm not even sure I'd want to if I could. What if he's getting spoiled?"

Libby raised an eyebrow. "Take a breath, Jules," she said. "You're dramatizing a little, don't you think? Calvin is a good kid, and it would take a lot more than a week or two of high living at the ranch to spoil him. Both of you are under extra stress—Calvin just started kindergarten, and you're back to teaching full-time, with your house under a tent because of termites—and then there's the whole Gordon thing…" Libby stopped talking, reached through the window to squeeze Julie's shoulder. "The point is—things will even out pretty soon. Just give it time."

Julie worked up a smile, tapped at the face of her watch with one index finger. *Easy for you to say*, she thought, but what she said out loud was, "Gotta go."

Libby nodded and stepped away from the car, raised a hand in farewell. She seemed reluctant to let Julie go, and a worried expression flickered in her blue eyes as she watched her back up, turn around and drive off.

Libby had done her little-girl best to stand in after their mother had abandoned the family years before. She'd given up finishing college and arguably a lot more besides when their dad, Will Remington, was diagnosed with pancreatic cancer. Libby had moved back to Blue River, started the Perk Up Coffee Shop—now reduced to a vacant lot across the alley from the house they'd all grown up in—and looked after their father as his illness progressed.

Of course, Julie had helped with his care as much as

possible and so had Paige, but just the same, most of the hard stuff had fallen to Libby. Sure, she was the eldest, but the age difference was minor—they'd been born one right after the other, three children in three years. The truth was, Libby had been willing to make sacrifices Julie and Paige couldn't have managed at the time.

Julie bit down on her lower lip as the town limits came into view, and she began reducing her speed. Their mother, Marva, had reappeared in Blue River months ago, moved into an apartment, and tried, in her own way, to establish some kind of relationship with her daughters. The results had been less than fabulous.

At first, Libby, Julie and Paige had resisted the woman's every overture, but even after deserting them when they were small, breaking their hearts and their father's as well, Marva was blithely convinced that a fresh start was just a matter of letting bygones be bygones.

In time, Julie and Paige had both warmed up to Marva somewhat, Libby less so.

The Cadillac bumped over potholes in the gravel parking lot behind Blue River High. The long, low-slung stucco building had grown up on the site of an old Spanish mission, though only a small part of the original structure remained, serving as a center courtyard. Classrooms, a small cafeteria and a gymnasium had been added over the decades, and during an oil boom in the mid-1930s, Clay McKettrick II, known as JR in that time-honored Southern way of denoting "juniors," had financed the construction of the auditorium, with its two hundred plush theater seats, fine stage and rococo molding around the painted ceiling.

Erected on school property, the auditorium belonged to the entire community. Various civic organizations held their meetings and other events there, and several different denominations had used it as a church on Sunday mornings, while their own buildings were under construction or being renovated.

The auditorium, cool and shadowy and smelling faintly of mildew, had always been a place of almost magical solace for Julie, especially in high school, when she'd had leading roles in so many plays.

Although she'd performed with several professional road companies later on, Julie had never wanted to be an actress and live in glamorous places like New York or Los Angeles. All along, she'd planned on—and worked at—getting her teaching certificate, returning to Blue River and keeping the theater going.

There was no room in the budget for a drama department—the high school theater group supported itself by putting on two productions a year, one of them a musical, and charging modest admission. Like her now-retired predecessor, Miss Idetta Scrobbins, Julie earned her paycheck by teaching English classes—the drama club and the plays they put on were a labor of love.

Julie was thinking about the next project—three one-act plays written by some of her best students—as she hurried down the center aisle and through the doorway to the left of the stage, where she'd transformed an unused supply closet into a sort of hideaway. Officially, her office was her classroom, but it was here that she met with students and came up with some of her best ideas.

Hastily, she tossed her brown-bag lunch into the small refrigerator sitting on top of a file cabinet, kicked off her flat shoes and pulled on the low-heeled pumps she kept stashed in a desk drawer. She flipped on her computer—it was old and took forever to boot up—locked up her purse and raced out of the hideout, back up the aisle and out into the September sunshine.

She was five minutes late for the staff meeting, and Principal Dulles would not be pleased.

Everyone else was already there when Julie dashed into the school library and dropped into a utilitarian folding chair at one of the three long tables where students read and did homework. The library doubled as a study hall throughout the school day.

Up front, the red-faced principal puffed out his cheeks, turning a stub of chalk end over end in one hand, and cleared his throat. Julie's best friend at work, Helen Marcus, gave her a light poke with her elbow and whispered, "Don't worry, you didn't miss anything."

Julie smiled at that, looked around at the half dozen other teachers who were her colleagues. She knew that Dulles, a middle-aged man from far away, made no secret of his opinion that Blue River, Texas, hardly offered more in the way of cultural stimulation than a prairie-dog town would have. He considered her a flake because of her colorful clothing and her penchant for putting on and directing plays.

For all of that, Arthur was a good person.

Like Julie, most of the other members of the staff had been born and raised there. They'd come home to teach after college because they knew Blue River needed them; high pay and job perks weren't a factor, of course. To them, odd breed that they were, the community's kids mattered most.

Dulles cleared his throat, glaring at Julie, who smiled placidly back at him.

"As some of you already know," he began, "the Mc-

Kettrick Foundation has generously agreed to match whatever funds we can raise on our own to buy new computers and special software for our library. Our share, however, amounts to a considerable sum."

The McKettricks were community-minded; they'd always been quick to lend a hand wherever one was needed, but the foundation's longstanding policy, except in emergencies, was to involve the whole town in raising funds as well. At the name *McKettrick*, Julie felt an odd quickening of some kind, at once disturbing and delicious, thinking back to her encounter with Garrett in the ranch-house kitchen.

The others shifted in their seats, checked their watches and glanced up at the wall clock. Students were beginning to arrive; the ringing slam of locker doors and the lilting hum of their conversation sounded from the wide hallway just outside the library.

Julie waited attentively, sensing that Arthur's speech was mainly directed at her, but unable to imagine why that should be so.

No one spoke.

Arthur seemed reluctant, but he finally went on. He looked straight at Julie, confirming her suspicions. "It's a pity the drama club is staging those three one-act plays for the fall production, instead of doing a musical."

The light went on in Julie's mind. Since the plays were original, and written by high school seniors, turnout at the showcase would probably be limited to proud parents and close friends. The box-office proceeds would therefore be minimal. But the musicals, for which Blue River High was well known, drew audiences from as far away as Austin and San Antonio, and brought in thousands of dollars.

The take from last spring's production of *South Pacific* had been plenty to provide new uniforms for the marching band *and* the football team, with enough left over to fund two hefty scholarships when graduation rolled around.

Arthur continued to stare at Julie, most likely hoping she would save him the embarrassment of strongarming her by *offering* to postpone or cancel the student showcase to produce a musical instead. Although her first instinct was always to jump right in like some female superhero and offer to take care of everything, today she didn't.

They'd committed, she and Arthur and the school board, to staging *Kiss Me Kate* for this year's spring production—casting and rehearsals would begin after Christmas vacation, with the usual three performances slated for mid-May.

She had enough on her plate already, between Calvin and her job.

The silence grew uncomfortable.

Arthur Dulles finally cleared his throat eloquently. "I'm sure I don't need to remind any of you how important it is, in this day and age, for our students to be computer-savvy."

Still, no one spoke.

"Julie?" Arthur prodded, at last.

"We're doing *Kiss Me Kate* next spring," Julie reminded him.

"Yes," Arthur agreed, sounding weary, "but perhaps we could produce the musical *now*, instead of next spring. That way it would be easy to match the McKettricks' contribution, since our musicals are always so popular."

Our musicals, Julie thought. As if it would be *Arthur* who held tryouts every night for a week, and then two months of rehearsals, weekends included. Arthur who dealt with heartbroken teenage girls who hadn't landed the part of their dreams—not to mention their mothers. Arthur who struggled to round up enough teenage *boys* to balance out the chorus and play the leads.

No, it would be Julie who did all those things.

Julie alone.

"Gosh, Arthur," she said, smiling her team-player smile, "that would be hard to pull off. The showcase will be ready to stage within a month. We'd be lucky to get the musical going by Christmas."

Bob Riza, who coached football, basketball and baseball in their respective seasons, in addition to teaching math, flung a sympathetic glance in Julie's direction and finally spoke up. "Maybe the foundation would be willing to cut us a check for the full amount," he said. "Forget the matching requirement, just this once."

"I don't think that's fair," Julie said.

Arthur folded his arms, still watching her. "I agree," he said. "The McKettricks have been more than generous. Three years ago, you'll all remember, when the creeks overflowed and we had all that flood damage and our insurance only covered the basics, the foundation underwrote a new floor for the gymnasium, in full, and replaced the hundreds of books ruined here and in the public library."

Julie nodded. "Here's the thing, Arthur," she said. "The showcase won't bring in a lot of money, that's true. But it's important—the kids involved are trying to get into very good colleges, and there's a lot of competition. Having their plays produced will make them stand out a little."

Arthur nodded, listening sympathetically, but Julie knew he'd already made up his mind.

"I'm afraid the showcase will have to be moved to spring," he said. "The sooner the musical is under way, the better."

Julie knew she'd lost. So why did she keep fighting? "Spring will be too late for these kids," she said, straightening her spine, hiking up her chin. "The application deadlines are—"

Arthur shook his head, cutting her off. "I'm sorry, Julie," he said.

Julie swallowed. Lowered her eyes.

It wasn't that she didn't appreciate Arthur's position. She knew how important those new computers were—while most of the students had ready access to the internet at home, a significant number of kids depended on the computers at the public library and here at the high school. Technology was changing the world at an almost frightening pace, and Blue River High had to keep up.

Still, she was already spending more time at school than was probably good for Calvin. Launching this project would mean her little boy practically *lived* with Libby and Paige, and while Calvin adored his aunts, *she* was his mother. Her son's happiness and well-being were her responsibility; she couldn't and wouldn't foist him off and farm him out any more than she was doing now.

The first period bell shrilled then, earsplittingly loud, it seemed to Julie. She was due in her tenth-grade English class.

Riza and the others rose from their chairs, clearly anxious to head for their own classrooms.

Julie remained where she was, facing Arthur Dulles. She felt a little like an animal caught in the headlight beams of an oncoming truck, unable to move in any direction.

He smiled. Arthur was not unkind, merely beleaguered. He served as principal of the town's elementary and middle schools as well as Blue River High, and his wife, Dot, was just finishing up a round of chemotherapy.

"It would be a shame if we had to turn down the funding for all that state-of-the-art equipment," Arthur said forthrightly, standing directly in front of Julie now, "wouldn't it?"

Julie suppressed a deep sigh. Her sister was engaged to Tate McKettrick; in his view, that meant Julie was practically a McKettrick herself. Maybe Arthur expected her to hit up the town's most important family for an even fatter check.

"Couldn't we try some other kind of fundraiser?" she asked. "Get the parents to help out, maybe put on some bake sales and a few car washes?"

"You know," Arthur said quietly, walking her to the door, pulling it open so she could precede him into the hallway, "our most dedicated parents are *already* doing all they can, volunteering as crossing guards and lunchroom helpers and the like. I know you depend on several women to sew costumes for the musical every year. The vast majority, I needn't tell you, only seem to show up when they want to complain about Susie's math grades or Johnny playing second string on the football team." He straightened his tie. "It isn't like it used to be."

"How's Do feeling?" she asked gently. Arthur's wife was a hometown girl, and everybody liked her.

Arthur's worries showed in his eyes. "She has good days and bad days," he said.

Julie bit her lower lip. Nodded. So this was it, she thought. The showcase was out, the musical was in. And somehow she would have to make it all work.

"Thank you," Arthur replied, distracted again. Once more, he sighed. "I'll need dates for the production as soon as possible," he said. "Nelva Jean can make up fliers stressing that we're going to need more parental help than usual."

Nelva Jean was the school secretary, a force of nature in her own right, and she'd been eligible for retirement even when Julie and her sisters attended Blue River High. But aged miracle though she was, Nelva Jean couldn't work magic.

Julie and Arthur went their separate ways then, Julie's mind tumbling through various unworkable options as she hurried toward her classroom, her thoughts partly on the three playwrights and their own hopes for the showcase.

She'd met with the trio of young authors all summer long, reading and rereading the scripts for their one-act plays, suggesting revisions, helping to polish the pieces until they shone. They'd worked hard, and were counting on the production to buttress their college credentials.

Julie entered her classroom, took her place up front. She had no choice but to put the dilemma out of her mind for the time being.

Class flew by.

"Ms. Remington?" a shy voice asked, when first period was over and most of the students had left.

Julie, who'd been erasing the blackboard, turned to see Rachel Strivens, one of her three young playwrights, standing nearby. Rachel's dad was often out of work, though he did odd jobs wherever he could find them to put food on the table, and her mother had died in some sort of accident before the teenager and her father and her two younger brothers rolled into Blue River in a beat-up old truck in the middle of the last school year. They'd taken up residence in a rickety trailer, adjoining the junkyard run by Chudley Wilkes and his wife, Minnie, and had kept mostly to themselves ever since.

Rachel's intelligence, not to mention her affinity for the written word, had been apparent to Julie almost immediately. Over the summer, Rachel had spent her days at the Blue River Public Library, little brothers in tow, or at the community center, composing her play on one of the computers available there.

The other kids seemed to like Rachel, though she didn't have a lot of time for friends. She was definitely not like the others, buying her clothes at the thrift store and doing without things many of her contemporaries took for granted, like designer jeans, fancy cell phones and MP3 players, but at least she was spared the bullying that sometimes plagued the poor and the different. Julie knew that because she'd taken the time to make sure.

"Yes, Rachel?" she finally replied.

Rachel, though too thin, had elegant bone structure, wide-set brown eyes and a generous mouth. Her waist-length hair, braided into a single plait, was as black as a country night before the new moon, and always clean. "Could—could I talk with you later?"

Julie felt a tingle of alarm. "Is something wrong?"

Rachel tried hard to smile. Second period would begin soon, and students were beginning to drift into the room. "Later?" the girl said. "Please?"

Julie nodded, still thinking about Rachel as she prepared to teach another English class. Probably because she'd had to move around a lot with her dad, rambling from town to town and school to school, Rachel's grades had been a little on the sketchy side when she'd started at Blue River High. The one-act play she'd written— tellingly titled *Trailer Park*—was brilliant.

Rachel was brilliant.

But she was also the kind of kid who tended to fall through the cracks unless someone actively championed her and stood up for her.

And Julie was determined to be that someone.

Somehow.

A PHONE WAS RINGING. Insistent, jarring him awake.

With a groan, Garrett dragged the comforter up over his head, but the sound continued.

Cell phone?

Landline?

He couldn't tell. Didn't give a damn.

"Shut up," he pleaded, burrowing down deeper in bed, his voice muffled by the covers.

The phone stopped after twelve rings, then immediately started up again.

Real Life coalesced in Garrett's sleep-fuddled brain. Memories of the night before began to surface.

He recalled the senator's announcement.

Saw Nan Cox in his mind's eye, slipping out by way of the hotel kitchen.

He recollected Brent Brogan providing him with a police escort as far as the ranch gate.

And after all that, Julie Remington, a little boy and a three-legged beagle appearing in the kitchen.

Knowing he wouldn't be able to sleep after Julie had taken her young son and their dog back to bed in the first-floor guest suite—the spacious accommodations next to the maid's rooms, where the housekeeper, Esperanza, stayed—Garrett had gone to the barn, saddled a horse, and spent what remained of the night and the first part of the morning riding.

Finally, when smoke curled from the bunkhouse chimney and lights came on in the trailers along the creek-side, Garrett had returned home, put up his horse, retired to his private quarters to strip, shower and fall facedown into bed.

The ringing reminded him that he still had a job.

"Shit," he murmured, sitting up and scrambling for the bedside phone. "Hello?"

A dial tone buzzed in his ear, and the ringing went on.

His cell phone, then.

He grabbed for his jeans, abandoned earlier on the floor next to the bed, and rummaged through a couple of pockets before he found the cell.

"Garrett McKettrick," he mumbled, after snapping it open.

"It's about time you picked up the phone," Nan Cox answered. She sounded pretty chipper, considering that her husband had stood up at the previous evening's fundraiser and essentially told the world that he and Mandy

Chante were meant to be together. "I'm at the office, and you're not. You're not at your condo, either, because I sent Troy over to check. Where *are* you, Garrett?"

He sat up in bed, self-conscious because he was talking to his employer's wife, one of his late mother's closest friends, naked. Of course, Nan couldn't see him, but still.

"I'm on the Silver Spur," he said, grabbing his watch off the bedside table and squinting at it.

Seeing the time—past noon—he swore again.

"The senator needs you. The press has him and the little pole dancer cornered in their hotel suite."

Garrett tossed the comforter aside, sat up, retrieved his jeans from the floor and pulled them on, standing up to work the zipper and the snap. "I can understand why you think this might be my problem," he replied, imagining Morgan and Mandy hiding out from reporters in the spacious room he'd rented for them the night before, "but I'm not sure I get why it would be *yours*. Some women would be angry. They'd be talking to divorce lawyers."

"Morgan," Nan said quietly, and with conviction, "is not himself. He's ill. We still have five children at home. I'm not about to turn my back on him now."

"Mrs. Cox—"

"Nan," she broke in. "Your mother and I were like sisters."

"Nan," Garrett corrected himself, his tone grave. "Surely you understand that your husband's career can't be saved. He won't get the presidential nomination. In fact, he will probably be asked to relinquish his seat in the Senate."

"I don't give a damn about his career," Nan said

fiercely, and Garrett knew she was fighting back tears. "I just want Morgan back. I want him examined by his doctor. He's not in his right mind, Garrett. He needs my help. He needs *our* help."

Although the senator was probably going through some kind of delayed midlife crisis, Garrett wasn't convinced that his boss was out of his mind. Morgan Cox wouldn't be the first politician to throw over his wife, family and career in some fit of eroticized egotism, nor, unfortunately, would he be the last.

"Look," Garrett said quietly, "I've given this whole situation some thought, and from where I stand, resignation is looking pretty good."

"Morgan's?"

"Mine," Garrett replied, after unclamping his jaw.

"You would *resign*?" Nan asked, sounding only slightly more horrified than stunned. "Morgan has been your *mentor*, Garrett. He's shown you the ropes, introduced you to all the right people in Washington, prepared the way for you to run for office when the time comes..."

Her voice fell away.

Garrett thrust out a sigh. *Would* he resign?

He wasn't sure. All he knew for certain right then was that he needed more of what his dad would have called range time—hours and hours on the back of a horse—in order to figure out what to do next.

In the meanwhile, though, Morgan and the barracuda were pinned down in a hotel suite in Austin, two hours away. The senator was obviously a loose cannon, and if he got desperate enough, he might make things even worse with some off-the-wall statement meant to appease the reporters lying in wait for him in the corridor.

"Garrett?" Nan prompted, when he didn't speak.

"I'm here," he said.

"You've got to do something."

Like what? Garrett wondered. But it wasn't the sort of thing you said to Nan Cox, especially not when she was in her take-on-the-world mode. "I'll call his cell," he told her.

"Good," Nan said, and hung up hard.

Garrett winced slightly, then speed-dialed his boss.

"McKettrick?" Cox snapped. "Is that you?"

"Yes," Garrett said.

"Where *the hell* are you?"

Garrett let the question pass. The senator wasn't asking for his actual whereabouts, after all. He was letting Garrett know he was pissed.

"You haven't spoken to the press, have you?" Garrett asked.

"No," Cox said. "But they're all over the hotel—in the hallway outside our suite, and probably downstairs in the lobby—"

"Probably," Garrett agreed quietly. "First thing, Senator. It is *very* important that you don't issue any statements or answer any questions before we have a chance to make plans. None at all. I'll get back to Austin as soon as I can, but in the meantime, you've got to stay put and speak to no one." A pause. "Do you understand me, Senator?"

Cox's temper flared. "What do you mean, you'll get back to Austin as soon as you can? Dammit, Garrett, where are you?"

This time, Garrett figured, the man really wanted to know. Of course, that didn't mean he had to be told.

"That doesn't matter," Garrett replied, his tone measured.

"If I didn't need your help so badly," the senator shot back, "I'd fire you right now!"

If it hadn't been for Nan and the kids and the golden retrievers—hell, if it hadn't been for the people of Texas, who'd elected this man to the U.S. Senate three times—Garrett would have told Morgan Cox what he could do with the job.

"Sit tight," he replied instead. "I'll call off the dogs and send Troy to pick you up. You're still going to need to lie low for a while, though."

"I want *you* here, Garrett," Cox all but exploded. "*You're* my right-hand man—Troy is just a driver." Another pause followed, and then, "You're on that damn ranch, aren't you? You're two hours from Austin!"

Garrett had recently bought a small airplane, a Cessna he kept in the ramshackle hangar out on the ranch's private airstrip. He'd fire it up and fly back to the city.

"I'll be there right away," Garrett said.

"Is there a next step?" Cox asked, mellowing out a little.

"Yes. I'm calling a press conference for this afternoon, Senator. You might want to be thinking about what you're going to tell your constituents."

"I'll tell them the same thing I told the group last night," Cox blustered, "that I've fallen in love."

Garrett couldn't make himself answer that time.

"Are you still there?" Cox asked.

"Yes, sir," Garrett replied, his voice gruff with the effort. "I'm still here."

But damned if I know why.

HELEN MARCUS DUCKED into Julie's office just as she was pulling a sandwich from her uneaten brown-bag lunch. Having spent her lunch hour grading compositions, she was ravenous.

At last, a chance to eat.

"Big news," Helen chimed, rolling the TV set Julie used to play videos and DVDs for the drama club into the tiny office and switching it on. Helen was Julie's age, dark-haired, plump and happily married, and the two of them had grown up together. "There *is* a God!"

Puzzled, and with a headache beginning at the base of her skull, Julie frowned. "What are you talking—?"

Before she could finish the question, though, Garrett McKettrick's handsome face filled the screen. Commanding in a blue cotton shirt, without a coat or a tie, he sat behind a cluster of padded microphones, earnestly addressing a room full of reporters.

"That sum-bitch Morgan Cox is finally going to resign," Helen crowed. "I feel it in my bones!"

While Julie shared Helen's low opinion of the senator—she actually mistrusted *all* politicians—she couldn't help being struck by the expression in Garrett's eyes. The one he probably thought he was hiding.

Whatever the front he was putting on for the press, Garrett was stunned. Maybe even demoralized.

Julie watched and listened as the man she'd encountered in the ranch-house kitchen early that morning fielded questions—the senator, apparently, had elected to remain in the background.

Helen had been wrong about the resignation. Senator Cox was not prepared to step down, but he needed some "personal time" with his family, according to Garrett. Colleagues would cover for him in the meantime.

"So where's the pole dancer?" Helen demanded.

"Pole dancer?" Julie echoed.

Garrett, the senator and the reporters faded to black, and Helen switched off the TV. "The *pole dancer*," she repeated. "Some blonde the senator picked up in a seedy girlie club. He wants to marry her—I saw it on the eleven o'clock news last night and again this morning." The math teacher rolled her eyes. "It's *true love*. He and the bimbette have been together in other lives. And there's our own Garrett McKettrick, defending the man." A sad shake of the head. "Jim and Sally raised those three boys of theirs right. Garrett ought to know better than to throw in with a crook like that."

Just then, Rachel Strivens appeared in the doorway of Julie's office. "I'm sorry," she said quickly, seeing that Julie wasn't alone, and started to leave.

"Wait," Julie said.

Helen had already turned off the TV set and unplugged it, rolling it back out into the hallway on its noisy cart. If Helen had planned on staying to talk, she'd clearly changed her mind.

Blushing a little, Rachel slipped reluctantly into the room.

"Rachel," Julie said quietly, "sit down, please."

Rachel sat.

"What is it?" Julie finally asked, though of course she knew. She'd announced the suspension of plans to produce the showcase—it was only temporary, she'd insisted, she'd think of something—in all her English classes that day.

Rachel looked up, her brown eyes glistening with tears. "I just wanted to let you know that it's okay, about the showcase probably not happening and everything," she said. The girl made a visible effort to gather herself up, straightening her shoulders, raising her chin. "I can't do any extracurricular activities anyway—Dad says I need to start working after school, so I can help out with the bills. His friend Dennis manages the bowling alley, and with the fall leagues starting up, they can use some extra people."

Julie took a moment to absorb all the implications of that.

Rachel hadn't said she wanted to save for college, or buy clothes or a car or a laptop, like most teenagers in search of employment. She'd said she had to "help out with the bills."

She wasn't planning to *go* to college.

"I understand," Julie said, at some length, wishing she didn't.

Rachel bit her lower lip, threw her long braid back over one shoulder. "Dad tries," she said, her voice barely audible. "Everything is so hard, without my mom around anymore."

Julie nodded, holding back tears. In five years, in ten years, in twenty, Rachel might still be working at the bowling alley—if she had a job at all. Julie had seen the phenomenon half a dozen times. "I'm sure that's true," she said.

Rachel was on her feet. Ready to go.

Julie leaned forward in her chair. "Have you actually been hired, Rachel, or is the job at the bowling alley just a possibility?"

Rachel stood on the threshold, poised to flee, but clearly wanting to stay. "It's pretty definite," she answered. "I just have to say yes, and it's mine."

Things like this happened, Julie reminded herself. The world was an imperfect place.

Kids tabled their dreams, thinking they'd get back to them later.

Except that they so rarely did, in Julie's experience. One thing led to another. They met somebody and got married. Then there were children and rent to pay and car loans.

Rachel was so bright and talented, and she was standing at an important crossroads. In one direction lay a fine education and every hope of success. In the other...

The prospects made Julie want to cover her face with her hands.

After Rachel had gone, she sat very still for a long time, wondering what she could do to help.

Only one course of action came to mind, and that was probably a long shot.

She would speak to Rachel's father.

CHAPTER THREE

TATE WAS WAITING at the airstrip in his truck when Garrett landed the Cessna around five that afternoon.

Garrett taxied to a stop outside the ramshackle hangar that had once housed his dad's plane and shut off the engines. The blur of the props slowed until the paddles were visible.

He climbed down, shut the door behind him and walked toward his brother.

They met midway between the Cessna and Tate's truck.

Obviously, Tate had heard about the scandal in Austin by then, and Garrett figured he was there to say, "I told you so."

Instead, Tate reached out, rested a hand on Garrett's shoulder. "You okay?"

Garrett didn't know what to say then. Flying back from the capital, he'd rehearsed another scenario entirely—and that one hadn't involved the sympathy and concern he saw in his brother's eyes.

He nodded, though he couldn't resist qualifying that with "I've been better."

Tate let his hand fall back to his side. Folded his arms. "I caught the press conference on TV," he said. "Cox isn't planning to resign?"

Garrett sighed, shoved a hand through his hair. "He

will," he said sadly. "Right now, he's still trying to convince himself that the hullabaloo will blow over and everything will get back to normal."

"How's Nan taking all this?"

"She's holding up okay," Garrett said. "As far as I can tell, anyway."

Tate took that in. His expression was thoughtful. "Now what?" he asked, after a few moments had passed. "For you, I mean?"

"I catch my breath and look for another job," Garrett replied.

"You quit?" Tate asked, sounding surprised. If there was one thing a McKettrick didn't do, it was desert a sinking ship. Unless, of course, that ship had been commandeered by one of the rats.

Garrett grinned wanly. Spread his hands at his sides. "I was fired," he said.

Now there, he thought, was a first. In living memory, he knew of no McKettrick who had ever been fired from a job. On the other hand, most of them worked for themselves, and that had been the case for generations.

The look on Tate's face would have been satisfying, under any other circumstances. *"What?"*

Garrett chuckled. Okay, so his brother's surprise *was* sort of satisfying, circumstances notwithstanding. It made up for Garrett's skinned pride, at least a little. "The senator and I had words," he said. "He wanted to go on as if nothing had happened. I told him that wouldn't work—he needed to fess up, stand by his wife and his kids, if he wanted to come out of this with any credibility at all, never mind holding on to his seat in the Senate. I agreed to handle the press conference because Nan practically begged me, but when it was over, the senator informed me that my services were no longer needed." Still enjoying Tate's bewilderment, Garrett started toward the Cessna he'd just climbed out of, intending to roll it into the hangar. He stopped, looked back over one shoulder. "You wouldn't be in the market for a ranch hand, would you?"

Tate smiled, but there was a tinge of sadness to it. "Permanent or temporary?"

"Temporary," Garrett said, after a moment of recovery. "I still want to work in government. And I've already had a couple of offers."

Tate's disappointment was visible in his face, though he was a good sport about it. "Okay," he said. "How long is 'temporary'?"

Garrett wasn't sure how to answer that. He needed time—thinking time. Horse time. "As long as it takes," he offered.

Tate put out a hand so they could shake on the agreement, nebulous as it was. "Fair enough," he said.

Garrett nodded, watched as Tate turned to walk away, open the door of his truck and step up on the running board to climb behind the wheel.

"See you in the morning," Tate called.

Garrett grinned, feeling strangely hopeful, as if he were on the brink of something he'd been born to do.

But that was crazy, of course.

He was a born politician. He belonged in Austin, if not Washington. He wanted to be a mover and a shaker, part of the solution. Working on the Silver Spur was only a stopgap measure, just as he'd told Tate.

"What time?" he called back, standing next to the Cessna.

Tate's grin flashed. "We've got five hundred head

of cattle to move tomorrow," he said. "We're starting at dawn, so be saddled up and ready to ride."

Garrett didn't let his own grin falter, though on the inside he groaned. He nodded, waved and turned away.

If Ron Strivens, Rachel's father, carried a cell phone, the number wasn't on record in the school office, and since Strivens did odd jobs, he didn't work in the same place every day, like most of her students' parents. In the end, Julie drove to the trailer he rented just across the dirt road from Chudley and Minnie Wilkes's junkyard, and found him there, chopping firewood in the twilight.

Seeing Julie, the tall, rangy man lodged the blade of his ax in the chopping block and started toward her.

Julie sized him up as he approached. He wore old jeans, beat-up work boots and a plaid flannel shirt, unbuttoned to reveal a faded T-shirt beneath. His reddish-brown hair was too long and thinning above his forehead, and the expression in his eyes was one of weary resignation.

"I'm Julie Remington," Julie told him, after rolling down the car window. "Rachel is in my English class."

Strivens nodded, keeping his distance. Behind him loomed the battered trailer. Smoke curled from a rusty stovepipe, gray against a darkening sky, and Julie thought she saw Rachel's face appear briefly at one of the windows.

"What can I do for you, Ms. Remington?" he asked, shyly polite.

Julie felt her throat tighten. Money had certainly been in short supply while she was growing up, and the family home was nothing fancy, but she and her sisters had never done without anything they really needed.

"I was hoping we could talk about Rachel," she said.

Strivens glanced back toward the trailer. The metal was rusting, and even curling away from the frame in places, and the chimney rose from the roof of a ramshackle add-on, more like a lean-to than a room. "I'd ask you in," he told her, "but the kids are about to have their supper, and I don't think the soup will stretch far enough to feed another person."

Julie ached for Rachel, for her brothers, for all of them. "I'm in sort of a hurry anyway," she said, and that was true. She still had to pick Calvin up at Libby and Tate's place, and then there would be supper and his bath and a bedtime story. "Rachel tells me she's taking on an after-school job."

Strivens reddened a little, nodded once, abruptly. He'd been stooping to look in at Julie through the window, but now he took a couple of steps back and straightened. "I'm right sorry she has to do that," he said, "but the fact is, we're having a hard time making ends meet around here. The boys are always needing something, and there's rent and food and all the rest."

Julie's heart sank. What had she expected—that Rachel's father would say it was all a big misunderstanding and what had he been thinking, asking a mere child to help support the family?

"Rachel is a very special young woman, Mr. Strivens. She's definitely college material. Her grades aren't terrific, though, and she's going to have even less time to study once she's working."

Pain flashed in his eyes, temper climbed, red, up his neck to pulse in the stubble covering his cheeks and chin. "You think I don't know that, Miss Remington? You think I wouldn't like for my daughter, for *all three* of my kids, to have a nice place to live and clothes that

didn't come from somebody's ragbag and a chance to
go on to college?"

"I didn't mean—"

Strivens glanced toward the trailer again. Softened
slightly. "I know," he said, sounding so tired and sad that
the backs of Julie's eyes scalded. "I know your intentions
are good. We've come on some hard times, my family
and me, but we're still—" he choked up, swallowed and
went on "—we're still a family. We'll get by somehow,
but only if we all do our part."

Avoiding Strivens's eyes, Julie opened the little memo
book with its miniature pencil looped through the top
and scrawled her cell and school numbers onto a page,
then handed it out the window. "If there's anything I can
do to help," she said, "please call me."

Strivens took the piece of paper, stared down at it for
a long moment, then turned away from Julie, shoving
it into his coat pocket as he did so. Prying the ax out
of the chopping block, he silently went back to work.

Half an hour later, when Julie pulled into one of the
bays of the McKettricks' multicar garage, it was already
dark. The door had barely rolled down behind her before Calvin was scrambling out of his car seat to dash
inside the house.

It would have been impossible not to note the contrasts between the mansion on the Silver Spur and the
single-wide trailer where Rachel lived with her father
and brothers.

Feeling twice her real age, Julie got out, reached into
the backseat for her purse and the quilted tote bag she
used as a briefcase. Harry, the beagle, could be heard
barking a joyous welcome inside the house, and that
made her smile.

The kitchen was warm and brightly lit, and fragrant with something savory Esperanza was making for supper.

Hungry and tired, Julie felt a rush of gratitude, smiling her thanks at the other woman as she stepped around Calvin and the dog to carry her things into the guest quarters in back.

After getting out of her skirt and sweater and putting on jeans and a long-sleeved royal-blue T-shirt, Julie washed her face and hands in the guest bath and returned to the kitchen to help Esperanza.

"How many places shall I set?" Julie asked, pausing in front of a set of glass-fronted cupboards. The number varied—sometimes, it was just Esperanza, Calvin and herself, but Tate and Libby and the twins often joined them for supper, even on weeknights, and it wasn't uncommon for a couple of ranch hands to share in the meal as well.

Esperanza turned from the stove, where she was stirring red sauce in a giant copper skillet. "Four of us tonight," she answered. "Garrett's back, you know."

Julie smiled. "Yes," she said, knowing how Esperanza loved it when any of her "boys" were around to cook for, fuss over and generally spoil.

Calvin, meanwhile, continued to wrestle with Harry.

"Go wash up," Julie told her son. "And don't leave your coat and your backpack lying around, either."

Calvin gave her a long-suffering look, sighed and got to his feet. He and Harry disappeared into the guest quarters.

Julie had just finished setting the table when she felt the prickle of a thrill at her nape and turned to see Garrett standing in the kitchen. He looked more like a cowboy than a politician, Julie thought, wearing jeans and old boots and a cotton shirt the color of his eyes.

Grinning, he rolled up his sleeves, revealing a pair of muscular forearms.

"Well," he said, in that soft, slow drawl of his, "howdy all over again."

Julie, oddly stricken, blinked. "Howdy," she croaked, froglike.

Esperanza, about to set a platter of enchiladas on the table, chuckled.

"Where is el niño?" she asked, looking around for Calvin.

"I'll get him," Julie said, too quickly, dashing out of the room.

When she got back, Calvin in tow, Esperanza was at the table, in her usual place, while Garrett stood leaning against one of the counters, evidently waiting.

Only when Julie was seated, Calvin on the bench beside her, did Garrett pull back the chair at the head of the table and sit.

Everybody bowed their heads, and Esperanza offered thanks.

Calvin had probably been peeking at Garrett through his eyelashes throughout the brief prayer, though Julie could only speculate. Grace seemed particularly appropriate that night.

The Strivens family was having soup. And not enough of it, apparently.

"Aunt Libby had the news on when Audrey and Ava and I got home from school today," Calvin told Garrett. "I saw you on TV!"

Garrett grinned at that, though Julie caught the briefest glimpse of weariness in his eyes. "All in a day's work," he replied easily.

Esperanza gave him a sympathetic glance.

"Tate says the senator ought to be lynched," Calvin went on cheerfully, his chin and one cheek already smudged with enchilada sauce.

Julie handed him a paper napkin, watched as he bunched it into a wad, dabbed at his face and wiped away only part of the sauce.

Garrett's grin slipped a little, Julie thought, and a glance at Esperanza revealed the other woman's quiet concern.

"Is that right?" Garrett responded, very slowly. "Tate said that?"

Calvin nodded, thrilled to be carrying tales. "He didn't know I heard what he said," the little boy explained, "but when Aunt Libby poked him with her elbow, he almost choked on his coffee." A pause. "That was funny."

Garrett chuckled. "I suppose it was," he agreed.

"What's 'lynched'?" Calvin persisted, gazing up at Julie. "Aunt Libby wouldn't tell me when I asked her. She said I'd have to ask you, Mom."

Thanks a lot, sis, Julie thought wryly. "Never mind," she said. "We're eating."

"Is it something yucky, then?"

"Yes."

"Will it give me bad dreams?"

"Maybe," Julie said.

Again, Garrett chuckled. "How old are you, buddy?" he asked, watching the child.

"Almost five," Calvin answered, proudly. "That's how come they finally let me into kindergarten. Because I'm almost five."

Garrett gave a low, exclamatory whistle. "I'd have sworn you were fifty-two," he said, "and short for your age."

Calvin laughed, delighted by the joke—and the masculine attention.

Julie felt a pang, barely resisted an urge to ruffle her son's hair in a fit of unrestrained affection. He would have been embarrassed, she thought, and the pang struck again, deeper this time.

Eventually Calvin finished eating, and excused himself to feed Harry and then take him outside. Julie knew he'd ask about lynching again, but she hoped she could put him off until morning.

Esperanza began clearing the table, and waved Julie away when she moved to help.

Calvin and the dog came back inside.

"Time for your bath, big guy," Julie said.

For once, Calvin didn't argue. Maybe he wanted to look good in front of Garrett McKettrick; she couldn't be sure.

Once the boy and his dog had vanished into the guest suite, and Esperanza had served the coffee, started the dishwasher and gone as well, Julie was alone with Garrett.

The realization was deliciously unsettling.

She cleared her throat diplomatically, but when she opened her mouth, intending to make some kind of pitch concerning the foundation's funding the new computers in full, not a sound came out.

Garrett watched her, amusement flickering in his eyes. He could have thrown her a lifeline, tossed out some conversational tidbit to get things started, but he didn't. He simply waited for her to make another attempt.

That was when Calvin reappeared, tugging at Julie's shirtsleeve and startling her half out of her skin. "Do I *have* to take a bath tonight? I had one *last* night and I hardly even got dirty today."

Garrett's smile set Julie back on her figurative heels.

Flustered, she turned to her son. "Yes, Calvin," she said firmly, "you *do* have to take your bath."

"But Esperanza and I were going to watch TV," Calvin protested, his usual sunny-sky nature clouding over. "Our favorite show is on, and somebody's sure to get voted off and sent home."

Julie turned back to Garrett. "Excuse me," she said, rising.

Garrett merely nodded.

She took Calvin to their bathroom, where Esperanza was filling the tub. The older woman smiled at Julie— she'd already gotten out the little boy's pajamas, and they were neatly folded and waiting on the lid of the clothes hamper.

Bless the woman, she went out of her way to be helpful.

Julie felt yet another rush of gratitude.

Harry sat on a hooked rug in the middle of the bathroom, panting and watching the proceedings.

"I'll make sure young Mr. Calvin is bathed and in his pajamas in time to watch our program," Esperanza said. Then she made a shooing motion with the backs of her fingers. "You go back to the kitchen."

Was Esperanza playing matchmaker?

Julie made a little snorting sound as she left the bathroom. Herself and *Garrett McKettrick*?

Fat chance.

The man was a *politician*, for cripes' sake.

Anyway, he had probably lit out for his part of the house by then, either because he'd already forgotten their encounter or because he'd guessed that she was about to ask for something—with all the pride-swallowing that would entail—and wanted to avoid her.

Garrett was still at the table, though, drinking coffee and frowning at the newspaper spread out in front of him. He'd recently topped off his cup—the brew steamed at his right elbow—and when he looked up, Julie saw that he was wearing wire-rimmed glasses.

For some reason, that struck her in a tender place.

Seeing her, he stood.

"I guess you must have heard about Senator Cox," Garrett said, with a nod toward the paper, his voice deep and solemn and very quiet.

Julie nodded. "I'm sorry," she told Garrett, and then she felt foolish. "If that's the appropriate sentiment, I mean," she stumbled on. "Being sorry, that is."

She closed her eyes, sighed and squeezed the bridge of her nose.

When she looked at Garrett again, he smiled, took off his glasses and folded down the stems, tucked them into the pocket of his shirt.

His eyes were the heart-bruising blue of a September sky.

His expression, unreadable.

"Did I read you wrong, or did you want to speak to me about something earlier, before the interruption?"

Oh, but there was a slight edge to his tone—or was she imagining that?

Totally confused, Julie raised her chin a notch. "Sit down," she said. "Please."

"Not until you do," Garrett said, grinning again.

Julie smiled, plunked herself down on the bench and waited until Garrett was back in his chair.

She was instantly nervous.

Her heart thrummed away at twice its normal rate, and she knew it wasn't just because she meant to look a gift horse in the mouth, so to speak.

"The foundation—your family's, I mean—has very generously promised to match any money the school district can raise to buy new computers and software for use in the library at Blue River High and—"

A sudden blush surged up Julie's neck and cut off her words. What was the matter with her? Why was she so self-conscious?

This just wasn't like her.

"And?" Garrett finally prompted, putting his glasses back on.

"We appreciate the gift," Julie managed lamely.

"You're welcome," Garrett said, puzzled now.

Damn her pride.

And for all she knew, Garrett wasn't even directly involved with the McKettrick family's foundation. Hadn't she read once that his cousin, Meg McKettrick O'Ballivan, who lived in Arizona with her famous country-singer husband, handled such things? She would have to do some research before she broached the subject again, could have kicked herself for not thinking of that sooner.

Garrett waited, and though he wasn't smiling, something danced in his eyes. He was enjoying this.

In the end, though, Julie outwaited him.

Presently, with a tap of one index finger to the front page of the newspaper, he asked, "As a voter, what's your take on the senator's future in politics?"

"I'm probably not the right person to ask," she said moderately, remembering their somewhat heated exchange after a mutual friend's funeral a few months before. It had been fairly brief, but they *had* gotten into a lively discussion of one of the major issues of the day.

"Why would you say that?" Garrett asked, sounding genuinely curious.

"I voted against the senator in the last election," she admitted. Her cheeks burned, not with chagrin but with lingering conviction. "And the one before that."

"I see," Garrett said, and his mouth quirked again, at the same corner as before.

"Why?"

Julie straightened. "Because I liked his opponent better."

"That's the only reason?"

Julie's shoulders rose and fell with the force of her sigh. "All right, no. No, it isn't. I never liked Morgan Cox very much, never trusted him. There's something… well, *sneaky*…about him."

"Something 'sneaky'?" Garrett challenged, a wry twist to his mouth, sitting back in his chair, watching her. He slid the newspaper in her direction, somehow directing her gaze to the photo spread—every shot showed Senator Cox with smiling children, or golden retrievers, or an adoring and much-admired *Mrs.* Cox or some combination thereof.

Julie hesitated, choosing her words carefully. "The whole thing seemed too perfect," she finally replied. "Almost as though he'd *hired* people to *pose* as his all-American family. And then there was that hot-tub incident. It was downplayed in the media, strangely enough, but it happened. I remember it clearly."

Garrett gave a hoarse chuckle at that. He didn't sound amused, though. "Ah, yes," he said, far away now. "That."

"That," Julie agreed. "Senator Morgan Cox in a hot

tub with three half-naked women, none of whom were his wife. It was a family reunion, he claimed, and they were all just a happy group of cousins. As if any idiot would believe a story like that."

Something changed in Garrett's face. "I can think of at least one idiot who believed it," he said quietly.

Julie wished she'd kept her opinions to herself, but it was a little late for that. "What happens now?" she asked, and this time her tone was gentle.

"I can't speak for Senator Cox," Garrett said, after a long time, "but I'll be staying on here for a while."

A strangely celebratory tingle moved through Julie at this news.

Not that she cared whether Garrett McKettrick was around or not.

"Well, good night," she said.

"Good night," Garrett replied.

Julie turned around too fast, bumped into the cabinet behind her, and gasped with pain.

Garrett caught hold of her arm, turned her to face him.

One wrong move on either of their parts, Julie reasoned wildly, and their torsos would be touching.

"Are you all right?" Garrett asked. His hands rested lightly on her shoulders now.

Their faces were only inches apart.

It would be so easy to kiss.

No, Julie thought. *No, I am* not *all right.*

"Julie?" Garrett prompted.

"I'm fine," she lied, easing backward, out of his grasp.

Julie turned around carefully that time, and walked, with dignity, out of the kitchen, managing not to crash into anything in the process.

Tomorrow, she told herself, *is another day.*

CHAPTER FOUR

DAWN ARRIVED LONG before Garrett was ready for it, and so did his brother. When he stumbled out the back door of the ranch house, after a brief shower, there was Tate, already waiting in front of the barn. He'd saddled old Stranger, their dad's roan, for himself, and a black gelding named Dark Moon for Garrett.

After flashing Garrett a grin, Tate swung up onto Stranger's back and took an easy hold on the reins.

"I'd kill for coffee," Garrett said, hauling himself onto Dark Moon, shifting around to get comfortable. He'd forgotten how hard a saddle could be, especially when the rider was less than thirty minutes from a warm, soft bed.

"It won't come to that," Tate assured him, still grinning. "But I know the feeling." He turned, pulled a medium-sized Thermos bottle from one of his saddlebags and tossed it to Garrett. "Made it myself."

Garrett chuckled. "I might have some just the same," he said, unscrewing the cup-lid and then the plug. He poured a swig and sipped. "Not bad," he allowed. "You wouldn't happen to have a plate of bacon and eggs in the other side of those saddlebags, would you?"

Tate chuckled and shook his head. "Sorry," he said. "We'd best get moving. Most of the crew is already on the range, ready to work."

Garrett resealed the coffee jug, rode close to hand it back to Tate, watched as his brother stowed it away again.

He hadn't had nearly enough java to jump-start his brain, but he supposed for the time being it would have to do.

Tate led the way through a series of corral gates, and by then the darkness was shot through with the first flimsy rays of sunshine. They crossed the landscape side by side, their horses at a gallop, and Garrett was surprised at how good he felt. How...right.

"You heard anything from our little brother lately?" Tate asked, slowing the roan as they neared the temporary camp, where a small bonfire burned. Cowboys and horses milled all around, raising up dust, and the cattle bawled out there in the thinning gloom as if they were plain dying of sorrow.

"No," Garrett answered. God knew, he had troubles of his own, but he worried about Austin. Their kid brother had taken his time growing up, and then he'd nearly been killed riding a bull at a rodeo over in New Mexico. Coming that close to death would have made some people a mite more cautious, but the effect on Austin had been just the opposite. He was wilder than ever.

Tate reined in a little more, and so did Garrett. "I figure if we don't get some word of him soon, we'll have to go out looking for the damn fool."

Garrett nodded, stood in the stirrups to stretch his legs. He'd be sore for the next few days, he supposed, but riding wasn't a thing a man forgot how to do. His muscles would take a little time to remember, that was all. "I'll do some checking," he said.

"I'd appreciate it," Tate answered.

A couple of the cowboys hailed them from up ahead, and the din and the dirt clouds increased with every stride their horses took toward the herd.

"Garrett?"

Garrett turned to his brother. "Are you going to jaw at me all day, Tate?" he joked. Of the three McKettrick brothers, Tate was normally the one least likely to run off at the mouth.

Tate grinned. "No," he said. "But I've got one more thing to say." He paused, adjusted the angle of his hat, pulling the brim down low over his forehead. "It's good to have you back."

With that, Tate nudged Stranger's flanks with his boot heels, and the horse bounded ahead, leaving Garrett to catch up.

And since Garrett was out of practice when it came to cowboying, he was pretty much catching up all morning long.

With a few minutes to go before she had to be at school, Julie followed an impulse and drove by the cottage she'd been renting since her return to Blue River, when Calvin was just a baby. The exterminator's giant tent still billowed around it like a big, putty-colored blob.

Watching the thing undulate from within, Julie didn't immediately notice Suzanne Hillbrand, of Hillbrand Real Estate. Her Mercedes was parked nearby.

Wearing high heels, a pencil skirt and very big hair, Suzanne was examining the spiffy new For Sale sign out by the curb.

The shock of seeing that sign struck Julie like a slap across the face. She cranked the Caddie into Park and got out, slamming the door hard behind her.

"Well," Suzanne trilled, beaming, "*hello*, Julie Remington!"

Suzanne's outgoing personality wasn't an affectation designed to sell properties; she'd always been that way.

Even in kindergarten. The big hair only went back as far as high school, though.

"Hello, Suzanne," Julie responded, not smiling. She indicated the sign with a motion of one hand. "Are you sure this isn't a mistake?"

"Why, *of course* I'm sure, darlin'!" Suzanne replied, with exhausting ebullience, shading her perfectly made-up eyes with one perfectly manicured hand. "It isn't as if there's a real estate boom on here in Blue River, after all. I've got this cottage and the old Arnette farm on the books, and that's it."

The flash of adrenaline-fueled annoyance that had propelled Julie from behind the wheel of her Cadillac dissipated in an instant. She bit down on her lower lip.

"I take it Louise didn't tell you she was putting the place on the market?" Suzanne asked quietly.

"She might have tried," Julie admitted, picturing her very efficient and quite elderly landlady. "I'm not sure she has my cell number, and I keep forgetting to check my voice mail."

Suzanne's smile came back full force. "We all know you and Libby and Paige came into some money a while back," she said. "Things like that get around, of course. Well, here's the perfect investment for you. Your very own cottage. Think how easy it would be. You wouldn't even have to pack up and move!"

In spite of herself, Julie smiled. She'd always liked Suzanne, and the woman's enthusiasm was catching. Plus, she'd often dreamed of buying the cottage—back when she didn't have the means, especially.

"What's the asking price?"

Suzanne named a figure that would nearly wipe out Julie's considerable nest egg.

So much for enthusiasm.

"No way," Julie said, backing up a step.

Suzanne stayed happy. "Louise is firm on the price," she said. "I told her she wouldn't get that much, considering the state the market's in right now, but she's not about to budge. The place is paid for, and she doesn't need the money. All that works in your favor, of course, because you'll probably have all kinds of time before it actually sells—to find somewhere else to live, I mean."

All kinds of time to find somewhere else to live.

Oh, right.

There weren't a lot of housing options in towns the size of Blue River.

Let's see. She could move in with Paige, who was in the process of renovating the small house they'd all grown up in, rent by the week at the seedy Amble On Inn on the edge of town, or make an offer on the Arnette farm, which was almost as much of an eyesore as the Wilkeses' junkyard.

A fixer-upper, Suzanne would call it.

In Julie's opinion, the only hope of making that old dump look better was a bulldozer.

For the time being, she'd have to stay on at the Silver Spur.

Darn.

Remembering the time, Julie checked her watch and turned to head back to her car. Calvin was in another mood, and she'd had to cajole him into getting out of bed, eating his breakfast, finding his backpack.

By the time she'd dropped him off at Libby's, so he could ride to school with the twins, Julie had been working on a mood of her own.

"You think about making an offer, now!" Suzanne called after her.

Julie waved, got back into her car and headed for Blue River High.

Okay, so the day was definitely going in the downhill direction, she thought, as she pulled into the teachers' lot and spotted a shiny blue SUV over in visitors' parking. Things could still turn around, if she just looked on the bright side, counted her blessings.

She had a wonderful, healthy son.

She had a job she loved, even if it was a bummer sometimes.

And, yeah, someone might come along and buy the cottage right out from under her and Calvin, but given the economic slowdown, selling would probably take a while. In the meantime, she and her little boy had a roof over their heads, and for the first time in Julie's life, thanks to a fluke, she had money in the bank.

A person didn't have to look far to see that a lot of other people weren't so fortunate. The Strivens family, for instance.

Julie parked the Cadillac, grabbed her tote bag and her lunch, and got out.

While she was locking up, she saw the driver's-side door of the strange blue SUV swing open.

Gordon Pruett got out.

She barely recognized him, with his short haircut, chinos and polo shirt. A commercial fisherman by trade, Calvin's father had always been a raggedy-jeans-and-muscle-shirt kind of guy.

Julie's stomach seemed to take a bungee jump as she watched the man she'd once loved—or *believed* she loved—strolling toward her as though they both had all the time in the world.

Like Calvin's, Gordon's eyes were a piercing ice-blue, and both father and son had light blond hair that paled to near silver in bright sunshine.

"Hello, Julie," Gordon said. He was tanned, and a diamond stud sparkled in the lobe of his right ear, making him look something like a pirate.

"Gordon," Julie managed, aware that she hadn't moved since spotting him moments before. "What are you doing here? Why didn't you call?"

"I did call," Gordon answered mildly, keeping his distance, squinting a little in the dazzle of a fall morning. "I've emailed, too. Multiple times, in fact. You've been putting me off for a couple of months now, Jules, so I figured we'd better talk in person."

Julie sighed. Her throat felt dry and raw, and her knees were wobbly, insubstantial. "Calvin isn't ready to see you," she said.

"If that's true," Gordon responded, "I'm more than willing to wait until he is ready. But are you sure our son is the reluctant one, Julie? Or is it you?"

Tears of frustration and worry burned in her eyes. She blinked them away, at the same time squaring her shoulders and stiffening her spine. "Calvin is barely five years old," she replied, "and you're a stranger to him."

"I'm his father."

Julie closed her eyes for a moment, drew a deep, deep breath, and released it slowly. "Yes," she said. "You're his father—biologically. But you didn't want to be part of Calvin's life or mine, remember? You said you weren't ready."

Gordon might have flinched; his reaction was so well-controlled as to be nearly invisible. Still, there *had* been a reaction. "I regret that," he said. "But I've taken care of Calvin, haven't I? Kept up the child support payments? Let you raise him the way you wanted to?"

Julie's throat thickened. She swallowed. Gordon wasn't a monster, she reminded herself silently. Just a flesh-and-blood man, with plenty of good qualities and plenty of faults.

"I have classes to teach," she said at last.

"Buy you lunch?"

The first-period bell rang.

Julie said nothing; she was torn.

"I could meet you somewhere, or pick up some food and bring it here," Gordon offered.

Already hurrying away, Julie finally nodded her agreement. "The Silver Dollar Saloon makes a decent sandwich," she called back. "It's on Main Street. I'll meet you there at eleven-thirty."

Gordon smiled for the first time since the encounter had begun, nodded his head and returned to the SUV.

Julie normally threw herself into her English classes, losing all track of time, but that day she simply couldn't concentrate. When lunchtime came, she grabbed her purse and fled to the parking lot, drove as fast as the speed limit allowed to the Silver Dollar.

Gordon's SUV was parked in the gravel out front; she pulled the battered Caddie up beside his vehicle, shaking her head as she looked over at his ride. Although he'd made a good living as a fisherman, Gordon had never cared much about money, not when she knew him, anyway. Instead of working another job during the off-season and saving up to buy a bigger boat, or a starter house, or—say—an engagement ring, as some of his friends would have done, Gordon had partied through every nickel he earned. By the time he went back to sea, he was not only broke, but in debt to his father and several uncles besides.

The SUV looked fairly new.

His clothes, while nothing fancy, were good.

Obviously, Gordon had grown up—at least a little—since the last time Julie had seen him.

Now, reflecting on these things, she steeled herself as she walked up to the door of the Silver Dollar, started a little when it opened before she got hold of the handle.

Gordon stood just over the threshold, in the sawdust and peanut shells that covered the floor, acting for all the world like a gentleman.

Maybe he truly *had* changed. For Calvin's sake, she hoped so.

She swept past him, waited for her eyes to adjust to the change of light.

The click of pool balls, the steady twang from the jukebox, the aroma of hot grease wafting from the grill—it was all familiar.

The Silver Dollar was doing a brisk business for a weekday, and folks nodded at Julie in greeting as she let Gordon steer her toward the back, where he'd scored one of the booths.

He waited until she was seated before sliding into the seat across from hers.

"You're as beautiful as ever," he said. "It's good to see you again, Julie."

The waitress appeared, handed Julie a menu. "The special is a grilled chicken sandwich, extra for cheese."

"I'll have that, please," Julie said. "Without the cheese. Unsweetened iced tea, too, with lemon."

Gordon asked for a double-deluxe cheeseburger with curly fries and a side of coleslaw, plus a cola.

"Fishing must be hungry business these days," Julie commented, to get the conversation going.

"I'm not fishing anymore," Gordon answered. "I'm in construction."

"I see," Julie said, though of course she *didn't*, not really.

"How is Calvin?" Gordon asked.

"Except for his asthma, and he hasn't had any problems with that for a while, he's healthy and happy. He has a dog, a beagle named Harry, and he's been learning to ride horseback out on the Silver Spur."

"I can't believe he's in kindergarten," Gordon said.

Their drinks came, and neither of them spoke until the waitress had gone.

"Believe it," Julie said. "Calvin can already read and do simple math, and he would have skipped kindergarten and gone directly into first grade if I hadn't refused to let him do that."

Gordon watched her pensively, stirring his tall, icy cola with his straw. "I'm not here to make trouble, Julie," he said.

"I didn't say you were," Julie pointed out.

He grinned. "No," he agreed, "you didn't. But you're not happy to see me, are you?"

"No," Julie admitted glumly.

Gordon chuckled at that. "Okay," he said. "That's fair. I appreciate the honesty."

The food came, and Gordon took the time to salt and pepper his burger, line up the little wells of ketchup for dunking fries.

Julie cut her sandwich in half to make it more manageable and surprised herself by eating a few bites.

"I think I told you about Dixie," Gordon began. "My wife?"

"You told me," Julie said. "Are you still living in Louisiana?"

Gordon shook his head. "Dallas," he said. "That's Dixie's hometown. Lots of construction going on, so I've been working steady."

"That's good," Julie said carefully.

She had lived with this man.

Made love with him, borne his child.

Even back then, in the throes of passion, she'd known so little about Gordon Pruett. Never met his parents and very few of his friends. She wondered, then and now, if he'd been trying to keep her a secret for some reason.

"Dixie's dad owns the construction company," Gordon explained, with no trace of apology or defensiveness. "We have a nice home in a good neighborhood and—"

"You can't have Calvin," Julie broke in, frightened again. Still. "I'm all he knows, and I won't just send him off to live with total strangers, Gordon."

Gordon raised both hands in a bid for peace. "Julie," he said, leaning toward her a little, his voice slow and earnest, "let's be clear from the beginning. I have no intention—*zero*—of going after full custody, or even *shared* custody. I'll continue to make the child-support payments. But I want to get to know Calvin, and have him get to know me."

Julie eased up a little. Although her appetite was gone, she made herself eat a little more, so her blood sugar wouldn't plunge in the middle of the afternoon.

"And how would you go about this? Getting acquainted with Calvin, I mean?"

Gordon smiled, and Julie was reassured by the kind twinkle in his eyes. "Very slowly and carefully at first," he replied. "Maybe we'd just go out for pizza in the beginning, or play some miniature golf. Of course, you'd be included in any outings Dixie and I planned for Calvin—we wouldn't expect you to be comfortable with any other kind of arrangement, at least in the beginning."

Julie's relief must have shown clearly in her face, because Gordon reached across the table, took her hand in a gentle grip and gave it a fleeting squeeze.

"Except for spending the night with one or the other of my sisters, Libby or Paige, Calvin's never been away from home," she said tentatively. "His asthma doesn't flare up very often, but when it does and it's bad, he's terrified. Usually the inhaler works, but sometimes he needs a ventilator."

Gordon's Calvin-blue eyes were solemn. Looking across the table at this man, this familiar stranger, Julie slipped into a time warp for just a fraction of an instant and saw her little boy, all grown up.

"Dixie's an RN," he said. "She knows all about medical equipment and medicines and the like. And she *loves* kids. In fact, we're expecting one of our own next April."

Julie felt a too-familiar ache on Calvin's behalf.

Gordon was excited about the baby he and Dixie were expecting. He was ready to be a father. Where had all this maturity been when *Calvin* was born?

On the other hand, shouldn't she just be grateful that Gordon wanted a relationship with his son at all? As absentee fathers went, he was surely one of the better ones.

"How long will you be in town?" she asked, after taking a long sip of iced tea to wet her nerve-parched throat.

"We've got to be back in Dallas by the day after tomorrow," Gordon answered. "I was hoping you and Calvin could have supper with Dixie and me tonight. The café at the Amble On Inn isn't much, but they serve a decent meal."

Julie would have liked a little more time to prepare Calvin for his first real meeting with his dad and step-mom, but since she'd sort of forced Gordon's hand by dodging his calls and emails for more than a month, the opportunity was clearly lost.

Gordon had been patient, even kind, but he was no-body's fool. If he and Julie couldn't work out a visita-tion schedule they'd both be able to live with, he would almost certainly take things to the next level and hire an attorney.

"Okay," Julie said, checking her watch again. Her lunch period was almost over, and after eleventh-grade English literature, she was meeting with Arthur Dulles and several school board members in his office. He was determined to make her set aside the three one-act plays she'd intended to showcase and put on a big, splashy musical instead, because those made more money. And he was rolling out the major cannons. "What time?"

"Let's meet at the café at six, if that works for you," Gordon said.

Julie nodded, pulling her wallet from her purse when the check arrived. Gordon picked it up and waved away her offer to at least pay the tip.

He stood.

She stood.

He said thank you.

She said he was welcome.

He walked her back to her car and waited until she was inside before turning to head for his SUV.

Julie immediately got out her cell phone headset and

speed-dialed Paige. "Are you busy?" Julie asked, steering with one hand as she pulled out onto the main road.

Paige, a highly skilled surgical nurse, worked in a private clinic an hour from Blue River, and her schedule was a bugger. She put in four twelve-hour days every week, and spent most of the other three sleeping off her exhaustion and overseeing the changes she was making in the house.

"Me, busy?" she joked. "Let's see. Just as I was getting off work last night, search and rescue airlifted an accident victim in from some farm in the next county. Kid chopped off his left arm trying to sculpt a bear out of an oak stump with a chain saw—but we're the best. Dr. Kerrigan sewed it right back on. I guess that constitutes 'busy.'"

Julie felt slightly queasy. "Thanks for sharing," she said. "If you don't have time to talk, just say so."

"I have time to listen," Paige said. "What's going on, Jules?"

"The cottage is up for sale," Julie answered. "I've been renting that house from Louise Smithfield for five years, and she didn't even bother to tell me she was putting it on the market."

"So we change the renovation plans for the house," Paige said easily. "We'll make it a duplex. You and Calvin can live on one side, and I'll live on the other."

Julie's palm was damp where she was clasping the phone.

"But you didn't call to tell me about the cottage, did you?" Paige prompted.

"It's Gordon," Julie said shakily. "He's in town. He finally just…showed up. Calvin and I are having dinner with him and his wife. *Tonight*."

"Julie?"

"What?"

"Take a breath. This is a *good* thing, sis."

"So why do I feel terrified?"

"Because you've probably been going over worst-case scenarios ever since you got that first email from Gordon."

Ah, yes, the worst-case scenarios.

Julie knew them all.

Gordon snatches Calvin and whisks him off to Mexico or some other third-world country, and Julie never sees her child again.

Gordon has a secret addiction—alcohol, gambling, drugs—maybe all those and more. Calvin is not only in danger when he visits his father, he's more prone to engage in said addictions himself.

Gordon is a perfectly good father, and Calvin loves him so much that he doesn't want to live even part-time with his mom anymore.

And those were the *cheerier* ones.

"All right, I admit it," Julie all but whimpered. "I'm scared to death."

"I know," Paige said, gentling down a little. "Listen, Jules, you're the best mother in the universe," she went on softly. "But be that as it may, Calvin still needs a father."

Julie had reached the school by then, and she maneuvered into her parking spot. "You're right."

Paige laughed. "Of course I am." A pause. "Did Libby mention our getting together, the three of us, on Saturday? She wants to start shopping for her wedding dress."

The thought of Libby and her happiness made Julie feel better instantly. "We talked about it a little this morning, when I dropped Calvin off at her and Tate's house."

"Do you not think it just a little strange that they want to live there instead of the mansion?"

"It's not strange, Paige. I'm sure the small house is cozier, better suited to family life. Anyway, you know Tate's never been much for high living, and neither has Libby."

"You're staying in the main house," Paige pressed. "What's it like?"

"You've been in the ranch house, Paige. At least as far as Austin's bedroom, not to put too fine a point on things."

"Ha," Paige said. "So funny. It was dark, we were young, and I wasn't exactly thinking about architectural detail."

"I don't suppose you were," Julie drawled back. "Gotta get back to work now. Thanks for listening."

"Keep me in the loop," Paige chimed in reply.

Goodbyes were said, and the call ended.

Julie dropped her phone into her tote bag and wove her way through a river of teenagers flowing along the hallway.

Their energy exhilarated Julie, made her smile. Parents and administrators could wear her down, but the kids themselves always energized her. Many nights, after a theater group rehearsal or a performance, she was high for hours, too excited to sleep.

The afternoon sped by.

The meeting with Arthur Dulles and two school board members went exactly as Julie had expected it to—the showcase was out, unless she wanted to stage the three one-act plays in addition to the musical.

That would be impossible, of course.

Which was exactly why she was going to do it.

CHAPTER FIVE

CALVIN.

On a midnight-black horse.

As Julie drove into the yard at Tate and Libby's place late that afternoon, the sight of her child made her heart catch. Calvin looked not just happy, but transported, perched in that saddle with Garrett McKettrick behind him.

The reins rested easily in Garrett's leather-gloved hand, and his hat threw his face into shadow, but Julie felt his eyes on her as she stopped the Cadillac, shut off the motor and got out.

Man, boy and horse.

The image, Julie thought, with a sort of exhilarated terror, would remain in her mind forever, etched in sunlight, with the creek dancing behind and the sky a shade of lavender-blue that scalded her eyes.

"Look, Mom, I'm riding a horse!" Calvin crowed.

Her boy, her baby, was safe within the steely circle of Garrett's arms, she could see that plainly. And yet Julie's heart scrambled up into the back of her throat and flailed there as she thought of all the terrible things that *could* have happened.

A snake might have spooked the horse, causing him to be thrown. Badly hurt, or even killed.

Or something—some dirt mote or bit of pollen—

could have brought on one of Calvin's rare but horrifying asthma attacks.

Did he have his inhaler handy, or was it still stashed in the bottom of his backpack, as usual?

She looked around, saw Tate on another horse nearby, Audrey riding in front of him, Ava holding on from behind. Libby smiled from over by the clothesline, where she was unpegging white sheets and dropping them into a basket.

Julie stared at her sister, amazed, angry, admiring. Libby's happy grin seemed to dim a little around the edges as she left the basket behind in the grass, billowing with what looked like captured clouds, and came toward her.

"Mom!" Calvin yelled again, evidently thinking Julie hadn't noticed him. "Look! *I'm riding a horse!*"

Julie's smile felt brittle on her face, and slippery, barely holding on to her mouth. *Be reasonable*, she told herself. *No need to panic.*

"Isn't that—wonderful," she said.

Libby was at her side by then. "He's all right," she said, very quietly, and with big-sister firmness. "Garrett wouldn't let anything happen to Calvin, and Tate and I were right here all the time."

Julie swallowed, watched as Garrett took off his hat, plunked it down on Calvin's head. The little boy's face disappeared inside the crown, and his muffled laugh of delight was sweet anguish to Julie.

Her Calvin.

It hurt to love so much.

"I guess this ride's over, pardner," Garrett told Calvin, reclaiming the hat and settling it back on his own head. All the while, the man's eyes never left Julie's face, and even caught up in a tangle of conflicting emotions, she would have given a lot to know what Garrett McKettrick was thinking just then.

Keeping one arm around Calvin's middle, Garrett swung his right leg over the horse's neck and jumped easily to the ground. Set Calvin on his feet.

Giggling, the little boy staggered slightly and whooped, "Whoa!"

Garrett was still watching Julie.

She marched toward him, gave another rigid smile and reached down to grab Calvin's hand.

"We have dinner plans," she said, and while she was looking back at Garrett, she was actually *speaking* to Calvin.

Wasn't she?

Calvin looked up at her. The sun lit his hair, and he shielded his eyes with one grubby little hand. "But Tate's going to barbecue," he protested. "Hot dogs and hamburgers and *everything*."

"Another time," Julie said.

Calvin jerked his hand free of hers, and she felt stung, somewhere down deep. "But I want to stay here!"

Garrett took off his hat again, held it in one hand as he crouched next to Calvin. "A cowboy always speaks respectfully to a lady," he told the boy, "especially when that lady is his mama."

Calvin's lower lip jutted out. "She's just mad because I got on a horse without permission," he said. He turned to Julie again, his round little face and baby-blue eyes full of rebellion. "Aunt Libby *said* I could ride with Garrett! And she's the boss of me when you're not here!"

Inwardly, Julie sighed. Outwardly, she kept her cool.

"We can talk about this in the car, Calvin," she said evenly. "Get your backpack, please. Right now."

Furious, Calvin pounded off toward the house to retrieve his belongings.

Garrett rose back to his full height. For a moment, it seemed he was about to say something, but in the end he just turned, stuck a foot in the stirrup and mounted again. He rode up alongside Tate, and one of the twins—Audrey, Julie thought—leaped from her dad's horse to her uncle's.

Garrett and Tate turned their horses and rode down the gently sloping creek-bank to let the animals drink.

Which meant Julie and Libby were alone for the moment, with Calvin still inside the house.

"If you didn't want Calvin to ride," Libby said mildly, "you should have told me."

Julie realized she'd been holding her last breath and let it out in a whoosh. "I'm sorry," she said. "I was just—startled."

Libby raised one eyebrow, watching Julie closely. "Startled?"

Julie bit her lower lip. "Gordon is in town," she said, very quietly, watching as Calvin stormed out of the house again, his backpack bump-dragging behind him. "Calvin and I are having dinner with him and the wife."

"Tonight?" Libby asked.

Julie nodded brusquely. "Yes. How do I prepare Calvin for this? What do I say, Libby? 'After five years, your father has finally decided he wants to meet you'?"

Libby put an arm around her, gave her a squeeze. "So *that's* why you were so peevish and unreasonable."

"I was *not* peevish and—"

"Yes, you were," Libby interrupted, smiling. "It's

okay, Jules. I know you get stressed out about Calvin sometimes. I understand."

Libby *did* understand, and the knowledge was so soothing to Julie that she finally began to relax.

"I was having fun!" Calvin declared, standing a few feet away now, and glaring up at Julie. "Until *you* came along, anyway!"

"Calvin Remington," Julie said, "that's quite enough. Get in the car."

"Goodbye, Aunt Libby," he said, with all due drama. "If I don't see you again, because my *mother* is mad at you for letting me *have fun*, and she sends me away to *military school*, I'll get in touch as soon as I'm eighteen!"

Julie held on to her stern face—Calvin's behavior was *not* acceptable—but there was a giggle dancing inside her all the same. Just like the one she saw twinkling in her sister's eyes.

Libby waggled her fingers at Julie. "See you tomorrow?" she asked.

"See you tomorrow," Julie confirmed, with a sigh.

"Is THAT HIM?" Calvin whispered, a little over an hour later, when Julie led him into the Amble On Inn's small café. Gordon rose from a table over by the jukebox as they entered, while the lovely blonde woman accompanying him remained seated. "Is that my dad?"

"Yes," Julie said. After giving Calvin a lecture for acting like a brat at Libby and Tate's house, she'd explained about their dinner plans. He'd been unusually quiet since then, hadn't even protested when she'd made him shower and change clothes. "That's him."

It all seemed surreal.

How many times, over the short course of Calvin's

life, had she hoped Gordon would change his mind, take a real interest in their son, be a father to him?

An old saying came to mind: *Be careful what you wish for....*

Gordon had crossed the room, and now he stood facing them. His gaze connected briefly with Julie's—he mouthed the word "thanks"—and then dropped to Calvin.

"Hey, buddy," Gordon said, putting out a hand.

Calvin studied his father's hand for a few moments, his expression solemn and wary, but finally, he reached out.

They shook hands. "Hey," Calvin replied, looking the stranger up and down.

Julie gave his back a reassuring pat. Silent-speak for *Everything's going to be okay.*

"Anybody hungry?" Gordon asked, gesturing toward the table, where the blonde waited, smiling nervously. She was dressed in a pale rose cotton skirt with a ruffled top to match, and her hair fell past her shoulders in a sumptuous tumble of spun gold. Her skin and teeth were perfect.

"We were *supposed* to have barbecue at Aunt Libby's," Calvin said gravely, though he allowed Gordon to steer him toward the blonde and the table.

The evening to come, Julie knew, would be pivotal, changing all their lives forever, even if it went well. If, on the other hand, things went badly...

Julie reined in her imagination.

"Hush, Calvin," she said, looking around. The scarred café tables, the patched-vinyl chair seats and backs, the crisply pressed gingham curtains—all of it was familiar, and therefore comforting.

"I'm Dixie," Gordon's wife said, as he pulled back a chair for Julie.

"Julie," she responded—warmly, she hoped—once she was seated. Calvin took the chair beside hers, and Gordon sat with his wife, the two of them beaming at Calvin, drinking him in with their eyes.

A sort of haze descended, at least for Julie. Later, she would remember that Gordon had been wearing a blue-and-white-striped shirt, and that Dixie had ordered a chef's salad with Thousand Island dressing on the side, and that nothing of staggering importance had been said, but she would not be able to recall what she'd eaten, or what Calvin had, either.

After dessert—there *had* been dessert, because Calvin had a smudge of something chocolate on the clean shirt he'd put on after his bath, back at the ranch house—Dixie produced a digital camera from the depths of her enormous cloth handbag and took what seemed like dozens of pictures—Calvin by himself, Calvin posing with a crouching, grinning Gordon.

Telephone numbers were swapped, and Dixie promised to email copies of the photographs as soon as she and Gordon got home.

Calvin, though polite, seemed detached, too.

After the goodbyes were said in the parking lot, and he was safely buckled into his car seat in the back of the Cadillac, Julie slipped behind the wheel and waited a beat before speaking.

"So," she said, as Dixie and Gordon went by in their big blue SUV, Gordon flashing the headlights to bright once, in cheery farewell. "That's your dad. What do you think?"

Calvin was quiet.

"Calvin?" Julie finally prompted, adjusting the rear-view mirror until her son's face was visible.

At some length, Calvin huffed out a sigh. "I thought it would be different, having a dad," he said. "I thought *he* would be different."

"What do you mean?" Julie asked carefully, making no move to start up the car, though she *had* pressed the lock button as soon as she and Calvin were both inside.

"I was hoping he'd turn out to be a cowboy," Calvin admitted. "Like Tate and Garrett and Austin."

"Oh," Julie said, at a loss.

"But he's a builder guy instead," Calvin mused.

"That's good, isn't it? Building things?"

"I guess," Calvin allowed, sounding way too world-weary for a five-year-old. "I bet he gets to wear a hard hat and a tool belt and cool stuff like that, but I kind of liked it better when I could still wonder, you know?"

She *did* know. Calvin's IQ was off the charts. Young as he was, he'd probably constructed a pretty imaginative Fantasy Father in that busy little head of his. Now, he was going to have to get to know the real one, and he was bright enough to see the challenges ahead.

"Yeah," she said, very gently. She hadn't hooked up her seat belt yet, and turned sideways so she could look back at Calvin instead of watching him in the rearview. "Is something else bothering you, big guy?"

Calvin took a long time answering. "Do I have to visit my dad someplace far away, like Audrey and Ava visit their mom in New York sometimes?"

Julie's heart slipped a notch. "Not unless that's what you want," she said, when she'd injected a smile into her voice. "And you don't have to decide for a long time."

"Good," Calvin said, and the note of relief in his voice brought tears to Julie's eyes—again.

She turned once more, facing forward now, waited a few breaths, hooked on her seat belt and started the car.

"I thought I wanted a dad," Calvin confided, when they were on the main road and headed out of town. "Now, I'm not so sure. I think maybe having Tate and Garrett and Austin for uncles might be good enough."

Julie swallowed. "Well," she said, with manufactured brightness, "like I said, you don't have to decide right away." The Welcome to Blue River sign fell behind them, and it seemed to her that the night was subtly darker, the stars a little closer to the earth.

"How come you got so mad about me riding the horse?" Calvin asked, when they were well out of town, almost to the tilted mailbox marking the turnoff to Libby and Tate's little house. "I wasn't all by myself, you know. I wouldn't have gotten hurt, because Garrett was right there, behind me."

"Tell you what," Julie offered, after taking another long breath. "I'll say sorry for reacting without thinking first and getting all overprotective when I saw you on that horse, if you'll say sorry for the rude tone."

Calvin considered the deal.

"Okay," he said, at long last.

"Okay," Julie agreed.

By the time they arrived at the ranch house, Calvin was sound asleep.

He'd had a very big day for such a little guy.

Garrett happened to be in the garage when Julie pulled in. He was standing on the front bumper of an old red pickup truck, the hood raised, doing something to the works inside.

Seeing Julie, he gave a grin that stopped just short of his eyes, got down off the bumper with the same grace as he'd descended from the horse in Tate's yard earlier, and reached for a rag to wipe his hands clean.

Julie looked him over, and didn't see so much as a smidgeon of grease. When her gaze came back to his face, and she realized he'd been watching her scan him from head to foot, she blushed.

"Need some help?" he asked, when she opened the back door of the car, about to hoist Calvin out of his safety seat.

The child was nodding, half awake, half deeply asleep.

He was heavy, and Julie suddenly felt the weight of all the things she carried, visible and invisible, as she moved out of Garrett's way. Allowed him to unbuckle Calvin and lift him into his arms.

Calvin yawned, laid his head on Garrett's shoulder and went back to sleep.

The sight of this man carrying her son struck Julie in a tender place, and she wondered why that hadn't happened when she'd seen Calvin and Gordon together earlier, at the restaurant.

Julie shut the car door and followed Garrett into the kitchen, across that wide space and into the hallway leading to the guest suite she and Calvin had been occupying since the exterminators had tented the cottage.

The apartment was comfortable, though small. It boasted two bedrooms, a full bath and a little sitting room with a working fireplace and large, soft armchairs upholstered in a floral pattern made chicly shabby by age.

Harry lay curled up on a rug in front of the cold

hearth, and looked up with a big dog yawn as they entered.

"You're quite a guard dog, Harry," Julie told the animal wryly.

Garrett chuckled at that, paused to look back at her.

"To your right," Julie said, in answer to the unspoken question.

He nodded, carried Calvin into the tiny bedroom.

Julie switched on the lamp on the pinewood dresser, rather than the overhead, and watched as Garrett put Calvin down carefully on the bed and stepped away, then out of the room.

Calvin stirred, blinking, his glasses askew.

Julie, now seated on the edge of his bed, set the specs aside and kissed the little boy's forehead.

"Do I have to wash and brush my teeth?" he asked.

"Yes," Julie told him. She got it then—Calvin had almost surely been pretending to be asleep all along, so Garrett would carry him. "And you have to put on your pajamas, too."

"What about my prayers?" Calvin negotiated, as Julie shifted to tug off his little tennis shoes. "Do I have to say them?"

"That's between you and God," Julie replied.

She stood, went to the dresser, took a set of yellow cotton PJ's from the top drawer, handed them to him.

Calvin was on his feet by then, resigned to washing up and brushing his teeth.

Julie waited, smiling to herself.

She heard the toilet flush, then water running in the sink.

When Calvin returned, Julie was sitting on the side of his bed and Harry was snugged in down by the footboard. Remarkably agile on his three legs, the dog had jumped up unassisted, just as he did every night.

Julie rose, and Calvin climbed into bed, staring soberly up at Julie while she tucked him in. She was oddly aware of Garrett nearby, either in the sitting room of the suite or beyond, in the big kitchen.

"I love you," she said.

Calvin grinned. "I love you more," he countered. It was a game they played, the two of them.

"I love you all the way to the moon and back," Julie replied.

"I love you twice that much."

"I love you *ten times* more," Julie batted back.

"I love you all the numbers in the world," Calvin finished triumphantly.

Julie laughed, accepting defeat gracefully. She could have thrown infinity at him, but he would merely have doubled it.

Her heart was full when she kissed Calvin once more, for good measure. She barely kept herself from hauling him into her arms and holding him tight, tight, tight.

Of course, that would have worried him.

"Can I ride on Dark Moon again tomorrow?" he asked as switched off the lamp. "If Tate is there, or Garrett?"

Julie debated silently for a few moments, then gave a suitably noncommittal answer. "Let me talk the idea over with your aunt Libby first," she said. "Maybe it would be better if you rode one of the twins' ponies instead of a big one. The ponies are more your size."

Calvin's smile, though tentative, was worth everything to Julie. "I wish I could have my own pony," he said, in an awed whisper. "My very own pony, black and white. I'd name him something cool, like Old Paint."

"Even if he wasn't old?" Julie teased. She knew she shouldn't have played along with the pony fantasy—not even for a few moments—since it wasn't one she could fulfill, but she didn't have the heart to throw cold water on the idea.

Calvin beamed. "He could be *Young* Paint, then, I guess," he said. Without his glasses he looked even younger than he was, and more vulnerable, too.

Again, Julie wanted to gather her baby into her arms and clutch him close to her. Again, for the sake of Calvin's dignity, she resisted the urge.

He yawned big and closed his eyes. Made a little crooning sound as he settled into his pillow, into his little-boy dreams.

Julie rose and went to the doorway, lingered on the threshold, listening as his breathing slowed and deepened.

He was asleep within moments.

And Garrett was still in the sitting room.

"Got a minute?" he asked.

Julie longed for a bath, a soft nightgown and eight full hours of sleep, but nodded.

"Sit down," Garrett said.

She took one of the shabby-chic chairs, and he took the other.

The chairs faced each other, and their knees, his and hers, almost touched.

"About today," Garrett began.

Julie put up a hand. "I overreacted," she said. "To the horse, I mean. I just—I don't know—a lot of things happened earlier, and I guess I just panicked—"

Garrett grinned. "You're the boy's mother," he added, when she fell silent. "If you don't want him riding horseback, that's certainly your prerogative."

Julie nodded, then shook her head, then blushed. What was it about being in this man's presence that made her feel so rattled and so confused, so off balance? No one else affected her that way—no one ever had. Not even Gordon, when they were together.

"Libby and Paige are always telling me I'm too protective of Calvin," she said. "And they're right. He has asthma, but it's not as if he's fragile or anything. I don't want him to grow up frightened of all the things that scare *me*."

"What scares you, Julie?" Garrett asked, resting one booted foot on the opposite knee and settling back in the big armchair. He was so wholly, uncompromisingly male, so at home in his own skin, that Julie began to feel warm again.

"The uncertainty, I guess," she answered, after giving the question some thought. "What if he gets hurt? What if he gets sick? What if—?" Julie stopped herself, shook her head. "You see what I mean."

Garrett nodded. "Libby looks out for Calvin when you're not around," he told her. "So does Tate."

"I know," she said.

Garrett leaned forward a little. Lamplight played in his longish dark blond hair. "Are you afraid of horses, Julie?"

She stiffened. "Afraid?"

"Afraid for yourself, I mean."

She shook her head. "I used to ride a lot," she said. "When I was younger."

That wicked, McKettrick-patented grin flashed. "But now that you're old and decrepit, you don't?"

She laughed. "It's been a while," she admitted, sobering.

"There's a bright moon out," he said. "How about a ride?"

The prospect, out-of-the-blue, off-the-wall *crazy* as it was, had more appeal than Julie would have expected it to. "Calvin's in bed," she said. "I can't just go off…"

"Esperanza's still up," Garrett said easily, when Julie ran out of steam in the middle of her sentence. "I heard her TV when we came in earlier. She could sit with Calvin for a while."

Julie shook her head. "I wouldn't want to impose."

Garrett was already on his feet, headed for the door. He seemed to have no doubt at all that the family housekeeper would agree to serve as an impromptu babysitter.

In the doorway, he stopped and looked back at Julie. "You'll want to switch that getup for jeans and a warm shirt, a jacket and boots," he said.

"But I—"

But Garrett had already left the room.

Within twenty minutes, Esperanza had settled herself on the sitting room couch, knitting and smiling while she watched TV, the sound muted.

Julie was wearing jeans, boots, a thick shirt and a denim jacket.

How did this happen? she asked herself, as she followed Garrett across the kitchen, out the back door, across the broad, grassy yard toward the barn. *How did I get here?*

The moon and stars were so bright that night, she could have read by them. Small print, no less.

"Is this even safe?" she asked. "Going riding? What if the horses can't see?"

Garrett glanced back at her. "Does everything you do have to be safe?" he countered.

"I'm the single mother of a very young child," she retorted, mildly defensive. "So, *yes*, everything I do has to be safe. As safe as I can make it, anyway."

"I'll put you on the tamest horse we have," Garrett replied, waiting until she caught up, fell into step next to him. "We'll stay on soft ground—not that Ladybug would ever throw you—and it's like daylight out here."

Julie said nothing. She didn't look at Garrett, didn't want him to see in her face that for all her misgivings, she was excited by the adventure. Maybe even a little thrilled.

"Unless, of course," Garrett went on, stepping in front of her just before they reached the entrance to the barn, blocking her way, causing her to look up at him in surprise, "it's not the horse you're afraid of."

Julie thrust out her chin, rested her hands on her hips, elbows sticking out. "If you're implying that I'm afraid of *you*, Garrett McKettrick—"

"No," he agreed, curving a finger under her chin and lifting, "but you might be a little scared of *yourself*."

She gave a huffy burst of laughter, though the truth was that she *was* scared. "Oh, right," she said, having no choice but to tough it out. "I'm *terrified*. I might be overcome by your masculine charms, lose control, throw myself at you. It could happen at any moment!"

Garrett laughed again, and for one lovely, dreadful skittering beat of her heart, she thought he was going to kiss her.

Instead, he took her hand and led her into the barn.

Various motion-sensor lights came on as they entered, but mostly the stalls were dark.

Julie sat on a bale of hay, trying to think of a way to get out of going riding in the dark without sounding chicken, wanting, at the same time, more than practically anything, *ever*, this ride, on this night, with this man.

Garrett whistled under his breath as he led two horses out into the wide sawdust-covered aisle between the long rows of stalls and saddled them.

And Julie wondered why she wasn't behaving like a sane woman, a teacher and a mother, soaking in a nice bath, or sipping a cup of herbal tea, or a glass of white wine, before climbing into bed.

"Ready?" Garrett asked, startling her a little.

She stood. "Ready," she said.

They led the horses out into a star-silvered night, and Julie mounted without waiting for Garrett. She hadn't ridden in years—not since high school, when she'd sometimes visited the McKettrick ranch with Libby. Even then, her sister and Tate had been in love, though they would have a lot of rivers to cross before they found their way back to each other.

Garrett climbed onto his own horse, and although she couldn't be sure, Julie would have sworn he winced a little as he lowered himself into the saddle.

A smile touched down on Julie's mouth, immediately flew away again. Of *course*, she thought, Garrett had been wearing a suit to work for years. Sitting at desks. Yes, he was a McKettrick through and through, and riding was in his blood, but she wasn't the only one likely to be sore in the morning.

He bent from the saddle to work the latch on a gate,

rode through and waited for Julie before shutting it again behind her.

They followed the shining ribbon of creek winding along the lower end of the range, and the lights of staff trailers and Tate and Libby's house gleamed distantly through the trees.

The peace was all-encompassing, and there was no need for words.

Julie drank it all in, the country quiet, the cloppity-clop of the horses' hooves, the babbling murmur of the creek, the sighs and whispers of the wind. The cattle were quiet, some lying down, dark lumps in the moonlight, others still grazing. Once in a while, one of them gave a low, mournful call.

She tilted her head back, breathed in not only fresh, cool air, but the very light of the stars and the moon, or so it seemed to her. She hadn't done anything this impulsive since—well, since she couldn't remember when. She was a single mother, a teacher. She loved her son, she worked and struggled and...she survived.

Moonlit horseback rides with a true cowboy, born and bred, were not part of her everyday experience.

When she and Garrett started back toward the ranch house after half an hour or so, Julie was sorry to see the odyssey end. As tired as she was, as emotionally wrung out from the evening with Gordon and Dixie, the ride left her feeling restored.

She would be ready for whatever came next.

CHAPTER SIX

JULIE STOOD FACING the big bulletin board in the high school cafeteria late the next afternoon, tacking up the printed notice announcing that tryouts for *Kiss Me Kate* would begin on Monday afternoon of the following week, as soon as the day's classes were over.

"So it's official, huh?" the girl asked, trying to smile. "The showcase is out and the musical is in?"

Julie had been inside all day, and she needed some fresh air. She felt frustrated and out of sorts—none of which was Rachel's problem. "I was thinking we could do a single performance of each of the plays—no props, no extras of any kind—and record them. Send digital copies—"

Rachel colored up so quickly that Julie fell silent.

The worst was true, then. Rachel had already given up on going to college.

"My little brothers need me," she said, at once shy and fierce. "They're having a really hard time without Mom, and Dad tries, but it isn't the same."

The last bell of the day shrilled, signaling dismissal.

Julie waited for it to stop, but even when it had, the din was joyously horrendous—kids poured out of class-rooms, locker doors squealed open and slammed shut again, exuberant plans were shouted, and most likely texted, from one end of the school's main corridor to the other.

Julie had always loved the sounds and the energy of kids. Her dad had often said, with a look of tired contentment in his eyes, that he'd been born to teach and Julie had never doubted he was right.

In that way, she was like Will Remington—teaching was her gift. She loved children, related to them, thrilled to the excitement some of them radiated when she finally got through, and they grasped some concept that had eluded them before.

Of course there were always others who, for one reason or another, couldn't be reached. She didn't want Rachel to be one of those kids.

But what could she say? In Rachel's place, she might have done the same thing. And it was sobering to think that, in some ways, Libby *had* been in a position similar to this young girl's.

Libby hadn't joined the school band or acted in plays or tried out for cheerleader. She'd come straight home every day, after her last class, to mother Julie and Paige.

Something buzzed, jolting Julie out of her reflections.

Rachel took a cheap cell phone from the pocket of her hooded sweatshirt and peered at the screen. The phone looked like a pay-as-you-go model, the kind sold in convenience stores, along with tacky cigarette lighters, energy boosters in little bottles and candy bars in faded wrappers.

Julie wasn't really surprised to see the cell, of course. Kids with virtually nothing else had phones. It was a sign of the times.

"Dad sent me a text," Rachel explained, though Julie

hadn't asked. "He wants me to go over to the elementary school and take the bus home with my brothers before I head over to the bowling alley for work."

Julie nodded. "I could give you a ride," she offered, wondering how Rachel planned to get back to the bowling alley after she took the boys home and if there would be anyone to look after them after she left.

But Rachel shook her head. "That's okay," she said.

Still, she didn't move to walk away.

"Was there something else, Rachel?" Julie finally asked.

"I just—I just wanted to say thank you, Ms. Remington. For picking my play to be in the showcase and everything. It really meant a lot to me." Sorrow shone in the girl's wide, luminous eyes, and a kind of determined bravery. "Guess I'd better get moving, or I might miss the elementary school bus." With that, Rachel was gone, hurrying through the crowds of departing kids, disappearing from view.

Julie was still pensive, half an hour later, when she stopped by Libby and Tate's to pick up Calvin.

He was down at the creek-side, with the twins and Libby, all of them wielding fishing poles.

Julie parked the pink bomb and got out, cheered by the sight.

"Have you caught anything yet?" she called, from the top of the bank, her arms folded against a chilly wind. It was bonfire weather, leaf-burning, blue-skied, hot-soup-simmering-on-the stove weather.

"Not one single fish," Libby called back, grinning. She wore jeans, a heavy sweatshirt, sneakers and a ponytail. Briefly, guiltily, Julie envied her sister, soon to be married to a man who loved her. "Guess it's beans and wieners for supper tonight!"

Julie laughed, because envy or no envy, she loved both her sisters. And she was happy for Libby, happy for Tate, happy for Audrey and Ava, the six-year-old twins who needed the stability their father and future stepmother provided.

Calvin seemed set apart from them all somehow, and Julie felt an ache of sadness as he reeled in his fishing line and turned to trudge up the bank behind Libby and the twins.

"Hi, Mom," he said, without particular enthusiasm.

Julie laid a hand on his head, ruffled his hair. "Hey," she said back.

"You might as well stay for supper," Libby said quietly, slipping an arm around Julie's waist and steering her toward the little house. She gave Julie a mischievous grin and a sisterly squeeze. "I'm not *really* serving beans and wieners," she said. "We're having stew, and it's been simmering in the Crock-Pot all day. It smells like heaven."

"*You* cooked?" Julie teased.

Libby laughed, sent the three kids around back to put the fishing poles away on the covered porch and take off their muddy shoes. "Now that I don't have the Perk Up to run, I'm developing all sorts of new skills."

Julie's insides warmed at the twinkle in her sister's eyes—and the aroma of savory stew, as they stepped into the living room. Until their mother, Marva, had driven Julie's Cadillac through the front wall and brought the whole place down, timber-and-brick, Libby had been the harried owner of a coffee shop on Main Street.

Three dogs—Libby's aging Lab, Hildie, and the twins' matching mutts, Ambrose and Buford—barked a greeting.

Libby shushed them, while Julie looked around at the living room, admiring the renovations anew, even though she'd seen the project unfolding all along. A row of floor-to-ceiling windows overlooked the creek and the towering oak trees in one direction, and the old orchard in the other. A fire crackled on the hearth of the natural stone fireplace, and the screen of Libby's new computer ran a perpetual slide show of photos she'd taken herself—Tate, the girls, Calvin, the breathtaking scenery that surrounded them on all sides.

"How's the online degree coming along?" Julie asked, as the dogs deserted them, en masse, for the kitchen, where the kids were entering from the back porch.

Libby looked back at her, shrugged. "It's coming," she said. "I've mostly been looking at pictures of other people's weddings online." She dropped into a cushy armchair, legs dangling over one side, looking more like a teenager than a woman about to be married. "Sit," she added.

Julie sat. The kids and the dogs were making a commotion in the kitchen, but it didn't seem to bother Libby, so Julie didn't worry, either.

"Are we still on for the shopping trip on Saturday?" Libby asked.

"Why wouldn't we be?" Julie countered. The snap in her voice surprised her as much as it did Libby.

Julie frowned.

Libby waited a few beats. "What's bothering you, Jules? Did dinner with Gordon and the missus go badly?"

Julie sighed. Shook her head. "It was…okay," she said. "I'm still worried about how this whole thing is going to be for Calvin, but for right now, anyway, I think I can feel my way through."

"Then, what?" Libby inquired gently. She wasn't pushy, but she wasn't going to be put off, either. "The cottage being under a tent? The job?"

Again, Julie sighed. "Arthur Dulles and the school board have spoken," she said. "I'd planned on showcasing the one-act plays—I told you about them—but a musical always brings in more money, so it's scratch the showcase and stage the umpteenth amateur production of a Broadway staple."

Libby smiled, looking a little puzzled. "I've never known you to balk at an excuse to sing and dance," she said. "Even vicariously, by directing instead of actually treading the boards."

Julie laughed, feeling better already, but the bittersweet sensation, like sadness but *not* sadness, lingered. "*Kiss Me Kate* will be lots of fun," she admitted. "But I was counting on the showcase to help those three kids get into college."

Libby raised an eyebrow. "Won't they get in anyway? They're all smart."

"Tim and Becky will," Julie nodded, thinking of the two young playwrights whose plays she'd planned to produce, along with Rachel's. Both of them were from middle-class families, and they had scholarships and loans in place. "I'm not so sure about Rachel."

Libby simply waited, so at ease sprawled in that chair.

Julie told her sister what little she knew about the girl's circumstances.

"You're afraid she won't go to college because her dad and her brothers need her?" Libby recapped, when Julie had finished.

Julie nodded.

Calvin, the twins and the three dogs all straggled in from the kitchen.

"Can we watch TV?" one of the twins asked. Both girls were beautiful, with their father's McKettrick-blue eyes. They wore mismatched jeans, boots, plaid flannel shirts and long, ebony-dark braids. They were alike— and at the same time, different.

"No, Audrey," Libby replied cheerfully.

"Not even if it's something educational?" the other twin asked, while Calvin looked on earnestly, his glasses a little crooked. He was still wearing his coat, though he'd left his shoes on the back porch, that being the house rule whenever the kids had been down by the creek or out in the garden, and was therefore padding about in his stocking feet.

Julie ached with mother-love, just looking at him. He was so beautiful—and he would be a little boy for such a short time.

For a moment, she wanted to stop every clock in the world, stop the universe itself. *Wait, wait. My baby is growing up too fast....*

She shook off the fanciful thoughts, gestured for Calvin to come to her.

He did, dragging his feet only a little along the way, and she unzipped his two-toned nylon coat. Pushed it back off his shoulders.

"We're staying for supper," she told him.

Calvin's face lit up instantly, and Julie felt another rush of helpless love for her boy.

"Yippee!" he yelled.

The dogs barked again, the twins echoed Calvin's shouts and Libby and Julie merely waited for the hoopla to subside.

The swooping roar of an airplane engine distracted everybody.

"I bet that's Uncle Garrett!" Ava yelled, dashing to the front door, wrenching it open and rushing outside, soon followed by the dogs and her sister and Calvin, still in his stocking feet.

Libby and Julie brought up the rear, Julie scooping Calvin off the ground with a laugh and a squeeze, all of them with their faces turned skyward.

Julie's heart lifted off like a rocket from a launcher, as she stood watching. The small plane flew low, tracing the crooked path of the creek for a few hundred yards, then circled back, tipped a wing twice and finally banked to zoom away over the range.

"It *is* Uncle Garrett!" Audrey whooped, beaming.

"I bet Dad's with him!" Ava agreed.

Libby laughed and held both girls against her sides for a moment, bending to kiss each of them on top of the head once before letting them go.

"We'd better get the table set," Libby told the kids. "There are at least two hungry McKettrick men headed our way."

The next few minutes were happy chaos—more dog-barking, more kid-laughter, a lot of washing of hands and faces, along with the clinking of silverware and the colorful everyday dishes Libby loved to mix and match.

When Tate came in, some minutes later, Libby and the twins flew at him, and he laughed and somehow managed to enfold them all. Garrett was right behind him, taking off his hat as he crossed the threshold, the gesture so old-fashioned that it almost made him seem shy.

Garrett's too-blue gaze caught on Julie as he hung his hat on a peg by the door, shrugged out of his faded denim jacket and hung that up, too. When he shifted his attention from her to Calvin, she felt it again—that same sensation of leaving the ground that she'd experienced earlier, while watching the airplane.

"Hey, buddy," he said. And then, with no hesitation at all, Garrett swept Calvin up, as he might have done with a boy of his own, and added, "How's my horseback ridin' partner?"

Calvin beamed, all but transported. "Pretty good," he said. Then, breathlessly, "Was that you and Tate in the airplane?"

Garrett nodded. "Sure enough was," he said. "Didn't you see us waving at you?"

"Yep," Calvin said, delighted. "I saw the wings tip, like you were saying hello. Will you take me flying with you sometime?"

Garrett's grin didn't falter, but his gaze moved from Calvin to Julie. "That's up to your mother," he said quietly.

Calvin seemed to deflate. "Oh," he said, dejected.

Garrett bounced him once before setting the child back on his feet. "Hello, Julie," he said, watching her.

Hello, Julie. It was a perfectly ordinary greeting, nothing more.

And yet, for just the length of a heartbeat, the floor—the earth itself—seemed to shift beneath Julie's feet.

It was all too easy, during that momentary interlude, to flash on another warm, bright kitchen, in some unknown house, homey like this one, with Garrett pulling *her* into his arms, just the way Tate was doing with Libby, and kissing her soundly. It was all too easy to imagine a *lot* of things.

She blushed.

"Can I go flying with Garrett, Mom?" Calvin demanded, breaking the spell.

"Someday," Julie said. Her son was standing right in front of her, tugging at the sleeve of her teacherly— make that *dowdy*—cardigan sweater. With it, she wore a long tweed skirt and a prim blouse. And just then, her gaze still locked with Garrett's, she had to shake off the odd sensation that she'd mistakenly put on someone else's clothes that morning—the garments of a much older person.

Garrett smiled.

She blushed harder.

"Someday?" Calvin protested.

"Someday," Julie repeated.

Tate lifted the lid off the Crock-Pot and drew in an appreciative breath, while the kids, including Calvin, scrambled into chairs at the big table in the center of the kitchen. Libby bent to take a baking sheet from the oven—*biscuits?*—and Tate gave his future wife a subtle pat on her blue-jeaned bottom.

Julie smiled at that, aware of Garrett still standing near enough to touch, near enough that she could feel the heat and the hard strength of that cowboy body of his.

"Hey," Libby said, making a face at Tate. "Cut it out, bucko."

Tate laughed.

"You made biscuits?" Julie marveled.

"There is no end to my talents," Libby replied.

"You can say that again," Tate told her, in a low growl, grinning the whole time.

"Little pitchers," Libby reminded him, singsong, indicating the kids with an eloquent nod of her head.

But the kids were oblivious, Audrey and Ava scrapping over who got to sit by Garrett, Calvin wistful behind the lenses of his glasses, which were steamed up after Libby passed the basket full of biscuits under his nose.

Julie sat down, and so did Libby, but Garrett and Tate remained on their feet until after they were settled. Garrett winked at the twins, and they each moved one seat over, as if by tacit agreement, leaving a space open next to Calvin.

Garrett dropped into the seat.

Grace was offered, and then everyone dove in, ravenous.

Julie prided herself on her cooking—it had always been *her* area of expertise—but Libby's stew and biscuits were wonderful, and she seemed so proud of the accomplishment that Julie was touched.

Overall, confusion reigned—there was a lot of laughter—and Calvin drank his milk without the usual complaints. He hated the stuff, rarely missed an opportunity to remind Julie that no other species on the planet drank milk after they were weaned *except* humans.

Five going on fifty-two, that was Calvin. Just as Garrett had recently remarked.

But tonight the little boy sported a milk-mustache and listened wide-eyed as Garrett and Tate talked about flying high over the Silver Spur, and how it was a handy way of knowing which part of the herd was where.

They'd seen part of a remote fence down, too, which explained some missing cattle, though there had been no sign of the cattle themselves. At first light, they meant to head out there in Tate's truck, a crew following, and have a closer look.

"Rustlers?" Libby asked. She'd been about to take a bite of stew, but she lowered the spoon back to her bowl then, looking worried.

"Maybe," Tate said, clearly unconcerned.

Garrett flung a look across the table at his brother, then turned to favor Libby and all three kids with an easy sweep of a smile, heavy on the McKettrick charm. "Fences," he said, "have been known to fall down on their own, with no help at all from rustlers. Sometimes cattle trample them, too."

Libby didn't look reassured, and Julie was with her on that one. Rustlers were still a problem on far-flung ranches like the Silver Spur. They herded other people's cattle into the backs of waiting semis now, under cover of darkness, instead of driving the creatures overland on horseback, as in the movies, but they were still criminals, and at least some of them still carried guns, too.

Julie and Libby exchanged glances.

The conversation turned to airplanes again. Back in college, Garrett had worked summers for a crop-dusting outfit. That was how he'd learned to fly. Calvin listened, spellbound, as Garrett and Tate swapped memories of some pretty wild adventures—including taking their dad's plane up once, when he'd gone to Houston on business, and nearly plowing that restored World War II bomber into the side of a mountain when the throttle got stuck.

Garrett had managed to pull out of the dive in time

and make a safe landing, but word of the exploit must have gotten back to Jim McKettrick, though he never mentioned it, because a week later, he'd sold the plane.

"You think he missed it?" Tate asked Garrett thoughtfully, settling back in his chair. He'd made a respectable dent in the stew, and consumed a few biscuits, too. "The bomber, I mean?"

Garrett chuckled. "Maybe," he answered, "but you know how Mom hated it when he went up in that thing. I like to think things were a little more peaceful here on the home front, when it was gone."

For a few moments after that, both men were quiet, probably remembering their parents, missing them. Jim and Sally McKettrick, Julie recalled sadly, had been killed in a car crash a decade before.

After the meal was over, Garrett and Tate cleared the table and loaded the dishwasher, while the kids got underfoot trying to help.

Libby smiled and shook her head at the sight, her face so full of love that, yet again, Julie's throat tightened.

Not for the first time, it struck Julie how reckless, how truly dangerous it was, to love with one's whole heart.

But what else could a person do?

Seeing that Calvin was finally starting to run down, Julie told him to gather up his things, they both said their thank-yous and Garrett grabbed his coat and hat from the pegs and came outside with them, into the deepening chill of an autumn twilight.

"Catch a ride back to the ranch house with you?" Garrett asked. Seeing him standing there in his cowboy getup, Julie could almost forget that he was really a politician, more at home in an expensive suit, making deals behind closed doors.

Sharing hot tubs with any number of half-naked women who were most definitely not his cousins.

Julie shook off the image; she was being downright silly.

And, anyway, Garrett wasn't married. He could cavort with all the women he wanted to, half-naked or otherwise.

"Sure," she answered finally, holding Calvin's backpack while he scrambled into his seat in the back. "We'd be glad to give you a lift."

Calvin was being so good. He normally made a fuss whenever they left Libby and Tate's place—it was as if he wanted to live there, instead of with her.

Grateful for small favors, Julie made sure he was properly fastened in before sliding behind the wheel.

"This is quite a car," Garrett said, settled in on the passenger side of the pink Cadillac.

"It's a classic," Julie said fondly. She'd always loved the pink bomb, but lately she'd been thinking of trading it in for something smaller and more fuel-efficient. "It burns a lot of gas, though."

"It's a dinosaur," Calvin contributed, from the peanut gallery. "Some woman won it, about a hundred years ago, for selling a lot of face cream and stuff."

Garrett chuckled at that.

Julie caught Calvin's eye in the rearview mirror and made a face at him.

Calvin was revved up again. "My grandma drove this car right through the front of Aunt Libby's coffee shop, and all that happened was it got a few dents and scratches."

"I heard about that," Garrett said. His voice was a low rumble of amusement, and Julie realized she was aware of him in a holographic sort of way—every cell in her body seemed to contain the whole.

Julie concentrated on driving. *Back up. Turn around. Point the headlights down the driveway, toward the main road. Don't go too fast. Don't go too slow.*

"This car is built like a tank," Calvin went on. "That's what Aunt Libby says."

Garrett smiled, adjusted his hat. "Is that right?" he asked conversationally, and Julie felt his gaze touch her in the relative darkness as they bumped over an old cattle guard.

The moon was out, as it had been the night before, when she and Garrett had gone riding. When they reached the mansion, Julie used the remote control Esperanza had given her to open the garage door.

Julie couldn't help flashing back on the previous evening, when she and Calvin had come back here after having supper in town with Gordon and Dixie, and Calvin had pretended to be asleep so Garrett would carry him inside.

The way fathers had always carried sleeping children into houses, generation upon generation.

That night, however, Calvin was mobile, clearly still trying to make a good impression on Garrett. Harry greeted them at the garage door, wagging hard and whimpering a little, and Garrett took the dog outside.

Calvin submitted to his nightly bath without significant fuss.

He brushed his teeth, took off his glasses and crawled into bed, hands clasped together, lips moving and eyes closed in silent prayer.

Julie bent and kissed his forehead. "I love you a lot, big guy," she told him.

"I love you, too, Mom," Calvin whispered, his eyes open wide now. "But I really think you should give me permission to go up in Garrett's airplane with him."

Harry came in and leaped up onto the foot of Calvin's bed to settle in for the night.

"You really think that, do you?" Julie grinned.

"Yes," Calvin said, blinking. Looking into the pale, innocent blue of her son's eyes, she caught a momentary glimpse of forever—her heart embraced his children and their children's children.

Because she was so moved, Julie's response came out sounding a little croaky. "Why?" she asked, genuinely curious. Calvin had always talked a lot about horses—he loved race cars and roller coasters, too, though he'd never had a direct experience with either—but he'd never shown any particular interest in airplanes.

Of course, he was young.

He still had a lot to discover.

Calvin's small shoulders moved beneath the cotton top of his pajamas as he executed a nonchalant shrug. "It sounds pretty exciting. Being able to wave at people from the sky and stuff."

Julie nodded in agreement. "A lot of things are exciting," she said, "but that doesn't mean we need to rush out and do them."

"Is that like when I used to say I crossed the road without permission because my friend Justin did, and you asked me if Justin jumped off a bridge, would I do it, too?"

She smiled. "Sort of," she said. "My point is, you've

got lots of time. You can do all the things you really want to do—eventually."

"But not now?" he sounded monumentally disappointed.

"Some now," Julie conceded, smoothing back his hair. "Some, later."

"Like that?" Calvin pressed. "Like what?"

"Riding horses," Julie heard herself say. "As long as Tate or Libby—" she paused, swallowed, because this was hard for her, as much as she trusted her sister and future brother-in-law "—or Garrett is around. No trying to ride by yourself or with just the twins around. I need your word on that, Calvin."

Calvin looked thrilled. "Will you tell them it's okay for me to ride even if you're not there?" he wanted to know. "Because Aunt Libby thought it was okay, because it's always been okay before, and then you saw me on the big black horse with Garrett and you got upset—"

Julie pressed a finger to Calvin's mouth. "Shhh," she said. "I'll tell them."

"Good!" Calvin said, burrowing down into his covers and his pillow and squinching his eyes shut tight, the way he did on Christmas Eve, because Julie had told him Santa wouldn't come until he was asleep.

Julie doubted that he still believed, but he was willing to pretend for a little while longer, and so was she.

She kissed him again, patted Harry good-night and stood.

Tired as she was, Julie knew she wouldn't be able to sleep yet; her mind was racing. After peeking into the kitchen to make sure Garrett wasn't there, reading the newspaper or something, she went back to her room, changed into her swimsuit, a black one-piece, clipped her hair up on top of her head, grabbed a towel and headed for the indoor swimming pool.

What she needed, she decided, was a little exercise.

Her body wasn't particularly sore from the horseback ride the night before, but her *mind* could use some unkinking, that was for sure.

After crossing the kitchen, Julie stood on the tiled edge of the magnificent pool and looked up.

The retractable roof was shut, but the light of the stars and moon shimmered through the glass panels arching two stories overhead, and danced on the dark water at her feet. She and Calvin had used the pool several times during their short stay, and it was usually lit from beneath, from a dozen different angles, but she didn't know where the switches were and saw no point in searching for them.

Julie dropped her towel onto a chaise longue and stepped into the pool at the shallow end. The water was perfect, not too cool, and not too warm, either, and she felt pure joy as she plunged forward and swam vertical laps back and forth, back and forth.

The flood of multicolored light rose up around her suddenly; it was as though she were inside a giant prism. She stopped, blinking, in the grip of the strange magic she'd begun to sense earlier, when she'd said good-night to Calvin.

"Oops," Garrett said. "Sorry."

Julie turned, saw that he was standing on the side nearest the kitchen, barefoot, tousle-haired, and wearing a terrycloth robe.

"You scared me," she said, without recrimination. And then she laughed, treading water in the middle of that gigantic pool, with all those shafts of colored light rising up around her.

He grinned. "Sorry," he said again.

Julie's gaze dropped. Was he wearing swimming trunks under that bathrobe?

Surely he was.

Wasn't he?

Before Julie could decide one way or the other, Garrett shed the robe, revealing a pair of trunks. He dove into the water and surfaced about a foot in front of her, droplets flying as he gave his head a shake. His eyelashes were spiky with moisture, and his mouth curved into a mischievous smile.

Julie's heart, still pounding from the start he'd given her by switching on the underwater light show, began to slow down a little, find its normal beat.

And then she laughed again, because Garrett did a couple of slow somersaults in the water, as deft as a seal, before surfacing again, this time closer. Close enough to make her breath catch, in fact.

Was he showing off?

No, she decided. Garrett was *reveling*, celebrating his own agility and the water itself.

And there was something so elemental, so sexy about that, that Julie felt a fierce grab of desire, unlike anything any other man had ever aroused in her, in a place so deep inside her that it went beyond the physical.

That was when she knew she was in big, *big* trouble.

CHAPTER SEVEN

As far as Garrett was concerned, kissing Julie Remington was as inevitable as drawing in his next breath. There, in the middle of the pool, he cupped his hands on either side of her face, bent his head and touched his lips to hers—lightly at first, in case she wanted to pull back—and then more deeply when she gave a soft moan and slipped her arms around his neck.

Garrett had kissed a lot of women in his time—he'd enjoyed all those kisses, even thrilled to some of them, but this one, *this one*, seemed to clutch at something deep inside him and hold on, squeezing the breath out of him.

When he finally came up for air, it was out of pure desperation, because his lungs demanded oxygen. He had an odd sense of settling back into himself after being catapulted to somewhere else, and when he opened his eyes and saw Julie staring back at him, looking as baffled as he felt, he laughed.

Julie eased back a little way, although she wasn't out of reach. Pink splotches glowed on her cheeks, and her wonderful chameleon eyes shifted between blue and violet as they drew color from the water.

Garrett longed to pull her close again, kiss her again, hell, do a *lot more* than kiss her. But he didn't move. She was as rattled as he was—all five of his known senses told him that, and a few besides. If he came on too strong, he'd scare her away, maybe for good.

"What just happened here?" Julie asked, her toned arms moving gracefully as she went on treading water.

Garrett couldn't hold back a grin. He was too damn happy. "I think you kissed me," he said, though he knew her question had been rhetorical.

He was rewarded by a widening of her eyes and an indrawn breath. "I beg your pardon, Garrett McKettrick," she said. "*You* kissed *me.*"

"So I did," he replied easily. "Now that we agree on what 'just happened' here, let's figure out what comes next."

"*Nothing* comes next," Julie said, turning and gliding toward the side of the pool. Gripping the tiled edge with one hand, she looked back at him.

Her spirally copper hair was coming down from the clip on the top of her head, but she didn't seem to notice, and that was fine with Garrett. In the shifting, watery light, she looked like the goddess of ice and fire. There was only one thing he wanted to do more than look at her, and that was touch her, all over, inside and out.

Whoa, he thought. *Go easy, cowboy.*

Julie moved toward the ladder, probably intending to climb out of the pool and flee.

"Wait," Garrett heard himself say. The voice, though his own, was strange to him, hoarse.

She'd reached the ladder, gripped one of the rungs. Looking back at him over one delectable and faintly freckled shoulder, she bit her lower lip, as though pondering some inner dilemma.

"If you say nothing happens next, Julie," Garrett told

her, keeping his distance, "then that's the way it will be. You don't have to run away."

She gave a little burst of laughter, part indignation and part relief, and let go of the ladder, moved away from the side of the pool, though she remained well out of Garrett's reach. Her hair escaped the clip and she raised both arms to attend to the problem, causing her perfect breasts to jut forward.

"Who says I was running away?" she asked.

The kiss had made Garrett hard; the lift of Julie's breasts sent scorching heat pounding through him, rendering him speechless. In a vain effort to cool off, he ducked under the water, considered staying down there long enough to drown himself, and then surfaced again.

When he did, Julie had secured her hair in the squeeze clip, though tendrils spiraled down around her cheeks, her shoulders, the side of her neck.

Garrett wanted to trace the length of that lovely neck with his lips, the tip of his tongue, find her earlobe and nibble at it, make her moan.

He didn't move, though. The water did little to cool his blood; in fact, he half expected the contents of that pool to come to a slow simmer around him.

"So," he said, "are you seeing anybody?"

Are you seeing anybody? Talk about hokey. Why didn't he just put on a bad toupee, one of those two-tone jobs maybe, hang a slug of gold chains around his neck, and ask what her sign was?

She smiled. "No," she said, after considering the question for a long moment. That was it, just "no," and then she left him to dangle.

Garrett might as well have been a kid again, he felt so awkward. Where, he wondered, was the mover and shaker, the bring-it-on guy, the smooth operator who could handle anything?

Someplace else, evidently.

Nobody here but a beautiful woman and a country boy making a damn fool out of himself, he thought.

Being a McKettrick meant never knowing when to quit, a trait that could be a blessing or a curse, depending on the situation. Garrett kept talking, when he might have been better off shutting up. "Maybe—we could—well—do something?"

Julie chortled at that—the sound was warm and throaty, made him imagine waking up next to her, deeply rested after a night of frenetic sex, followed by hours of exhausted sleep. She turned, moved to the ladder and climbed up it. Water sluiced off her in iridescent sheets, and her backside swayed slightly. Things ground together inside Garrett, an achy shift in a place where he hadn't known there *was* a place, up to now.

Sitting on the edge of the pool, Julie reached for a towel, wrapped it around her shoulders, idly moved her feet in the water. She was shivering a little.

"What kind of 'something' do you have in mind, Garrett?" she asked, in her own good time.

She knew, of course, that she was getting to him. And she was enjoying it.

The single mother, devoted to her son.

The teacher, dedicated to her students and her work.

It amazed him that she was the same person as the offbeat girl he'd known in high school.

Julie Remington was all those things, and a lot more besides. There was mischief in her, and fire, and the rare, lasting mystery that just keeps on unfolding, indefinitely. A man could spend a lifetime, he realized with a jolt, maybe longer, just uncovering all the layers of who she was, what she wanted, what she had to give.

The prospect enticed him and, at the same time, scared the hell out of him. At no time in his life, in no situation, had he ever felt out of his depth.

He did now.

"Garrett?" she prompted, raising one eyebrow slightly.

"I was thinking maybe we could go out to dinner," he said, and was surprised by his own ability to speak coherently. Inside, all was chaos—collisions, things sparking off each other and igniting. "Maybe to a movie."

"Dinner," she repeated, still swinging her legs back and forth. "Where?"

Except for the café at the Amble On Inn, the Silver Dollar Saloon, a snack bar in the bowling alley and a few fast-food places, Blue River didn't have much to offer in the way of restaurants. "Paris?" he asked.

Julie smiled. She probably thought he was kidding.

The weird thing was, he wasn't.

He was thinking "private jet." Sex in swanky hotel rooms with views of the Seine, room service champagne, more sex.

"Be serious," she said.

"How about Austin, then?" Garrett persisted, though he made up his mind, then and there, that he would take Julie Remington to Paris, sooner rather than later. "Or maybe San Antonio?"

While he waited for her answer, Garrett let himself imagine what it would be like to pleasure this woman. The thought of her buckling against his mouth or under his hips in the last frantic throes of an orgasm turned his hard-on from problematic to out-and-out painful.

Something sparked in Julie's eyes, putting Garrett in

mind of a tigress, living fierce and free in some jungle. He knew in one dizzying flash of insight—or perhaps it was pure animal *instinct*—that here was a woman capable of throwing her whole self into the fire, of abandoning inhibition, of giving in completely to her own responses and those of the man lucky enough to be making love to her.

If it hadn't been for the little guy, Calvin, snoozing away in his room in the guest quarters, Garrett figured he would simply have gotten out of the pool, whisked the tempting Ms. Remington up into his arms and carried her upstairs, Rhett Butler-style. He'd have had her in the shower first, after peeling away that clinging wet bathing suit and shedding the swim trunks.

But Calvin was a reality.

"It would probably be easier," she mused, "if I just cooked dinner for you." She bit her lower lip. "Us. You and me and Calvin, I mean—"

She was as nervous as he was. Garrett found that reassuring.

You and me and Calvin...

Garrett shook off the momentary daze he'd slipped into, thinking about Julie naked in his private shower, warm and slick and, unless he missed his guess, hyperorgasmic.

"Wouldn't you rather go to a restaurant?" he asked. The passing moments, it seemed to Garrett, were marked by the beat of his own heart.

The atmosphere was humid, almost sultry, and the play of lights, having gone through a programmed sequence, slowed and then stopped, throwing the pool and the area surrounding it into something akin to twilight.

"Julie?" he said, low, because she'd been silent for so long, pondering.

She slipped forward, eased back into the water, waited by the side. Either she couldn't speak or she'd chosen not to—Garrett could guess which one.

He went to her, but slowly. Ever so slowly.

"Kiss me again," she murmured, when he was facing her.

He pressed his mouth to hers, all but pinning her body against the smooth-tiled wall of the pool. Everything in him ached to have her—*here, now*—but even then, lost in that second, deeper kiss, he was careful.

No sudden moves, he thought.

When the kiss ended, leaving both of them breathless, Garrett kept the hard angles of his frame close against Julie's curvy softness, but without pressure. He said her name again, nibbled at the side of her neck, tasted her earlobe, the way he'd wanted to do earlier, delighted in the little moan she uttered.

"Garrett," she whispered. He felt her palms flatten against his chest, but she didn't push. "It's too soon— we have to stop, and I don't think—I don't think I can do that if you don't help me out a little here."

He drew back far enough to leave a space between them, probably no thicker than the fabric of her swimsuit. His breath was ragged, and he gripped the pool's edge on either side of Julie, not to trap her, but to keep himself from sinking.

"Okay," he rasped out. "Okay."

She planted a wet kiss in the cleft of his chin, then ducked under his left arm, grabbed hold of the ladder again and climbed out of the pool.

He couldn't bear to watch her this time. That trim

waist, that perfect backside—dammit, there was a limit to what one man could take without going crazy.

"Good night, Garrett" he heard her say.

Garrett closed his eyes, rested his forehead against the tile, held on to the pool's edge with both hands. A verbal response was more than he could manage—he merely nodded once, and listened as she hurried away.

After a long time, he returned to his own part of the house, stood in the long living room, with its row of floor-to-ceiling windows, looking out over the darkened range. Although he hadn't been around a lot since going to work for the senator right after law school, it wasn't because the quarters lacked creature comforts.

He turned, taking in the huge natural rock fireplace, the full-sized kitchen beyond the dining area. There were two bedrooms, each with its own bath, in addition to the master suite. The apartment covered nearly five thousand square feet, and it had two exits of its own, one leading to the garage on the lower level, one to a set of stone stairs ending in the yard.

After their folks' death, Garrett recalled grimly, one of them—Austin or Tate or himself, he didn't know— had suggested dividing the big house into sections.

The idea had seemed like a good one at the time, Garrett thought now, with a rueful smile. The kind of thing young men tend to come up with, he supposed, when they've just lost their folks and feel a need to dig their roots in deeper and hold on to their piece of ground.

Garrett had draped a towel around his waist before leaving poolside, but he was dripping on the slate-tile floors. He made his way into the master bath, opened the shower door and stepped inside.

The space boasted a stone bench and fully a dozen different sprayers that could be angled to suit.

If Julie had been there, he might have done some fancy sprayer-arranging, but since it was just him—dammit—he used only the big round one, overhead. He took off the swim trunks and let them hit the shower floor with a soggy plop, and switched on the water.

He soaped and rinsed, but shaving seemed like a waste of time, since he'd have to do it again in the morning.

Scrubbed, smelling of soap and shampoo, Garrett snatched a towel, dried himself rigorously and walked out of the bathroom with the towel hooked around his waist.

He was hungry.

He meandered into his kitchen—since he rarely bothered to stock the shelves or the refrigerator, preferring to cadge meals from Esperanza when he was on the ranch—and checked out the supply situation.

It amounted to meager—or a little less than that.

The fridge was empty except for half a loaf of blue-crusted bread and an egg carton with an expiration date that made Garrett hesitant to lift the lid.

He chucked both items into a garbage bag, nose wrinkled, and headed for the inside staircase, planning to dispose of it in one of the trash bins outside the garage.

Realizing he was naked except for the towel, he paused at the top of the stairs, garbage bag in hand, debating the wisdom of going down there in what practically constituted the altogether.

Running into Julie would be one thing—he took a few moments to savor the fantasy—but meeting up with Calvin or Esperanza would be another. With a sigh, Garrett set the bag down, returned to his bedroom and pulled on a pair of jeans.

Then he took the garbage downstairs and outside, where the chill bit into his bare chest and the soles of his feet, so that he did a hopping little dance back into the kitchen.

He washed his hands at the nearest sink, checked the multiple refrigerators for leftovers, and wound up munching on cold cereal because nothing else appealed to him.

He was just sticking his empty bowl into a dish-washer when the dog padded out on his three legs, wagging his tail.

Garrett acknowledged the animal with a smile, was about to head back upstairs, where he *might* get some sleep, when Harry pressed his beagle-snout to the crack between the outside door and the frame.

He glanced toward the guest quarters, half expecting—hell, *hoping*—that Julie would be there.

Only she wasn't.

The dog gave a benign little whimper.

Garrett sighed. "It's *cold* out there," he protested.

The dog whimpered again.

He bent, checked the tags on the mutt's collar. "Listen, *Harry*," he said, drawing on his negotiation skills, "maybe you wouldn't mind doing your thing on some newspaper, just this once—"

Harry gave an urgent whine, raised one of his front paws to scratch at the door—he had two legs in front and one in back—and he teetered a little, trying to stay balanced.

"Oh, *all right*," Garrett said, steeling himself for a second barefoot, naked-chested venture into the night air.

He waited, shivering, while the dog took care of business.

"I THINK GARRETT asked me out," Julie confided in Libby, bright and early the next morning, when she stopped by with Calvin. She didn't say it, of course, until her little boy had joined Audrey and Ava, who were playing in the leaves beneath the oak trees on the other side of the yard.

Libby chuckled. "What do you mean, you *think* Garrett asked you out?" she replied. "Either he did or he didn't."

Julie bit back the admission that he'd kissed her, too. Twice. There wasn't much she didn't tell her sisters, but she had yet to make sense of what had happened in the pool the night before.

And something *had* happened.

"He mentioned dinner in Austin or San Antonio," Julie said.

Libby raised one eyebrow, her eyes twinkling. "And you said…?"

Julie's face burned. "And I said maybe I should cook instead," she murmured.

Libby folded her arms; it was chilly that morning. Tate's truck wasn't in its usual place in the driveway; he must have gotten an early start, as Garrett had. Watching through one of the kitchen windows at the main ranch house, Julie had seen him drive off before the coffee had finished perking.

"It's not like you to blush over a man," Libby pointed out, grinning and giving her a light jab with one elbow. Her eyes rounded with a sudden and delighted realization. "You're *interested* in Garrett—sexually, I mean."

"Libby!" Julie protested, pained.

Libby laughed. Shook her head. "This is *so* not you. This reticence thing, that is. Of the three of us, you've always been the bold one, the adventurous one—and now the idea of making dinner for a man has you turning red?"

"Okay, so I'm *interested*," Julie blurted. With a slight motion of her head, she indicated Calvin, happily plunging in and out of the gloriously colored leaf piles across the yard. "I can't just have a fling with Garrett McKettrick—I have to think about my son."

"As if there's any danger that you *won't* think about Calvin," Libby said gently. "You're a great mother, Jules. The little guy knows you love him, knows you'd go to the wall for him."

"It was just a kiss—okay *two kisses*—but Libby, the things Garrett made me feel..."

Her voice fell away.

Libby smiled, gave her a brief, tight hug. "I know all about what a man can make a woman feel, Jules," she said. "A *McKettrick* man, anyway."

Julie gnawed at her lower lip for a moment, watching Calvin and the twins and the happy dogs, frolicking in rustling mounds of orange and yellow and crimson leaves, scattering them in all directions. "Garrett and I live under the same roof," she reminded Libby. "Things could get really awkward, really fast."

Libby's blue eyes were alight with love as she watched the kids and the dogs. "So much for the two hours I spent raking the yard yesterday afternoon," she said good-naturedly. Then she turned and looked directly at Julie again. "Is this my frankly sensual sister speaking? The one who lamented, not all that long ago, the lack of hot stand-up sex in her life?"

She was going to be late for work if she didn't hurry.

Hedging, Julie got into the Cadillac and turned the key in the ignition until it made a grinding sound. Then she gunned the engine a couple of times before responding to what Libby had said. "I'm going to lose my mind if I think about stand-up sex, hot or otherwise, so don't remind me, okay?"

"I think stand-up sex is *always* hot," Libby speculated mischievously.

Julie couldn't help laughing, and that expelled some of the tension that had been building up inside her since the night before.

Temporarily, anyway.

"And of course you speak from experience," Julie teased, making Libby laugh. "You lucky woman."

With that, she shifted the Caddie into Reverse, tooted the horn in farewell and waved to Libby and to the kids jumping in the leaf piles under the oak trees.

Calvin was too busy having a good time to wave back.

HAVING APPROPRIATED AUSTIN'S battered old red pickup from the garage at home, since the Porsche wasn't suitable for the kind of day he was bound to have, Garrett pulled up behind Tate's blue Silverado, parked across the road from the downed fence line the two of them had spotted from the airplane the day before, late in the afternoon.

A pair of horses grazed nearby, while Tate and two of the ranch hands crouched, examining something in the dirt.

The sinking sensation in Garrett's gut told him it was nothing good, even before he got there and saw the tread marks sunk into the soft dirt on the shoulder. They'd been left by a big rig, those tracks, not a car or a pickup.

The dirt around the fallen fence was churned up, pocked with the impressions of a few hundred hooves.

Seeing Garrett approach, Tate straightened, stood. "Well," he said grimly, "it's official."

"Rustlers," Garrett confirmed, with a nod. "Any idea how many cattle we're missing?"

Tate sighed. "Henson and Bates are running a quick tally right now," he answered, gesturing toward two distant men on horseback. "Offhand, though, I'd say fifty to a hundred head."

Since even a semi wouldn't hold that many cattle, the thieves must have made several trips, maybe even over a period of days. The Silver Spur rambled on for miles in all four directions, like a giant patchwork quilt spread over a lumpy mattress, and while there were great, grassy expanses of open range, there were also stands of oaks and other deciduous trees hiding shallow canyons and old wagon trails and even a dry riverbed.

A crew arrived to repair the fence, began setting the posts back in their holes and packing dirt and rocks in around them. Once that was done, they'd secure them with cement and then string new wire.

Tate put a call through to Brent Brogan on his cell phone, walking toward his truck as he explained the situation to the lawman and gesturing for Garrett to come along.

When the call ended, Tate had the driver's-side door open and one foot up on the running board. "Let's take that plane of yours up again, have another look around. Maybe we missed something last time."

Garrett nodded. "Meet you at the hangar," he said, turning and sprinting back to Austin's pickup.

Twenty minutes later, they were in the sky.

Tate's voice came through Garrett's headphones,

sounding tinny and a lot farther away than one seat over. "Let's make a pass over the oil field," he said.

Garrett nodded and banked the plane to the right, began a gradual decline, and swung in low over the rusty derricks and the two long Quonset huts where equipment had been stored in the old days.

The shacks built to house the workers were gone now, just bits of foundation jutting out of the grass here and there. Once, though, there had been *homes* on this piece of land—nothing fancy, but clean and sturdy and warm in winter. Folks had laughed and fought and loved and raised kids, made a community for themselves— there had even been a church and a one-room school-house, way back when.

During the Great Depression, when so many men and women were desperate for work, the oil had just kept on coming, and the shantytown had been a haven for several dozen workers and their families; back at the main ranch house, there were boxes of old pictures of the place and the people.

It gave Garrett a hollowed-out feeling, thinking how there could be so much life and energy in a place, and then—nothing.

They made a wide loop and then passed over the area again.

Not so much as a blade of grass moved down there; the broken foundations, the Quonset huts, the time-frozen derricks…the place was as still as any ghost town.

Just the same, Garrett felt uneasy, and when he glanced at Tate, he saw that his brother was frown-ing, too.

"Can you land this thing down there?" Tate asked.

"I can land anywhere," Garrett answered.

The wheels bumped and jostled over the hard-packed dirt when they touched down a couple of minutes later, rolling to a stop a few dozen yards from one of the huts.

"This," Tate said, indicating the larger of the two Quonset huts with a nod of his head, "would be a damn good place to hide a semi between raids on the herd."

Garrett braked, shut down the engine, pulled off his earphones. He'd never run from trouble in his life, and there was no sign of any that he could see, but he knew something was off, just the same. Maybe it was because he hadn't gotten much sleep, thanks to Julie Remington and all the fantasies she'd inspired.

"It can't hurt to look around," he said, his voice gruff.

The two brothers climbed out of the plane, walked toward the tail, in order to avoid the still-spinning blades on the wings.

Here there were no tracks to indicate the comings and goings of any kind of rig, big or otherwise. The padlocks securing the roll-up doors on the Quonsets were not only fastened, but rusted shut, and the panes in the windows remained intact.

So why were the little hairs on his nape standing straight up like a dog's hackles? Garrett wondered. He glanced at Tate, saw his brother wipe off a corner of one of the windows to look inside.

Garrett turned, scanning the immediate area.

He saw old derricks, tumbleweeds and not much else.

And it gave him the creeps.

"See anything?" he asked, when Tate stepped back, dusting his hands together.

Tate shook his head. "Just cobwebs and a lot of dust," he answered.

"Is it just me," Garrett pressed, "or is there something about this place that doesn't feel right?"

Tate's teeth flashed as he grinned. "You spooked?" he asked.

"No," Garrett said, too quickly. As kids, they'd explored this area on horseback, he and Tate and Austin. The dry bed of an ancient river cut through the land just beyond a nearby rise, and there were a number of caves around, too, though most of them had probably fallen in a long time ago. "*Hell*, no, I'm not spooked."

Tate chuckled, slapped Garrett on the back. "Remember when you and Austin and I used to camp out here sometimes, with Brent Brogan and Nico Ruiz?"

Garrett nodded, relaxed a little. "We liked to scare the hell out of each other with yarns about ghosts and guys with hooks for hands," he said. "That one time, when you were twelve and I was eleven and Austin was ten, we told our baby brother we were going to sneak back home as soon as he dropped off to sleep, and he was so worried about being left alone in camp that he didn't shut his eyes for the rest of the night and kept us awake, too, saying one of our names every five minutes."

Tate grinned. "We had to do all the usual chores the next day. Damn, I was too tired to spit. Served us right, I guess."

Garrett laughed. "You and I and Brent and Nico did chores," he corrected. "Austin got to go to the cattle auction with Dad, if I recall it correctly."

Tate seemed to enjoy the recollection as much as Garrett did, though neither of them had thought the experience was funny back then. Remembering, he chuckled and shook his head.

"That little runt must have snitched on us," Garrett said, referring to Austin. "How else could Dad have known we gave him a hard time?"

Tate slapped him on the shoulder. "After all these years," he jibed, though not unkindly, "you still haven't realized that we just *thought* we were all by ourselves out here? Dad and Pablo Ruiz took turns bedding down within a hundred yards so they could keep an eye on us."

Garrett *hadn't* known, and he figured Tate hadn't, either, at least not until after the fact, because they'd talked about practically everything in the relative anonymity of country-dark nights, staring up at that endless expanse of stars. Neither their dad nor Pablo had ever let on that they'd overheard.

He smiled, but at the same time his throat went so tight that his voice came out sounding raw, as if it had been scraped off his vocal chords. "I miss Dad," he said. "Mom, too."

Tate nodded, tightened his fingers on Garrett's shoulder for a few moments, then let go. "We were damn lucky to have them as long as we did," he said hoarsely.

Garrett, having left his hat in Austin's pickup, shoved a hand through his sweaty hair and looked away, struggling to compose himself. "I thought Morgan Cox was like Dad," he said, unable to meet Tate's gaze. Contempt for the senator and for his own judgment roiled up inside Garrett. "It galls me that I believed it, even for a minute."

"Maybe you *needed* to believe it for a while," Tate said quietly.

By tacit agreement, they walked toward the riverbed and the caves they'd loved to explore as kids. They'd found arrowheads there, some of them ancient, along with colorful bits of crockery from the shantytown years. In those days, according to their mother, things like oatmeal and flour and tea and laundry soap had been sold with premiums inside—cups and saucers and sugar bowls and the like.

Boys being boys, they would have discarded the shards of old dishes—the arrowheads were a lot more interesting—but Esperanza liked to glue the prettiest china pieces to plant pots and tabletops, so they'd lugged them home to her in plastic grocery sacks.

The riverbed had been dry for a thousand years, if not longer, but if he closed his eyes and concentrated, Garrett could almost hear it flowing by, almost smell the water. He bent, picked up a stick and flung it hard, the way he would have done alongside any of the creeks crisscrossing the ranch.

At some point, long, long ago, the river had changed course. It ran on the other side of the clustered oaks now, through the canyon it had carved into the land over centuries.

Tate watched him, squinting a little against the sun.

"I'd swear I remember when that river ran through here," Garrett said.

Tate, probably guessing that something else was on Garrett's mind, simply waited. He'd always been the quiet type, Tate had, but since he and Libby had reconnected a few months before and gotten engaged to be married, his thoughts seemed to run deeper.

Or he was just more willing to share them.

"Maybe you can tell me," Garrett said, "how I could have grown up around Blue River, gone through school with Julie Remington, from kindergarten to graduation from high school, and never noticed that she's beautiful."

Tate chuckled. They walked one dusty bank of the river, though Garrett couldn't have said what they were looking for, beyond some sign of trespassers.

"So you're taken with Julie, are you," he said. It was a comment, not a question.

"I didn't say I was *taken* with her, Tate," Garrett pointed out, instantly on the defensive. "I said she was beautiful."

"She's that, all right," Tate agreed. Again, without ever voicing the decision, they were headed somewhere in particular—back to the plane.

Without intending to, Garrett asked, "Is Calvin's father in the picture?"

Tate sighed, rubbed his chin with one hand. Like Garrett, he had a stubble coming in, though Tate's was dark, like his hair, while Garrett's was golden. "According to Libby, the guy—Gordon Pruett is his name—hasn't shown much interest in Calvin until recently. He paid child support and remembered birthdays, so I guess you could say he was trying, but he definitely kept his distance."

Picturing Calvin, squinting up at him through the smeared lenses of those very serious glasses of his, Garrett ached. How could a man father a child and then just ignore him, except for writing a check once a month and sending birthday gifts?

"Until lately," Garrett said.

"Pruett wasn't around," Tate nodded. "Until lately. Now, I guess he's decided he wants to be part of Calvin's life, and Julie's pretty concerned, according to Libby."

"Why the change?" Garrett asked. They'd reached the plane and the glare off the metal sides made him pull his sunglasses from the pocket of his work shirt and put them on.

"I guess because he got married," Tate said. "Pruett, I mean. Now, all of a sudden, he's a family man."

Garrett felt a combination of things, none of which he wanted to examine too closely right at that moment. "How's Calvin taking all this?"

Tate raised and lowered one shoulder in a nearly imperceptible shrug. "He's like any little kid," he said. "He wants a dad."

"This Pruett—he's all right?"

Tate opened the door on his side of the plane, climbed in. "As far as I know," he replied. "Libby stands up for him. And she's a pretty good judge of character."

Garrett laughed. "Oh, yeah? She's marrying *you*, isn't she?" he joked, rounding the plane to hoist himself back into the pilot's seat. "Just how good a judge of character can she be?"

Tate grinned. "You've got a point," he said.

"You're one lucky bastard," Garrett told him. "You know that, don't you?"

Tate nodded. "Sure do," he answered.

CHAPTER EIGHT

WHEN JULIE AND CALVIN arrived at the McKettrick house that evening, Garrett was in the kitchen again, chatting up Esperanza while she put the finishing touches on one of her simple but wonderful suppers. Tonight it happened to be fried chicken, mashed potatoes with gravy and steamed corn.

Harry scrambled up off a rug in front of the crackling fire on the hearth to greet Calvin with face licks and tail wagging and a low, eager whine that meant he wanted to go outside.

Calvin gave Esperanza and Garrett a jaunty wave, then took Harry into the backyard. Julie, thrown by Garrett's presence for no reason she could identify, nodded to him, smiled at Esperanza and sped off into the part of the house she and Calvin shared.

Her heart was pounding, as if she'd had some sort of close call, and she felt the sting of a blush in her cheeks. Chiding herself for being silly, she dumped her purse and tote bag—briefcase, got out of her cloth coat and headed for "her" room.

The master bedroom in the guest suite was twice the size of the one she slept in at the cottage. There were cushioned window seats under the bay windows, and an unimpeded view of rangeland and foothills unfurled from there.

If she'd had the *time* to sit and dream, Julie silently lamented, she'd have chosen that spot for the purpose.

Alas, she seemed to have less and less free time these days, and more and more responsibilities. With the high school musical to cast, rehearse and stage—a task she usually undertook when she had the momentum of spring fever working for her—with her rental house officially on the market and Gordon Pruett dead set on being part of Calvin's life—

Well, it would be easy to feel overwhelmed.

Since that wasn't an option, either, she sucked in a deep breath, blew it out, and murmured one of her favorite, if most irreverent, mantras.

Shit happens.

After kicking off her low-heeled pumps and shedding the tailored gray pantsuit she'd worn to work that day, Julie hastened into worn jeans and a blue-and-white-striped T-shirt with long sleeves.

She had never been shy, but that dreary autumn afternoon, the temptation to hide out in the guest quarters required some overcoming on her part.

It didn't help, knowing she was acting like an adolescent. But the moment she'd stepped into the house and locked gazes with Garrett McKettrick a couple of minutes before, every cell in her body had begun to buzz with awareness. Although the vibrations were beginning to slow—she splashed cold water on her face at the bathroom sink to help the process along a little—the second they were in the same room together again, she knew she'd feel as though she'd stuck a finger into some cosmic light socket.

Julie had worn her hair up that day, pinned into a thick bun at the back of her head, and now, standing in front of the bathroom mirror, she let it tumble down around her shoulders.

Instantly, she regretted the action.

Wearing her hair down when she wasn't working was normal for Julie, but that afternoon, it seemed to say, *Come hither.*

She didn't want Garrett to think she was a red-hot mama with almost as many erogenous zones as she had freckles. Of course she *was*, or at least had been, but— that was *beside the point.*

Julie drew in another breath, gathered her hair back into a ponytail, grabbed a rubber band to secure it.

There, she thought. *You don't look the least bit sexy.*

She didn't look the least bit like herself, either. So she removed the rubber band, finger-fluffed her hair, and turned purposefully away from the mirror to march right back out into the main kitchen.

Since when had she based her hairstyles on a *man's* opinion—for or against? She'd left that kind of stuff behind at the end of junior high, hadn't she?

Upon reaching the kitchen, she saw that Calvin and Harry were back from the yard—Calvin's cheeks were pink from the cold and the lenses of his glasses were fogged up. He'd apparently gotten his jacket zipper stuck, because Garrett was crouched in front of him, trying to work the tab.

Both of them were laughing, and the sound snagged in Julie's heart, a sweet pain, too quickly gone.

Esperanza smiled at Julie, but Garrett and Calvin hadn't noticed her.

"Stick 'em up, Pilgrim," Garrett told the child, when the zipper remained immovable.

Calvin laughed again and flung both his hands up in

the air, and Garrett lifted the partially zipped jacket off over the child's head, jostling his glasses in the process.

Calvin took off his specs, wiped them with the tail of his shirt and stuck them back on his face. Julie knew he'd seen her, but all his attention, it seemed, was reserved for Garrett.

Garrett, giving Julie a sidelong look, handed her the jacket and then scooped Calvin up, tickling as he lifted him high.

Calvin's laughter rang like bells on a clear summer day.

Harry barked in delight.

Esperanza chuckled and shook her head, her eyes misted over.

And Julie just stood there, watching, stricken with some combination of joy and sorrow, wonder and caution.

Catching something in her expression, Garrett carefully set Calvin back on his feet, ruffled his hair.

"He shouldn't get overexcited," Julie explained, as though Calvin weren't there, or didn't comprehend the English language. Even as she said the words, she regretted them, but they came out automatically. "He has asthma."

Calvin spared her a single glance, wounded and angry, and then turned away, ruffling Harry's ears and asking loudly if the dog was ready to have some supper.

Julie let out her breath, and her shoulders drooped, and the hem of Calvin's jacket brushed the floor. "Too bad real life doesn't have a Rewind button," she told Garrett miserably.

Garrett, cowboy-handsome in clean boots, newish jeans and a fresh-smelling, long-sleeved Western shirt, quirked up one corner of his mouth, underscoring the grin that was already twinkling in his impossibly blue eyes.

"Supper's ready," he said, relieving her of Calvin's jacket, setting it aside, and steering her toward the table, one hand resting lightly against the small of her back.

The gesture was subtle—barely a touch of his fingers—and at the same time, utterly masculine. Julie loved the way it felt.

Calvin, having filled Harry's kibble bowl and given him fresh water as well, disappeared, without being told, to wash his hands.

He returned holding them up as evidence that he'd followed the rules, well-scrubbed and a little damp.

He'd even slicked a wet comb through his hair.

"You look very handsome," Julie told her son sincerely.

Calvin favored her with a forgiving smile. "Thanks," he said, straightening his glasses before climbing onto the chair beside his. Then, after making sure both Esperanza and Garrett were paying attention, he wriggled his right front tooth.

"Sthee?" he lisped. "It's going to come out."

"Calvin," Julie corrected gently. "Not at the table."

After that, everyone bowed their heads and Esperanza offered a brief prayer of thanksgiving.

"Esperanza," Garrett said, having made sure the chicken platter went around the table before helping himself to two large pieces, "I haven't even tasted this food yet, but I can already tell you've outdone yourself. Again."

The older woman beamed, enjoying the praise. "Shush," she said, pleased.

A distant grinding sound alerted them to the rising of one of the garage doors.

Harry, just finishing his kibble, perked up his ears and gave an uncertain bark.

As guard dogs went, Harry was a wuss, but he liked to go through the motions.

A couple of beats passed, during which no one spoke, and then the door between the kitchen and the garage swung open and Austin stepped over the threshold.

The youngest of the McKettrick brothers, Austin was just as good-looking as Tate or Garrett, and famous on the rodeo circuit. Even when he was being friendly, it seemed to Julie, who didn't know him all that well, there was a go-to-hell look in his eyes.

"Well," Garrett said easily, settling back in his chair to survey his brother, "you look like five miles of bad road, but welcome home anyhow."

"Let me get you a plate!" Esperanza told Austin, already on her feet.

Austin stopped her with a tired gesture of one hand. "I had a burger outside of San Antonio," he said. He took off his hat, which looked as though it had fallen into a chute at the rodeo and been stomped on, and hung it on a peg.

His light brown hair was shaggy, curling above the collar of his denim jacket, and his boots were nothing fancy. That night, he looked more like a drifter hoping for a berth in the bunkhouse than a McKettrick son and heir.

Austin grinned at Calvin, then the dog. His McKettrick-blue eyes were weary when he looked at Julie, but he smiled. "Hello, Julie," he said. "Good to see you."

She smiled back and nodded. "Hi, Austin."

Esperanza was all aflutter, even though she'd sunk back into her chair at Austin's wave. "You'll be hungry later," she insisted.

"When that happens, I'll come down here looking for grub," Austin teased.

What was it about him that made Julie's throat tighten, and tears burn behind her eyes? She stole a glance at Garrett and saw that he was frowning a little as he studied his brother.

"In the meantime," Austin said, opening one of the refrigerator doors and pulling out a long-necked bottle of beer, "I just want to take a hot shower and crash in my own bed."

Nobody responded to that.

Austin nodded a farewell, taking them all in, and headed up one of the three sets of stairs rising from the kitchen to the second floor.

Esperanza sat stiffly, staring down at her food.

Garrett wasn't eating, either, and Julie, hungry as she was, didn't pick up her fork.

Only Calvin, gnawing happily on a drumstick, seemed to have an appetite.

Austin's footsteps echoed overhead.

Garrett pushed back his chair, exchanged glances with Esperanza and muttered, "Excuse me."

Rising, he left the table and then the room, taking the same stairs Austin had used moments earlier.

"Do you think you can fix my zipper?" Calvin asked. "Because I'm going to need that jacket tomorrow to go to the horse sale with Tate and Audrey and Ava, while you and Aunt Libby and Aunt Paige are in Austin shopping for Aunt Libby's wedding dress."

Julie blinked, refocused her attention on her son and

even picked up her fork to resume her supper. "I can fix the zipper," she assured him. "But it's time you had a new coat, anyway. Maybe I'll pick one up at the mall."

A protest took shape in Calvin's earnest little face. "Not without me," he said, and then swallowed. "You might get something geeky-looking."

Julie chuckled, and Esperanza smiled, too.

"Gee, buddy," Julie said, mussing up Calvin's hair with one hand, "thanks for the vote of confidence. When was the last time I bought you something 'geeky-looking'?"

Calvin straightened his spine. "At Christmas," he replied. "You gave me that sweater with that lame duck on the front."

Julie defended herself. "That was Santa."

Calvin blew through both lips and then said, "Pu-leeeeze, Mom."

So he had been humoring her—he didn't believe in Santa anymore. And he was only five. She'd hoped for one more believing Christmas, just one more, but apparently it wasn't to be.

The backs of Julie's eyes stung again, the way they had when she'd looked at Austin a few minutes earlier, but she managed a smile.

"Finish your supper," she said. "We'll figure out the new-jacket thing later."

By the time Garrett returned, Julie and Esperanza had cleared the table, except for his plate and utensils, and Calvin was happily splashing away in the bathtub in the guest quarters, with Julie checking on him every few minutes.

Returning from one of these runs, she paused to look at him for a moment, wondering what to say, if anything, before she gave up and began helping Esperanza load the dishwasher.

With a sigh, Garrett sat down.

"I could heat that food up for you," Esperanza offered, watching him.

He smiled, but he looked tired. "I could heat it up for myself," he said. "But there's no need."

"Is Austin all right?" Esperanza asked, in the tone of a woman who has held back a question as long as she was able.

Garrett didn't answer right away. When he did speak, his voice was low and slightly rough. "Probably not," he said. "I tried to get him to talk, and he told me to leave him the hell alone, so that's what I plan on doing. For tonight, anyhow."

Esperanza lifted worried eyes toward the ceiling. She murmured something, probably a prayer, and shook her head.

"He'll be fine in a few days, Esperanza," Garrett said quietly.

Esperanza opened her mouth, closed it again.

"I'll finish cleaning up," Julie told her, very gently. "You've been working all day."

"So have you," Esperanza pointed out, cheering up a little, reaching back to untie her apron. With a sigh, she added, "But I think I'll take you up on your kind offer, Julie. Put up my feet and read for a while before bed. There's nothing decent on TV."

Julie took the apron from Esperanza's hand, nodded.

After the housekeeper had gone, Garrett got up from the table and put his plate into the microwave, pushed a few buttons.

Meanwhile, Julie wiped down counters, rinsed out

the sponge, washed her hands and applied lotion. The air trembled with that now-familiar tension, and she stole several glances at Garrett, trying to figure out if he was feeling it, too.

The microwave timer dinged, and he took out his plate, returned to the table, sat down to eat. Sighed before picking up his fork.

From the looks of things, he'd forgotten Julie was even in the room.

She suppressed a sigh and started for the doorway. It was time to get Calvin out of the tub, into his pajamas, oversee the tooth-brushing ritual.

"Julie?"

Garrett's voice stopped her on the threshold of the corridor leading to the guest quarters and to Esperanza's living area. She straightened her spine, waited for him to go on, but didn't turn around or speak.

"Would you mind coming back here after you tend to Calvin?" he asked quietly. "Just to keep me company for a little while?"

There was nothing needy in his tone, and nothing demanding, either. Garrett was making a simple request.

She turned her head, felt an actual impact when their two gazes met. If she hadn't figured out instantly that something was happening when he kissed her the night before in the pool, she'd have known it then.

"Okay," she replied, in a smaller voice than she'd used in a long time.

Since the next day was Saturday, and Calvin was looking forward to spending the time with Tate and the twins, he was unusually tractable about brushing and flossing, being tucked in and kissed and saying his prayers. Libby, Paige and Julie would be away for hours, visiting a whole series of bridal shops in search of Libby's wedding dress.

Harry jumped up onto the bed and curled up at Calvin's blanketed feet, starting to snore practically the moment he'd settled in.

Calvin squeezed his eyes tightly shut, determined to sleep. The sooner he fell asleep, he probably reasoned, the sooner it would be morning.

Julie chuckled and kissed his forehead. "You're trying too hard," she whispered.

Calvin's eyes popped open, wide and faintly dazed because he wasn't wearing his glasses. "It's *never* going to be morning!" he fretted.

Julie smoothed his hair lightly, remembering when she was little, looking forward to something, counting the days till it finally came—Christmas, or a birthday, or the last day of school, or the *first* day of school.

Back then, she and her sisters had wanted to speed time up.

Usually, their dad would smile wistfully and tell them not to wish their lives away.

"It *will* be morning," Julie reminded her eager son.

"When?" he asked fitfully.

She leaned down, kissed his forehead just once more. *"When it's morning,"* she answered. "Happy trails and sweet dreams, cowboy."

Calvin huffed out a sigh, but he grinned at her before turning onto his side, snuggling down into his pillow and his covers and squeezing his eyes closed again. "'Night, Mom."

Julie lingered in the doorway, savoring this child, this fleeting place in time. It was all too easy, she reminded herself, to get caught up in causes and concerns and plans for the future and forget what truly mattered—loving and being loved, in the present moment.

She closed the door softly, took her time returning to the kitchen.

Garrett was putting his plate, glass and utensils in the dishwasher when she arrived, and she noticed that he'd set out a bottle of red wine and two glasses.

Catching her looking at them, he chuckled, turned to face her, leaning back against the counter and folding his arms. His dark blond hair looked especially shaggy, and his beard was coming in, bristly and golden. His blue eyes twinkled with a certain benevolent mischief.

"It's okay, Julie," he told her, in a tone he might have used to reassure a skittish mare, indicating the wine with a slight inclination of his head. "I'm not out to seduce you."

An unspoken *yet* hovered between them.

"A glass of wine would be nice," she said, struggling to find her equilibrium.

"Good," Garrett said. He picked up the wine in one hand and caught the stems of the glasses together in the other, then led the way onto the indoor patio on the near side of the pool.

The lighting was soft, the water was a great sparkling rectangle of turquoise, and the retractable roof was open to the silvery dance of a zillion stars spread across the night sky.

Garrett chose one of several tables, set down the things he was carrying, and drew back a chair for Julie to sit.

She hesitated—it was here, after all, in this very swimming pool where she'd felt a degree of desire she'd never even imagined to be possible—and the equation was obvious. Sexy man plus starlight plus wine and privacy equaled extreme vulnerability on her part.

Sex was one thing—it would be beyond good with Garrett, no doubt about that—but emotional entanglement was another. Easy manner, cowboy getup and horseback riding aside, he was a man with serious political aspirations—everybody in Blue River knew his association with Senator Cox was an apprenticeship of sorts, a way of learning the ropes.

And the fact of Garrett's association with a man Julie had always considered a scoundrel sent up all kinds of red flags in her mind. If Garrett had respected Cox enough to work for him from the time he finished law school and passed the bar, which he had, until their recent break in the midst of the pole-dancer scandal, what did that say about Garrett's judgments and values?

Once she took a chair, Julie just sat there, feeling like a lump.

Garrett gave a small, rueful smile, wry at the edges, and poured wine into her glass, then his own.

"We need to talk," she blurted, and immediately felt like four kinds of fool.

Garrett sat back comfortably in his chair—hell, he was damnably comfortable in his skin—and waited indulgently for her to go on.

She reached for her wineglass, nearly spilled it and set it down again, without taking so much as a sip.

Garrett smiled again, though his eyes were solemn. And still he waited. Wine by the pool under a universe full of shimmering stars had been *his* idea, but now that she'd opened her big mouth and clearly regretted it, he wasn't going to let her off the hook.

She cleared her throat, picked up her glass again, and sloshed back a gulp that nearly choked her.

Garrett didn't say one word, but a hint, a shadow, of amusement lingered on his mouth, and his eyes never left her steadily reddening face.

Julie took a second sip of wine, this time slowly, stalling in the hopes that her composure would return.

It did, sort of.

"What happened last night," she said, nodding toward the pool, "our kissing each other and everything…"

She ran out of steam.

Garrett chuckled, sipped his wine. Set his glass down and took his sweet time picking up the conversational ball. "At least you're willing to admit it was mutual," he said. "Last night, you seemed bound and determined to put all the blame on me."

Julie's cheeks pulsed with heat. She knotted her fingers together in her lap. "I'm not denying there's a certain *attraction*," she ventured, and then had to stop and clear her throat, which was mortifying.

Garrett gave an almost imperceptible nod of agreement. Or encouragement. Or *something*. But he went right on letting her dangle.

"Feel free to jump in and contribute to this exchange at any time," Julie said, annoyed.

That made him laugh. It wasn't just a chuckle—oh, no. Garrett McKettrick threw back his head and gave a husky shout of amusement.

Turnabout, Julie decided, was fair play. *She* waited now.

He watched her for a long time, and his regard felt, she thought, like a caress. Which was just ridiculous, in her opinion, because he wasn't touching her.

Thank *God*, he wasn't touching her.

"It seems reasonable to assume," he said, after a long time, "that you and I might wind up in bed together one of these days—or nights—since there's a *certain attraction* here. You've probably guessed that the whole idea works for me, on every possible level, but it has to work for you, too, Julie—because if it doesn't, it can't happen at all."

Julie hadn't been involved with a lot of men, but she wasn't naive, either. Garrett's blunt honesty was new, in her admittedly limited experience, and she didn't know quite what to make of it.

Did he actually *mean* what he said?

Would he *really* back off if she told him this wasn't the right time in her life for a—well—a fling?

Garrett picked up the bottle, leaned, topped off her glass. "What?" he prompted, watching her face, raising one eyebrow.

"We're very different," Julie said.

He grinned. "In all the right places," he replied.

"That isn't what I mean and you know it." She steadied herself with another sip of wine. It was a very nice wine, she thought. A shiraz, maybe, or a merlot. Even without peering at the label—which she refused to do—she knew the full-bodied red was way out of her price range.

And Garrett McKettrick, her pragmatic side pointed up, was out of her league. Not because he was better—of course he wasn't—but because he traveled in different circles, normally. Very sophisticated ones. Not that Julie couldn't fit in, if she made the effort, but that was the problem. She didn't want to change.

She liked her life a lot—teaching English in a small

high school, despite all the attendant problems, and running the drama club.

She loved her sisters.

Most of all, she loved Calvin, and she wanted to raise him in the little town of Blue River, where she'd grown up herself.

Garrett smiled, evidently enjoying her frustration. "Talk to me," he said.

"You're not working for Senator Cox anymore?" she asked, back in blurting mode.

Dammit, she thought. She was intelligent. She was certainly competent. Why did her IQ make a swan dive whenever she spoke to or even looked at this man?

"No, that's over," he replied.

"What about your career?"

"What about it?"

Her temper flared in the way Libby and Paige swore made her hair crackle. "Surely your *career* isn't over," she said. "We didn't run in the same crowd in school—you were a popular rodeo jock and I was artsy and a little weird—but—"

Again, one of his eyebrows rose. "A *little* weird?" he teased. "You wore white lipstick all through junior year."

Taken by surprise, Julie spoke without thinking. "You noticed that? The white lipstick phase?"

Garrett laughed. "It was hard to miss, especially since you dressed like Morticia Addams most of the time."

"I did *not* dress like Morticia Addams!" Julie protested, laughing too. "I just wore a lot of black, that's all. I was making an existential statement."

He rolled his marvelous eyes. "Whatever."

The muscles linking Julie's shoulders to her neck let go in a sudden burst of relaxation; the swiftness of it made her feel light-headed.

This was *some* wine.

She finally looped back to where she'd left off—Garrett's career. "My point is, even in high school you were interested in politics. You wanted to serve in the U.S. Senate, if not be president. Has all that changed?"

Garrett stopped smiling. Turned his wineglass slowly on the tabletop, by the stem. Then he looked straight into her eyes. "The truth is, I'm not really sure," he said. "Why do you ask?"

Why *was* she asking?

Because she needed to know his long-term plans, if she was going to get involved with Garrett, even on a temporary basis.

To a man, a fling was a fling, and when it was over, it was over. But Julie knew that if she shared her body with this particular man, there was a good chance her heart would jump ship, too.

Julie was a risk taker by nature, or, at least, she *had* been, until Calvin was born. Now, she was more careful, because if her heart got broken, Calvin's surely would, too. And she had to stay strong to be the kind of mother to him that her own had never been to her or to her sisters.

It would make a lot more sense to simply walk away, right now, before things got any more out of hand.

Except that she was a normal woman, not yet thirty, with healthy desires and needs that made her body ache with a singular loneliness sometimes—okay, *often*—in the depths of the night.

"I have a son," Julie said, very quietly and at considerable length. "What I do affects him. We're between homes, Calvin and I, and he just met his father for the first time since he was a baby. I don't want to confuse him. He looks up to Tate, and now you, and like any little boy, he's impressed by airplanes and all the rest—"

She was rambling.

Tears sprang to Julie's eyes at that moment, and she was completely unprepared for them.

Garrett reached over, took her hand and pulled her easily onto his lap.

"Hey," he said. "Everything's going to be okay."

"That," Julie sniffled, making no move to get back to her own chair, "is easy for *you* to say. For you, everything *will* be okay, because you're a man, and a *McKettrick* man, at that."

Garrett cupped her cheeks in his hands, let the pad of his right thumb brush lightly over her mouth.

"Don't you dare kiss me," Julie said, thinking she'd die if he didn't do exactly that.

"I can wait," he told her, his voice a sleepy, rumbling drawl. "Because sooner or later, Julie Remington, I mean to kiss you all over, and I'm only *starting* with your mouth."

A hot shiver went through her.

It was going to be one of those achy nights, and there wasn't a damn thing she could do about it.

Garrett traced the edges of her mouth with his thumb again. "Did you mean it when you offered to cook for me?" he asked, his voice slow and low. His face was so close to hers that she could feel the warmth of his breath against her lips.

She nodded. There was no sense in denying it. When

Julie offered to cook for a man, it was a big deal. "Yes," she said.

"Tomorrow night?" he prompted. "My place?"

Julie swallowed hard. On the inside, she felt like a pinball machine on *tilt.* "I'm going shopping with my sisters tomorrow," she said. "For Libby's wedding gown."

"I see," Garrett said, barely breathing the words. "And you won't be in the mood to—cook—after a long day on the town?"

"I have to consider Calvin," she reminded him.

"Calvin likes spending the night over at Tate and Libby's place, doesn't he? With the twins?"

Julie was almost hypnotized. She knew what was happening—she was being seduced—and she was going along with it. She was letting Garrett lead her, however circuitous the route, right to his bed.

"Your place?" she asked. She knew he had a condo or a house or something in Austin.

He raised his chin, looked briefly toward the ceiling. "Upstairs," he said.

Julie had been curious about Garrett's private quarters. Now she was going to get the tour.

Sort of.

"No strings," she warned. "On either side."

Garrett tipped his head a little to the right, nibbled briefly at the side of her neck. "No strings," he agreed.

Julie nearly cried out, the pleasure of his mouth on her skin was so intense. "We're both adults here," she said, breathlessly.

Who was she reminding—Garrett or herself?

"Consenting adults," Garrett said.

Julie got shakily to her feet. The irony was, she would

have fallen back into Garrett's lap if he hadn't steadied her by taking a firm grip on her hips.

When he bent forward and nipped at her, very lightly, where the legs of her jeans met, she couldn't hold back a groan of desire so keen that it spiked through her like a bolt of lightning.

He chuckled. "I thought so," he mused, almost under his breath.

Julie regained her senses—mostly—and stepped away from him. She still tingled where he'd put his mouth to her, ached to give herself up to him then and there.

She didn't, of course.

She still had some dignity, *some* self-control.

But not much.

CHAPTER NINE

It was an achy night.

Julie barely slept, and when she arrived at Libby and Tate's place the next morning, with an excited Calvin in tow, Paige was there ahead of her. Bright-eyed and dressed for marathon shopping in jeans, running shoes and a long-sleeved red T-shirt, Paige looked even younger than her twenty-eight years.

Happy chaos reigned in the small kitchen—dogs barked, the twins squabbled and Tate gave a shrill whistle to get everybody's attention.

The dogs and the kids went silent, stricken with what appeared to be awed admiration. After all, not everybody could whistle like that.

It was impressive.

Tate was impressive.

"Breakfast!" Tate announced, as a follow-up to the whistle, setting a platter piled high with pancakes in the center of the table, alongside a dish of scrambled eggs and a plate of crisp bacon.

Since Calvin's jacket zipper was still stuck, he threw the whole shebang off over his head, disappeared into the nearest bathroom to wash his hands and scrambled to join in the meal as soon as he got back to the kitchen. The way he dug into that food, Julie thought with rueful affection, a casual observer would think he was being starved at home.

Libby, dressed in dark slacks and a long-sleeved white blouse, looked pretty spiffy compared to her sisters; like Paige, Julie had elected to go casual, wearing jeans, comfortable shoes and a lightweight sweatshirt.

Libby and Tate exchanged a light kiss, in the midst of all that breakfast hubbub, and there was something so sizzly-sweet in the way they looked together that Julie's throat went tight and her eyes stung.

Paige gave her a light elbow bump. "Libby is getting married," she said. "Can you believe it?"

"*I* can believe it," Tate said, when another, longer kiss ended, smiling down into Libby's happy eyes. "And it's none too damn soon, either."

Paige was driving that day—her car was a four-door and easy on gas.

There was a flurry of departure—goodbyes, reiteration of plans and assigned chores for the day—and then the Remington sisters were outside, ready to roll.

When Libby climbed into the back of Paige's late-model compact, Julie shrugged and took the front passenger seat, feeling a lot more awake and ready for the day now that the three of them were setting off on their own.

Paige slid behind the wheel, started the engine and reached to switch off the radio when country music blared into the car.

"You're growing your hair out," Julie observed, with some surprise, noticing that Paige's dark, glossy cap of hair was getting longer.

"It's been too long since you two have seen each

other," Libby remarked, from the back, "if you're just now noticing that Paige changed her hair, Jules."

Paige backed up the car, turned it around and started down the bumpy dirt driveway toward the main road. "It has definitely been too long," she agreed. "We need to do this more often. Get together, I mean, just the three of us."

Julie wondered at Paige's words, though they sounded lighthearted. As different as they were from each other, the bond between the sisters had always been tight. Since Libby and Tate had fallen in love, though, things weren't the same.

They had always been busy with their separate lives, but they'd spent more time together before.

Briefly adjusting the rearview mirror for a quick look, Julie saw Libby's eyes looking back at her.

"Are you feeling neglected, little sister?" Libby asked, addressing Paige. Her voice was gentle—as the firstborn, she'd looked after Julie and Paige, especially after their mother, Marva, deserted the family when they were small.

Before Paige could answer—she'd surely been about to say yes—they met Garrett, driving Austin's red truck, about halfway down the long driveway.

Julie, unnerved, would have preferred just to wave as they passed, but Paige stopped her car and rolled down the window, prompting Garrett to stop, too.

Julie stared straight ahead while they exchanged pleasantries.

Just the night before, she'd let this man kiss her— heck, she'd kissed him *back*—and they'd made plans to have sex and supper, though possibly not in that order—

and the night before *that*, they'd gone horseback riding in the moonlight.

Considering all that, Julie couldn't bring herself to even look at Garrett, let alone make small talk. What would she say, after all?

She imagined the conversational possibilities.

I don't usually plan *sex—it's always been an impulse thing with me.*

How could I have known you all these years, Garrett McKettrick, and never noticed how hot you are?

I'm worried—you might have the power to break my heart.

All discards, of course.

Soon, mercifully, Paige and Julie had finished the informal country-road chat with Garrett, and they were off again.

Julie snuck a glance at the rearview, watching as Garrett barreled on up the driveway, a plume of dust churning behind the old truck.

"Phew," Paige said, "when I first saw that red truck—"

"You thought it was Austin," Libby finished for her. "You two have been out of high school for ten years now. The breakup, spectacular as it was, is water under the bridge. Don't you think it's about time you stopped avoiding each other? Especially now that you're going to be family?"

Remembering Austin's mood the night before, when he'd shown up during supper, Julie felt her spirits dampen a little. Something was definitely wrong there, and it made her sad.

"Family," Paige scoffed. "Austin will be part of *your* family, Lib, not mine."

"Meaning if Austin is going to be at our place for,

say, Thanksgiving dinner, you'll stay away?" Libby asked, sounding hurt.

Paige and Julie exchanged glances.

And then Paige softened a little, braking for the stop sign at the bottom of the hill and signaling a left turn, toward town. Their favorite mall, outside of Austin, was nearly two hours away, but they'd agreed to stop for breakfast at a roadhouse between Blue River and San Antonio.

"I promise to be civil to Austin McKettrick if I can't avoid him," Paige said, raising one hand as if to swear an oath. "Fair enough?"

"Fair enough," Libby replied, though Julie knew she was still troubled. Then, after an eloquent sigh, Libby added, "You know, Paige, you need to mellow out."

"*I* need to mellow out?" Paige repeated, with a giggle. "Easy for you to say, Lib—*you're* getting regular sex."

Julie scooted a little further down in her seat, hoping the subject would change before she felt compelled to blurt out to her sisters, with whom she shared pretty much everything, that she had decided to go to bed with Garrett McKettrick.

"It's not just *regular* sex," Libby said, amused. "It's extremely good sex."

Julie, who usually would have jumped on the topic with more aplomb than either Libby or Paige, remained silent. Miserably silent.

"What's the matter with you?" Libby finally demanded, poking her in the shoulder from behind.

"Nothing," Julie lied. "Nothing whatsoever is the matter with me."

"We're talking about sex and you haven't said anything outrageous," Paige told her. "Who are you and what have you done with our sister, Julie?"

Finally, Julie laughed. She couldn't help it. Nor could she hide the note of despair underlying her amusement. A tear streaked down her cheek, and she wiped it away with the back of one hand—though not quickly enough to keep Paige from seeing.

Paige pulled the car to the side of the road and flipped on the safety blinkers.

"All right, spill it," she told Julie.

With her brown eyes and dark hair, Paige looked the most like their father. The resemblance gave her an odd authority, at least some of the time.

"What's going on?" Libby demanded, unhooking her seat belt and scooting forward to shove her head between the seats and study Julie.

Julie sniffled. "I'm going to sleep with, of all people, Garrett McKettrick," she burst out. "And I don't even have the excuse of not knowing any better!"

Libby began to laugh.

Paige beamed. "Wow," she said. "You and *Garrett*?"

"There is no 'Garrett and me,'" Julie countered quickly. "This is only about sex."

"I can't believe I'm hearing this," Libby said. "'This is only about sex'?"

"Hot damn," Paige said, clearly delighted. Then she repeated, more slowly that the first time, *"You and Garrett."*

"Maybe we can have a double wedding!" Libby chimed in, thrilled.

"No double wedding," Julie was quick to say. "Garrett and I aren't like you and Tate. This isn't a love match—it's pure lust. We don't have the same goals, or even the same values, unless I miss my guess."

"Garrett's a hunk and you could really use a man in your life," Paige put in, careful to keep her eyes mostly on the road, though she did sneak a few glances in Julie's direction. "Goals can be adapted, and let's face it, the McKettricks are known for being straight shooters, so there shouldn't be any problem with values."

"He's a politician," Julie reminded her sisters.

"Think of how great this would be for Calvin," lobbied Paige.

"Garrett is a politician," Julie repeated.

"You make it sound like he has a case of leprosy," Libby said.

"That might be an improvement," Julie insisted. "Garrett is aligned with Senator Cox, and Senator Cox, in case you haven't been watching the news, has the morals of an alley rat."

"But you're planning to *sleep* with the man," Paige said, in a let-me-get-this-straight tone of voice. "Despite an obviously low opinion of his political affiliation?"

"His *former* political affiliation," Libby put in. "Garrett doesn't work for Morgan Cox anymore."

"We've admitted there's an attraction, that's all," Julie tossed into the verbal jumble, making her tone lofty. "Since we're both consenting adults, we've decided to go to bed together. It's just that simple."

"Straight to bed?" Paige teased, shutting off the blinkers and easing carefully onto the road again. "Without passing go and collecting two hundred dollars?"

Julie rolled her eyes at the reference to the board game they'd played throughout their childhood. Paige had always been the one to buy up all the little green houses and red hotels, erecting them on the most expensive properties, too. A shark, winding up with piles of pastel-colored money at the end of every session.

She'd been downright ruthless when it came to collecting the rent.

"I'm cooking dinner for him first," Julie said.

"Well," Libby said, drawing out the word and waving both hands for emphasis, "*that's* different, then. You're going to cook a gourmet meal for Garrett and *then* fall into bed with him. Where, pray tell, is Calvin going to be during this—this *escapade*?"

Julie turned in the seat and found herself almost eye to eye with Libby. Libby's words had been inflammatory, but now Julie saw that her sister's baby blues were twinkling with mischief.

"I hope," Julie answered, "that Calvin will be at your place, spending the night."

"That's it?" Paige marveled, sounding thrilled. "Take Calvin to a babysitter, cook a meal and hit the sheets? That's your plan?"

"I'm not a babysitter," Libby said, miffed. "I'm Calvin's aunt."

"That's the plan," Julie admitted.

"I like it," Paige said, with enthusiasm.

They all laughed then.

The topic of conversation turned to breakfast, and the day ahead—which bridal shops and upscale department stores ranked highest on Libby's list, what color their bridesmaids' dresses should be.

Audrey and Ava would be junior bridesmaids, and Calvin was the official ring bearer.

During breakfast at the roadhouse, they talked about the cottage Julie had been renting being put on the market, and the whole tenting-for-termites experience, and Paige, an RN, confided that she'd been offered a job at Blue River's clinic. It paid less than she was making now, but the benefits were good and the hours were shorter, and she wouldn't have to commute fifty miles every day, and that was worth something, wasn't it?

Libby and Julie agreed that it was.

They visited two different malls and three bridal shops before they found The Dress.

It was a cloud of gossamer silk, that dress, with a fitted bodice and lovely full sleeves and tiny ivory pearls and pinpoint rhinestones setting it alight, as though it had been fashioned from some long-ago snowfall. The veil seemed to be made of air and candlelight.

Libby stood frozen on the sidewalk in front of the small Austin boutique when she spotted it in the window, a fairy-tale gown, more fantasy than fabric.

Trying it on only magnified the magical effect.

Of course, there would be alternations—the dress was too big through the waist and too small in the bodice—but the sight of Libby swathed in all that soft glory brought tears to Julie's eyes, and to Paige's.

They stared at their sister in wonder, outside the dressing room, marveling. Libby seemed translucent; like a human pearl, she glowed with soft, creamy brilliance.

Happiness looked good on Libby, and so did that marvelous dress.

The exquisite gown, the saleswoman explained, was vintage, on consignment from the costume department of a movie studio. As far as she knew, no one had ever actually worn it in a film, but Julie pictured Loretta Young wearing it, and then Vivien Leigh, and neither of them could compare to Libby.

Paige snapped a photo with her cell phone, planning to zap it off to Tate, but Libby absolutely forbade that. The dress had to be a surprise, she maintained—her groom was not to see her in that gown until their wedding, scheduled for New Year's Eve.

The save-the-date cards had already gone out, and the caterers had been hired.

The honeymoon had been planned, the flowers selected and ordered.

Except for finding Libby's dream dress, which had involved a lot of research, both online and in magazines—and those Julie, Paige, Audrey and Ava would wear—everything was done.

"That's a silly superstition," Paige protested, but Libby was adamant.

"It's bad luck," Libby insisted.

Paige merely shook her head.

Julie smiled at Libby, so happy for her sister that she thought she might burst. "You're going to be the most beautiful bride *ever*," she said.

The antique dress rustled as Libby hugged her.

Libby paid for the dress, and she and the store owner set up an appointment for the first of several fittings.

Next, the three sisters had lunch in a favorite Mexican restaurant.

"You don't really believe in bad luck, do you?" Paige pressed, over guacamole and chips. "That's just an old wives' tale, you know—that something terrible will happen if Tate sees you wearing the dress before you walk down the aisle."

Libby considered the question, shrugged slightly. "I'm not taking any chances," she said.

"Good idea," Julie said, smiling across the table at Libby. "Better safe than sorry."

Paige gave a small snort of laughter. "Since when have you lived by *that* motto?" she asked, turning to look at Julie, who sat beside her in the restaurant booth.

"Since Calvin," Julie answered.

The mood shifted.

"When is the big supper-and-sex date?" Paige asked, her dark eyes tender now, and luminous with affection.

"Garrett suggested tonight," Julie said, squirming a little.

Libby's eyes rounded.

"Yes!" Paige said, punching the air with one fist.

"I didn't say I agreed," Julie pointed out reasonably.

The waitress came and they took their orders—the three of them would share a plate of nachos, heavy on the goop.

"I'm bringing Calvin home with me tonight," Paige decided. "We'll take in a movie, the big guy and me, and go out for pizza. I've been working so much—this is the first weekend off I've had in months."

"I thought Calvin was going to stay with Tate and the girls and me," Libby said.

"I haven't said yes," Julie reiterated.

"But you're going to," Paige reasoned. "It's written all over you. You're hot to trot. Ready to tango."

"Stop," Julie pleaded, blushing.

Paige and Libby both giggled.

"What are you planning to cook?" Paige asked.

"What will you wear?" Libby wanted to know.

Since both of them had spoken at once, Julie took a moment to untangle their words.

"It's more about what she's *not* going to wear," Paige observed, in the gap.

"I thought I'd cook something very simple," Julie said, her cheeks burning now. "And I will be fully dressed, thank you very much."

"That's only important if you're frying something," Libby said. "Otherwise, cooking naked can be—"

Both Julie and Paige stared at her, grinning.

Now it was Libby who blushed.

The nachos arrived, and the waitress refilled their ice tea glasses.

Libby started picking off hot peppers and setting them aside.

The food was delicious, fattening and delightfully messy to eat. The three of them clowned around a little, Paige karate-chopping a long strand of cheese stretched between the plate and the loaded chip she raised to her mouth.

Libby accidentally got a slice of hot pepper and drank from all three of their water glasses in turn.

Julie laughed and shook her head. She loved spicy food—the hotter, the better. "Wimp," she said, with love.

"Food," Libby sputtered, after filling her mouth with ice and sluicing it around before chewing and swallowing, "should not be painful."

After lunch, they returned to one of the bridal shops they'd visited earlier, to take a second look at a bridesmaid's dress that had caught Libby's eye.

It was way too ruffly, and tied in a big bow at the back.

What was it, Julie wondered, that drew otherwise sensible brides to dresses seemingly designed to please Little Bo Peep?

"It comes in a lot of colors," Libby mused, studying the tag.

"You're my sister, and I love you," Paige told her. "I'll do anything for you, Lib. Dance barefoot over hot coals. Donate a kidney. Throw myself in front of a train. *Anything* but wear that god-awful dress."

Libby looked so discouraged that Julie slid an arm around her older sister and gave her a quick squeeze. Naturally, the wedding meant a lot to Libby, and she must have been feeling pressure to tie up all the loose ends.

"You found the perfect wedding gown," Julie reminded Libby. "That's progress."

Paige nodded in agreement. "The right bridesmaids' dresses are out there somewhere," she put in, "and we'll find them."

"Just not today, probably," Julie added gently.

Libby smiled and nodded, and her whole face seemed to light up. "Let's go," she said.

They stopped at a supersize discount store on the way back to Blue River—Libby wanted a big bag of dog food, Paige planned to pick up some toiletries and Julie was in the market for a play jacket for Calvin.

"Is this geeky-looking?" she asked, holding up a blue and beige coat, when Paige wheeled her cart up alongside Julie's.

"Everything looks good on Calvin," Paige replied. Then, after a beat, "So what's on the menu for the romantic rendezvous with Garrett?" She leaned in a little way, lowered her voice. "Besides you, I mean."

Julie swatted at her. Of course, on some level, she'd been rifling through her mental recipe collection since the night before, considering one dish, then deciding against it and moving on to another.

Her specialty was lasagna, but that took hours to prepare, and she didn't have that kind of time. Besides, Garrett had already eaten her lasagna, albeit as leftovers.

"Why did I agree to make dinner for him?" she whispered to Paige. "I could at least have given myself some time!"

Paige grinned. "Come on, relax. You're a great cook—everything you make is delicious."

"Help," Julie pleaded miserably.

Libby showed up then, with a huge bag of kibble filling up her cart. "Are you two about finished with your shopping?"

Paige rammed Julie's cart with her own, though gently. "Our sister is on the horns of a dilemma," she said, turning to Libby. "She promised Garrett a dinner, and she can't decide what to serve."

"Meatballs," Libby said helpfully. "You make the *best* meatballs."

"Too messy," Julie said, imagining herself up to her elbows in a mixture of ground beef, spices, onions, bread crumbs and raw eggs.

"Fried chicken?" Paige suggested. "Most men love fried chicken."

"Esperanza made that last night," Julie replied.

"The man's not thinking about food, anyway," Paige said. "Why don't you just buy a frozen entrée and nuke it in the microwave?"

Julie made a face and pushed between Paige's cart and Libby's, rolling on into the aisle, and headed for the grocery section. At that moment, she almost wished she hadn't told her sisters *anything* about her plans for the evening.

Paige and Libby trailed after her, whispering and giggling between themselves the way they would have done back in high school.

Cowboys liked steak, didn't they? Julie wondered, reaching the meat counter and peering at the selection of beef.

For all she knew about Garrett McKettrick, she realized, he could be a vegetarian.

That didn't seem likely, given that the McKettricks were cattle ranchers and had been for more than a hundred years, but still.

"Your chicken spaghetti," Libby said, selecting a package of poultry and tucking it into a plastic bag, "is bound to be a hit." She dropped the works in Julie's cart, taking care that it didn't land on Calvin's new jacket.

Julie's gratitude was all out of proportion to the favor Libby had done her. She felt teary and overly sentimental. Why hadn't *she* thought of chicken spaghetti on her own? She'd won prizes for the stuff, and she knew all the other ingredients she'd need were in Esperanza's pantry back at the ranch.

"What?" Paige asked, plucking a tissue from the little package she carried in her purse and handing it to Julie.

Julie dabbed at her eyes, sniffled, shoved the crumpled tissue into her jeans pocket. "This is crazy," she said.

"Come on," Libby said, pulling at the front of Julie's cart while pushing her own forward at the same time. "If we hurry, we can beat the weekend traffic."

"What's crazy?" Paige asked, squeaky-wheeling it

alongside Julie as they all moved toward the checkout counters at the front of the store.

Julie made a face. "My plans for the evening," she said primly, aware of other people, all of them strangers, crowding in around them. Possibly listening.

Paige's eyes twinkled. She'd probably considered responding with something like, *Your plans? Oh, yes, I forgot. You're going to sleep with Garrett McKettrick.* Fortunately, she didn't.

They were in the parking lot, stuffing their purchases into the trunk of Paige's car, when Libby spoke up.

"You were crying in there," she said to Julie, her tone matter-of-fact.

"Definitely hormonal," Paige commented.

"What if you're ovulating?" Libby wanted to know. "You could get pregnant."

"Will you lower your voice?" Julie demanded, annoyed. "And while you're at it, give me credit for the sense God gave a goose."

They all got into the car, spent a few noisy moments juggling their purses and fastening their seat belts.

"What if you get pregnant?" Paige insisted.

"I'm not going to get pregnant," Julie snapped.

"That's what you said when you and Gordon hooked up," Libby reminded her. "And, presto!" She snapped the fingers of both hands. "Heeeeeere's Calvin!"

"Will you stop?" Julie begged.

"Are you on the Pill?" Paige asked, ever the nurse. She was busy navigating the crowded parking lot, working her way toward one of several exits.

"No," Julie said, after a few moments of internal struggle.

"Some other form of birth control?" Libby pressed, popping her head between the seats again.

"Don't you think this conversation is getting a little personal?" Julie countered. "Even for sisters?"

"We're just trying to help," Libby said.

Julie closed her eyes, drew in a deep breath, and let it out again. "Unlike some people I could name," she said evenly, "I happen to know exactly where I am in my cycle at all times. And, anyway, I've decided to call the whole thing off. I don't know what I was thinking, agreeing to such a thing."

"Do I still get to keep Calvin for the rest of the weekend?" Paige asked.

"Yes," Julie said. "And if he thinks the coat I bought him is 'geeky,' I'm going to tell him *you* picked it out."

After a few more minutes of sisterly banter, the Remington women were all talked out. They lapsed into a comfortable silence, and Paige tuned the radio to an easy-listening station.

There was still a little light when they reached the outskirts of Blue River, and the cottage was just two streets over, so Julie automatically glanced in that direction, expecting to see the giant exterminator's tent looming against the darkening sky.

It was gone.

"Drive by the cottage," Julie said, turning to Paige. If the tent had been taken down, she and Calvin could move back in, at least until the place was sold.

Paige signaled and they left the main highway.

Sure enough, the tent had been deflated, but not removed. It bulged and rippled all around the little house, like a garment on top of an open heat vent.

Julie had barely taken that in when Paige nudged her. "Look," she said, pointing.

It was then that Julie spotted the real estate sign. Suzanne Hillbrand had scored—there was a big, red Sold sticker plastered across the other information.

"Sold," Julie whispered, her heart sinking. She guessed she hadn't really believed it would come to this.

"They can't just kick you out," Paige said quickly, and a little angrily as well. "You have a lease. Your landlady has to serve adequate notice."

"I thought it would take a while to sell the cottage," Julie said, as though her sister hadn't spoken. "You know, with the market the way it is and everything. And I *don't* have a lease—it's month to month."

Libby reached forward from the backseat to place one hand on Julie's shoulder and squeeze lightly. "Were you planning on making an offer yourself?" she asked, very quietly.

Julie sniffled, shook her head no. She felt bruised and somehow bereft.

For all intents and purposes, she and Calvin were homeless.

They couldn't stay on the Silver Spur forever, and the house she and Libby and Paige had grown up in was under renovation.

By tacit agreement, they headed for the ranch.

At Tate and Libby's, they were greeted by a crowd of eager children and yipping dogs. Audrey and Ava flung themselves at Libby, wrapping their arms around her waist, making her laugh.

Calvin, Julie noticed, hung back a little, keeping to the fringe of things. It made her heart hurt.

"Don't get mad, okay?" he said, when Julie approached her small son and drew him close for a hug, there in the yard.

"Okay," Julie said cautiously, looking him over more closely now, in the light spilling from Libby and Tate's front porch, and the tall, wide windows on either side of the door.

No casts. No stitches. No bandages, blisters or burns.

Calvin's chin wobbled as he looked up at Julie. "I was down at the creek by myself," he blurted, "and I fell in."

Julie's heart nearly stopped. The creek wasn't particularly deep, nor did the water move especially fast, but it had been cold all day.

Automatically, she checked his forehead for a fever, but his temperature was normal. His clothes, though wrinkled, were dry.

"Garrett was here and he waded in and got me," Calvin hastened on. "I had to take a warm shower and wear one of Tate's shirts until my clothes came out of the dryer. *And* I had a time-out."

Tate appeared, shooing kids, dogs and women toward the house. There was no sign of Garrett.

Tate hung back, once everybody was inside, and Julie paused, too, both of them standing just inside the threshold. He shut the door and spoke quietly.

"I'm sorry, Julie," he said. "The kids were playing soccer in the yard, after we got back from the stock sale this afternoon, and, well, Calvin chased the ball right into the creek."

Julie sighed. Obviously, Tate expected her to be angry with him. Instead, she stood on tiptoe and kissed his cheek.

"Calvin's okay," she reminded her future brother-in-law, the man who had already brought her sister so much happiness. "That's what's important."

Tate nodded, looking relieved. Beyond, in the kitchen, Libby and Paige and all three of the kids seemed to be talking at once.

"Did she find the dress?" he asked. Often, when Tate spoke of Libby, a note of hoarse reverence came into his voice. It happened then, too.

Julie smiled. "Yes, and it's fabulous," she answered.

Tate's grin was as swift and as lethal as Garrett's, though it didn't have the same effect on Julie as Garrett's did. "*Libby's* fabulous," he said.

"No argument there," Julie replied.

Paige appeared in the doorway from the kitchen. "It's okay for Calvin to come home with me, right?" she asked. Calvin was pressed up against his aunt's side by then, clinging to her and gazing hopefully at his mother.

Calvin loved to spend time with either or both of his aunts, but he and Paige had a special bond.

Julie folded her arms, frowned a little and tapped one foot. "I don't know," she said, pausing to run her teeth over her lower lip. "There *was* that whole creek incident, requiring a time-out."

Paige ruffled Calvin's hair and made a face at Julie.

"Oh, all right," Julie relented, as though making a great concession.

By then, she'd decided to tell Garrett she'd changed her mind about everything but making supper.

Julie loved cooking, and she was good at it.

For tonight, Garrett McKettrick would just have to be satisfied with food.

CHAPTER TEN

AUSTIN, CLAD ONLY in faded black sweatpants and a shit-eatin' grin, turned from the refrigerator in the main kitchen to give Garrett an idle once-over. After a low whistle of exclamation, he plucked a can of beer from a shelf and shut the door, popped the top on the beer and raised it in a mocking toast.

"Dressed like that, big brother," Austin drawled, "you're either announcing your candidacy for something, or fixing to charm some woman into the sack."

Considering that he'd gone to some trouble to strike a casual tone, Garrett was not pleased by this observation—particularly since it struck so close to the bone. After he'd gotten back from Tate's place an hour or so before, he'd showered, dressed in moderately new jeans, a long-sleeved Western shirt open at the throat, with the sleeves rolled up to his elbows, and donned a pair of decent boots.

He glared at Austin's beer, then at Austin.

"If anybody around here is a candidate for anything," he replied, "it's you. You've been elected the resident lunatic by a landslide."

Austin, suffering from a bad case of bed-head—on him, even that looked good, dammit—gave a companionable belch and took a long swallow from the brew. "So it's the woman, then," he said. "Julie Remington, I presume?"

No comment, Garrett thought.

"How about making yourself scarce?" he said aloud.

Austin mugged like he was wounded to the quick and pretended to pull a blade from his chest. He was scarred where a whole team of surgeons had put him back together after a bad turn with a mean bull on the rodeo circuit earlier that year, but that probably appealed to women, rather than putting them off.

"Well," he said now, "*that* ain't neighborly."

"We're not neighbors," Garrett pointed out, casting an anxious glance toward the door leading in from the garage. "We're brothers. Get lost—and spare me the hillbilly grammar while you're at it."

Instead of obliging, Austin padded over to the huge table in the middle of the room, drew back a chair and sat down. "I know it's inconvenient at the moment," he said, "but I *live* here."

Even looking like he did—he might have been sleeping on the floor of somebody's tackroom closet for a week—Austin had a way about him, especially with women. It would be just like him to wangle an invitation out of Julie to join them for supper, and then hang around for the rest of the night, knowing damn well he was getting in the way.

Garrett resisted an urge to shove a hand through his hair. He'd just combed it after his shower, gotten rid of the crease left by his hat. He'd spent the day helping the fence crew drive postholes and string wire, except for a stop at Tate's place on the way back home.

He smiled, recalling that. Maybe all wasn't lost, after all.

He'd fished Calvin out of the creek, though the kid

had never been in any serious danger of drowning, and that might have earned him a few points with Julie.

"Okay," Garrett said, almost sighing the word. "What's it going to cost me to get you the hell out of here for the rest of the night?"

Austin's eyes twinkled with a faint reflection of the old mischief, then hardened slightly. "You've been kow-towing to Morgan Cox for too long, brother," he said. "Not everybody has a price, whatever your boss may have led you to believe."

Garrett's back molars ground together. He stood be-side the table, gripping the edge, and did his best to loom. Not that Austin was intimidated, the little bas-tard—he was cocky as a rooster.

"Maybe I'll pretend you didn't say that," Garrett said slowly and evenly. "The fact is, right about now I'd just as soon drown you in the pool as anything else."

Austin chuckled, but the sound was raspy and there was no amusement in it. He shook his head once, and then leaned back to drain the beer can. That done, he stood up so fast that his chair nearly tipped over. He caught it before turning toward Garrett.

"Bring it on," he challenged. His blue eyes flashed with temper, and with pain.

"Some other time," Garrett replied quietly. Some-thing was sure as hell eating his kid brother alive, but whatever it was, Austin wasn't ready to talk about it.

Austin raised an eyebrow. "Scared?"

In the near distance, one of the garage doors rolled up.

"You know I'm not," Garrett said. "I happen to have other plans, that's all, and they don't include getting into a pissing match with you, little brother."

Some of the granite drained out of Austin's eyes and his jawline; he looked almost like his old self again.

Almost, but not quite.

He slapped Garrett on the shoulder and headed for one of the stairways, and by the time Julie stepped into the kitchen, carrying one plastic grocery bag and her purse, Austin was gone.

"Where's Harry?" she asked, looking around the kitchen.

It took Garrett a moment to realize she was referring to the dog.

He smiled, crossed the room and took the bag from her hand. "He's taken to hanging out in front of my fireplace," he explained. "I hope that's all right with you."

"I wouldn't have thought he could manage the stairs," Julie said, her tone fretful and her gaze straying up the steps.

"I carried him," Garrett said. And just then, the three-legged beagle appeared on the landing above, making a happy whining sound down deep in his throat and wagging his tail and both hips.

Julie seemed strained and pretty tired, but a smile transformed her face. "You carried him?" she asked, as though she wasn't sure she'd heard him correctly.

"Yeah," Garrett admitted, puzzled. The dog was about to start down the stairs, a decision that could prove disastrous, considering the critter's anatomical limitations, so he said, "Hold it right there" and bounded up there to head Harry off.

He caught the mutt in the curve of one arm, hoisted.

Julie stood at the bottom of the stairs, looking up at them, that soft smile still gracing her face. For a moment, it seemed to Garrett that she glowed like a stained-glass Madonna in a church window.

The sight of her made his breath catch and then swell in his throat.

"I hear you saved Calvin in the face of certain survival," she quipped, the smile turning to a grin. "Thanks for that, Garrett."

He chuckled. "You're welcome," he answered, frozen where he was, at the top of the stairs, with a dog under his arm and a grocery sack dangling from his other hand. His voice came out sounding hoarse. "Come on up," he said. "Whatever's in this bag, we'll cook it together."

She hesitated, set her purse aside on a countertop and mounted the stairs, looking down at her feet as she climbed. It was only when she'd reached the landing that Garrett saw the heat burning in her cheeks.

She was still wearing her coat, and the rich autumn-brown color of the cloth turned her changeable eyes to a smoky shade of amber. "About what we were planning—for after supper, I mean—"

Garrett set Harry down, and the dog greeted Julie with a few jabs of his nose to her shins, then turned and trotted off toward the double doors opening into Garrett's living area.

Garrett shifted the grub-sack to his other hand and pressed his palm lightly into the small of Julie's back, steering her toward the well-lit privacy of his living room. He meant the gesture to reassure her, and she did seem to relax a little. At the same time, he felt energy zipping through her like electricity through a wire.

"Wow," she said, after crossing the threshold.

A fire crackled on the hearth, and the tall windows overlooking the range seemed speckled with stars. Lamps burned here and there, switched to "dim," giving the room a welcoming glow.

Garrett grinned at her, but proceeded to the kitchen, where he looked into the bag, saw that it contained a package of boneless, skinless chicken breasts, and tossed the works into the refrigerator.

He'd opened a good shiraz earlier, to let it "breathe," though he was secretly skeptical about the respiratory capacity of wine, no matter how fancy its label.

He slid two wineglasses from the built-in rack under one row of cupboards, holding them by their stems, and set them on the counter as Julie slid out of her coat and draped it over the back of one of the barstools at the counter.

Garrett washed his hands at the sink, remembering that he'd been holding the dog, dried them on a dish towel, and gave Julie a questioning look as he reached for the wine bottle.

She nodded, met his eyes as he handed her a glass and then clinked his own against it, very lightly.

"To a friendly supper," he said huskily, wanting to put her at ease, "between two friends."

Julie looked relieved, but a little disconcerted, too, as she nodded and then sipped. Closing her eyes, she said, "Ummm," and things ground inside Garrett, like rusted gears freshly oiled and just starting to turn again.

If it hadn't felt so damn good, he reflected, it would have hurt like hell.

"Are we friends, Garrett?" she asked.

"I hope so," he answered.

As if that settled something, Julie set the wineglass down, washed her hands and opened the fridge door to retrieve the bag. "Let's cook," she said. "I'm starved."

Right on cue, Garrett pulled a baking sheet lined with stuffed mushrooms from the oven. They'd been warming there for a while, thanks to Esperanza, but they weren't shriveled, and they smelled fine.

Julie's eyes widened. "You cook?"

If only he could have lied and taken the credit. Alas, Garrett came from a long line of compulsive truth-tellers. "I know how to fry eggs," he confessed. "Esperanza keeps a stash of frozen finger foods on hand at all times. Her theory is, You never know when a dinner party might break out."

Julie laughed at that. Reached for one of the mushrooms and lifted it to her mouth, taking a delicate sniff before she bit into it.

"Ummmm," she said again, just the way she had before, when she first tasted the wine. She *breathed* the sound, and there was something so sensual about it that Garrett's brain turned to vapor inside his skull and then seemed to dissipate like mist under a hot sun.

In that moment, the sophisticated Garrett McKettrick, former top aide to a U.S. senator, forgot everything he'd ever known about women, except for one thing: He loved them.

Loved the way they looked, the way they smelled, the way they felt.

Or maybe it was just this particular one he loved.

He was still standing there, dumbstruck by the implications, when Julie opened those marvelous, magical eyes, looked straight into his, and suddenly popped a mushroom into his mouth.

It was an ordinary gesture, entirely innocent.

And it struck Garrett with all the wallop of a punch.

It was only by superhuman effort that he refrained

from taking the wineglass out of her hand, pressing her body against the wall or the refrigerator door, with the full length of his own, and kissing her like she'd never been kissed before.

Even by him.

"Whoa," he ground out, amazed that it was so hard to rein himself in.

Julie gave a breathy little giggle and fluttered a hand in front of her face like a fan. "Phew," she said. "Esperanza must have stuffed those mushrooms with jalapeños."

Garrett laughed as some new and startled kind of joy welled up inside him and broke free. His heart pounded and his breath came shallow and raspy.

He loved Julie Remington.

No, he instantly corrected himself. He couldn't *possibly* be in love with her—it was too soon.

And he was in transition.

"We'd better cook," he said, desperate to distract her.

And equally desperate *not* to.

Julie giggled again and put her wineglass on the counter, then slid both arms around his neck. He felt her breasts, soft against the hard wall of his chest. "Oh," she said, "I think we're *already* cooking."

Garrett, like his brothers, like his father and his grandfather and a whole slew of greats, had been raised to be a gentleman.

Cursing his upbringing, he took a very light grip on Julie's wrists and brought her arms down from around his neck. He held on to her hands, though. Squeezed them.

"Food first," he said, and the rumble in his voice reminded him of the pre-earthquake sound of tectonic plates shifting far underground.

Julie's cheeks glowed and something flashed brief and bright in her eyes. But then she swallowed visibly and nodded.

"Food first," she agreed.

THE WHOLE TIME she and Garrett were assembling that batch of chicken spaghetti, Julie was torn between equally strong impulses to run in the other direction, as fast as she could, and fling herself at him again.

Not that putting her arms around Garrett's neck really qualified as *flinging herself at him*, she thought. On the other hand, what *else* could she call it?

She couldn't blame it on the wine. Two sips weren't enough to make her brazen.

No, it hadn't been the wine.

She'd raised that stupid stuffed mushroom to his mouth—what had possessed her to do such a forward thing she would never know—and he'd taken it from her. Moreover, he'd sucked lightly at her fingers as she withdrew.

That was the moment it happened. The moment she lost her mind.

They worked reasonably well together, Julie thought, taking occasional and very slow sips from her wineglass, and chatted like the old friends they most definitely were not while she slipped the casserole into the preheated oven and set the timer, after musing over the dials and buttons a little.

While the main course baked, Garrett threw together a very decent salad, and Julie watched, munching on another stuffed mushroom.

"And you said all you could do was fry eggs," she said.

Garrett winked. "Oh, I can do *lots* of things besides fry eggs," he told her.

The kitchen was big, though not as enormous as the one downstairs, and wired for sound. When an old Patsy Cline ballad melted in through the speakers, like some shimmering liquid, nearly visible, Garrett turned the volume up and the lights down and pulled Julie into his arms, waltzing her around the perimeters of the island in the center of the room.

If he'd kissed her then, she would have been lost. But he didn't.

He simply danced with her.

Until the song ended and she was dizzy, and her breathing was all messed up.

Silently, Julie reminded herself that Garrett was only passing through—even this legendary ranch wasn't big enough to accommodate his ambitions. He wanted to play on the world stage, and when he left, she couldn't— and wouldn't—go with him.

Still, she'd been alone for so long.

And Garrett had roused things in her that no other man had even stirred.

Her body—every cell of it—was suddenly asserting itself, making demands, crying out for things her mind would have called foolish. And among those things was the simple solace of being held by a man.

Just held.

In a last-ditch effort to resist, to override flood-tide passion with common sense, Julie did the opposite of what her entire physicality craved: She pulled out of Garrett's arms, turned from him, and stood leaning against the counter opposite the door, her head down, gasping for breath.

And her body wept.

Garrett moved to stand behind her, rested his hands on her shoulders, barely touching her, but touching her just the same. Touching her in a way that caused her very essence to gather within her and then surge, like some sparkling force summoned by a wizard, into the rein-roughened palms of his hands.

The sensation was so deliciously compelling, so utterly unnerving, that Julie sagged, suddenly boneless, and might have collapsed if Garrett hadn't held her upright, turned her in his arms, held her against his chest.

She was trembling.

"Shhh," he murmured. It was what she needed—*holding*—and somehow he knew that.

Garrett curved a finger under Julie's chin and lifted, so she was looking into his eyes.

Without a word, he kissed her.

There was undeniable wanting in that kiss, but it was exquisitely controlled. It made promises, that sweet pressure of his mouth on hers, but demanded nothing in return.

I'm losing my mind, Julie thought, feeling swept away.

Garrett stretched—she realized he was switching off the oven—and then swung her easily up into his arms.

"If you say 'stop,'" he told her, "if you even *think* 'stop,' I will."

She nodded to let him know she understood, and rested her face in the curve where his neck and shoulder met, loving the smell of his skin, the warmth and substance and strength of him.

He carried her into a darkened room, and she knew by the fresh-air, Garrett-scent of the place that this was where he slept.

She felt dazed, needy, incredibly safe.

Garrett stood her beside the shadow of a bed. "Where's Calvin?" he asked.

Julie swallowed, scrounged around in the depths of herself until she found her voice. "With Paige," she answered. "For the weekend."

He began peeling away her clothes, and the touch of his hands seemed reverent, rather than forceful. "Good," he said, and the word vibrated down the length of her neck, because he spoke it into the hollow beneath her right ear. "That's good."

She didn't have to be strong, Julie thought, bedazzled. For once, for a little while, she didn't have to be strong.

Garrett was strong enough for both of them.

Garment by garment, Garrett bared Julie, then himself. He took a condom from the nightstand.

"Just hold me," she whispered, as they sank together into rumpled sheets, fragrant with detergent and sunshine and Garrett.

He stretched out beside her on the bed, drew her close, so that their bodies fit together.

But he did not kiss or caress her.

Not then.

Honoring his tacit promise, Garrett simply *held* Julie in the strong, warm circle of his arms. He propped his chin on top of her head, and she took comfort in the steady meter of his breathing. He said nothing. Asked for nothing.

Gave everything.

Julie lay there, in Garrett's easy embrace, and felt no shame, no sorrow and no need of anything more than what she had, in that precise moment.

After a long time, she spoke his name, whispered it, like a plea.

And he understood, and eased on top of her, bracing himself on his elbows and forearms.

"Are you sure, Julie?" he asked.

She bit her lower lip, nodded.

From Julie's perspective, there was no need for foreplay. Her surrender to Garrett was a gift, and not a fulfillment of any desire she possessed. She eased her thighs apart, lifted her hips just slightly, delighting in the groan the motion elicited from him.

"I'm sure," she told him.

He eased inside her.

Julie cried out, not in pain, but in celebration—the friction, the fit, was perfect. It sent her spinning away from herself, in a glittering spiral of light and heat, and the sounds she made were expressions of awe and delight.

He was so big.

So strong.

So hard.

Julie gave herself up to the most primitive aspects of her own femininity, let herself be lost in Garrett.

He entwined his fingers with hers, pressed her hands into the pillow on either side of her head and pumped hard with his hips.

Julie kept pace, meeting him stroke for stroke, thrust for thrust.

The climb was a sacred quest, every new level intensified the pleasure.

Their bodies flirted, then danced, then slammed into each other, fierce in their need for union, for the deepest kind of contact, for satisfaction.

When the climax came, it was simultaneous. Garrett

tensed on top of Julie, with a guttural shout, a warrior's cry of conquest and triumph. Julie, in turn, flung herself upward to meet him, to take him deep inside her, to clench around him and wring from him everything he had to give to her, and then still more.

That first, apocalyptic release was followed by a series of progressively smaller ones, soul-wrenching and utterly involuntary.

When it was over, a long, long time had passed, and Garrett and Julie lay still, exhausted.

Julie was glad of the darkness, because suddenly her eyes were awash in tears—not of sorrow and certainly not of regret, but of wonderment and awe. When had she last felt those things, soared like that?

Never, that was when.

The thought jolted Julie; she sneaked up a hand to dry her cheek. And she began to rationalize.

She'd responded in the soul-shattering way she had because it had been so long since she'd had sex, that was all.

It wasn't Garrett, she insisted to herself. Any reasonably skilled man could have satisfied her just as thoroughly as he had.

Probably.

Garrett lay sprawled beside her, where he'd fallen, one leg draped across her thighs. When he moved to switch on the lamp, his upper arm brushed against the side of her face, and he felt the moisture on her skin.

He looked solemn as he gazed down at her. "Are you—? Did I—?"

She smiled, touched his beard-bristled cheek, ran the pad of her thumb over that sensuous mouth of his. And she shook her head. "I'm all right, Garrett," she said.

He leaned over her, kissed her right cheekbone, and then her left. "Stay there," he told her.

He got off the bed, and Julie heard a rustling sound. Though she couldn't bring herself to look at him, she knew he was pulling on his jeans.

As soon as he'd left the room, Julie got up and scrambled for the master bathroom.

When Garrett returned, though, she was back in bed, wearing her shirt and her jeans, the covers pulled up to her chin in a way that was, once she had time to think about it, pretty ridiculous.

Garrett, carrying a plate piled with Esperanza's stuffed mushrooms, chuckled when he saw her. Then he maneuvered until he was sitting beside Julie, his back to the pillows fluffed between him and the headboard, and offered her a morsel.

She hesitated, feeling self-conscious, and then her stomach rumbled.

Garrett laughed, touching the mushroom to her mouth.

Julie took it. Chewed for a long time, finally swallowed.

"I turned the oven back on," Garrett said. "How long do you think it will take for the spaghetti to finish cooking?"

Now it was Julie who laughed, though more with relief than because anything was funny. She didn't know what she'd expected from Garrett—regret? Dismissal, or even contempt?

It hadn't been a perfectly ordinary question about dinner, that was for sure.

"Maybe fifteen minutes," she said, feeling incredibly awkward, fully clothed and hiding everything but her head under the covers.

Garrett smiled, tossed a mushroom into his mouth and offered Julie another one. When she shook her head, he set the plate aside on the bedside table.

Then he slid an arm under Julie's back and eased her against his side.

His chest was bare, lightly dusted with hair the color of brown sugar.

Julie wanted to place her palm in the center of his taut belly, spread her fingers wide, but she refrained. Contented herself with resting her head on his shoulder.

"So why were you crying?" he asked, very quietly and after a long time.

Julie sighed. "Because it was so good," she admitted.

He chuckled, a low and entirely masculine sound that struck some tender places hidden away in Julie's heart. Whatever else he might be—an expert at spin, Blue River, Texas's, favorite son—Garrett was a cowboy, too.

The real deal, born and bred on the Silver Spur Ranch.

Raised to be all man and yet capable of a degree of tenderness, at least while making love, that made Julie marvel just to recall it.

She was glad when the timer dinged out in the kitchen, because she was just about to cry again. Instead, she leaped out of bed as eagerly as if supper came around once a month instead of every day.

Garrett stayed behind in his room long enough to pull a T-shirt on over his head. It was plain, with a hole in one side seam, but clean.

They ate sitting cross-legged on the floor in front of Garrett's fireplace, Harry snoozing nearby and opening one eye every now and then, probably hoping for a scrap.

"Damn," Garrett said, with an appreciative grin. "You can cook."

Julie's cheeks ached with heat as she stared down at her plate. "Thanks."

A companionable silence ensued. Garrett picked up his wineglass, which he'd set on the coffee table earlier, and took a sip, but Julie was off the sauce, at least for the evening.

Why was it so easy to fall into this man's bed, and so hard to talk to him afterward?

"Hey," he said, when he'd taken both their plates to the kitchen and returned to sit on the rug again, facing her. "Are you ever going to look at me?"

Julie blinked, made herself meet Garrett's eyes. She was acting silly, she knew that, but she couldn't seem to figure out how to stop.

"You're a woman," Garrett said, holding her gaze, the firelight flickering over the strong angles of his face, the powerful set of his shoulders, "and I'm a man. What just happened between us—happened. And that's okay, Julie. It's a lot *better* than okay, in fact."

"I don't usually—" She paused, miserably embarrassed. Where was the old, confident, sensual Julie? "I mean, you must think—"

Garrett cupped his hand under her chin, and her skin tingled where the tips of his fingers touched. "I *think*," he told her firmly, though his voice was gruff, "that you are one hell of a woman, and *I'm* one lucky son of a gun to be spending an evening with you."

An evening. He was lucky to spend *an evening* with her.

Well, what had she expected?

A lifetime commitment, an avowal of undying love?

After one roll in the hay?

"It *was* good," she admitted, wondering when she'd be able to shake off the strange shyness possessing her now.

"Ya think?" Garrett teased, raising one eyebrow slightly.

Julie laughed, and just like that, the tension was broken, the shyness gone. Still, a part of her wanted to ask, *Now what?*

More sex?

More wine?

More chicken spaghetti?

Was this a fling, or an affair, or just a one-night stand?

And what was the difference between a fling and an affair?

Julie sighed and pressed her fingers to her temples. And she blurted it right out.

"Now what?"

Garrett scooted forward, so their knees touched. Then their foreheads.

"Now," he ventured, "we take a shower together and make love again?"

"You can't possibly be serious," Julie said.

Garrett tugged her T-shirt up until her breasts were uncovered. She'd forgotten to put her bra back on.

"Hot damn," he said, admiring her for a long, delicious moment before he ducked his head and took her nipple into his mouth. He suckled until she moaned, then turned and thoroughly attended to her other breast before meeting her eyes again. "Still think I'm not serious?" he asked, lifting the T-shirt off over her head and arms and tossing it away. "If you need more convincing, I'll be happy to oblige."

She felt beautiful, powerful, even slightly dangerous, like some nomadic princess about to enjoy a captive lover, sitting there on Garrett's floor, with their knees and shins touching, and her naked breasts bathed in the dancing light of his fire.

Mischief widened her eyes and made her smile saucy. "You know," she said, "I'm just not sure—I think I *might* actually need some convincing."

He laughed and eased her backward onto the floor, then luxuriated in her breasts, kissing them, caressing them, weighing them in his hands. "Then maybe," he said, after making a slow circle around each of her nipples with the tip of his tongue, "I'd better have you again, right here and right now, while I've got you on your back."

"That was such a sexist thing to say," she gasped.

He was kissing her belly, working the snap on her jeans, and then the zipper. "You're not on your back?" he teased, his voice sleepy and slow.

"You know what I mean," Julie whimpered, as he slid down her jeans. She'd forgotten her panties, too, she realized, not just her bra.

"Ummmm," he murmured.

And then he made Julie call out his name, not once, not twice, but half a dozen times before he finally took her.

CHAPTER ELEVEN

JULIE LAY PERFECTLY STILL, her eyes closed, reorienting herself. It was a slow process, grasping at wispy fragments of consciousness, trying to fit them into some sensible pattern.

She wasn't in her usual bed—which wasn't her usual bed, either, to be perfectly accurate—the directions and the angles were all wrong.

And then it all fell into place, and Julie sucked in a sharp breath.

Oh, God. She'd had sex with Garrett McKettrick—crazy, sweaty, unbridled, *consequences?—what consequences?*—sex.

Now, the proverbial chickens had come home to roost. It was time to pay the piper, face the music.

Welcome to the dreaded Morning After.

The mattress shifted. "Open your eyes," Garrett drawled. He smelled of soap and aftershave, and his breath was minty.

Julie was fairly certain hers wasn't.

He knew she was awake—there was no point in trying to fake it so he'd go away and leave her alone long enough to get her act together.

Not that she had any idea how to go about doing that, at the present moment, at least.

"Julie?"

She opened her eyes. Wide.

Garrett was so close that their noses were almost touching.

"Mornin'," he said, one corner of his mouth crooking upward in a teasing grin.

"Mmmm," Julie said, with a nod, clasping one hand over her mouth. "Breath," she explained, through her fingers.

Garrett chuckled, shook his head once, and placed a brief, smacking kiss on her forehead before rolling off the bed and landing on his feet with that grace peculiar to people who've spent a lot of time on horses, cowboys in particular.

He was wearing jeans and nothing else.

Tossing her a blue cotton bathrobe, heretofore draped over the back of a leather-upholstered wingback chair, he said, "Coffee's almost ready."

The moment he left the room, Julie pulled the robe under the covers, wriggled herself into it, and even tied the belt before throwing back the blankets to rise.

Given that the horse was already out of the barn, she thought ruefully, it was a little late to be closing the barn door.

Garrett's bathroom was large, and there was travertine tile everywhere—on the walls and the floor and the long counter with two bronze sinks set into it. The matching faucets, beautifully cast, were shaped like horses' heads, and although Julie quickly found a new toothbrush and toothpaste in a drawer, it took her a while to figure out how to turn on the water.

Once she'd accomplished that, she scrubbed her teeth with a fury.

A sound startled her—a masculine rap of knuckles on wood.

Julie went to the door, opened it an inch and peeked out.

Garrett was standing there, holding a neat stack of folded clothing. Jeans. A lightweight gray sweatshirt. Socks and even underwear.

Julie recognized the garments—vaguely—as her own things.

He chuckled, noting her reluctance to open up.

This was, after all, *his* bathroom. And it wasn't as if she had anything he hadn't already seen. She was behaving like an idiot, and she couldn't seem to help it.

"Don't you want to get dressed?" he asked.

Julie flushed, nodded, opened the door just far enough to reach out and grab her clothing. Where had he gotten these things?

Garrett must have seen the question in her face, because he answered it.

"I told Esperanza you needed something to wear," he said, "and she fetched this stuff from the laundry room."

Julie's eyes widened. "You *told* Esperanza…?"

"Oops?" Garrett inquired. There was a distinct twinkle in his eyes.

Julie made a growling sound of frustration, and he laughed, and she shut the door in his face and turned the lock for good measure.

"I was kidding," Garrett called through the closed door. "I found your gear in a basket in the laundry room. Esperanza's not around—she always goes to church on Sundays."

Julie rested her forehead against the panel, smiling a little. "Okay," she replied, after letting out a long breath. "Thanks."

But she didn't unlock the door.

She used Garrett's fancy shower—the one they'd

shared the night before—between making love on the living room floor and making love *again* in bed.

Julie's knees weakened a little as she took off the borrowed robe, stepped into the shower, adjusted the spigots. She tried not to think of the things she and Garrett had done in that steamy cubicle, but of course that would have been impossible.

She washed quickly, trying not to get her hair wet, used a monogrammed bath sheet to dry off, and hastily pulled on the clean clothes Garrett had rustled up for her.

She finger-combed her hair—fortunately, it hadn't frizzed overmuch—tidied up the bathroom and unlocked the door.

Julie found Garrett in the kitchen, scrambling eggs on the stovetop set into the island.

He was wearing a blue chambray shirt and boots now, along with the jeans.

"You look like a man about to swing up into the saddle and strike out for other parts," Julie remarked, willing herself not to blush again.

And she didn't.

Two thick slabs of bread popped out of the toaster, and Garrett slid the skillet of eggs off the burner before deftly buttering the slices.

Harry, Julie noted, was eating kibble out of a bowl in a corner.

Fresh clothes for her, dog food for the beagle. Garrett, it seemed, had thought of everything.

"Tate called a little while ago," he said, in belated answer, plopping the eggs and the toast onto two plates and carrying them to the breakfast bar. "We've been having some trouble with rustlers lately and he wants to make a few passes over some of the canyons in my plane—see if we can spot anything."

A little niggle of dread curled in Julie's stomach, like smoke.

We've been having some trouble with rustlers lately...

Rustlers were criminals.

Criminals tended to be dangerous.

And although Tate and Garrett probably thought they were invincible, since they were rock-ribbed McKettricks, they could be hurt, like anyone else.

"Shouldn't the police handle things like this?" she asked, in a cracked-china voice.

Garrett, perched on the stool next to Julie's, sat with his fork suspended in one hand, watching her as though she represented a dozen delightful curiosities to be puzzled out, one by one. "Tate's been keeping Brent Brogan up to speed," he said, his tone as thoughtful as his expression. "Brent's just one man, though, and the Silver Spur is our worry—Tate's and Austin's and mine—not his."

Julie's jaw tightened. She relaxed her face by force of will. "This isn't the Old West, Garrett," she reasoned. "You and your brothers don't have to stand against these—these cattle thieves, all by yourselves."

There it was again, that registered-weapon of a grin. Garrett narrowed his true-blue eyes slightly as he studied her. "Why, ma'am," he joked, heavy on the Texas twang and the schlock, "are you frettin' your pretty little head over a ring-tailed polecat like me?"

She laughed, though reluctantly, and moved one hand a little, as if to swat at him. "Stop it," she said. "This is serious. What if someone gets hurt?"

Something tender moved in his eyes. "It happens," he said quietly. Maybe, like Julie, he was thinking of Pablo

Ruiz, the longtime ranch foreman and a close friend of the McKettricks. Pablo, a good man and a much beloved member of the community, had been *killed* a few months before, trying to unload a half-wild stallion from a horse trailer.

"Yes," Julie agreed, "it happens."

I don't want it to happen *to Libby's future bridegroom, the man she loves, body, mind and soul.*

I don't want it to happen *to you, Garrett McKettrick.*

The silence stretched between them, drawn taut, about to spring back on itself.

"We'll be careful," Garrett said.

Julie pushed her plate away—the eggs weren't bad, but she'd lost her appetite—and looked down at her hands, knotted together in her lap. Yes, she'd spent the night with Garrett, and to say they'd been intimate would have been the understatement of the century.

But the reality was, she had no claim on Garrett, no say in how he ran his life. If he wanted to put himself in danger, to play hero instead of calling in the authorities to deal with the rustlers, there wasn't a damn thing she could do about it.

She didn't have to like it, though.

And she couldn't seem to shut up.

"Just remember," she said, tearing up a little, "that Tate has children. Audrey and Ava need him. And my sister, *my sister*, loves that man with everything she has and everything she is. If anything happened to him—"

"I haven't forgotten the twins, Julie. They're my nieces and I love them." Garrett's eyes were solemn, his hand strong when he laid it over Julie's. Only when his fingers squeezed hers did she realize she'd been shaking. "I know what Tate means to Libby," he went on, his voice husky, "and what she means to him. Trust me when I tell you that I'll watch his back."

And who will watch yours? Julie wanted to ask, but she didn't, because she couldn't get the words out and, anyway, she already knew what his answer would be. Garrett and his brothers would watch out for *each other*, the way brothers—and sisters—did.

Suppose it wasn't enough?

Seeing that Julie was finished eating, Garrett collected their plates and silverware and carried them to the sink.

Harry, having scarfed up his morning kibble, nudged Julie's ankle with his muzzle and whimpered to let her know he needed to go outside.

Mundane as the task was, Julie was glad to have something to occupy her. She slid off the high barstool and sighed. "Come on, dog," she said. "Let's go."

"He might have some trouble with the stairs," Garrett said, his voice unusually deep, as though he'd just had a testosterone rush. With that, he leaned down, whisked Harry up into his arms and headed for an outside door.

Before stepping through it, Garrett took an old jeans jacket from a peg on the wall and handed it to Julie.

"Put this on," he said. "It's probably chilly out there."

Julie shrugged into the coat, at once comforted and unsettled because Garrett's scent rose from the denim.

There was a small landing, then a set of stone steps leading down to a cozy, grassy yard, walled in with stucco. Julie followed Garrett down onto the private lawn, folded her arms against the cold while Harry sniffed around, looking for a place to relieve himself.

"I didn't know this was here," Julie remarked, because the silence made her antsy. "It's almost like a secret garden."

Garrett's side-tilted grin reappeared. "Yeah," he agreed, "except for the—er—*garden*."

Harry was taking his sweet time finding just the right place to lift his leg.

Smiling, Julie stood in the center of the yard and turned in a slow circle, closing her eyes to dream of roses and peonies and all manner of other colorful plants and bushes.

A white wrought-iron bench would be lovely, too, and perhaps a small fountain, and a birdfeeder or two.

Suddenly dizzy, Julie stopped turning and opened her eyes and was startled to find Garrett standing so close to her that she could feel the hard man-heat emanating from his flesh.

Her breath caught.

Garrett chuckled hoarsely and set his hands on her hips, holding her in a way that brought back a flood of steamy memories from the night before.

"I won't be gone long, Julie," he said, his mouth very close to hers, his warm breath dancing on her skin, "just an hour or two."

He kissed her then, so gently that some new and unnamed emotion surged up within her, rendering speech impossible.

"I have to make lesson plans," she blurted out, the moment their mouths parted. "And call my landlady. Get Calvin ready for a new week—"

Garrett had not released his grasp on her. She could feel the press of his thumbs on her hipbones, the spread of his fingers over her buttocks, even through the relatively heavy fabric of her jeans. Her whole body remembered their lovemaking then, in a visceral rush of echoed sensation, and she gasped slightly and felt heat thrumming in her face again.

Garrett smiled, as though he'd read all of that and more in her expression, and maybe he had.

It was a disconcerting thought.

"Make your lesson plans and call your landlady while I'm gone," he told her. "Because I've got a few plans of my own for when I get back."

Garrett hadn't exactly issued a command, Julie reasoned, but he wasn't making a request, either.

"Like what?" she asked, because she couldn't just let him get away with a thing like that. Whatever that thing was.

If there even *was* a thing.

Again, that slow and patently lethal cowboy grin. "You really want me to tell you? Right here and now?"

"No," she said quickly.

Yes, protested everything besides her voice.

Just then, Harry made it known that his errand had been completed. He was ready to go back in the house and lose his dog-self in the depths of a nap, preferably near a warm, crackling fire.

All was well in Harryworld.

With a chuckle, Garrett bent to ruffle the dog's ears. "This way, buddy," he said. But instead of heading back up the stairs, he led Julie and the dog out of the hidden yard by a side gate.

There was the barn, the concrete driveway leading to the multicar garage, the acres of grass.

Garrett walked up to the back door, turned the knob and opened it.

Harry rushed into the otherwise empty kitchen, found his water dish in its usual place and started lapping like crazy.

Garrett waited patiently until Julie, oddly shaken,

feeling as though she'd just traveled between two worlds instead of two parts of the same huge house, remembered she was wearing his jacket and took it off.

She handed it over.

"I'll be back in a while," Garrett said, shrugging into the garment.

Thinking of the rustlers again, Julie felt an almost overwhelming need to get him to stay, whether by coaxing or cajoling or even coercion. She bit down hard on her lower lip to keep from nagging.

"I might not be around," Julie said casually, although she was feeling anything *but* casual.

She'd made a terrible mistake, sleeping with Garrett McKettrick.

She'd lowered her defenses, and he had breached them.

And now he was inside, possibly to stay.

If he hadn't been standing right there, looking directly into her face, Julie might have covered said face with both hands and wailed in frustration and chagrin.

Garrett merely arched an eyebrow, waited for her to go on.

"I'll probably go to town," she said. "Stop by the cottage and see if the place is habitable, now that the exterminators are finished."

He chuckled, gave her a light kiss. "It's too late to run away now, Julie," he said. "We're in too deep for that."

Julie opened her mouth to protest, realized she didn't have a leg to stand on, so to speak, and closed it again. And again, heat pulsed in her cheeks.

At least he'd said *we're* in too deep.

"It was only sex," Julie felt compelled to argue. After all, that was the rationale she'd used to justify the indulgence to herself.

"'Only'?" he teased in response. "Not a word I would use to describe what happened between us."

Julie didn't trust herself to reply—the likelihood that she'd put her foot in her mouth was entirely too high.

Garrett turned and headed for the door to the garage then, and Harry gave a little whine of sorrow at his going. Julie barely stifled a mournful whimper of her own.

"Hush," she said to Harry, her voice husky. "You mustn't get attached."

Standing there in the vast McKettrick kitchen, Julie closed her eyes and swayed against a sudden rush of sadness.

Harry *was* attached to Garrett.

So was she.

And so, most worrisome of all, was Calvin.

She had to step back, move out of the ranch house, do whatever was necessary to put some distance between herself and Garrett.

Resolute, Julie found her address book, unplugged her cell phone from its charger and punched in her landlady's number.

Julie and Calvin's rental had been Louise Smithfield's "honeymoon cottage," until Mr. Smithfield's death twenty years before.

Unable to stay where there were so many memories, Louise hadn't been prepared to let the place go, either. She'd decided, she'd told Julie, to visit a cousin in Austin for a while, get some perspective before she made any big decisions.

One thing led to another, of course, and Louise made new friends in Austin, found a job she liked and eventually bought a condo there.

The honeymoon cottage became a rental, and Louise was content to let it pay off its own mortgage. Julie, the latest in a long line of tenants, had loved the place, allowed her heart to feel at home there.

"Hello?" Louise croaked, in her rickety old-lady voice, startling Julie out of her reverie. "Who is this? If you're a telemarketer, I'm on that list and you'd better not call me again."

"Mrs. Smithfield?" Julie interrupted, with a timorous smile, "I'm not selling anything. It's me, Julie Remington."

Mrs. Smithfield was quiet.

"Your tenant?" Julie prompted.

"I know who you are," Mrs. Smithfield said crisply, but not unkindly. "I'm sorry, Julie. You've been a marvel, taking such good care of the cottage, always paying your rent on time. I'm not getting any younger, though, and it's time for me to liquidate some of my assets."

Julie's throat ached. She *had* been happy at the cottage. "When does the sale close?" she asked.

Louise sighed. "The buyers are paying cash," she replied. "The transaction can be completed as soon as—as soon as you've moved your things out, dear." A pause, slightly breathless, belied what she said next. "Not that there's any hurry."

Julie closed her eyes for a moment, dazed by the prospect of packing all her and Calvin's belongings and leaving the cottage for good.

Where would they go?

She supposed she could put the furniture and the pots and pans and all of their other stuff into storage, wedge into Paige's apartment on a temporary basis, start watching the classified ads for that rarest of Blue

River phenomena, a house or apartment whose lease was coming up and whose tenants were leaving.

Or she could stay right there on the Silver Spur, continue to go to bed with Garrett McKettrick whenever Calvin wasn't around, and risk breaking not just her own heart, but her little boy's, too.

The dog whimpered and scratched at the door Garrett had passed through minutes before.

"Julie?" Mrs. Smithfield said, sounding concerned. "Are you still there?"

"Yes, Mrs. Smithfield," Julie answered. "I'm still here. The cottage is definitely sold, then?"

"Yes," the landlady replied, sounding both relieved and defensive. "Frankly, I was a little surprised that *you* didn't make an offer, Julie."

There was no point in saying that the asking price had been too high; after all, someone had met or even exceeded it. Someone who could pay cash, no less.

"If the sale falls through for any reason," Julie responded gently, "I hope you or Suzanne will get in touch with me."

Louise promised to do that, and Julie promised to be out of the cottage by the first of the month, a date barely two weeks in the future.

She did not need this, she thought, hanging up after a cordial goodbye. Not on top of the musical she had to stage at school, her disappointment over shoving the showcase of one-act plays to a back burner and Gordon Pruett suddenly deciding he wanted to play a role in Calvin's life after all.

Among other things.

Julie's gaze rose briefly to the ceiling.

What is it with you, Remington? she asked herself.

Your life wasn't complicated enough, without adding Garrett McKettrick to the mix?

Julie shook the thought off. She hadn't been fibbing when she told Garrett she had things to fill her time that day besides going back to bed with him.

The thought of which made her nipples harden, her knees weaken and her insides melt.

"Enough," she told herself and Harry, who sat at her feet now, head tilted to one side, ears perked up.

Resolutely, Julie marched into the quarters she and Calvin shared. She was a whirlwind, dusting and vac-uuming, putting fresh sheets on the beds, clean towels on the rack in the bathroom.

All too soon, the rooms were spotless.

How long had Garrett been gone? she wondered, checking her watch. If he got back before she'd either picked Calvin up at Paige's place in town, or Paige had brought him home, well, it didn't take a rocket scientist to predict what would happen.

Before she knew what hit her, she'd be on her back in Garrett's bed, bare-ass naked, boinking away.

She felt herself go moist with longing.

"Get a grip," she said.

Harry, who had followed her from room to room during the brief cleaning frenzy, wagged his tail and watched her with interest. Clearly, he was expecting something to happen.

"Come on," Julie told him, taking his leash from the top drawer of the small antique bureau in the hallway between her bedroom and Calvin's and clipping it to his collar. "We're going on a reconnaissance mission."

As soon as he saw the leash, Harry was beside him-self with joy.

It did not take much to please Harry.

Julie grabbed a casual jacket before leaving the house—her regular coat, along with yesterday's clothes, was still upstairs in Garrett's hideaway, she remembered with more burning of the face—and tracked down her purse.

By the time she had installed Harry in the backseat of her Cadillac and raised the garage door using the remote Tate had given her when she moved in, Julie almost felt like some sort of crook fleeing the scene of a crime.

Once out and pointed in the right direction, she ferreted through her purse for her cell phone headset, put it on and speed-dialed Paige's number before heading down the driveway.

She got her sister's voice mail.

"It's Julie. I'm on the way over to the cottage to start getting ready to move, and I'll probably be there for a while, so maybe you can drop Calvin off there and save yourself a trip out to the ranch. Call me when you get this. 'Bye."

The phone rang just as she reached the main gates, which, fortunately, were standing open.

"Paige?" she said, instead of hello.

"Libby," her other sister replied, with a smile in her voice. "Listen, I'm making a big potato salad, and Tate took a *bunch* of steaks out of the freezer before he went to meet Garrett at the airstrip, so it just makes sense to throw a big barbecue, don't you think?"

Julie chuckled, carefully looking both ways before pulling onto the main road. "What else can you do," she joked, "*besides* throw a big barbecue?"

"My thoughts exactly," Libby said, with a laugh.

She sounded so happy, Libby did.

What would it be like to be that happy?

"You'll be here, then?" Libby prodded, when Julie didn't speak again right away.

"Sure," she said. Most likely, Garrett would be invited, and that might be a little awkward, but Calvin would be around, too, and Paige, and the rest of the crowd. She would have buffers. "What time, and what should I bring?"

"Six-thirty," Libby answered, "and just bring yourself."

Julie smiled. "Have you spoken to Paige? She didn't answer her cell phone."

"She's here," Libby said, "with Calvin. Her phone is probably in the bottom of her bag, and the kids are playing a video game and making so much noise nobody heard it ring. Why don't you swing by?"

Julie considered the offer. As short as her time apart from Calvin had been, she missed him. Still, with less than two weeks to go before she had to have everything out of the cottage, she needed to do some serious planning and maybe even pack some boxes.

"I have some things to do at my place," she explained. "Even though the exterminator's tent is down, I'm not sure what the air quality is like inside, and with Calvin's asthma—"

"Enough said," Libby interrupted gently. "Calvin is right here, and he's fine. Join us when you can."

"Thanks, Lib," Julie said, genuinely grateful. "I'll be there later on."

"Jules?"

Julie, about to end the call, hesitated. "What?"

"Are you okay? You sound sort of—I don't know—*distracted*."

No worries, Julie imagined herself explaining. *It's*

*just that I spent most of the night twisting the sheets
with Garrett McKettrick, and now I'm wondering what
the hell I was thinking.*

"I'm fine," she said instead. But she couldn't resist
adding, "This rustling thing. How serious is that, do you
know?"

"To a rancher," Libby replied, "rustling is *always*
serious. According to Tate, they've lost as many as a
hundred cattle, by the latest estimate, and since the crit-
ters are currently going for around a thousand dollars a
head, that's a lot of money."

"You're not worried?"

"About the cattle?" Libby countered.

"About Tate and Garrett going after the rustlers instead of sending the law," Julie clarified, somewhat im-
patiently. Libby knew damn well what she meant.

Libby was quiet for a few moments, interpreting Julie's words and her tone and drawing conclusions. "So
I guess it's safe to assume the big date went off okay?"
she finally asked.

She wasn't about to dish with her sister. Not while
she was driving, anyway. And certainly not when there
was even the remotest chance that Calvin might over-
hear. "It was—okay," she said.

"Just 'okay'?"

Julie sighed. "Not now, Lib," she said.

"But later?" Libby persisted. "You'll tell us—Paige
and me—all about it later?"

"Not *all* about it," Julie said.

Libby laughed. "My imagination is already filling in
the blanks," she said.

"*Goodbye*, Libby," Julie said. The Cadillac was rolling
along at a pretty good clip, and the town limits would be

coming up pretty soon. She needed both hands and all her attention to drive.

"See you soon," Libby practically sang, and the call ended.

When Julie reached the cottage, she saw that the tent had been taken away. The little house looked forlorn, standing there, with a Sold sign in the front yard and no sign of light or life at any of the windows.

Julie pulled into the gravel driveway—there was no garage—and shut off the car. She sat for a few moments, just staring at the tidy brick building she and Calvin had moved into while he was still a baby.

Calvin had never lived in any other house.

Even Harry, realizing where they were, began scrabbling at the inside of the car door behind Julie, eager to run through the grass again, or dig up one of the many bones he'd stashed in various places around the yard.

Feeling overly emotional, Julie got out of the car, opened the door for Harry and pulled the keys from the ignition.

The lock on the front door proved stubborn—nothing new there—and Julie drew a deep breath of fresh air before turning the knob and pulling.

A strong chemical smell struck her immediately, and she was glad she hadn't brought Calvin with her. He hadn't had a serious asthma attack in a long time, but she never knew what would set one off.

She left the front door standing open to air the place out a little and stepped inside. Harry was busy exploring the yard—the grass needed mowing.

The small living room was dusty, and there were ashes on the hearth from the first fire of the season. She and Calvin had roasted marshmallows over the flames that night after supper, Julie recalled fondly, and made some preliminary plans for Calvin's Halloween costume.

He wanted to dress up as Albert Einstein.

Julie smiled sadly and ran one hand over the afghan draped over the back of her couch. Paige had crocheted the coverlet, choosing yarn in the lush autumn shades Julie loved, during what Paige called her Earth Mother phase.

The desk over by the windows was empty—Julie had taken her PC with her when she and Calvin went to stay on the Silver Spur—and the sight made her feel strangely forlorn.

Sure, it was an inconvenience, having to move, a big one. But it was hardly a tragedy, now was it?

So why was she so emotional?

It was no great leap to identify the reason: Garrett. The way he'd made love to her had touched her on so many levels.

She couldn't help taking the whole thing seriously, she thought, and wasn't now a fine time to think of that?

Garrett, of course, would suffer no pangs of guilt or regret over the night just past, and the things it might have set in motion. He was a man, and used to getting what he wanted, when he wanted it.

He would get bored soon, and go back to his life in the fast lane, and that would be the end of it.

For Julie, the parting wouldn't be so easy.

Sometime between that first kiss and breakfast this morning, she'd fallen in love with Garrett McKettrick.

And she was under no illusion whatsoever that she'd be falling *out* of love with him anytime soon.

CHAPTER TWELVE

TATE AND GARRETT covered most of the Silver Spur in Garrett's plane that morning, and they found more downed fences, the carcasses of half a dozen cattle near a remote watering hole and no sign whatsoever of the rustlers.

At least, nothing visible from the air.

"Son of a bitch," Tate rasped, leaning in his seat as if straining for a closer look at the dead animals. "Put this thing on the ground."

That section of the ranch, nestled against the foothills as it was, happened to be especially rugged, pocked with gullies and gorges, and honeycombed with waist-deep ruts.

Garrett eyed the area dubiously. Shook his head. "Now that would be one stupid thing to do," he said. "We'd better go back to the barn and trailer a couple of horses. I wouldn't be averse to bringing along a rifle or two, either."

"Now how many times have you told me you could land an airplane anywhere?"

"My aim in this instance," Garrett said, "is to land the plane *and* live through it."

Tate scowled at him, impatient with the delay, though he didn't argue the point any further.

They returned to the airstrip, landed and headed for the main place in Tate's dusty Silverado, leaving Austin's rattletrap truck where it was, parked alongside the hangar. A plume of good Texas dirt billowed out behind them as they raced over country roads, both of them silent, occupied with their own thoughts.

Garrett was thinking of Julie, and how he'd promised her he'd keep Tate safe, for Libby's and the twins' sakes, and it took him a while to realize he was grinding his back molars together fit to split his jawbones.

Except for a rotating skeleton crew of three or four men, none of the ranch hands worked on Sundays, but that day, it seemed that everybody on the payroll had gathered around the smallest of several corrals adjoining the barn. Cowboys crowded the fence rails and looked on from the haymow, high overhead.

"If I didn't know better," Garrett remarked, as Tate slammed on the truck's brakes, "I'd swear there was a rodeo going on, right here on the Silver Spur."

Tate frowned and climbed out of the Silverado, leaving the driver's-side door ajar in his haste to find out what was going on. For the moment, the dead cattle out there on the range must have slipped his mind.

As it turned out, there *was* a rodeo going on.

Of the one-man variety.

Garrett didn't figure Tate was really any more surprised than he was. He slipped his sunglasses down a little way and peered over the rims, watching as Austin leaped from the top rail of the inoculation chute on the far side of the corral and straight onto the bare back of a bronc Garrett didn't recognize.

The stallion was magnificent, for all that there were burrs tangled in his mane and tail and old battle scars marking his flanks and breast and front legs. Garrett wondered if the wild horse had been caught on their own rangeland or purchased for breeding purposes.

Tate spat a curse, then started up the slats of the fence as if he meant to go right on over and haul Austin down off the back of that horse in front of God and everybody else.

Garrett caught Tate by the back of his denim jacket and pulled him back. "Let him ride," he said quietly, relieved that most of the men were too busy watching Austin and the bronc to notice Tate's attempt to intervene. "Let him ride."

The bronc stood quiver-flanked inside that chute, with his four legs straddled out as wide as the limited space allowed. His ears crooked forward and its head was down.

Austin sat that horse with the same idiotic confidence he'd shown riding Buzzsaw, the bull that had nearly killed him in front of a packed rodeo arena and a TV audience numbering in the hundreds of thousands.

"Turn him loose," Austin said clearly, after calmly resettling his battered, sweat-stained hat.

One of the men swung the chute gate open, and Garrett held his breath as the animal stood there, evidently deciding on a course of action.

When he'd made up his mind, he sprang out into the corral, pitched forward to kick out both hind legs and splinter the gate behind him with that one powerful thrust.

Delighted, Austin let out a celebratory whoop and nudged the bronc with the heels of both boots.

Watching, Tate shook his head. "I'll be goddamned," he muttered, measuring out the words. "Is he *trying* to kill himself?"

Garrett, standing next to Tate there by the corral fence, slapped him on the shoulder, but he never took his eyes off Austin. One thing you had to say for the crazy little bastard—he could ride damn near anything.

That stallion went up and he went down. He went sideways, and then he spun like a tornado. When that didn't unseat his rider, he switched directions, the motion sharp as the hard crack of a whip.

Austin stayed on him, covered in dirt, waving his hat and grinning as if he had half the sense of a fence post.

The bronc finally bucked himself out and stood with his chest heaving in the middle of the corral.

Casual as could be, Austin swung a leg over that critter's neck and leaped to the ground, landing on his feet with the grace of a cat.

Wearing that infamous shit-eatin' grin of his, he approached the fence, the whites of his eyes in stark contrast to the dusty grime masking his face.

The crew kept its collective distance, probably because Tate was throwing pissed-off-boss-man vibes fit to singe the bristles from a hog. "Easy," Garrett told Tate. "Take it easy. He's all right."

Tate glared at Austin, ignoring Garrett altogether. His knuckles were white where he gripped the fence rail, as if he wanted to vault over it, grab their kid brother by the throat and throttle him right on the spot.

But it was Austin who came over the fence, standing there, cocky as a rooster, with his dust-caked hair stuck to his neck with sweat and that fuck-you look in his eyes.

"Where the hell is my truck?" he demanded.

Garrett suppressed a chuckle, but Tate looked mad enough to bite the ends off carpet tacks and spit them clear to the far side of the creek.

He moved to grip Austin by the front of his shirt, but

stopped just short of follow-through. His fingers flexed and unflexed, but he didn't make fists.

"Your truck?" The way those words tore themselves from Tate's throat, it was a wonder they didn't take the hide with them. "You just rode a horse you don't know anything about, and you're worried about your *goddamn truck?*"

Austin's eyes shot blue fire. After that ride, the adrenaline was still surging through his system, and he was spoiling for a fight.

Obviously, Tate was inclined to oblige.

The stallion, meanwhile, trotted back and forth in the corral, nickering and tossing his head, raising up five acres of dust in the process. He wanted a piece of somebody, that bronc, that was for sure.

Garrett, not usually the peacemaker, stepped between his brothers.

"I took your truck," he told Austin. "Screw your damn truck. We've got trouble, plenty to go around. We sure as hell don't need trouble with each other on top of it."

Austin swallowed hard. His gaze darted past Garrett's face to sear into Tate's flesh like a hot branding iron, then swung back, reluctant. Resigned.

"What kind of trouble?" Austin asked slowly, grudgingly.

"Dead cattle trouble," Tate said tersely. "More downed fences, too."

"We spotted the carcasses from the plane a little while ago," Garrett added.

"Shit," Austin said, with conviction, shoving a hand through his hair. "Why are we just standing here, if we've lost livestock?"

Tate thrust out a sigh and tilted his head back for a moment.

Garrett gripped Austin's shoulder with one hand and Tate's with the other, just in case they were to change their minds about the tacit truce and spring at each other all of a sudden. He'd sure as hell seen it happen before.

"I'll get the rifles while you two saddle the horses," Garrett said.

Tate nodded grimly and spoke to the cowboys standing silently at the bulging periphery of his McKettrick temper. As Garrett turned to head into the house, he heard Tate give Austin a brief explanation of the carnage they'd seen on the range.

SOMETHING IN THE weight of the atmosphere inside the kitchen told him Julie wasn't anywhere around, though Esperanza was back from church, sporting an apron and fixing to shove a couple of chickens into the oven for Sunday dinner.

While Garrett was relieved not to be gathering guns and ammo while Julie was there to raise questions, let alone an objection, he felt oddly bereft at her absence, too. It was a cold thing, missing her, and it blew through him like a bitter wind.

Esperanza hadn't spoken, but as he passed through the kitchen on his way to the nearest of several gun-safes around the place, the housekeeper slammed the oven door shut with a force no prudent man would ignore.

Grinning to himself, Garrett walked into the study that had been his father's, his grandfather's, his great- and great-great-grandfather's. There, he uncovered the safe not-so-subtly hidden behind a bookcase on hinges and spun the dial to the first digit of the combination.

He opened the heavy steel door, colorfully emblazoned with the name McKettrick Cattle Company, and reached inside, bringing out one rifle, then another, then a third.

Garrett took out a box of shells, too, and then set the rifles aside long enough to close and lock the safe. When he turned around, he nearly jumped out of his hide, because Esperanza was standing so close behind him he might have trampled her, and he hadn't even heard her come into the room.

He bit back a swear word and took a firmer hold on the rifles.

Esperanza's dark eyes followed his every move. "What are you doing?" she asked, folding her arms.

"It's just a precaution, taking the rifles along," Garrett said, starting around her. "Nothing to worry about."

"Nothing to worry about?" Esperanza argued, staying right on his heels as he strode out of the room. "It was bad enough that Austin had to risk his fool neck out there in the corral, riding that wild horse. Now the three of you are up to something that calls for *guns?*"

Lying to Esperanza would do no good. She'd been with the family since before Tate was born, and she knew the McKettrick brothers too well to be deceived by bullshit denials.

"There are some cattle down," Garrett explained, slowing his words but not his pace. "It could be bad water or some kind of poison weed that got them—we only saw the carcasses from the air—but since some more fence lines have been cut in that area, it's a safe bet that somebody shot them."

For a hefty woman, Esperanza was quick on her feet. She got ahead of him somehow as he started across the kitchen, and blocked his way. "I don't see a badge pinned to your shirt, Garrett McKettrick," she said. "Have any of you lunkheads troubled yourselves to call Brent Brogan and report this?"

"Brogan knows about the rustling," Garrett said, shuffling the three rifles and then going around her, which took some doing because she'd set her feet and dug in her heels. "It's not as if we're playing posse here, Esperanza. Most likely, whoever cut those fences and slaughtered a half dozen of our cattle for what seems like no reason but pure meanness is long gone. Just the same, if Tate and Austin and I have to defend ourselves, or each other, we'd prefer to be ready."

"Wait, Garrett," Esperanza said, very quietly. "Don't take the law into your own hands. Let Chief Brogan handle this. He can bring in the state police, if need be, but you've got no business heading out there with guns."

He hesitated, opened the outside door. "I'm sorry," he said, and he meant it. Esperanza was a lot more than an employee; she was a member of the family, and her intentions were good.

She wanted to protect Jim and Sally McKettrick's boys—that was all.

"Be careful," she said. Her dark eyes were luminous with sorrow. "You just be careful, and make sure your brothers are, too."

He nodded. Stepped out onto the side porch, started down the steps.

One of the trailers had been hitched to Tate's truck, and Austin and another man were loading saddled horses inside.

Tate came out of the barn, saw Garrett with the rifles and walked toward him, his expression grim.

"Esperanza," Garrett said, "is not real happy with any of us right about now."

Tate gave up a spare grin. "I don't suppose she is," he agreed.

They stored the rifles and the ammunition in the backseat of the Silverado, since there were no gun racks.

Tate got behind the wheel when Austin called that the horses had all been loaded, and Garrett grabbed the shotgun seat. That left the back for Austin.

Moments later, they were rolling down the long driveway. Just before they reached the main gates, Tate took a left turn onto a narrow utility road that wound along the front of the property and then forked out onto the range in three directions.

"What the hell were you doing back there?" Tate bit out, after steaming in silence for a while.

Garrett gave his brother a sidelong glance but said nothing. Tate wasn't talking to him, after all, but to Austin.

"Back where?" Austin asked, baiting him. He knew damn well what Tate wanted to know, unless Garrett missed his guess, and that was why he'd ridden a bucking bronc, and a wild one fresh off the range in the bargain. It hadn't been that long since Austin had undergone extensive emergency surgery—his survival had by no means been a sure thing—and even after his release from the hospital, he'd spent several months in physical therapy.

Sure, he was Texas tough, and he was only twenty-eight, so he had youth going for him, but he was a long way from his old self, too.

"If you want to die," Tate rasped furiously, "why don't you just say so, straight out?"

Austin spat a curse. "Why don't *you* stop being such a grandma?" he retorted. "Maybe nobody's ever mentioned it to you, but there are times when you carry this big-brother bullshit too damn far, Tate."

Tate checked the side mirror, taking his half of the road out of the middle, since the trailer was wide and heavy with good horseflesh. He made a visible effort to calm down. "There isn't a damn thing you need to prove," he said evenly.

Even without looking back at him, Garrett knew Austin was still plenty riled.

"Is that what you think I was doing, Tate?" Austin snapped. "Trying to *prove* something?"

"Weren't you?" Tate challenged. The question probably would have been less inflammatory if he'd yelled it, instead speaking softly, in a tone he might have used to calm a skittish horse or a frightened dog.

Garrett sighed inwardly, but he didn't say anything. Too much had been said already.

Austin swore and shifted around in the backseat like he wanted to bust out of there or something. "I don't need to prove anything to *you*," he answered, after drawing and huffing out a few audible breaths.

Something had gotten under his hide, no doubt about it. But Garrett figured there was more going on here than Austin's need to show the world—and himself—that even though that bull had torn him up good and put him in the hospital for a long time, he was back. He still had it.

Instinct said that wasn't all.

Garrett had tried to find out the whole truth, but Austin wasn't in the mood to confide in anybody. Ten to one, though, their kid brother's mood had more to do with some woman than Buzzsaw, the bull.

"Can we work this out later?" Garrett asked.

"Out behind the barn, maybe?" Austin interjected.

Then he laughed, a ragged sound, like nothing was funny, and Tate gave up a gruff chuckle with about the same degree of good humor. And the tension inside that truck cab tightened like a screw.

"So, Garrett," Austin said, after a few beats, his tone deceptively affable, even hearty, "I hear the senator shit-canned your career right along with his own."

Garrett stiffened, adjusted his sunglasses.

Tate gave a little snort.

"Where'd you hear that?" Garrett asked, with a mild-ness that probably didn't fool either of his brothers.

"Hell," Austin replied, "it's all over the internet. The word on the web is that you've had a lot of job offers already, and turned them down."

One of the ranch pickups was coming toward them along the private road; the driver pulled to the side to make room for Tate's truck and the horse trailer, tooted the horn and waved as they passed.

Tate tapped the Silverado's horn once, in response.

"Is that true?" he asked, glancing Garrett's way.

"Is what true?" Garrett countered.

"That you've had job offers," Tate said, with an ex-aggerated effort at patience.

Garrett shrugged. "I've had a few calls," he said. "Nothing I was interested in."

"You're needed here," Tate said carefully, downshift-ing as they came to a wide cattle guard set into the road. The wheels of the truck and then the trailer it was pull-ing bumped over the wooden grate as they crossed it.

"You've gotten by just fine without me, up to now," Garrett pointed out. Then he jutted a thumb over one shoulder to indicate Austin. "And Billy the Kid here is even more dispensable than I am."

"Gee," Austin said, "thanks."

Tate's shoulders strained beneath his shirt and denim jacket. "I'm serious," he said. "It's a lot of responsibility, running this place, especially now that Pablo Ruiz is gone. I've got two kids and I'm about to get married. Libby and I want to get a baby started ASAP. And what I'm getting at here is this—you two each own a third of the Silver Spur, just like I do—and you're drawing dividends for it—but you're not carrying your fair share of the load."

Garrett was surprised, though upon reflection he could see Tate's point.

"You hard up for money, Tate?" Austin joked, possibly as clueless as he sounded, but more likely just obnoxious. "If you are, I'll be glad to help you out with a few bucks."

Tate eased the truck to a stop alongside the road, mindful of the trailer and the horses riding inside it. They were probably two miles from the place where they'd seen the dead cattle and the breached fence lines, but that was as close as they could get in a rig. It was time to unload the horses, mount up and ride in.

Shoving his door open, Tate got out of the truck and stood waiting for Austin.

Austin climbed out, too.

They faced each other on that dirt road, Tate and Austin, like a pair of gunslingers about to draw.

The air was crackling again.

Garrett rounded the front of the truck at a sprint, but he was too late.

Tate had grabbed Austin by the front of his shirt and slammed him hard against the door of the pickup.

Austin bounced off it and lunged into Tate's middle with his head down.

Garrett dove between them and caught somebody's fist hard under his right eye.

He staggered, seeing stars. He was going to have a shiner, at the very least.

"Shit!" he yelled, furious, pressing the back of his hand to his cheekbone. It came away bloody.

"Sorry," Austin said.

Tate's hoarse chuckle turned to a guffaw.

Austin laughed, too.

"I'm glad you two think this is funny!" Garrett yelled. So much for keeping the peace. If his eye hadn't been swelling shut already, he'd have gone after both of them at once and settled for trouncing whichever one he got hold of first.

"I think it's freakin' *hilarious*," Austin said, and then hooted again.

Garrett glared at him.

Tate grinned, flashing those movie-cowboy teeth of his, and slapped Garrett on the shoulder just a mite too hard. "Hope there aren't any press conferences on your schedule, Mr. President," he said. "There isn't enough pancake makeup on the planet to cover up the black eye you're going to have about five minutes from now. You definitely aren't ready for prime time."

"It was such a pretty face, too," Austin observed, in a voice an octave higher than his real one.

"Shut up," Garrett growled. The whole right side of his head ached.

Tate merely chuckled and shook his head.

Several ranch trucks pulled in behind them, and Austin started back to help unload the horses.

"When I figure out which one of you hit me," Garrett vowed to his brothers, reaching into the truck for the rifles, "I'm going to kick his ass from here to the Panhandle and back again."

Austin chuckled and walked away.

Tate grinned and followed.

Within a couple of minutes, they were all on horseback, with loaded rifles in the scabbards affixed to their saddles, as were the men who'd come along to help.

While the state of Garrett's face drew a few glances, nobody was stupid enough to make a comment.

They rode uphill, single file, nine men in all, putting Garrett in mind of an old-time posse heading out to round up outlaws.

Normally, he would have smiled at the picture that took shape in his brain, but between the punch he'd taken, Tate's complaint about running the ranch without help and the dead cattle waiting up ahead, Garrett wasn't feeling especially cheerful.

It took half an hour or so to reach the first dead cow; shot through the neck, the animal had bled out on the ground. Flies swarmed, blue-black and buzzing.

There were five more cattle just ahead, killed the same way.

Tate was the first to dismount. He crouched beside one of the carcasses, seemingly heedless of the flies, and touched the critter's blood-crusted side with his right hand. Something about the motion—gentleness, maybe—tightened Garrett's throat.

"What kind of sick son of a bitch shoots an animal and leaves it to rot?" Austin ranted, taking in the scene.

Garrett shook his head, having no other response to offer at the moment, and swung down from the saddle.

The ranch hands rode on, looking at the other slaughtered cattle and keeping their thoughts to themselves, as cowboys usually do.

He looked around, but the ground was hard and dry, and if there had been any tracks—a man's, a horse's or those of an off-road vehicle of some kind—the wind had already brushed them away.

Garrett leaned down to pick up a spent shell, showed it to Tate and Austin, then dropped it into his jacket pocket.

Tate rose from the crouch next to the cow. Austin remained on his horse, silhouetted against a dry, blue sky.

Austin adjusted his hat, surveyed the far distance and then looked down at his brothers with eyes the same color as the sky behind him. "Now what?" he asked.

Tate walked back to his horse, stuck a foot into the stirrup and remounted. "We do the next logical thing," he answered wearily.

"Which is?" Garrett asked, returning to the saddle himself. The skin around his eye throbbed, and he wondered what Julie would think when she saw he'd been hurt.

Maybe, he thought, mildly cheered up, he was in line for a little feminine sympathy.

Yes, sir, he could do with some of that.

"It wouldn't be right to leave these animals to be picked apart by buzzards and coyotes," Tate answered grimly. "We'll burn the carcasses and then ride the fence lines, see if we can pick up some kind of trail."

Once again, Austin fiddled with his hat, as he always did when something stuck in his craw and there was no other way to react. "Cattle thieving is one thing," he said, gazing off into the distance, "and killing for the hell of it is another. Whoever did this is carrying a mean grudge."

Garrett nodded in grim agreement. Now and then, especially when times were hard, somebody killed and butchered a McKettrick cow, but it was generally to feed his family.

That was understandable, at least.

This was wanton slaughter.

He felt a lot of things, sitting there in the saddle, with the stench of shed blood filling his nostrils and making his gut churn with the need to do something about it.

It didn't seem possible that, not so many hours ago, he'd been in bed with Julie Remington. She'd driven him outside of himself, Julie had, and as many women as he'd been with in his life, he couldn't recall ever feeling the things she'd made him feel, even once.

They rode on, past the other fallen cattle.

There were signs of horses on the other side of the downed fence line, and more spent cartridges scattered on the ground.

Bile scalded the back of Garrett's throat. Who hated Tate—or all the McKettricks—enough to massacre living creatures for the sport of it?

He scanned the other men, the ones who'd loaded horses of their own back at the main place, followed in trucks, come along to help if they could. As a kid, Garrett had known everybody who worked on the Silver Spur, but now that he'd been away so much, a lot of them were strangers.

In fact, Charlie Bates was the only one he knew. A crabby old bachelor, Bates had lived on the ranch for years, and he'd always been a hard worker.

Tate spoke to Bates, and the other man nodded and

sent two riders off on some errand. They returned with gas cans and shovels fetched from the trucks down on the road.

Tate took one of the shovels and turned up a shovelful of dirt all around one of the cattle, making it known what he wanted done.

Once these precautions had been taken, the carcasses were doused in gas and burned.

The smoke burned the eyes, and the smell of singed hide and charred beef-flesh damn near turned Garrett into a vegetarian on the spot. For a while, he thought, he'd stick to chicken and fish—assuming he could bring himself to eat at all.

He ached, watching those flames.

He helped to quell them with shovelfuls of dirt, when the time came to do that.

Two men stayed behind to make sure there were no flare-ups; the rest rode back down to the dirt track below.

On the way out, they'd argued, Garrett and Tate and Austin.

On the way back, nobody said one word.

Not one.

At home, Austin and Bates and a few of the other men unloaded the horses from the trailer and led them to the barn. Tate backed the trailer into the equipment shed, and then unhitched it, while Garrett returned to the house with the rifles.

This time, Esperanza wasn't alone in the kitchen.

Calvin was there, perched on a barstool at the long counter, with a plate of cookies and a glass of milk in front of him. At the sight of the guns, the kid looked wide-eyed.

Garrett gave the boy a friendly nod and kept walking.

In the study, he locked the rifles up again, along with the box of ammunition he'd shoved into his jacket pocket earlier.

When he got back to the kitchen, Esperanza was basting the roasting chickens, and the scent of them made Garrett's stomach rumble with hunger.

Pausing by the stove, he lifted the lid off a pot and looked inside, pleased to see potatoes, peeled and salted and ready to boil up and mash.

"Yes," he muttered.

Esperanza looked at him over one shoulder as she closed the higher of two wall ovens. She was clearly still in a peckish mood; Garrett half expected her to tell him he needn't let his mouth get to watering over her crispy-skinned chicken, thick gravy and mashed potatoes, because he wasn't sitting down to any meal *she'd* fixed.

"Is your mom around?" Garrett asked Calvin, who was watching him with an expression akin to fascination.

Garrett had forgotten the shiner either Tate or Austin had given him out there on the road. From the look on Calvin's face, it was a dandy.

And it explained some of Esperanza's annoyance, too.

Calvin shook his head. "She's at the cottage, packing up our stuff. What happened to your eye?"

"I ran into something," Garrett hedged, his gaze snagging on Esperanza's and then breaking away. He opened one of the refrigerators and pulled out a bottle of beer.

"Want a cookie?" Calvin asked, pushing the plate toward him.

"Ought to go great with beer," Garrett grinned, tak-

ing the stool next to Calvin's and accepting the offer
by helping himself to a couple of oatmeal-raisin cookies. He munched a while before speaking again. "How
come your mom is packing up all your stuff?" he asked.

Calvin leaned in a little, squinting up at Garrett's
shiner with the sort of interest little boys usually reserved for dead bugs and dried-up snakeskins. "We
have to move," he answered. "You didn't really run into
something, did you? You got in a *fight*."

Esperanza glared at Garrett over the top of Calvin's
blond head. Her expression said he was setting a poor
example for the boy.

"It wasn't a fight," Garrett told Calvin. "Not exactly,
anyhow. Where are you moving to?"

Calvin's small shoulders stooped a little then, and
he ducked his head. "Don't know," he mumbled. "Aunt
Paige didn't tell me that."

Garrett frowned, confused.

"She thought Mom was here," Calvin explained.
"Aunt Paige did, I mean. That's why she brought me
to the Silver Spur. When Mom called her on her cell
phone and told her she was at the cottage instead, Aunt
Paige asked Esperanza to watch me for a while, so she
could go help Mom."

"I see," Garrett said, though he was still pretty much
in the dark.

Calvin sighed. "I wish we could live here," he said
in a small voice, after a long time had passed. "I wish
Mom and Harry and me could stay on the Silver Spur
forever."

The earnest way the kid spoke wrenched at something deep inside Garrett.

Maybe because he was starting to wish the same thing.

CHAPTER THIRTEEN

EXCEPT FOR THE marshal's office, which was a minor tourist attraction, the fire station was the oldest public building in Blue River. The engine itself dated back to 1957, but it still ran, and so did the old-fashioned, hand-cranked siren.

Harry howled when the alarm sounded the first long, tinny wail, and Paige and Julie, busy in Julie's kitchen, both stopped wrapping dishes in newspaper to press their hands to their ears.

The siren droned to silence, then wound up again.

Harry did his beagle-best to drown it out, singing along.

Paige rushed for the back door, that being the nearest exit, and Julie followed, after leaning down to give Harry a brief and reassuring pat on the head and instructing him, in vain, to hush up.

By tradition, the intended warning could be anything from a lost child to a full-scale invasion by space aliens.

The smell of smoke was sharp in the air, but Julie couldn't tell where it was coming from until she and Paige ran around to the front yard.

A black, roiling cloud of the stuff loomed against the afternoon sky.

Fire, Julie thought, strangely slow-witted. Then, of *course* it was fire.

She gave in to a moment of pure panic before pulling herself together to focus on her first and highest priority—Calvin.

Her son, she reminded herself, as if by rote, was on the ranch. Paige had taken him there before returning to town to help Julie get ready for her imminent move. The smoke, to her relief, was rising in the opposite direction from the Silver Spur.

The siren revved up once more, and Harry bayed in concert.

Around town, other dogs had joined in, a yip here, a yelp there. The bell on the fire engine clamored in the near distance, a resonant clang in the heat-weighted, acrid air.

The volunteers, rallied by the emergency siren, were on the job then, already racing down Main Street. The old truck rarely saw action, except each year on the Friday after Thanksgiving, when it carried the Lions Club Santa to the tree-lighting ceremony in the park.

Paige, shading her eyes with one hand, assessed the growing plume.

"What do you suppose is burning?" Julie asked. She was good at a lot of things, but reading smoke signals wasn't among them.

Mercifully, the siren had finally gone silent, having alerted everybody in the county that there was Some Kind of Trouble, and so had Harry and the canine chorus.

"Probably, it's Chudley and Minnie Wilkes's place, or somewhere pretty near it," Paige answered, looking worried.

Cars and pickup trucks raced by, two streets over on the main drag.

Paige dashed into the cottage, summoned Harry to

follow, shut him inside and came out jingling her car keys at Julie. "The dog will be fine," she said. "Let's go!"

Julie nodded, feeling slightly sick as she scrambled into Paige's car on the passenger side and snapped on her seat belt. Chudley and Minnie lived in a pair of single-wide trailers, welded together, just a few miles outside of town.

The Wilkeses' home was surrounded by several acres of rusted-out wrecks, most of them up on blocks, but it was the mountain of old tires that worried Julie now. If all that rubber caught fire, it might literally burn for *weeks*, and the greasy smoke would be a respiratory hazard for just about everybody.

Especially Calvin, with his asthma.

Practically everybody in the county was headed for that fire, or so it seemed—more than a few were gawkers, like Paige and Julie, with no real business showing up at all—but many wanted to help put out the flames and contain the blaze before it spread. Or simply be on hand to do whatever might need doing.

Wildfire was always a danger in dry country—it could race overland for miles, in all directions, if it got out of hand, gobbling up people, livestock and property, anything in its path.

Up ahead, Brent Brogan and his two deputies were running what amounted to a roadblock, letting only certain vehicles through.

Julie peered through the windshield of Paige's car, watching as the chief of police lifted a megaphone to his mouth.

"Folks," his voice boomed out, full of good-natured authority, "we just can't have all these rigs clogging up the road now. There's an ambulance on its way over from the clinic right this minute, and you don't want to hold it up, do you?"

Paige, a registered nurse with a lot of experience in emergency medicine, nosed her car right up to the front, tooting her horn.

Chief Brogan looked furious, until he recognized Paige. Immediately after that, he gestured for her to proceed.

Paige rolled down her window as they pulled up beside the frazzled lawman.

"It's that trailer Chudley rents whenever he can find a sucker," Brent said, bending to look inside the car. His fine-featured brown face glistened with sweat. "Everybody's out, but the girl and the little boys are pretty shaken up. For my money, all three of those kids are in shock."

Paige nodded and drove on, while Julie sat rigid on the seat, Brent's words echoing in her mind.

The girl—the little boys—all three of those kids are in shock.

It finally penetrated. Rachel Strivens and her brothers—they were the kids Brent had been talking about. They lived, with their father, in a house trailer rented from Chudley Wilkes.

"Oh, my God," Julie said. "Rachel—she's in one of my English classes—"

The fire engine was parked broadside, its bulky hose bulging with water, helmeted volunteers all around.

Paige got out of the car and ran forward, and Julie was right behind her.

The flames were out, though smoke churned through the roof of the trailer, having burned part of it away. The structure had been reduced to a blackened ruin, with strips of charred metal curling from it like oddly placed antennae. Hometown firemen, ranchers and farmers and store owners and insurance agents, among others, were everywhere, wielding axes and shovels, and there seemed to be no air left for breathing.

Julie's eyes burned as though acid had splashed into them, and so did her lungs and her throat, and she was so frightened for Rachel and her brothers that her heart began to pound in painful thuds.

She and Paige spotted the three children at the same moment, sitting huddled together on the ground under a tree on the far side of the property. Norvel Collier, a retired pharmacist who looked like he might need medical attention at any moment himself, kept thrusting an oxygen mask at them, and getting no takers.

"Norvel," Paige greeted the old man, with a businesslike nod.

Norvel nodded back. "Hello, Paige," he said, blinking at her, his eyes reddened from the smoke.

"You'd best let me take over there," Paige told him. "You go rustle up some more oxygen for me, why don't you? And a few blankets, maybe?"

Norvel didn't protest. He nodded, and Julie helped him to his feet. She received a grateful, faltering smile for her effort.

"Much obliged," he said.

"What can I do to help?" Julie asked Paige.

Paige had already persuaded the smaller of the two boys to let her place the oxygen mask over his nose and mouth. "Stay out of the way," Paige answered, her tone brisk but not unkind.

Rachel sat slumped, with one arm around each of her brothers, her clothes sooty and her hair singed. She locked gazes with Julie, but said nothing.

Despite Paige's instructions, Julie knelt to pull Rachel into a brief hug.

"Everything will be all right," she told the child. "I promise."

And then she got to her feet again, and stepped back out of the way.

The ambulance was making its way through the traffic on the gravel road, its siren giving short, uncertain bleats, like a confused sheep separated from the flock and calling out to be found.

"My kids!" a man's voice yelled, full of anguish. *"Where are my kids?"*

An instant later, Ron Strivens came into view, having torn his way through the crowd of firemen and able-bodied locals. He looked around wildly, spotted Rachel and the boys, and hurried toward his children.

Dropping to his knees, but not touching any of them, Strivens focused on the oxygen mask covering his youngest son's face. The glance he threw at Paige, who was overseeing the process and lightly stroking the boy's hair in an effort to keep him calm, was nothing short of frantic.

The man's skin was gray with fear, his lips pressed into a tight blue line.

"They'll be fine," Paige assured him, with the firm, in-control confidence Julie and Libby had always admired in their younger sister. Even before she'd gone through nursing school, graduating at the top of her class, Paige had been the type to keep her head in any kind of emergency.

Nothing and no one had ever caused her to lose her composure.

No one except Austin McKettrick, that is.

"How did it start?" Strivens croaked, sparing a glance for what remained of the mobile home but mainly concerned, naturally, with the well-being of his family.

Rachel started to answer, but before she got a word out, her little brother pulled the oxygen mask from his face long enough to say, "It wasn't Rachel's fault, Dad—"

Gently, Paige shook her head and replaced the mask.

The older of the two boys took up where the younger one had left off. "Rachel brought half a pizza home from the bowling alley when she got off work," he explained eagerly, his face as filthy as his sister's, his voice high and rapid. "She said we could have some, soon as she heated it up in the oven. But she wanted to change her clothes first, and that always means she's going to take forever. Me and Colley didn't want to wait, because we was *real* hungry, but the pilot light was out in the oven, so I lit it and—"

Once again, Colley pulled off the mask. He shouted, "Boom!" before Paige got it back in place.

Tears welled up in Rachel's eyes, already red and irritated from the smoke. "The place went up so fast," she told her father. "All I could think of was getting Max and Colley out of there—"

"You did good," Ron Strivens told her, reaching out to squeeze her shoulder.

By then, the paramedics had arrived.

Paige spoke to them briefly and went to stand with her upper arm pressing against Julie's. All their lives, the Remington sisters had communicated silent strength to each other in just that way.

The EMTs crouched to examine Rachel and the boys, and it was decided that while all three children were probably going to be fine, it couldn't hurt to take them on over to the clinic and let one of the doctors have a look to make sure.

"Where are we going to live, now that the trailer's gone?" Colley asked his father, who had hoisted the younger boy into his arms to carry him to the ambulance.

A paramedic trotted behind, holding the oxygen tank.

Julie didn't hear Ron Strivens's reply, but her gaze connected with Paige's.

It was a good question. Where *was* the family going to live?

Julie knew well, of course, how hard it was to find housing in and around Blue River. Except for the town's one apartment complex, which was always full to capacity, there simply weren't any rentals.

Paige merely spread her hands.

Chudley Wilkes appeared in the junker-choked field, driving an ancient tractor with a high metal seat, Minnie riding on one running board, her heavy cloud of gray hair billowing in the sooty breeze. They made for a colorful sight, Chudley and Minnie on that tractor.

About to head for Paige's car, Julie stopped to watch their approach, as did her sister.

Chudley's grizzled old face was hidden in shadow, since he was wearing a billed cap, but his neck seemed to bulge above the collar of his grungy shirt, the veins engorged, the flesh a frightening mottle of purple and red.

"Lord," Paige breathed, "that old fool is going to have a stroke right here if he doesn't calm down." She went back to the car and returned quickly with a blood-pressure cuff and a stethoscope.

Chief Brogan, who was a hands-on sort of cop, walked over to meet Chudley, and because Paige followed him, so did Julie.

"Chudley Wilkes," Paige said, as soon as he'd shut off the tractor motor and it had clunked and clattered and popped to silence, "have you been taking your blood-pressure medicine?"

"Never mind my blood pressure!" Chudley yelled in response. "I'm ruined! I'm bankrupted! Why, there ain't nothin' left of my trailer but the axles!"

Shaking her head, Minnie got down off the running board to examine the wreckage. "You ain't ruined, you damn fool," she said. Then, addressing Chief Brogan and the rest of them, she added, "Pay him no mind. He's just tightfisted, that's all. Why, he could bail out a middlin'-sized *country* with the money he's got stashed."

"Now, you hush up, Chudley Wilkes," Paige ordered, taking Minnie's place on the running board and wrapping the blood-pressure cuff around Chudley's tattooed upper arm with dispatch. She listened through the stethoscope and watched the digital meter while the inflated band slowly deflated.

"Just what I thought," Paige clucked, turning to Brent. "You'd better get Chudley to the doctor right away, Chief. He's in real danger of blowing a gasket."

Chudley grayed under his crimson flush and the grime that was probably as much a part of his skin as the pigment by this late date. He moved to fire up the tractor again.

"Minnie," he called to his wife, "get back on here, right now! We got to get me to the clinic!"

Minnie started toward the tractor, but Brent stopped her. "I'll drive you in the squad car," he said.

Chudley looked the chief over suspiciously, and Julie could just imagine what he was thinking. Never mind that Brent had been part of the community since he was a little boy—his dad had worked for Jim McKettrick out on the Silver Spur—never mind that he'd served bravely in the military and done a creditable job as the chief of police.

Perceptive, Brent sighed. "Come on, Chudley," he said.

Chudley looked down at Minnie, who waited in silence. "You got your purse with you?" he demanded.

"You see any *purse* in my hand, Chudley Wilkes? My purse is up there to the house, where I left it when you dragged me away from my Sunday afternoon TV movie to watch this here old trailer go up in smoke!"

"Well, we've got to get it, then," Chudley insisted, though he did allow Brent and one of the volunteer firemen to help him down off the high seat of that tractor. "I'll be needin' my Medicare card, and it's in your wallet, Minnie, and your wallet is *in your purse!*"

"You been into it for beer money, that's how you know what's in my *wallet*, you mangy old hoot owl!" Minnie retorted, bristling.

Julie began to fear for Minnie's blood pressure, as well as Chudley's.

"Let's just head on over to the clinic," Brent interjected reasonably. "Folks know you in Blue River, Chudley. You can give them your Medicare number later."

"That trailer had a good ten years left in it," Chudley complained, though he allowed Brent to steer him toward the squad car. The fire was out by then, and the volunteers were stowing the hoses and putting away shovels and picks.

The structure was a total loss, that was plain to see.

"Nobody got hurt," Brent told him. "That's what's important here."

Chudley shook his head as he stooped to plunk himself down in the passenger seat of the police car. Brent stood by patiently, holding open the door.

"That's easy for you to say," Chudley growled in response. "You didn't lose a perfectly good trailer."

Once again, Brent sighed, loudly this time, and with a visible motion of his broad shoulders. "Now, Chudley, you know damn well," Julie heard him tell the old man, "that trailer ought to have been condemned years ago."

Minnie had tarried there by the tractor, frowning as though she might be debating whether she wanted to accompany her husband to the clinic or not. When she made a move in that direction, though, Brent quickly opened the back door.

She had long since resigned herself to life with Chudley Wilkes—everyone in Blue River knew that.

Julie, watching the scene, started when she felt Paige's elbow nudge her lightly in the side. "Ready to call it a day?" she asked.

"Oh, yeah," Julie said.

Paige drove her back to the cottage, so Julie could fetch Harry and lock up. She wanted to see Calvin, hold him in her arms, ruffle his hair and kiss the top of his head.

Of course, she'd have to disguise her affection as a tickle attack—as young as he was, Calvin was already reticent about getting hugs and kisses.

"Thanks for letting Calvin visit over the weekend," Julie told her sister, when Paige pulled up in front of the converted Victorian mansion where she rented an apartment. Conveniently, Paige's place was right across the street from Julie's cottage. "He always has such a good time with you."

Paige nodded, but there was something vague about

her smile, and her eyes were watchful. "We didn't talk about it while we were packing dishes," she said, "but that doesn't mean I don't want to hear all about last night's big date."

Julie blushed. Looked away. Made herself look back. "It was—a date," she replied.

"It was more than a date," Paige insisted good-naturedly. "But we can talk about it tomorrow, after the school day is over, while we're packing up your kitchen."

Julie shook her head. "The tryouts start at three-fifteen—for the musical, I mean. I'll be busy at school until at least seven o'clock."

"What about Calvin?" Paige asked, pulling her purse and the blood pressure gizmo from the backseat of her car.

"He'll be with Libby and Tate," Julie said, feeling unaccountably guilty.

Paige nodded. The impish light in her dark eyes had faded, though, and her expression was pensive. "This unexpected move—I know it's stressful—" She stopped and made another start. "What I mean is, there's a lot going on, what with Gordon turning up out of nowhere and your having to stage a musical at school now in-stead of in the spring, when you'd planned, and then Libby's wedding—"

Julie chuckled, rounded the back of the car and gave her sister a hug. "I'm really, truly all right, so don't be a fussbudget."

Paige smiled, and her eyes glistened with moisture. "'Fussbudget,'" she repeated. "I haven't heard that word in years. Not since before Grammy died."

After their mother had abandoned the family, their

paternal grandmother had done her best to fill in the emotional gaps, but Grammy's health had already been failing, and she simply hadn't had the energy to deal with young children for any length of time.

Julie felt a pang of loss, remembering Grammy, a sweet, well-meaning woman, fragile as a bird. She'd kept her little house down the street from theirs impeccably tidy, Elisabeth Remington had, and baked cookies for them whenever she was feeling well enough.

"Maybe *I'm* the one who should be asking if something is wrong," Julie said, resting her hands on Paige's shoulders. "What's up, Paige?"

Paige looked away, looked back. Bit her lower lip.

"Tell me," Julie said firmly.

"I thought it was such a good idea to change jobs," Paige confessed. "I'm so tired of commuting. The renovations on the house are coming along well—we could all move in there, Julie, you and Calvin and me—even though we'd have to rough it for a while—"

Julie, taller than her sister, bent her knees to look more directly into Paige's face. "Wait," she said. "Hold it. Let's get back to how you *thought* it was a good idea to work at the clinic here in town instead of driving fifty miles each way, but now—what? You don't think that anymore?"

"But now Austin McKettrick is back," Paige said. She tried for another smile, but it was spoiled by the bleak expression in her eyes.

"Oh," Julie said.

"Yeah," Paige agreed ruefully. *"Oh."*

"I didn't realize you knew Austin was home."

Across the street, inside the cottage, Harry began to bark his come-and-get-me bark.

"Word gets around," Paige said.

Julie nodded. "But it's more than that, right?"

Paige sighed. "I seem to have radar, as far as Austin's concerned. If he gets within fifty miles of me, I can feel it."

"You still care about him, then?" Julie asked, miserable on her sister's behalf.

Austin was charming and he was handsome and he was sexy as hell. He was also a wild man, a renegade. He was all wrong for practical Paige, the nurse, the devoted aunt and sister, the career woman who secretly yearned for a home and a family.

Oh, yes, Austin was all wrong for Paige.

As wrong as *Garrett* was for *her.*

Julie closed her eyes for a moment. Drew a deep breath.

"No," Paige said, "I *don't* still care for Austin. It's just that—well—I don't particularly want to run into him in the supermarket and at the dry cleaner's—"

A corner of Julie's mouth kicked up in a grin. "I doubt if Austin does much of the grocery shopping or hangs around the cleaner's a lot, Paige."

Pain moved in Paige's exquisitely beautiful face. "With Libby marrying Tate, and now you getting involved with Garrett—Austin and I are bound to be thrown together more often than either of us wants. Julie, *what* am I going to do?"

Julie's face heated, and a protest rose in her throat, but she was more concerned about her sister's feelings than setting Paige straight by pointing out that she most definitely *was not* "involved" with Garrett.

She was just—well—*having sex* with him.

"It's true that things could get awkward," she said

moderately, "now that Libby and Tate are getting married, but Austin doesn't spend all that much time on the Silver Spur, let alone in Blue River, does he?"

Paige took a half step back. Tugged the strap of her purse up over one shoulder and tucked the blood pressure gear under one elbow. She was already in retreat, Julie knew, though she was trying to be subtle about it. "You're right," she said, too quickly. "I don't know why I'm so worried about bumping into Austin. The man wants to avoid me as much as *I* want to avoid *him*."

Julie wasn't so sure about that. She also wasn't fool enough to say so. Harry was barking, and she needed to go home to Calvin, prepare herself to get through the week to come.

"Call me," she told Paige, in parting.

Half an hour later, she and Harry arrived in the driveway of the main ranch house on the Silver Spur.

Calvin waved at her from his high perch on Garrett's shoulders as they came through the open doorway of the barn.

Harry, beside himself with joy, demanded to be released from the car, and by the time Julie had gotten out herself, opened the rear door and lifted the beagle to the ground, Calvin and Garrett were standing next to her.

"We've been feeding the horses!" Calvin crowed.

Julie's first impulse, whenever Calvin was around any animal other than Harry or Tate and Libby's three dogs, was to worry that the dander might trigger an asthma or allergy attack in her son. Seeing the delight on Calvin's somewhat grubby face, she caught the knee-jerk protest before it could leave her mouth.

Feeling oddly shy, in light of the deliciously scandalous things she and Garrett had done together the night before, Julie managed to avoid the man's gaze, for the moment, at least.

"You were?" she smiled. "You were feeding horses? Calvin Remington, I am *impressed*."

The happiness in the child's small, earnest face was sweet to see, but it also sent tiny cracks splintering through Julie's heart. Calvin *was* thrilled that he'd helped with grown-up chores, but simply being in Garrett's presence mattered more.

It was natural, she supposed, for a little boy, especially one raised without a father, to look up to a man like Garrett McKettrick.

But what if Calvin was growing attached to him?

Garrett reached up, removed his hat and set it on Calvin's head with unerring accuracy. Julie felt Garrett's gaze on her face and made herself meet it.

She saw a pensive expression in his eyes, along with gentle humor and a kind of—well—patience, a willingness to wait, that moved her in a way she wouldn't have anticipated. His face was badly bruised, as if he'd been in a fight, and Julie instinctively skirted the topic. She would ask about it later.

Harry, a dog wanting his boy, bounded around them, yipping cheerfully.

Garrett grinned and set Calvin on the ground. Still wearing Garrett's hat, Calvin giggled as Harry leaped up to lick his face and sent the both of them tumbling in the grass.

Julie's sinuses burned, and she had to blink a couple of times.

Garrett rested a hand lightly against the small of her back, urging her toward the house.

"I have to put the car away," she said.

"I'll do that later," Garrett responded.

A noise coming from the direction of the service road down by the gates made all of them turn to look.

A flatbed truck came into view, pulling half of a double-wide mobile home.

Julie watched it for a few moments, putting two and two together in her stress-and-sex-addled brain, and turned her eyes back to Garrett. The motion was quick and sure, like the needle of a compass swinging toward true north.

"Brent called," Garrett explained, sounding almost shy. "He said there was a fire in town, and it left a family with no place to live."

Before Julie could respond, Calvin tugged at the sleeve of her coat, thus commanding her attention. "Esperanza roasted two whole chickens for supper," he said. "And that's a lot of food, so Libby and Tate and Audrey and Ava are coming over to eat with us."

The way her child said the word *us* made Julie's throat go tight again.

Inside, the big kitchen was warm and glowing with welcoming light, and the atmosphere was savory with the aroma of Esperanza's roast chickens. A poignant sense of gratitude struck Julie in that moment, but it was bittersweet.

Was she getting too comfortable in this temporary place? With this very temporary man?

Suddenly aware that her clothes and hair must smell like smoke, Julie excused herself to take a quick shower and change her clothes.

When she returned from the guest apartment, perhaps twenty minutes later, Libby and Tate had arrived with the twins, and Austin, looking spiffy in clean jeans and a pale blue T-shirt, was setting the table for a crowd.

Julie took a moment to savor the scene, a happy family—or a *mostly* happy one, anyway—gathered to share a meal on a chilly fall evening. If Paige had been there, she thought, it would have been perfect.

A smile twitched at the corner of her mouth, lightening her mood. Well, maybe not perfect, she thought.

Could any space contain *both* Austin McKettrick *and* Paige Remington without bursting into flames?

Garrett bumped her lightly from behind, stopping just short of wrapping his arms around her waist—or that was the feeling she had, anyway. Maybe it was her imagination.

Or some serious wishful thinking.

"What?" he asked, after shifting to stand beside her.

Calvin was still wearing Garrett's hat, making sure Audrey and Ava noticed it.

Don't, Julie pleaded silently, watching her son. *Don't care too much.*

"Nothing," she lied. She couldn't have explained what she was feeling to GarrettMcKettrickit was all so complicated, she didn't understand it herself.

Libby and Tate were helping the twins out of their coats, taking off their own.

Libby turned her head, caught Julie's eye.

Julie watched as her sister's glance moved to Garrett, no doubt noticing how close the two of them were.

A smile twitched at Libby's mouth, and she widened her eyes at Julie, as if to say, *Well, now...what have we here?*

Self-consciously, Julie moved away from Garrett just a bit.

He chuckled at that, and shook his head.

Esperanza oversaw all this, but when it was time to sit down and eat, she pleaded a full schedule of must-see TV, took a plate and left the kitchen for her own sitting room.

Julie couldn't help noticing that Calvin, who usually sat beside her, had squeezed in between Garrett and Austin at the other side of the table. Thankfully, Austin had casually relieved him of the oversize hat, setting it aside on a nearby breakfront.

The fire at the Strivenses' place was the first topic of conversation.

"It's just lucky one of the staff trailers was empty," Libby said. Tate was next to her, and she paused to give him a look that said he'd not only hung the sun and the moon, but the stars, too.

Watching Libby, Tate looked wonderstruck, as though he couldn't believe his good fortune in being loved by such a woman.

Julie, seeing all this, made herself look away, not because she was envious, exactly, but because suddenly she yearned—oh, yes, *yearned*—to find what Libby and Tate had together. And in looking away, she immediately snagged gazes with Garrett.

It was a struggle, breaking free.

The air almost crackled between them.

And for just a little while, Julie allowed herself to pretend it would last.

CHAPTER FOURTEEN

"Are we going to pretend last night didn't happen?" Garrett asked.

Julie, startled half to death, stopped on the threshold of her small sitting room, one hand pressed to her heart. She'd just tucked Calvin into bed and listened to his prayers.

"You scared me," Julie said, although that was probably obvious.

Garrett sat, relaxed, on the sofa, with Harry snuggled right beside him. The dog's muzzle rested on Garrett's thigh and, barely acknowledging Julie's arrival, the animal casually rolled his luminous brown eyes in her direction but otherwise didn't move a muscle.

Not exactly protective.

"Sorry," Garrett said, but the grin quirking at the corner of his mouth belied the sincerity of his apology.

Julie didn't retreat, but she didn't move forward, either. She just stood there, and this was not at all like the self she knew, and that was irritating to the nth degree. Of all the men who might have breached her defenses, why did it have to be this one?

"Julie?" Garrett prompted, stroking Harry's ears, evidently willing to wait as long as necessary for an answer to his question.

"It might be better if we *did* pretend that last night didn't happen," she said.

Garrett studied her in silence for a long moment. Then he shook his head. "I don't believe that," he decided aloud, "and I don't think you do, either."

Julie bit down on her lower lip, wedged her hands, backward, into the hip pockets of her jeans, and rocked back, ever so slightly, on the heels of her sneakers.

"Come here," Garrett said, patting the Harry-free side of him on the sofa.

She hesitated. Pulled a hand free of its pocket to cock a thumb over one shoulder, indicating that Calvin was just down the hallway. The little dickens hadn't had time to fall asleep, and if he'd heard Garrett's voice, caught even the timbre of it, he was surely listening in.

"Calvin," Julie mouthed.

Garrett chuckled and shook his head again. "I wasn't planning on saying—or doing—anything ungentlemanly," he said.

"You *did* mention last night," she pointed out.

"So did you," Garrett reasoned, sitting there looking all cowboy-hunky, with his boots and his jeans and his Western shirt open at the throat. "Just now."

Julie narrowed her eyes, rested her hands on her hips. Harry had rolled onto his back for a tummy rub. Traitorous dog. Next, he'd be living upstairs with Garrett and riding around with him in trucks.

"Just remember," she said, "that Harry is *my* dog."

"Don't kid yourself," Garrett replied, still amused. His eyes seemed to drink her in in big guzzling gulps. "He's *Calvin's* dog, through and through." He glanced fondly down at Harry, who lay surrendered, all three legs in the air. "He's also something of a hedonist, it would seem."

Julie did not join Garrett on the sofa—that would have been giving too much ground, tantamount to sprawling on her back, like Harry, in hopes of a tummy rub.

Or something.

She did perch on the arm of a nearby chair, though. She folded her arms and tried to look as though the man hadn't turned her entire universe on its ear with one night of lovemaking.

"So the decision is…?" Garrett said, after watching her a little longer.

"There's supposed to be a decision?" she countered, stalling.

Garrett sighed. After easing Harry aside, he got up off the couch, walked to the archway leading into the small corridor, no doubt to make sure Calvin wasn't crouched just outside the glow of the hallway nightlight, eavesdropping.

Returning—the coast must have been clear—Garrett stood in front of Julie.

He gripped her shoulders, very gently, and raised her to her feet.

And then, slowly, and with a thoroughness that proved he meant business, Garrett McKettrick kissed her.

Julie practically swooned. There were now two categories of kissing in her personal lexicon—being kissed by Garrett McKettrick and being kissed by any *other* man in the world.

The first had totally ruined the second, for all time.

Julie had tears in her eyes when it ended. "You'll just go away," she blurted out in an anguished whisper, and instantly regretted the outburst.

Garrett curved his fingers under her chin. "I always come back," he said, his voice husky, his gaze tender on her face. "And you might like some of the places I go. Did you ever consider that?"

What was he saying? What did *And you might like some of the places I go* actually mean?

"I have a son," she said, taking a tremendous risk with her pride. He'd know she'd interpreted his remark as an invitation of sorts, or at least a suggestion that she might be traveling with him in the future—and that was way more than she was ready to acknowledge. "I have a job and two sisters." Julie's gaze dropped to Harry, still on the couch, though now curled contentedly into a furball. "I'm pretty sure I still have a dog. In other words, I'm not a jet-setter like you, or the people you know, Garrett. I'm a hometown kind of gal."

He frowned, apparently puzzled. A fraction of a second later, though, she saw his wondrous, dark-denim eyes widen with some realization he might or might not be willing to share. "I see," he said.

"I'm not sure you do," Julie replied, without meaning to say anything at all.

Her dad would have said her tongue was hinged at both ends, the way she kept blathering on. Why couldn't she just shut up?

The recollection of her gentle, often sad father brought the faintest hint of a smile to Julie's mouth.

Garrett merely raised one eyebrow, waiting for her to go on.

"You and I come from different worlds, Garrett," she told him finally.

He actually had the nerve to roll his eyes. "That is so corny," he said. "'You and I come from different worlds'? Have you been watching soap operas or something?"

Garrett was mocking her, Julie decided, and she should have been angry—or at least indignant. Instead, this ridiculous and completely unfounded happiness burgeoned inside her, and she almost laughed.

Now, the new-jeans eyes were twinkling. It was disconcerting how quickly he read her, Julie thought—and how well.

"You know what I mean," she insisted, determined to salvage something of the perfectly reasonable argument she was trying to make. "There are some pretty obvious contrasts between us, after all."

"Umm-hmm," Garrett agreed. He was about to kiss her again; she could feel his breath, a pleasant tickle on her mouth. "Viva la contrasts, baby."

Julie pressed her palms to his chest then, meaning to push him away, or at least hold him at a little distance. Instead, though, her hands slid, as if of their own accord, to join at the back of his neck.

The second kiss left her swaying.

Garrett's hands rested, strong and sure, on either side of her waist. Then he gave a long, comically beleaguered sigh. "Good night, Julie," he said, the words blowing past her ear like the softest of summer breezes.

He walked away then, and as soon as he turned his back, Julie rested one hand on the back of the armchair, just to steady herself, afraid she was going to hyperventilate.

Harry, still on the couch, lifted his head, thumped at the cushions a few times with his tail, and jumped, with remarkable grace, to the floor.

The dog hesitated, watching her with something like sympathy, then toddled off down the hall, headed for Calvin's room.

Julie followed, quietly opening the door, careful not to let the light from the hallway fall on her little boy's face.

Harry trotted in and bounded up onto the mattress on his own, settling into a sighing heap at Calvin's feet.

Julie blew a kiss to her sleeping son, slipped out of the room and softly closed the door.

"YOU'RE LIVING WITH this guy?" Gordon asked the next morning, his voice grating at Julie through her headset. She'd just dropped Calvin off at Libby and Tate's, and she had a full day of teaching ahead, to be followed by the first round of tryouts for the musical.

You're living with this guy?

The question was so off the wall that Julie was thrown by it.

That particular reaction was short-lived. "What did you just ask me?" she retorted.

Gordon sighed. "Look, as lousy as my track record is, I *am* Calvin's father," he said. "I'm concerned about his…environment, that's all."

Julie actually trembled, and for a moment she thought the cheap plastic housing of her cell phone might actually crack, she was squeezing it so tightly. She pulled over to the side of that country road, for her own sake and that of other drivers, put the car in Park, flipped on the blinkers.

With a conscious effort, she loosened her grip on the phone and lightened up on the pressure against her skull.

"His *'environment'*?"

"You know what I'm talking about," Gordon said, but with less certainty than before.

"No, Gordon," Julie countered, "I do *not* know what you're talking about." She did, actually, but she wasn't going to make this easy.

Gordon had been the one to initiate the call.

And he'd made her sound like some kind of tramp, shacking up with this guy or that one and leaving Calvin to manage on his own.

Another sigh came then, gusty and long-suffering. "Maybe I could have been more diplomatic," he ventured.

"Think so?"

Gordon sounded suitably remorseful. Even sad. But Julie knew from experience how quickly his mood could change. "I never knew how to talk to you, Julie. That was our main problem."

In her opinion, their "main problem" had been Gordon's complete inability to commit himself to either her or their son. Fortunately for Dixie and the new baby, due in April, he had evidently changed.

Tension stretched between them, almost palpable.

The invisible rubber band finally snapped.

Just as Julie had expected, Gordon retrenched. "Are you or are you not living with a man you're not married to?" he demanded.

So much for his concern about being more diplomatic.

"I'm not *living with* Garrett McKettrick," Julie said, "not that it would be any of your damn business if I was. I hardly feel any compunction to account to you for my behavior, Gordon."

"You're right," Gordon allowed, after a few beats. "What you do in your—romantic life—isn't my concern. It's just that Calvin told me—"

"When did you speak with Calvin?" Julie broke in.

She glanced into the rearview mirror and saw an old red pickup pull up behind her. It was the same truck Garrett had been driving on Saturday, when she and Libby and Paige were heading out to shop for Libby's wedding dress.

Great, she thought.

"I gave Calvin my cell number the other night, when we all had supper together," Gordon said. "He's called me a couple of times since then."

This was news to Julie. Calvin hadn't mentioned calling his father.

What did it mean—if anything?

She watched as the driver's-side door of the red truck swung open.

Julie's breath caught. "Listen, I'm due at work. Maybe we could talk later?"

"All right," Gordon said. "When would be a good time?"

"Later—I'll call you later. Sometime—"

Gordon clicked off, after making a disgruntled man-sound in her ear.

Julie felt a little jolt when she turned her head and saw Austin standing beside her car, instead of Garrett. It was both a disappointment, she decided fitfully, and a relief.

She rolled the window down.

Austin bent, grinning at her. "You having car trouble or something?" he asked.

"No," Julie said, embarrassed. "I was just—talking on my cell phone and—"

The man's smile was wickedly boyish, Julie thought, detached from Austin's charms in a way she couldn't seem to manage with Garrett. No wonder Paige wanted to steer clear of her old flame—when it came to this guy, the needle on the cute-o-meter was bobbing into the red zone, and there was a distinct danger of spontaneous combustion.

For Paige, anyway.

Austin tugged genially at his hat brim, every inch the cowboy. "I'll be on my way, then," he said, "if you're sure you're all right, that is."

Julie nodded to indicate that she was fine. "Thanks for stopping," she said.

Austin grinned and sprinted back to the truck.

Julie straightened her shoulders, drew in and released a few deep breaths, and drove on.

At school, the halls were jammed.

Even though phone calls, texts and emails had probably been flying back and forth among them all weekend, the kids were eager to discuss the latest calamity—the fire at the Strivenses place—face-to-face.

Julie wove her way through the crowd, catching a snatch of conversation here and there.

...the McKettricks gave them a trailer to live in, and it's practically brand-new...

...the marching band wants to give a concert to raise money for groceries and stuff...

...my mom says the Quilters' Guild is planning to raffle off the project they worked on over the summer...

By the time Julie stepped into her classroom, she was smiling.

Kids could be ornery, no doubt about it, but deep down, they cared about each other, as did their parents. This was the Blue River Julie had known and loved all her life, the community that invariably rallied in the face of trouble, stood shoulder to shoulder, and saw things through to the finish.

"Ms. Remington?"

Julie was only mildly surprised to turn and see Rachel Strivens standing quietly next to one of the bookcases. "Good morning, Rachel," she said, careful not to examine the child too closely or reveal any of the sympathy she felt.

It would be only too easy for Rachel to mistake sympathy for pity.

And pity was the last thing the girl needed.

Rachel wore jeans that didn't quite fit though they were good quality, along with a green sweater set with tiny matching buttons. She gazed earnestly at Julie for a long moment, swallowed and then said, "Do you think you could talk to my dad about—about how folks don't mean any harm by giving us things?"

Julie set her tote bag and purse in her desk chair, took off her coat and draped it over the back to deal with later. Before she could think what to say, Rachel went on.

"He says we don't need charity from the McKettricks or anybody else," she said miserably. "My brothers, they think it's Christmas, because people have been dropping stuff by since the men from the Silver Spur set the trailer down, just in front of the old one. They even hooked up the water and had the lights turned on. Folks bring groceries by the pickup load—clothes—new things, still in the boxes—you wouldn't believe it."

"I believe it," Julie said, with a small smile. She'd been born and raised in Blue River, and she could recall a number of times when the entire town had stepped up. Whether it was a fire, a lost job, a tragic accident or a grave illness—as in her own father's case—the locals invariably wanted to help.

Tears welled up in Rachel's eyes. "Dad's got his pride," she said. "He's already talking about moving on, just as soon as he can get the rig running right."

Julie rested a hand on Rachel's shoulder. The sweater set was soft—probably cashmere. She'd seen Cookie Becker in sophomore English wearing one much like it, and often. Cookie's widowed father didn't own a fancy ranch, practice a profession requiring advanced degrees or own stock in a technology firm or a software company. He worked at the tire store.

"Will you talk to my dad?" Rachel asked again. "I don't want to leave Blue River. Colley and Max don't want to, either. Especially not now that we've got that nice trailer to live in and all these new clothes and good things to eat—"

"I'll talk to him," Julie confirmed. "But that's all I can promise."

Yes, she'd seen the community rise to occasions like this one, some easier, some more difficult, time and time again. Generally, people were grateful, glad to have the help. But she'd also seen folks on the receiving end get their backs up, shake their fists at anything smacking of charity and anybody offering it.

Ron Strivens apparently fell into the latter group.

"Thanks," Rachel said, with more gratitude than the favor warranted, considering success was by no means a sure thing. After all, Julie hadn't accomplished much the *last* time she'd tried to talk to Rachel's dad.

The first period bell rang then, the door of Julie's classroom sprang open and her students poured in, a noisy river of laughter and slang, pushing and catcalls.

Rachel took her usual seat, meeting no one's eyes, keeping her slender back straight and her chin high.

Her father wasn't the only one in the family with pride, Julie thought.

What had it taken for the child to ask for help?

GARRETT WAS SORE as hell, but he saddled his horse anyhow and led it out of the barn, following behind Tate and the gelding, Stranger, into the morning sunshine. A large horse trailer waited in the yard, already hitched to a flatbed truck loaded with spools of barbed wire and various equipment.

Today, they'd be riding the downed fence lines up near where they'd found the dead cattle the day before.

Garrett had suggested taking the plane up again—it seemed like a good idea to him—but Tate refused, maintaining that the rustlers weren't likely to be working in the daylight. The thing to do now, he figured, was fix fences.

Tate was the eldest brother, and he was foreman.

When it came to ranch work, he gave the orders. That was only right, Garrett figured, since Tate was the one holding down the fort while he and Austin ran loose.

Garrett led the horse he'd chosen for the day up the ramp and into the trailer. He secured it among the half dozen others that had already been loaded and he and Tate walked back out into the light together.

Garrett's cell phone rang in the pocket of his jacket.

Tate gave him a wry look, partly disgusted, but offered no comment.

Seeing a familiar number in the panel, Garrett flipped the phone open and answered instead of letting the call go to voice mail, as he might have done otherwise.

"Hello, Nan," he said.

Nan Cox was smiling; Garrett felt the force of it as surely as if she'd been standing in front of him.

"Garrett," the senator's wife practically sang. "It's *so good* to hear your voice." What she meant: *Shouldn't you have called me?*

Tate shook his head, turned and walked away, leaving Garrett to hold the conversation in relative privacy.

"How are you?" Garrett asked quietly. "How are the kids?"

"Well, it's nice of you to *ask*, Garrett." *Finally.* "We're all fine, considering that my husband and their father has evidently lost his mind." A pause. "I really didn't expect you to bail out like this. I was counting on you to help me straighten this thing out."

Garrett moved well away from the action surrounding the horse trailer and the flatbed truck. "I didn't bail out, Nan," he said. "Morgan fired me."

"As I said," Nan replied, "my husband is out of his mind."

"I'm sorry," Garrett said. "That you and the children have to go through this, I mean."

"I didn't think you were apologizing for the other part," Nan said, with a sniff.

Garrett said nothing. Tate and the others were ready to head out now; he was holding up the show.

"Garrett," Nan went on, "have you been watching the national news? Reading the papers? Surfing the web? Surely you know what's going on."

He knew, all right.

The party had been pressuring Cox to resign, but the senator was still resisting the idea. According to Garrett's private contacts, who emailed regular updates from various places behind the scenes, the power brokers were getting impatient. Pretty soon, they'd throw the bureaucratic equivalent of a butterfly net over the guy and shuffle him off to some hospital or rehab center.

"I've got a pretty good idea," he admitted, watching Tate, who was watching him back. He knew Nan was calling because she wanted a favor. He also knew she wouldn't bring it up until she was ready, and there was no point in trying to hurry her along.

One foot on the running board of his truck, Tate waved the driver of the flatbed on ahead. Watching as the trailer loaded with horses went by, tires flinging up dust, Garrett recalled what his brother had said about running the Silver Spur with little or no help, and he felt a stab of guilt.

Garrett strode in Tate's direction.

"I need your help, Garrett," Nan said, at long last.

"Short of rejoining your husband's staff," Garrett said, pulling open the passenger-side door of Tate's truck and climbing into the seat, "I'll do anything I can. You know that."

Tate, behind the wheel now, slanted a look in Garrett's direction before turning the key in the ignition.

Nan finally laid it on the line, the real reason for her call. "Morgan is…on his 'honeymoon,' as he put it," she said. "He called me a couple of minutes ago from some swanky ski resort in Oregon, expecting me to share in his joy, I guess."

"Wouldn't that be bigamy?" Garrett asked.

Nan's chuckle was bitter. "Apparently, they decided to throw the honeymoon before the wedding. Morgan says he's going to divorce me and marry Mandy. Morgan and Mandy, married in Mexico. On top of everything else, it's alliterative." She paused, collecting herself. "By some miracle, the press hasn't picked up on any of this yet, but all hell will break loose when they do. That's why I need you to help me."

"I don't work for the senator anymore," Garrett reiterated, though gently.

"I understand that, Garrett. I'm asking you to work for *me*. I'll pay you whatever you were getting before, plus 20 percent."

"That's generous," Garrett said cautiously.

"Think about it," Nan answered, sounding more like her old self again. She was quick on her feet; the daughter of a former Texas governor as well as the wife of a senator, she'd spent a lifetime on the fringes of politics. She knew the ins and outs. "And don't take too long. The you-know-what is about to hit the fan. Besides, there are some other things we need to discuss in person. I've said more than I'm comfortable saying on a cell phone as it is."

Tate's shoulders were tense, and though he kept his eyes on the road and his hands on the wheel, Garrett could *feel* his brother stewing over there on the other side of the gearshift. Clearly, he'd picked up on the gist of the conversation.

"I'll be in touch," Garrett told Nan mildly.

"Make it soon," was Nan's answer. In the next moment, she clicked off.

Garrett shut his phone, tucked it away.

Both he and Tate were silent for a long time.

Scenery rolled by, but the trailer and the flatbed truck veiled most of it in one continuous cloud of road dust.

"What I said before," Tate began gruffly, flexing his fingers on the steering wheel.

Garrett noticed that the knuckles were white. "Yeah?" he prompted, when his brother stopped talking, right in the middle of a sentence. He was always doing that, Tate was, but Garrett did it, too, and so did Austin.

It seemed to run in the family.

"About needing some help from you and Austin, I mean," Tate said, then shut up again.

Winding up this conversation was going to be a delicate process, Garrett figured, like pulling porcupine quills out of tender flesh.

"Yeah," Garrett said, keeping the conversational door ajar. "I remember."

The tires of the truck thunked over the ruts in the road, and then the cattle guard.

"I didn't mind it so much before," Tate confessed. "Before Libby and I got together, I mean, and Audrey and Ava were spending every other week with their mother, but now—" He turned his head briefly, met Garrett's eyes. "I was so lonesome back then, I was glad to put in the hours."

Garrett felt something thicken in his throat. For Tate, who had always played his cards close to his vest, this was unprecedented. "And now?"

"Now, I want a life, Garrett. With Libby, with the kids." He drew a deep breath, huffed it out. "I love this place. It's been in the family for better than a hundred years. But I'd rather sell my share and move on than kill myself trying to run it alone."

"You'd *sell?*" Garrett couldn't believe his ears. The Silver Spur was home. There were generations of Mc-Kettricks buried in the private cemetery just a mile from the house, including their parents. Their own kin had fought and died to *hold on to* that ranch for over a hundred years, through droughts and the Dirty '30s, a dozen recessions and two world wars. And Tate was willing to *pull out?*

"Like I said," Tate told him gruffly. "I love this ranch. But I love Libby and the kids a lot more."

"You know damn well some big consortium would buy the place in a heartbeat—open the oil wells up again— clear out all the cowpunchers and their families—"

Tate didn't answer.

They'd reached the place where they had to pull over, help unload the horses from the other truck, mount up and ride in. Once they got out of Tate's rig, there would be no privacy.

So Garrett stayed put.

And when Tate moved to open his door, Garrett got him by the arm and held on, steely-strong.

"I thought better of you, Tate," he ground out. "I really thought better of you."

"What the hell do you mean by that?" Tate snapped, turning to face Garrett straight on.

"You'd never sell your share of the Silver Spur. You know Nan offered me a job just now, and you're trying to goad me into turning it down."

The look in Tate's eyes came as near to contempt as Garrett had ever seen, at least in his own brother's face. "You know what, Garrett?" he asked, his voice low and dismissive. "If you think I operate like that, well, you can just go to hell."

"Tate—"

Tate turned away, shoved the door open and got out. Slammed it behind him.

Not to be outdone, Garrett slammed the door on *his* side, too.

Charlie Bates, the man who'd no doubt expected to be ranch foreman after Pablo Ruiz died, stood behind the horse trailer, giving orders as the animals were led down the ramp, one after another. His small eyes darted from Tate to Garrett and back to Tate again, and a weird feeling burrowed into Garrett's stomach lining like a red-hot worm.

"You two look fit to butcher frozen beef without a knife," Bates observed. "Is there something I ought to know?"

Tate wouldn't look at Garrett, but he glowered at Bates. "When I feel inclined to discuss my private life with you," he said, "you'll be the first one I tell."

Bates's features seemed to contort a little, but it might have been an illusion, Garrett decided. The man wasn't exactly the expressive type.

Garrett's horse came down the ramp, saddled, and he took the reins from the hand of the cowboy leading the animal and swung up onto its back.

"Let's get this show on the road," he said, echoing words he'd often heard his dad utter, back in the day. "We're burnin' daylight."

Bates got on his own horse, made it bump sides with Garrett's.

"You giving the orders now, Dos?" Bates asked.

Dos. Garrett hadn't been called "Two" since he couldn't remember when, and the reference to his place in the McKettrick pecking order pissed him off, especially coming from Charlie Bates.

"Some of them," he answered, adjusting his hat.

Bates spat tobacco, careful to just miss Garrett and his horse. "And what would those be?" he drawled.

"Well, one of them would be to mind your own business."

"That so?" Bates grinned. Spat again, coming closer this time. "There's another?"

"Yeah," Garrett said. "Clean up."

With that, he rode away, just naturally falling in alongside Tate and his horse, even though they weren't speaking to each other at present.

CHAPTER FIFTEEN

ALL THAT MORNING, the call from Gordon nibbled at the back of Julie's mind, making concentration doubly difficult. Was it true that Calvin had been calling his dad without telling her? And if so, why?

Was something troubling Calvin—how could she not have noticed?—and why had he confided in Gordon, a virtual stranger, and not in her?

Okay, there were things a boy didn't want to tell his mom, but Calvin could have talked to Libby or to Paige. He had a good relationship with Tate too, and Garrett, if he'd wanted to confide in a man.

Why would he choose Gordon?

Julie was burning to speak to Calvin, make sure everything was all right in his small but busy world, reassure him if he was frightened or disturbed about something.

But she still had classes to teach, and the first round of tryouts scheduled for that afternoon and evening. Plus, she'd promised Rachel she'd have a word with Ron Strivens, try to smooth his pride-ruffled feathers, possibly get him to understand the difference between neighborly help and charity.

And frankly, that galled her a little—no, a *lot*.

Men and their damnable pride. She had too much to

do already, and now she'd committed herself to yet another task, one that would probably prove impossible.

By the time lunch hour rolled around, Julie was, as the old saying went, fit to be tied.

Even deep breathing, usually her mainstay, didn't help.

Instead of eating in the cafeteria or the teacher's lounge, Julie ducked into her tiny office in the darkened auditorium, got out her cell phone and called Gordon back.

"Julie?" he said, sounding surprised.

"I hope this isn't a bad time," Julie replied, and then wished she'd said something else. *Anything* else. It wasn't as if her ex would be doing her some big favor by taking her call. *He'd* been the one to initiate things, not her.

"I'm straddling the ridgepole on a roof at the moment," Gordon said, with a smile in his voice. "Nailing down shingles."

Julie remembered that Gordon worked in construction now. "I guess I could call back later," she said uncertainly. There was the school day to finish, then the first set of tryouts for *Kiss Me Kate*, then picking up Calvin, getting him through his bath and his prayers.

As much as she wanted to ask her little boy about calling Gordon—it was paramount for Calvin to understand that he'd done nothing wrong by telephoning his father—there probably wouldn't be time or energy for it. Not that night, at least.

"Julie," Gordon said quickly, earnestly, "stay on the line. Please. I'm wearing a headpiece, so I've got both hands free for hanging on."

Julie smiled at that, a smile muted to sadness by

memories of another time and place, when she and Gordon had expected to be together forever.

Or, at least, that had been *her* expectation. Gordon's take on the situation might have been entirely different from hers, right from the very beginning.

"I'm here," she said, quietly and at some length.

Gordon's voice was gruff when he replied. "About that phone call this morning," he said. "I'm sorry, Julie. I didn't mean to imply that you were—well—that I think there's anything wrong with the way you're raising our son. From what little I've seen of him—and I know that's my own fault and not yours—Calvin is a great kid."

Julie's eyes burned. Furious heartache rose up into her throat and expanded there, painfully.

Our son, Gordon had said.

The phrase made her feel fiercely territorial, a tigress backed into a corner with her cub, so it was probably a good thing that she was too choked up to speak.

She might not have been able to hold back all the damning questions she wanted to hurl at Gordon Pruett in those wretched moments: *How dare you say* our son? *Where were you when he nearly died of an asthma attack during Thanksgiving dinner? Where were you when he was teething, when he had the flu and couldn't keep anything down? Where were you when he was asking why he didn't have a dad to take him camping and fishing, like his friend Justin does?*

"Hey," Gordon said, when she didn't speak. "Are you still there?"

Julie managed to croak out a "Yes."

There was a pause, then Gordon launched cheerfully into the real reason he'd gotten in touch with her that morning, when she was driving to work. "My folks are visiting Dixie and me next week, and they want to meet Calvin." He paused, reining it in a little. "If that's okay with you, I mean."

Julie straightened her spine. Drew a deep breath and let it out without making a sound. "It depends on what you have in mind," she replied, pleasantly surprised by how calm and together she sounded. Everything inside her seemed to be jostling about, competing for a chance to jump onto a hamster wheel and run like hell. "I think it would be wonderful for Calvin to meet his grandparents."

On her side of the family, there was only Marva, since her father was gone. Marva was an interesting grandmother, in an Auntie Mame sort of way—but there was no getting around the undeniable fact that she was a character.

The one and only Marva.

"But?" Gordon prodded, not unkindly.

Julie sighed, but this time she made no effort to be quiet about it. "But you'll all have to come here, to Blue River. And if I can't be there personally, throughout the visit, then I want one of my sisters to be."

"I'm not planning on kidnapping the little guy, Julie," Gordon said, his tone reasonable, but shot through with some vexation, too. "My mom and dad have never seen him."

Whose fault is that? demanded the part of Julie's brain she was trying so hard to control.

"Those are the terms, Gordon."

"Take it or leave it?" Gordon asked, sadly amused.

"Pretty much, yeah," Julie answered.

"Okay," Gordon agreed. "We'll book a couple of

rooms at the Amble On Inn, then, and drive down from Dallas on Friday—Thursday if I can get the time off. I'll let you know when the plans are firmed up."

"Okay," Julie said.

Gordon chuckled. "Julie?"

"What?"

"I know it's hard, adjusting to my being back in your life, but I'm not your enemy. I'm not trying to steal Calvin away, or turn him against you. I blew it, big time, and I'm the first to admit it. You'll never know how much I regret not being there f . Calvin and for you, because if there are words to describe it, they're ones I've never learned." A pause, an indrawn breath, a sigh. "I just want a chance to know my son, Julie. That's all. Just to know him."

"And your parents," Julie pointed out, strangely compelled to cross t's and dot i's.

In all the time they were together, she and Gordon, he'd never introduced her to them. She'd wondered, back then and not very often, if it was because he was ashamed, either of dear old Mom and Dad—or of her.

The wild, unconventional girl from Blue River, Texas.

Full of spirit and confidence in those days, either singing and dancing with professional theater companies or waiting tables between semesters of college, always paying her own way, Julie had never *seriously* entertained the possibility that Gordon's folks might not approve of her.

She did now.

"And my parents," Gordon affirmed.

They said their awkward goodbyes then, and, mercifully, the call ended.

Julie had barely caught her breath when Libby dialed in. Calvin, through with kindergarten for the day, would be over at the community center by now, no doubt listening to a story or scaling the walls of the remarkably authentic toy castle Tate and his daughters had donated.

Unless something was wrong.

"Hey, Julie," Libby said.

Anxiety washed over Julie. "Is everyone all right?"

"Yes," Libby was quick to reply. "Mostly, anyway. I just got a call from the school—Audrey and Ava seem to have come down with identical cases of the flu. I'm off to pick them up in a couple of minutes, and I'll be taking them by the clinic, of course, since they're running fevers. What it all boils down to is this—I don't think we should expose Calvin."

Julie closed her eyes for a moment, already shaking her head. "No," she agreed.

"I know you were counting on us to look after Calvin until you get home from the tryouts for the play—"

"Don't worry about it, Lib," Julie broke in. "I'll figure something out. Maybe Paige can help."

"I'm so sorry, Jules."

"Don't be sorry," Julie said. "Just take care of Audrey and Ava. And let me know what the doctor says, will you?"

Libby promised a full report and rang off, only to call again before Julie had even managed to set the phone down.

"Garrett's here," Libby told Julie, without any sort of preamble. "He says he can pick Calvin up and bring him to you or out to the ranch—whatever works for you."

Julie's heart did a funny little flip, and she silently scolded herself for making a big deal out of nothing.

"Ask him to please bring Calvin here," she said. "To the auditorium, I mean."

Libby relayed this to Garrett, then asked, "What time?"

"Three?" Julie said. Classes were dismissed at 2:45; this way, she'd have fifteen minutes to "unfrazzle," a term her friend and fellow teacher Helen used, before coming face-to-face with Garrett McKettrick.

Libby repeated the time to Garrett, then confirmed, "He'll be there."

"Tell him thanks," Julie told her sister. "I really appreciate this. And don't forget I want an update on the twins, once they've seen the doctor."

"I won't forget," Libby promised.

Julie speed-dialed the community center, told one of the day-care workers that Calvin wouldn't be riding the bus home with the McKettrick twins the way he usually did. Instead, Garrett would stop by to pick him up.

"This is going to sound real silly," Soliel Roberts said, "since you and Garrett and I all grew up together and everything, but I'm going to need written permission to turn Calvin over to anybody besides you or Libby or Paige, dated and signed. You can fax it over, if you like. The fax number is 555-7386."

"I'll do that," Julie replied gently. "Thanks, Soliel."

Soliel said she was welcome, goodbyes were exchanged and Julie rooted in her lunch bag for the half sandwich she'd packed that morning, in the ranch-house kitchen. She'd already wolfed down the apple during her morning break.

The afternoon passed quickly, and Julie was grateful, considering that the second part of the day often seemed twice as long as the first.

At three o'clock, she was consulting with Mrs. Chambers, the music teacher, and a few of the most dedicated kids were already lolling in the front row of seats, texting each other while they waited to get up on stage and strut their stuff.

Calvin came racing down the middle aisle, his face flushed with excitement and the chill of a fall afternoon. "Garrett came and got me at school today!" he shouted, unable to contain his exuberance. "And it was *just like having a dad!*"

Julie's cheeks stung a little, though she smiled and bent down for Calvin's hello hug. Over the top of his head, she caught sight of Garrett, standing in the shadows at the back of the auditorium.

She couldn't see his face, but that didn't matter.

The familiar jolt went through her anyway.

While Calvin remained at the base of the stage, showing Mrs. Chambers his papers from school, Julie approached Garrett.

"Thank you," she said, peering cautiously at his badly swollen right eye. From a distance, she hadn't been able to see the damage. Up close, he looked as though something with hooves had kicked him in the face. "What happened to you?"

Garrett folded his arms, and his mouth—oh, his dangerous *mouth*—crooked up at one side. "I ran into a door?" he said.

"You were in a fight," Julie guessed aloud, keeping her voice down so Calvin, Mrs. Chambers and the theater kids wouldn't hear.

"You should see the other guy," Garrett joked.

She wanted to touch him. She wanted to fuss and fret and fetch an ice pack.

Which was why she was so careful to keep her distance.

"Does it hurt?" She couldn't resist asking him that.

He chuckled. "A little. Mostly, I'm numb."

"I appreciate your bringing Calvin over from school."

"It might be a long haul for the little guy," Garrett observed. "Hanging around here until you're done, I mean. I could take him on home if that would be better."

Julie glanced back at Calvin, knew he'd be better off at the house, with Esperanza and Garrett, rather than hanging around the auditorium until all hours, either bored out of his skull or creating a distraction or both.

"I couldn't ask you—or Esperanza—"

Garrett silenced her by resting the tip of one index finger against her lips, so lightly and so briefly that afterward she was never sure that he'd touched her at all. "You're not asking," he said. *"I'm offering."*

Julie's heart filled with something warm and sweet, and then overflowed. She hoped Garrett hadn't guessed that, just by looking at her. He'd think she was a sentimental sap if he had.

Just then, Calvin raced up the aisle and leaned against Julie's side. "I'm hungry," he said.

Garrett looked down at him, ruffled his hair. "Me, too," he agreed. "What do you say we go home and see if we can charm Esperanza into rustling up some grub?"

Calvin practically vibrated with eagerness. "That would be cool," he said. Then he looked up at Julie, his little face screwed up with studious concern, his glasses slightly askew, as they so often were. "Aren't you hungry, too, Mom?" he asked.

If she hadn't known it would embarrass her little

boy, she would have pulled him into her arms, then and there, and hugged him tight.

"I'll be fine," she said. "Somebody ordered pizza."

Calvin mulled that over. "Harry probably needs to go outside," he concluded at last. "And he'll be needing some kibble and some fresh water pretty soon."

"I'm sure you're right," Julie replied seriously.

"You don't mind if I go on to the Silver Spur with Garrett, then?" Calvin sounded so hopeful that Julie ached. "Instead of staying here with you?"

"I don't mind," Julie said, choking up a little.

Just then, her gaze connected with Garrett's.

"Have you heard anything from Libby? About Audrey and Ava, I mean?" Julie's cell phone was in the bottom of her purse; if her sister had called with news about Tate's girls and their twin cases of flu, she hadn't heard the ring.

"Tate called a little while ago," Garrett said. "It's the usual prescription—bed rest, children's medication and plenty of fluids. The twins will be fine in a day or two."

"But in the meantime," Calvin interjected, with energetic distaste, "they're really *germy.* I could be *contaged* just by being in the same room when they cough or sneeze."

"Sounds ominous," Garrett remarked, giving Calvin's shoulder a light punch, guy-like.

"Let's go," Calvin said, obviously impatient to be on his way, with Garrett.

Inside Julie, sorrow squeezed hard. It would be *years* before Calvin was old enough to leave home. Why was she always so conscious that the clock was ticking?

Garrett ducked his head slightly, to look into her face. "You okay?" he asked.

Julie swallowed hard, then nodded. Smiled. "I'll see you both later—around eight o'clock, I expect."

"See you then," Garrett said. His eyes seemed to caress her, warming her flesh, awakening her tired nerves.

Ten minutes ago, she'd been looking forward to the end of the day, when she could take a warm bath and then crawl into her bed.

Now she was only interested in the bed, and it was *Garrett's* bed she wanted to slip into, not hers.

Julie shook off a cloud of stars, nodded again, then bent to kiss the top of Calvin's head. "Be good," she said.

Calvin gave a sigh that seemed to rise from the soles of his little high-top sneakers. "I'm *always* good," he said. "It gets boring."

Garrett chuckled at that. "Come on, pardner," he said, getting Calvin by the hood of his new nylon jacket and steering him in the general direction of the main doors. "We've got things to do out on the ranch—nothing like doing chores to put an end to boredom—and your mom has things to do here."

"Garrett?" His name came fragile from her throat, shimmering and iridescent, like a soap bubble.

He'd turned away, engaged with Calvin, who was already recounting some incident that had taken place on the playground at school, but when Julie spoke, Garrett turned his head to look back at her.

She moved close to him, unable to help herself, touched her fingertips to the bruised skin under his eye. "You'll tell me what happened? Later on?"

"I'll tell you what happened," Garrett said, almost sighing the words.

Moments later, he and Calvin were gone.

Julie turned back to the task at hand—back to the

kids and the stage and Mrs. Chambers's piano-pounding musical style.

Kiss Me Kate wasn't going to cast itself, after all.

UPSTAIRS IN HIS own kitchen, Garrett hoisted Calvin onto the countertop, where the kid could watch the proceedings without being too close to anything hot or sharp. Buzzing with kid-energy, Calvin bounced the heels of his shoes against the cupboard door, stirring the dog, Harry, to a three-legged frenzy of yelping excitement.

"Whoa," Garrett said good-naturedly. "Sit still."

Calvin stopped kicking. Earlier, they'd fed the horses together, out in the barn, and the boy's glasses had fogged over from the cold. Now they were clear again, magnifying his pale blue eyes.

"Do you think the doctor made Audrey and Ava get *shots?*" he asked Garrett, looking horrified at the prospect.

The dog quieted down, went back to his kibble bowl.

"Don't know," Garrett said, peeling the foil off the pan of chicken tamales Esperanza had left downstairs in the oven for supper. Turned out, she had a meeting at church.

"I *hate* shots," Calvin told him.

"Well, now," Garrett said reasonably, taking two plates down from a cupboard, "a cowboy always takes his medicine, if the doctor says he needs it."

Calvin considered that, his eyes wide. "Did you ever cry, when you were little, and you had to have a shot?"

"No," Garrett answered honestly, "but I ran out of the clinic once, when I was about your age, and hid in the men's restroom of a gas station across the street, until my mom walked right in there and got me by the ear."

He grinned at the memory.

He'd barely felt the injection, given a few minutes later, he'd been so impressed that his mother wasn't afraid to march herself straight into a men's room to collect him.

"And she made you get the shot?"

"It had to be done," Garrett said, dishing up tamales.

Plates filled, he hoisted Calvin back down off the counter and set him on his feet.

They washed up, then took their meal to the table over by the wall of windows looking out over the dark range. The boy ate a few bites and then started blinking rapidly, like he had something in his eyes.

Garrett hid a smile, aware that Calvin was having a hard time staying awake.

"You tuckered out?" he asked the little guy.

Calvin yawned widely, set down his fork. "Yeah," he admitted. "But I don't want to go to bed yet, because my mom isn't home and Esperanza isn't either, and this is a big house to be alone in."

He was there, and Austin probably was, too, which meant that, technically, Calvin wouldn't be alone, though he might as well have been, Garrett supposed, considering the size of the place.

"I guess you could stretch out on my sofa till your mom gets back," Garrett offered.

"Would the lights be out?" Calvin asked. "Would you be right there?"

"I'd be right there," Garrett confirmed.

"In the living room, where I could see you?"

"In the living room, where you could see me."

Calvin looked relieved. "I guess that would be all right, then," he decided.

Then, "You wouldn't tell anybody that I'm scared of the dark, would you?"

The earnest expression in the little boy's face touched something in Garrett, caused another shift, one he couldn't begin to describe. It roughened his voice, the strange emotion he felt then.

"I wouldn't tell," he promised.

Calvin pushed his plate away. "I'm full," he said.

"No need to keep eating, then," Garrett replied.

He got a soft blanket and a pillow from the linen closet in the hallway, and made a bed for Calvin on the sofa. Lamps burned at either end, dimmed down to a yellow glow. Garrett switched on the TV, with the volume low, and kicked back in his favorite chair.

The dog immediately started trying to jump up onto the sofa with Calvin. It was a pitiful sight, given that the poor critter was missing a leg.

Garrett got up, hoisted the mutt onto the couch with Calvin and sat down again.

As usual, TV didn't have much to offer, but Garrett had made a promise—he'd stay with Calvin until his mother came home—so he flicked through the channels until he found a rodeo-retrospective on ESPN and settled on that.

His brain immediately divided itself into three working parts.

One level focused on the rodeo unfolding in front of his eyes.

Another, the lovely problem of Julie Remington, her boy and her dog, and all the ways they might change his life.

Still another went over and over that day, out on the range. They'd fixed fences, he and Tate and the other cowboys, but they'd found nothing that might lead them to the rustlers.

Or the sons of bitches who'd shot those six cattle and left them for the flies. The recollection sickened Garrett; it was hard to fathom why anybody would kill a living thing for no reason.

Nan's call had complicated everything, of course.

Fired or not, he knew he'd have to help her straighten out the mess Morgan and the pole dancer were stirring up. Not only had Garrett worked for her husband since law school, his mother and Nan had been college roommates and very close friends.

As far as he knew, Morgan hadn't hired anybody to replace him as yet—the august senator from the great state of Texas had been too busy romancing the pole dancer to do anything about the sudden vacancy on his staff, other than ask other staffers to cover the responsibilities that had been Garrett's.

It was only logical for Garrett to take up the slack.

Besides, he liked Nan. She was mentally, emotionally and physically sound. She knew the issues. She knew the people, cared about what they wanted and what was best for them, not only in the present, but generations hence.

Looking back over the years he'd worked for Senator Morgan Cox, Garrett was astounded at how many dots he hadn't noticed, let alone connected.

Nan was the strong one, not Morgan.

Nan was the force of nature, the skilled politician, the one with A Plan.

Why hadn't he seen that?

The thing Nan hadn't wanted to discuss over the cell phone? She was planning to call in all her markers and run for Morgan's Senate seat when the next election rolled around in a little over two years.

She meant to hire him, Garrett, as her right-hand man.

McKettrick, Garrett told himself, glowering at the TV screen above the fireplace, *not much gets by you. You have the political instincts of a pump handle.*

On the couch, Calvin stirred, made a soft, kid-sound in his sleep.

Garrett's heart actually seized.

He closed his eyes, just to shut out the light for a few moments.

When he opened them, Julie was sitting on the arm of his chair, smiling down at him.

"So," she whispered, keeping her voice down so Calvin wouldn't wake up, "what happened to your eye? Remember, you promised you'd tell me."

Garrett chuckled hoarsely. Julie Remington had no idea how down-home sexy she was. No idea at all.

"Either Tate or Austin punched me," he said.

Julie's wonderful, changeling eyes widened. She moved to smooth his hair back from his forehead, hesitated, then went ahead and did it.

Electricity shot through Garrett; all of a sudden, he was wide awake, every nerve reporting for duty, ready for action.

"'Either Tate or Austin'?" She smiled. Her fingertips rested lightly on his bruises, and he felt some kind of sacred energy surge through him. "You don't know which one?"

Garrett grinned. If the boy and the dog hadn't been sleeping on the couch, just a few feet away, he would have tugged Julie onto his lap. "Could have been either one," he said. "They were about to go at it, and I was fool enough to get between them."

She laughed, and the sound was silvery and pure, almost spiritual, like Christmas bells ringing out over miles of unmarked snow.

"Did Calvin behave himself?" she asked.

God, she was so beautiful. There are perfect moments in life, he thought, and this was one of them.

"He's a good kid," Garrett answered presently, and somewhat hoarsely, with a nod. "Did you know he's scared of the dark?"

"Most kindergarteners are," Julie said.

"I guess you've got a point."

Julie looked over at her son, curled up on the couch with his dog. The perfect moments just kept on coming, and that was fine with Garrett. "Would you mind carrying him downstairs for me?"

Garrett was on his feet. He would have carried the whole *sofa* downstairs, kid, dog and all, if she'd asked him to. He'd have staggered under the weight of just about anything, in fact, just for the light in her eyes and the way she held her mouth, as if she wanted to smile but wouldn't let herself do it.

"Sure," he said. He scooped the boy up, blanket and all.

"Is my mom home?" Calvin asked sleepily.

Julie fetched the boy's glasses from the end table where he'd left them. "Your mom is definitely home," she told her son.

Harry jumped down to follow.

"Keep the dog here," Garrett said, at the top of the staircase leading down into the ranch-house kitchen. "I'll come back for him."

Instead, Julie brought Harry downstairs herself.

The kitchen was dimly lit, and Garrett had no trouble navigating it.

When he laid Calvin down on his bed, his arms ached, objecting to the letting go.

Garrett waited in the sitting room while Julie settled her son in for the night, murmuring mother-words.

Garrett McKettrick marveled.

All his life, he'd wanted to be a U.S. senator and, eventually, president.

Now, incomprehensibly, he couldn't seem to think beyond being a husband, a father and the master of a three-legged dog.

What the hell was wrong with him?

JULIE DECIDED, once she'd tucked Calvin in and kissed him good-night, Harry properly settled in his place at the foot of the bed, that it would be all right to fuss over Garrett's black eye *just a little*. As long as she didn't get carried away, what harm could it do?

She was pleased to find him still in the apartment when she returned from Calvin's room.

"Now," she said, "let's have a better look at that eye."

"I'm all right," Garrett said, though not with a lot of certainty.

She took his hand—where had her bone-deep tiredness gone?—and led him into the big kitchen.

"Sit down," she said.

Garrett dropped into a chair.

Briskly—*just call me Nurse Julie*, she thought, with a silent chuckle—she found a plastic bag with a zip-top, filled it with ice and approached him.

Garrett winced when she touched the ice pack to his eye, then relaxed with a long sigh.

Julie smiled, overwhelmed by tenderness.

Garrett took hold of the ice pack, lowered it and buried his face in her middle, just long enough to start a wildfire blazing through her veins.

"I'll be going away in a few days," he said, very quietly.

Time itself seemed to stop the instant Garrett spoke those words.

At least, for Julie it did.

Why was she so shocked, so shaken? Garrett McKettrick was—Garrett McKettrick. He had another life, away from the ranch, away from Blue River.

Away from her.

"Julie?" Garrett's hands rested on her hips, holding her in place. Not that she could have moved to break away; she was in statue-mode. Frozen.

She didn't answer.

Garrett pulled her down, onto his lap.

She did her best not to look at him; that was all the resistance she could muster at the moment, it seemed.

She'd worn her hair up that day, in what Paige called her "schoolmarm do," secured by a sterling silver clip.

Garrett opened the clip, and all those spirally curls tumbled down.

"So go," she finally managed to croak out. "Nobody expects you to stay."

"Will you look at me?"

"Actually, no. I'd rather not."

He took her chin in one hand, gently, and turned her head. Short of squinching her eyes shut like a child, there was no way to avoid meeting his gaze.

"Senator Cox is about to resign," he said, very quietly. "That's a very big deal, Julie. I have to be there."

"Okay," Julie said.

"I'd like you to come with me."

She blinked, startled. "I can't," she managed, after a long moment of wild consideration. "There's Calvin, and my job—"

"We're talking about one or two days, max," Garrett reasoned. Splaying the fingers of his right hand, he combed them through her hair. "Think about it, Julie."

"I couldn't," she said.

"Just the two of us," Garrett drawled, his voice dream-like, almost hypnotic. "You and me. Together. Naked a lot of the time."

Julie swallowed hard.

"Think about it," Garrett repeated.

As if she could *help* thinking about it.

CHAPTER SIXTEEN

NAN'S PHONE CALL woke Garrett in the middle of the night.

He sat up, grumbling, and groped for the receiver beside his bed.

"Yeah?" he growled.

"You've got to come," she said.

Sleep still fogged Garrett's head. He'd been dreaming about Julie, the sort of erotic—and thwarted—dream it wasn't easy to leave behind.

"What? Where—?"

"There's been an accident, Garrett," Mrs. Cox replied, and now he could tell that she was struggling to maintain control. "Morgan and the—the woman, Mandy? They were skiing at some resort in Oregon—"

He felt a sickening sense of déjà vu. He couldn't help remembering another call, in the middle of another night, about another accident, of a different kind. That time, the caller had been Tate, and the news was beyond bad.

Their folks had been airlifted to Houston, after a car crash.

Neither was expected to live.

And neither had.

Garrett swore silently and swung his legs over the side of the bed, groping for the jeans he'd tossed aside earlier, after tearing himself away from Julie. God, he'd wanted to share her bed, spend the whole night loving her, wake up with her beside him. But there was Calvin to consider. He was not quite five years old; he couldn't be expected to understand.

She hadn't said Morgan was dead, he remembered. She'd said there had been an accident. "Exactly what happened, Nan?" he asked. "And how bad is it?"

"As I understand it, Mandy is all right," Nan answered woodenly, sounding detached now, as though she were watching the event unfold on a movie screen no one else could see. Of course she must have been in shock. "Morgan—Morgan is in bad shape. You know what a good skier he was—*is*—but—"

"Nan?" Garrett broke in, firmly but not unkindly. "What happened?"

She gave a strangled little laugh, void of humor and hard to hear. "He was probably showing off for that—that *pole dancer*. Skiing too fast—on a trail too advanced for a middle-aged man, out of shape—" Nan stopped. Made that sound again. Then, "Morgan collided with a tree, Garrett. He's—he's comatose."

Bile scalded the back of Garrett's throat. *Comatose.* He struggled into his pants, wedged the cordless receiver between his shoulder and his ear.

"But he's alive," Nan choked out. "People *do* come out of comas—sometimes."

Garrett closed his eyes, but the images wouldn't be shut out. Morgan Cox had been a brilliant man, a Rhodes scholar. Now, it seemed, he had been reduced to a vegetative state.

"Where are you?"

She named a hospital in Austin. "I asked them to

bring him here," she said. "I just hope he makes it, so I can say goodbye, tell Morgan I f-forgive him—"

Nan broke down then.

"I'll be there as soon as I can," Garrett told her, aching inside. "Hold on, Nan." He paused. The question had to be asked. "Are there reporters?"

Another ragged sob burst from Nan's throat. "Of *course* there are reporters," she blurted out. "There are *always* reporters."

"No statements," Garrett warned. It was a real bitch, trying to talk on the phone and get dressed at the same time. He felt like a one-legged man attempting to stomp out a campfire. "Don't say *anything*. I'll handle the press when I get there."

"Hurry," Nan pleaded.

Garrett said goodbye, thumbed the off button and tossed the receiver onto his rumpled bed.

He didn't shower and he didn't shave.

He just pulled on a shirt, socks and boots, grabbed his cell phone, and scrambled out of his room and down the stairs into the kitchen.

Austin was sitting at the table in a pair of sweatpants, shirtless, squinting at the screen of a laptop.

Seeing Garrett, he narrowed his eyes. "What the hell…?"

"Put a shirt on," Garrett snapped. "There's a lady in this house, and a little kid."

The admonition made Austin grin slightly, but his eyes were still troubled. "What's going on?"

"There's been a skiing accident," Garrett said, grabbing the Porsche keys from the hook next to the door leading into the garage. "Morgan isn't expected to live."

Austin gave a low whistle of exclamation, but he didn't say anything.

Even in his distracted state, Garrett noticed the haunted look that fell across his brother like a shadow, at the mention of the word *accident*. Of course, Austin was remembering the night their parents died.

They'd all taken the deaths hard, but Austin, maybe because he was the youngest, had taken them hardest of all.

"Do me a favor?" Garrett asked gruffly, about to go out the door, get in his Porsche and head for his Cessna.

"Sure," Austin said. A news site flickered on the screen of his laptop now, bluish in the dim light. "What do you need?"

"I know you and Tate are getting on each other's nerves and you want to lock horns," Garrett said, choosing his words with as much care as his rush would allow. "But Tate needs our help, Austin. It's not just this rustling thing—he's talking about selling out and moving off the ranch."

Austin's mouth dropped open. He closed it, then blurted, *"Selling out?"* A pause, rife with blinking disbelief. "He can't be serious."

"I've got a feeling our big brother is *dead* serious, Austin. The ranch matters to Tate, but Libby and the kids are more important, and he wants more husband-and-dad time."

Austin still looked as though he'd been sucker punched. "He'd never do it," he said, pale. Half sitting and half standing now, unable, it seemed, to make up his mind and choose one direction, up or down. "Tate would *never* sell his share of the Silver Spur!"

Garrett sighed. "We've got a choice to make—you

and I," he said in parting. "Either we step up and help Tate run this place, or he moves on."

Austin left the table, followed Garrett all the way out to the Porsche. Stood there, barefooted and bare-chested, while Garrett pushed a button to raise the garage door behind his car and started the engine.

"I could come along," Austin offered, when Garrett rolled down his window. "If you need somebody to ride shotgun or something—"

Garrett rummaged up a smile. "Thanks," he said, shaking his head even as he spoke. "It'll be better if you stay here and help Tate as much as you can. When I get back, the three of us will sit down and figure out what to do next."

Austin swallowed visibly, then nodded, stepping back from the Porsche and giving a halfhearted wave of one hand as Garrett backed out.

He reached the airstrip within five minutes, and after a quick safety inspection and an engine warm-up, Garrett drove his plane out of its hangar, lined up the nose and zoomed down the short, bumpy runway.

Once aloft, Garrett set his mind on reaching Austin.

He'd called Nan back on the drive to the airstrip, given her an ETA and asked her to have Troy meet him with a car.

In the near distance, the small grid of lights that made up the town of Blue River twinkled in the darkness.

The river and the creeks looked like black ribbons, snaking through the night, silvery with the moon's glow.

Tate's place was dark, Garrett noticed.

That gave him a lonely feeling.

He automatically scanned the horizon, though he could have charted the course to Austin or any one of a dozen other places with his eyes shut. And that was when he spotted the snarl of headlights over near the dry riverbed he and Tate had checked out a day or two before.

He banked in that direction, frowning, not wanting to take the time, knowing he wouldn't be able to see much from the air, heading there anyway.

He swung low over the trailer of a semi surrounded by a number of smaller rigs. Several sets of headlights—all but the semi's—blinked out like fireflies going into hiding, but not before Garrett spotted the dark figures of men scattering to flee.

He reached for the handset of the radio, but drew back without taking hold of it. Instead, he fumbled for his cell phone, jammed into his shirt pocket just before he left the house.

He thumbed in Tate's number, then reconsidered and cut off the call.

The rigs below scattered, driving blind. Garrett made an executive decision and stuck to the semi, its trailer probably loaded down with McKettrick cattle.

Tate called him back in two seconds, half-asleep and in no mood to be gracious. "What?" he growled. "You call, you let the phone ring *once*, and then you *hang up?*"

"Sorry about that," Garrett said. "Second thoughts." If he mentioned the semi to Tate now, the damn fool would probably come running out here in the middle of the night, planning to chase the crooks to the farthest corner of hell if he had to—and maybe get hurt or killed in the process.

Below, the semi driver jolted toward the main road, traveling fast, over rough ground.

Garrett hoped the cattle jammed into the back were all right. At the same time, it gave him that old rodeo feeling, tailing that fleeing semi from the air. Even with all that was going on, he could barely hold back a whoop of pure yeehaw.

"You're not getting off that easy," Tate said. "Why did you call me?"

It was easy to tell that he was a man in love, because as pissed-off as he was, he still tried to keep his voice down so he wouldn't wake Libby.

"Garrett," he demanded, in a loud whisper, "are you drunk or something?"

Garrett laughed outright then. It was a broken sound, part tragedy. "No," he said. "I'm not drunk." He was going to have to give up something, he could see that; Tate wouldn't leave him alone until he did. "I'm on my way to Austin," he said. He told Tate what little he knew about the senator's tragic mishap on an Oregon ski slope.

"I'm really sorry," Tate said, when Garrett had finished.

Garrett didn't answer.

Below, the semi pulled onto the main road, heading south.

"Gotta go," Garrett said.

"I could meet you at the hospital—"

Garrett cut him off. "No," he replied, his voice gruff. "Look, I'll call you tomorrow. Bring you up to speed."

The brothers said their goodbyes, and rang off, and Garrett put through a quick call to Brent Brogan. Brent promised to send the state police after the semi, but without a license number or any identifying characteristics other than the direction the rig was headed in, there wasn't much hope.

Just then, there didn't seem to be a whole hell of a lot of hope for much of anything.

Garrett felt a raw and confounding sadness, brief in duration but carving deep, and it had little or nothing to do with the senator's tragedy.

Below, the semi lumbered right, onto a state highway.

The driver could be headed anywhere—Arizona, Oklahoma, or even toward the Mexican border.

Reluctantly, Garrett changed course.

He was needed in Austin.

It was still dark when he landed the plane. Troy, the senator's driver, waited on the tarmac, beside the usual Town Car.

The two men shook hands, and then Garrett sprinted around to the passenger side and slid into the front seat.

"Has the senator arrived yet?" he asked, dreading the answer, as Troy settled behind the wheel.

Troy nodded wearily. "He was holding on when I left the hospital, but as soon as they unhook all those machines—"

Garrett's voice was hoarse. "How's Nan?"

"Mrs. Cox is hanging in there."

"Have the kids been told?"

"I don't think so," Troy answered, with a shake of his head. "Mandy, now, she's been spilling her guts to the media. Telling them more than even *they* want to know, probably." With a thin attempt at a grin, he added, "What happened to your *face*, man?"

"I was kicked by a horse," Garrett lied.

Troy's eyes rounded, then rolled. "You are so full of shit," he said.

"I missed you, too," Garrett said, leaning to punch

his friend in the shoulder. "How long's it been since we've crossed paths, old buddy? Three days? A week?"

Troy laughed, but there was a note of harsh grief in the sound. "Damn," he muttered. "This is bad, Garrett."

"Yeah," Garrett agreed, tilting his head back and closing his eyes.

"The state police came to the house to tell Mrs. Cox the news in person," Troy said. He lived in an apartment over Nan and Morgan's garage, so he'd be available whenever a driver was needed. Technically, he was on call 24/7, but he had a lot of downtime, too. "I heard a ruckus, so I got out of bed and dressed and scrambled downstairs to find out what was going on." Troy thrust out sigh. "He's not going to make it, Garrett."

After that, there wasn't much else to talk about.

They arrived at the hospital within a few minutes, and Garrett noticed several news vans in the parking lot.

He sighed inwardly.

"You might as well go on home and get whatever rest you can manage," Garrett told Troy quietly, bracing himself inwardly and pushing open the car door. He hadn't missed dealing with reporters during his brief hiatus on the ranch. "However things come down, tomorrow is bound to be a real mother."

Troy hesitated, then nodded. "You tell Mrs. Cox to call if she needs me."

Garrett promised to pass the word, got out of the car, squared his shoulders and headed for the hospital entrance.

As expected, reporters and cameramen were waiting in the lobby, and Mandy Chante, tragic in her black stretch ski pants and fluffy pink sweater, was holding court.

Garrett shook his head, skirted the scene and headed for the elevators.

"That's some shiner, handsome," purred Charlene Bishop, a freelancer who sold mainly to the tabloids, stepping directly into his path. He and Charlene had dated for a while, a few years back, nothing serious. Last he'd heard, she was married to a chiropractor and trying to get pregnant.

Garrett smiled, took the woman lightly by the shoulders and eased her aside. "Nice to see you again, Charlene," he said, moving on toward the elevators. "How's the husband?"

She kept pace, managed to slip into the elevator beside him, along with a guy wearing a backwards baseball cap and balancing a huge camera on one shoulder.

"Turn that thing on," Garrett warned him, "and I'll shove it up your—nose."

The guy grinned. "I've been threatened with a lot worse than that in my time," he retorted.

"You want worse?" Garrett asked. "I can give you *worse.*"

"Testy," sniped Baseball Cap.

"Shut up, Leroy," Charlene said, elbowing the guy aside, shifting to stand toe-to-toe with Garrett, so her breasts pressed against his chest. "I need this story," she confided, looking up at him with enormous powder-blue eyes.

Garrett raised an eyebrow. "You didn't notice Mandy Chante in the lobby?" he asked. "You're slipping."

Charlene huffed in disgust. "All she's doing is blowing smoke up everybody's butt," she said, dismissing the other woman with a slight wave of one hand. "Look, freelancing is a tough racket. You know that." She stepped in close, so her breasts pressed into his chest, and wriggled slightly. "How about an exclusive, for old times' sake?"

Leroy crowed at that last part.

Garrett stepped back, irritated, but being careful not to let that show.

The elevator doors opened and he was the first one out.

Troy must have called ahead to let Nan know they'd arrived, because she appeared immediately, slipped her arm through Garrett's and rested her head against his upper arm for a moment.

Her silver hair was pulled back and secured with a barrette, and instead of her trademark designer suit, she wore baggy brown corduroy pants and a heavy beige sweater.

Leroy aimed the camera.

Garrett glared him into retreat.

And Charlene clicked alongside Garrett and Nan, the pointy heels of her shoes tap-tap-tapping on the corridor floor.

"Mrs. Cox," she said breathlessly, "is it true that the senator got a quickie divorce in Mexico and then turned right around and married Miss Chante? She—Miss Chante—says they were on their honeymoon when the accident happened—"

"Charlene," Garrett broke in.

She blinked up at him. "What?"

"Shut up."

"But—"

"Beat it, Charlene. I'll give you a statement later."

Charlene's plump pink lower lip wobbled. "You promise?"

"I promise," Garrett replied tightly.

A security guard was approaching, probably intending to eject Charlene and Leroy from the Intensive Care Unit.

"Where? When?" Charlene pressed, walking backward.

Garrett sighed, rattled off his cell number. "Call me in a couple of hours," he said. "I won't talk to anyone else first. You have my word."

Charlene scribbled down the number, rushed over in a last-minute burst of moxie and shoved a card at Garrett. "Here's my number," she said. "*You* call *me*."

Garrett nodded.

The security guard arrived, taking Charlene's elbow in one hand and the back of Leroy's T-shirt in the other and propelling them both into the elevator.

"Thank God you're here," Nan said wearily.

"How's Morgan?" Garrett asked.

"He died five minutes ago," Nan answered. "His... prospective bride wasn't with him at the time. She was too busy enjoying her fifteen minutes of fame downstairs, it would seem." Her gaze was faraway, and a faint smile, sadder than tears, tugged at the corner of her mouth. "*I* was with him, though. I held Morgan's hand and I told him I understood, and he should just go if he was ready—the children and I would be all right."

Garrett had to sit down. He found a chair over by the wall and dropped into it. "My God, Nan," he rasped out. "I'm sorry."

Nan's eyes swam with tears, but she managed a brave smile. "Me, too," she said, taking the chair beside Garrett's. "The children will be devastated, of course."

Garrett could only nod.

"He wouldn't have wanted to live," Nan went on quietly, resting her hands on her knees. Her spine was very straight, and she held her chin high. "He was much too badly hurt."

Garrett put his arm around the woman's shoulders.

She trembled, allowed herself to lean against him, though just for a moment. "We'll have to make some kind of statement soon," she said.

Garrett nodded again, at a loss for words.

Nan gave a teary smile and tilted her head to one side as she studied him.

"What?" Garrett asked.

"What happened to your eye?" Nan countered.

THE NEWS WAS all over the TV, all over the internet.

Senator Morgan Cox was dead.

His grieving mistress, Mandy Chante, was already angling for her own reality show.

Julie stared at the TV, a cup of Esperanza's coffee raised to her lips. They were in the ranch-house kitchen, Calvin still sleeping, Esperanza watching the morning news as she started breakfast.

Julie felt a jolt of emotion, all of it unidentifiable, when Garrett's head and shoulders filled the screen. His hair was rumpled, his right eye was blackened and nearly swollen shut, his clothes more suited to the barn or the range than national TV. On top of all that, he needed a shave.

Her heart turned over inside her.

I love you, she told him silently.

"Senator Cox passed away at 2:33 a.m.," he said, into a cluster of microphones. He looked weary and grief-stricken and Julie longed to put her arms around him, and hold him, and chase away all the reporters.

All the demons.

"Madre de Dios," Esperanza muttered, pausing to cross herself.

Julie continued to watch Garrett, willing him to be strong.

"Mommy?" Calvin stood in the doorway to the guest suite. He was still wearing his pajamas, his hair was mussed and his cheeks were too pink by at least three shades.

Plus, he rarely called her "Mommy" these days.

She'd been demoted to "Mom" sometime after his fourth birthday.

"I don't feel good," Calvin said. Then, to prove his point, he threw up.

Julie hurried to her son, and Esperanza switched off the TV set.

"He's burning up," Julie told Esperanza, resting the backs of her fingers against Calvin's forehead.

Esperanza rushed to fill a bucket and grab a cleaning rag. "Back to bed," she said. "There can be no going to school like this!"

Calvin vomited again.

"Oh, Calvin!" Julie cried, alarmed by the violence of his illness.

"Am I in trouble?" he asked desperately, blinking as he stared up at her.

"No," Julie said, gathering him to her, mess and all. "*No*, sweetie. Come on, let's get you into some clean pajamas and back in bed."

Calvin cried and then wailed.

Harry, ever sympathetic, whimpered his concern.

Julie swept her son up into her arms and carried him back to their bathroom. There, she quickly stripped him, sprayed him down in the bathtub and bundled him into fresh pajamas.

Calvin had quieted down by then, but Harry cried continuously, the poor thing. He seemed to think his little master was being punished for some horrible misdeed.

Julie had no more than tucked Calvin into bed when he threw up again, all over everything.

Because Audrey and Ava were still sick, and therefore in what amounted to quarantine, she'd planned to take the boy to town herself, drop him off for kindergarten before her first-period class, and bring him back to the high school until tryouts were over.

All that was clearly out of the question now.

While Esperanza changed Calvin, and the sheets and blankets on his bed, Julie showered and changed her own clothes, then made a quick call to Arthur Dulles. The principal wouldn't be happy, since the tasks of overseeing her classes, along with that day's phase of the tryouts for *Kiss Me Kate*, were sure to fall to him.

Julie was relieved to get her boss's voice mail, although she dutifully left her callback information.

Next, she called Calvin's pediatrician.

The office nurse told her to put him to bed, dose him with children's aspirin and bring him in if he got worse.

Discouraged, she got in touch with Paige next, describing Calvin's symptoms.

"I'm on my way," her sister, the RN, responded.

"What about your job?" Julie asked, worried.

"I'm between one and the other," Paige replied. "And this is *Calvin* we're talking about here."

Julie let out her breath, relieved and grateful. "Thanks," she murmured.

She sat with Calvin, who was fitful, until Paige arrived, looking a little frazzled, which was unlike her.

It took Julie a moment to realize that her sister must have encountered Austin when she entered the house.

Paige's expression transformed in a twinkling, though, as she focused her attention on Calvin. "Hey, little buddy," she greeted her nephew, "what's the deal?"

"I spewed," Calvin said miserably. *"Everywhere."*

"It happens," Paige answered matter-of-factly, tossing a wan grin in Julie's direction. "Hi, sis. How about getting me a cup of coffee? I didn't get a chance to grab my usual caffeine fix this morning."

Julie nodded, reluctant to leave Calvin even long enough to pour Paige's coffee, but she knew he couldn't have been in better hands.

When she reached the kitchen, Austin was there, leaning against a counter and sipping coffee from a mug while Esperanza tried to persuade him to sit down and have a good breakfast before he went off to spend the day "playing cowboy."

Disreputably handsome in his work clothes and scuffed boots, Austin hadn't shaved, and if he'd combed his hair at all, he'd used his fingers. He looked pale and deeply weary, Julie thought, and even in her agitation over Calvin, it gave her pause.

Of course there had been an encounter between him and Paige, she concluded, both intrigued and saddened.

He'd been just as rattled by it as Paige.

"You heard about the senator, I guess," Austin said, his voice rough as sandpaper, cocking his head toward the TV. "Garrett will be taking this hard."

Julie nodded. She got a mug and filled it with coffee for Paige. "It's awful."

"Esperanza says your boy is under the weather," Austin said, watching Julie. "Is there anything I can do? Drive to town to fetch a prescription at the drugstore or something?"

Julie smiled, touching Austin's arm to let him know she was grateful for the offer. "Thanks," she said. "Now that Paige is here, I think we'll be all right."

The change in his face was barely perceptible, and he looked away quickly, but Julie saw it and recognized it for what it was.

He still cared for Paige—and he didn't like it.

"I've got my cell phone," he said, glancing briefly at Esperanza before turning his gaze back to Julie. There was a sort of unfolding in the way he moved, getting ready to leave, spend a day outdoors, working hard. "The number's over there on the message board. Call if you need anything."

"I will," Julie promised.

Remembering her errand, she hurried off then, with Paige's already cooling coffee.

"TOOK YOU LONG ENOUGH," Paige said, dropping her stethoscope back into her big purse. She was still sitting on the edge of Calvin's bed, and Harry stood with his muzzle resting on the mattress, soulful eyes rolling slowly between Julie and her son.

Do something, the dog's expression seemed to say.

Calvin lay with a thermometer jutting out of his mouth.

He was flushed, and his hair was all spiky, and Julie thought if she loved the child any more than she already did, she'd burst with it.

She handed Paige the coffee.

Paige took a sip, her eyes skirting Julie's.

Julie sat down in the one chair in the room, knotted her hands together.

"So," she said.

"So," Paige agreed, looking down at her watch, then back at Calvin.

Julie waited.

Presently, Paige took the thermometer from Calvin's mouth and checked the numbers.

"One-o-one," she said, ruffling her nephew's hair gently and setting the thermometer aside. "No skydiving for you, bud. And I'm afraid running with the bulls and spacewalking are out of the question, too."

Calvin blinked. He wasn't wearing his glasses, so Paige and Julie were probably blurry. "What about school?" he asked, very seriously.

"No school, either," Paige said, smoothing his covers.

Calvin's lower lip jutted out slightly, and he folded his arms.

Harry made the leap and snuggled up next to him.

"It's my turn to be class monitor," Calvin protested. "The monitor gets to pass out papers and everything."

"Sorry about that," Paige answered, patting his little shoulder. "Try to get some shuteye, big guy. The more you sleep, the faster you're going to recover."

"Read me a story?" Calvin wheedled.

Julie handed over his favorite book, and Paige took it.

Calvin wriggled down into his pillows, pleased.

Within five minutes, he was asleep.

Paige closed the book and she and Julie crept out of Calvin's room, Julie shutting the door softly behind them.

"What do you think?" she asked, worried. "A hundred and one is a pretty high temp, isn't it?"

Paige smiled, perched herself on the arm of one of the sitting room chairs, folded her arms in much the same way Calvin had. "If it goes up, we'll worry. It's not unusual for a child to run a fever, Julie, and this one isn't all that high. And he was vaccinated against the more serious strains of influenza, wasn't he?"

Julie nodded. "Of course," she said. She watched her sister for a long moment, then sat down on the couch, facing her. "I guess you must have run straight into Austin when you got here, huh?" she asked, finally.

The smile faded and Paige looked away. "Yeah," she admitted. "He opened the back door when I knocked."

"I'm sorry," Julie said, very softly.

Paige shrugged. "Don't be," she replied, with a lightness she obviously didn't feel. Finally, her gaze connected with Julie's. "It's bound to happen, with Libby and Tate getting married and you—"

A silence fell.

"And me?" Julie prodded, a few moments later.

"Come on, Jules," Paige said, spreading her hands wide. "I know there's something going on between you and Garrett."

Julie admitted nothing. She just raised one eyebrow.

Paige grinned, though sparely. "You're glowing like you swallowed a strand of Christmas tree lights. Besides, I'm psychic as far as you and Libby are concerned." She leaned forward a little and spoke with quiet drama. "You can have no secrets from me."

Julie rolled her eyes in the direction of Calvin's room, indicating that Paige should be careful what she said.

"He's asleep," Paige said, referring to her nephew. "And, anyway, give him some credit. My man Calvin is a perceptive guy, even if he *is* only five years old.

He's probably figured things out by now, and even if he hasn't, it would be better just to tell him that you and Garrett are dating."

"We're *not* dating," Julie whispered fiercely.

Paige widened her eyes in that same mocking way that had driven both Julie and Libby crazy when they were all younger.

"Oh, *right*," she scoffed.

Julie bit her lower lip, stuck for what to say next.

Paige giggled at her discomfort. "What is it with you?" she teased. "Of the three of us, you were always the boldest one. Why can't you admit that you and Garrett are—?" Her voice dropped to a whisper. *"Doing it?"*

"Paige!" Julie protested.

Paige shook her head, and her sleek dark hair gleamed in the thin light flowing in through the windows. It wasn't even October yet, but the weather was wintry.

"You're in love with him," Paige insisted.

Julie thought of Senator Cox, and the dreadful accident, and the look she'd seen in Garrett's eyes when he announced his mentor's death to a television audience.

Tears filled her eyes, spilled down her cheeks.

Paige left the arm of the chair to sit beside Julie on the couch and slip a sisterly arm around her.

"What, Jules?" she asked. "What is it?"

Julie sniffled. Straightened her spine. "I can't fall in love with Garrett McKettrick," she said. "I *won't* fall in love with him."

Paige's voice was gentle. "Why not?"

"Because," Julie answered, groping a little, finding her feelings hard to put into words, "it would hurt too much to fall back out again."

CHAPTER SEVENTEEN

A DEATH IS a complicated thing, and the details took a couple of hours to manage.

Nan's sister and brother-in-law arrived at the hospital within minutes of being summoned and squired her home, where she needed to be. Although the ordeal was just beginning, Nan looked worn through, almost transparent, like the fabric of an old shirt.

Garrett hoped the family would step up, surround her, hold her and the children up until the shock waves stopped coming.

He made calls to various high-level officials, including the president of the United States. He set up a press conference for two o'clock that afternoon, but gave Charlene Bishop the promised lead in the race to break the story first.

Finally, he arranged for Senator Cox's body to be removed to a local funeral home and took a cab to his downtown condo. Overlooking Town Lake and the Congress Avenue Bridge, probably most noted for its periodic eruption of flying bats numbering in the hundreds, the space was large and airy and sparely furnished.

Standing just inside the front door, Garrett took a moment to reorient himself to a place that should have seemed a lot more familiar, given that he'd owned it since he graduated from law school. But he might have lived there in another incarnation, as an entirely different man, for all the connection he felt to those rooms.

He wandered through to the master bedroom, rifled through his closet, chose a suit from his collection and tossed it onto the bed. In the adjoining bathroom, he showered and shaved, but he couldn't quite bring himself to put on the fancy duds, not yet, anyway.

Garrett still had almost two hours before the press conference, so he dressed in jeans and a black T-shirt and boots. He was standing in front of his refrigerator, studying the contents and feeling totally uninspired, when his doorbell chimed.

Custom-designed, the gizmo tripped through the first few lines of Johnny Cash's "Ring of Fire."

Frowning, Garrett left the fridge—there was nothing in there he felt brave enough to eat anyhow—crossed the kitchen and entryway and pulled open the door, braced to face down a reporter, if not a pack of them. Austin wasn't a big city; just about everybody in the news business knew where to find him.

But Tate and Austin stood in the corridor, looking too big for the space, with their wide shoulders and their cowboy hats.

"We thought you might need a little moral support," Tate announced to Garrett, pushing past him.

Austin followed, took off his hat and sailed it onto the surface of the foyer table. "Whether you want us or not," he added, in a drawl, "here we are."

Garrett shoved a hand through his hair, momentarily stuck for something to say. Several possibilities came to mind, but they were all too sappy.

He shut the door.

Tate looked him over as he passed, heading for the living room. "You clean up pretty well," he observed.

Austin got there ahead of them both.

"Thanks," Garrett said, belatedly.

"You even shaved," Austin remarked, making himself comfortable by dropping into the best seat in the condo, a leather wingback chair custom-tooled with the name McKettrick and the Silver Spur brand. "I'm impressed."

Tate set his hat aside and wandered into the kitchen. His question echoed back to Garrett, who was still in the living room. "You got anything to eat in this place?"

"Nothing that might not have medicinal properties," Garrett replied. The situation was still bad, that hadn't changed, but the rest of the day would be a little easier, now that his brothers were there.

Austin took his phone from the pocket of his denim jacket and tapped at the screen a few times with one index finger. "Hey, Pedro," he said affably, after a moment or two, a grin spreading across his face. "It's me, Austin McKettrick—"

While Austin placed an order for Mexican food, Tate meandered back from the kitchen. Looking around, he shook his head.

"Not very homey," he said.

Garrett sighed. "It doesn't have to be 'homey,'" he countered. "It's just a place to shower and sleep when I'm in town."

"Get you," Tate said, with a note of good-tempered mockery. "Keeping a fancy place like this just for a place to crash when you're in this part of the country. You got another one just like it in Washington, D.C.?"

"Extra jalapeños," Austin told Pedro. "Sure, I'd appreciate that," he told the restaurant owner, who happened to be an old friend of the family. "Send the grub on around the corner to Garrett's place when it's ready." A pause. Austin's blue gaze flicked to Garrett, and some of the shine went off him. "Yeah. Yeah, it's a pity about the senator. Yeah. I'll pass the word, Pedro. Thanks."

"I stay in residence hotels when we're in Washington," Garrett snapped, in answer to Tate's question. Too stressed to sit, he paced instead.

"Just like regular folks," Tate joked.

Garrett plunked down on the arm of yet another chair, assessing his brothers. "What do *you* know about 'regular folks'?" he jibed. "Until you took up with Libby and moved into the Ruiz place, you were living pretty high on the hog yourself, over at the main house."

Tate grinned, but his eyes remained solemn.

Except for a slight shrug of his shoulders, he gave no reply.

Austin, evidently bored with the conversation, had taken to scrolling through stuff on the screen of his phone, frowning as though the future of the free world depended on whatever was behind all those colorful icons.

"About that call I woke you up with last night," Garrett began, folding his arms.

"Denzel called me this morning," Tate said, *Denzel* being his nickname for his good friend, Chief Brent Brogan. His tone was flat and a little terse. "Why didn't you tell me you were buzzing rustlers in your plane while we were talking?"

"I figured you'd do something stupid if I did," Garrett replied.

Tate arched one dark eyebrow. "Like…?"

"Like going after them and getting yourself shot."

A muscle bunched in Tate's jaw. "So you just figured I didn't need to know somebody was on the Silver Spur, looting our herd?"

"I figured you didn't need to know it right *then*," Garrett said, grinning. "Thanks to Brogan, you know it now, and I'll bet you've already checked out the scene of the crime. Did you find anything?"

"Tracks," Tate answered flatly. "No more dead cattle, so that's a plus."

"Bates figures the loss at around fifty head this time," Austin remarked, reluctantly dropping the phone back into his jacket pocket. "If that's a 'plus,' then I'd say we're pretty damn hard up for good news around our outfit."

Fifty head of cattle represented a serious chunk of change, but it wasn't the loss of money that galled Garrett. It was the goddamn, brass-balls *effrontery* of cutting a man's fences, trespassing on his rangeland, thieving from his herd.

He swore and looked away. He was developing a headache, and there was still the press conference to get through. Wearing a suit.

The food arrived, delivered by one of Pedro's many teenage daughters, nieces or cousins, the majority of whom seemed to be named Maria.

Austin footed the bill and flashed a grin at the girl as he tipped her.

The poor kid would probably still be blushing come the middle of next week. She was so busy looking back at Austin on her way out the door that she nearly crashed into a wall a couple of times before finally clearing the threshold.

Tate disappeared into the kitchen and came back carrying three plates with silverware piled on top. He'd jammed a roll of paper towels under one arm, to serve as napkins.

"It's good to know he's still got it," Tate quipped, inclining his head toward Austin, who was just closing the door behind Maria, but looking at Garrett.

Garrett grinned. "You were worried that he didn't?"

In the next few minutes, they fell to eating, the three of them gathered around Garrett's table. It was sort of like the old days on the ranch, when the whole family had eaten together almost every night.

Garrett's distracted mind wandered—he thought about the upcoming press conference, the senator's funeral, soon to be held, the inevitable transfer of power—so he snagged on a remark Austin made like a leaf spinning downstream and catching behind a rock.

"—so I open the door and Paige Remington is standing there, big as life, come to take care of Julie's boy—"

Garrett made his reentry into the here-and-now with a jolt. "What's wrong with Calvin?"

"Flu, I guess," Austin said, scraping a cheesy pile of Pedro's unparalleled nachos onto his plate. "According to Esperanza, the poor little guy was heaving like a drunken sailor at the end of a three-day shore leave."

Tate pretended to wince, but he went right on shoveling in the ole enchiladas. "Audrey and Ava are just getting over that stuff," he said. "It's a sumbitch while it's going on, but it doesn't last long."

Garrett frowned, setting down his fork. "How's Julie?" he asked, and by the time he realized what he'd revealed by raising the question, it was too late.

Austin widened his eyes at Garrett, indulged in a

long, slow grin before troubling himself to make a reply. "She looked all right to me," he said, letting the words roll over that glib tongue of his like so much butter and honey. "*Better* than all right," he finally clarified.

By then, Garrett was glaring at him. "Paige showed up, huh?" he said, just to get under Austin's hide.

And it worked.

The hinges of Austin's jaws got stuck, or so it appeared, and his eyes narrowed. He looked like he was about to push back his chair, jump to his feet and challenge Garrett to a gunfight, like some old-time gambler in a saloon.

So much for the twinkle and the boyish charm.

"Hey." Tate waved a hand between them. "Do you think maybe you two could get through lunch without arguing?"

Garrett had largely forgotten about his shiner, but now, for no reason he could rightly make sense of, it reasserted itself, aching like hell, and in perfect rhythm with the beat of his heart.

Austin, who had the instincts of a shark scenting blood in the water, relaxed, grinning again. "I'll read a statement for you at the press conference," he offered, "if you don't want the whole state of Texas speculating as to who might have punched your lights out for you in the recent past."

"*Nobody* punched my lights out," Garrett said, through his teeth.

Austin flexed the fingers of his right hand, watching them move as though there were something downright fascinating about it. He had a pretty good scrape abrading his knuckles, Garrett noticed.

So Austin had been the one to hit him. It freaking figured.

"If it's any comfort," Austin said to Garrett, "I was aiming to deck Tate, not you."

"It isn't," Garrett said.

Tate and Austin both chuckled.

Like it was funny or something.

Garrett scowled. "If you'd like a shiner to match mine, little brother," he told Austin, "I can arrange it."

"If we're going to argue," Tate broke in, very quietly, but with the authority that came with being the eldest of the three, even if it was only by a year, "let's argue over something worthwhile. Like whether you two plan on ranching or playing at rodeo and politics for the rest of your lives, like a couple of trust-fund babies."

Silence.

Garrett pushed his plate away. He was riled, but Julie was tugging at the edge of his mind, too. Was she all right? Was Calvin?

Watching Tate now, Austin flushed. "I've still got things to do," he said, his voice low and hard-edged. "People to see. Bulls to ride."

Tate sighed. "So I guess that's an answer, even if it isn't what I was hoping to hear. You're not ready to settle down and help run the Silver Spur."

"I'll hire somebody to do my share," Austin said.

"Don't bother," Tate replied. "No stranger is going to give two hoots and a holler about the Silver Spur." He turned his gaze to Garrett, made him feel pinned where he was, like somebody's dusty science project, a dead bug, maybe, tacked to a display board. "Might be, it's time to call it good, go our separate ways. Hell, both of you have been doing that since Mom and Dad were killed anyhow. Might as well make it official and sell out."

Austin went pale behind his tan. "I'm not selling my third of the ranch," he said.

"Fine," Tate retorted. "Maybe you'd like to buy *me* out, then. The old Arnette farm is up for sale—I could pick it up for a song. Bulldoze that shack of a house and raze the barn, then rebuild. I might even raise some crops."

If they hadn't gone over this ground earlier, he and Tate, Garrett would have thought Tate was just jerking Austin's chain. Since they had, he was pretty sure Number One Brother was serious.

Even if Austin bought Tate's share of the ranch and hired a whole crew of management types to run it, it wouldn't be the same.

"Why the urgency, Tate?" Garrett asked his older brother, genuinely curious as well as quietly alarmed. Who would he be without that ranch? Who would *any* of them be? "The Silver Spur has been in this family since Clay McKettrick bought the original parcel of land a hundred years ago. Now, all of a sudden, you want everything decided and the property lines redrawn before when? Yesterday?"

"What happened to all that talk about how your daughters needed to grow up on the ranch, because they're McKettricks?" Austin threw in. He'd been pale before, now he was flushed.

"Things change," Tate said gravely. "People change."

"And you expect us to believe that *you've* changed that much?" Austin retorted, coldly furious. "Goddamn, if this is what love does to a man, then I hope I die a bachelor!"

Garrett rubbed his face with both hands, realized

his beard was already starting to come in again—and it hadn't been more than an hour since he'd shaved. The fatigue hit him between one moment and the next with the impact of a speeding truck.

Back in the day, Tate's temper would have flared up like an oil well set aflame right about then, but loving Libby had mellowed him.

"We can talk about this some other time," he said wearily. He met Garrett's gaze. "I'm sorry," he added. "Austin and I came here to help you in any way we could, and here we are squabbling instead."

Austin let out his breath. Reached over to squeeze Garrett's shoulder without looking at him. "Much as I hate to admit it," he muttered. "Tate's right."

The spread of Mexican food, delicious as it was, had lost its appeal.

By tacit agreement, the meal was over.

Austin and Tate cleared away the debris, while Garrett went into his room and exchanged the comfortable clothes he'd been wearing for the dark suit he'd left on the bed earlier.

Standing in front of the mirror on the inside of the closet door, he straightened his appropriately sedate tie, shrugged his shoulders to make the jacket sit right across his back.

Except for the black eye, he thought, with a rueful shot at a smile that went wide of the mark, he looked dignified enough to be a dead senator's spokesman.

He'd have been a lot more comfortable in jeans and boots, though.

WHEN JULIE HURRIED into her classroom the next morning, moments before the bell would bring a tsunami of first-period English students flooding in, Rachel was already at her desk in the second row.

"I was worried," she told Julie. "When you didn't come to school yesterday, I mean."

Julie felt a pang, even as she managed a harried smile. A glance at the wall clock told her she had roughly thirty seconds before the wave of adolescent humanity would make landfall. "My son didn't feel well," she said. "I had to stay home and care for him."

"Is he better?" Rachel asked.

"Yes," Julie answered, with a sigh of relief. Calvin wouldn't be able to attend kindergarten for the rest of the week, but he'd been well enough that morning to ride into town with Julie. He and Harry were spending the day at Paige's apartment, where they would surely be fed and tended, fussed over and spoiled within an inch of their lives.

Mindful of just how much this child had been through in her young life, Julie trained her full attention on the girl. "How about you, Rachel? How are you doing?"

Rachel shrugged, looked away. "Well enough," she said.

The bell rang.

The doors banged open and students streamed in.

The day had begun in earnest, and Julie didn't get another chance to speak to Rachel until after the last class of the day. Even then, the interlude was brief, because Julie had tryouts to oversee in the auditorium, and Rachel was in a hurry to get to her job at the bowling alley.

"If you need to talk about the fire or anything," Julie said, standing next to Rachel's locker while the girl shoved books onto the overhead shelf and reached for the lightweight jacket hanging on a hook, "I'll listen."

Rachel's spine straightened, and something flickered in her eyes, a sort of shutting-down. "Right," she said, in a that's-what-they-all-say tone.

Kids streamed past them.

"Rachel," Julie said, catching hold of the girl's arm when she would have turned away, "I mean it. We can talk, anytime."

"Really?" Rachel asked, with the first note of sarcasm Julie had ever heard from her. Considering that the girl was a teenager, that was saying something. "Like you were going to talk to my dad, you mean? About how maybe he could set aside his stupid masculine pride for once and let people give us stuff my brothers and I have been doing without our whole lives?"

Julie took a moment before answering. "Rachel," she said at last, kindly but firmly, "I want to help, I truly do, but I've been especially busy lately and, well, the last time your dad and I talked, he wasn't exactly receptive."

All the bluster seemed to go out of Rachel then; she literally deflated. "I know," she said. "It's just that I can't think of anybody else to ask, and Dad's talking about how he's ashamed to show his face in public, what with folks bringing us clothes and food and even a real nice trailer to live in, like he can't take care of his own family—and he's making noises about moving on again, too—"

"I'll try again," Julie broke in gently, laying a hand on the girl's shoulder. "I promise."

"I don't know what we'll do if he won't listen to you," Rachel fretted.

With that, she nodded a farewell, put on her jacket and hurried away.

As Julie had learned that morning, Mr. Dulles had

simply canceled the tryouts the night before, instead of putting Mrs. Chambers in charge in Julie's absence or taking over the task himself. That meant, of course, that they'd made no progress at all.

She listened dutifully to every song.

She paid earnest attention to every reading.

And the evening seemed endless.

When the first round of tryouts was finally over, some two hours after they'd begun, Julie was tired and hungry, and she still needed to pick Calvin up at Paige's apartment.

Ron Strivens was waiting outside the auditorium, with Rachel and the boys, when she paused to lock up. Mrs. Chambers stayed close to Julie's elbow, smiling nervously at the ragged little family.

Julie smiled at them, too.

"My girl said you wanted to talk to me," Strivens said to Julie, pushing away from the lightpost he'd been leaning against to stand straight. "Here I am, Ms. Remington. I'm listening."

"Shall I stay?" Verna Chambers asked, hesitating as she pulled her car keys from her handbag.

"No, no," Julie said, patting her friend's arm. "It's all right."

Reluctantly, Verna nodded a good-night to all concerned and headed for her car.

"Would you like to go in?" Julie asked the Strivenses. "We could all sit down—"

"Right here's good," Strivens said, indicating a nearby bench. He turned to his daughter. "Rachel, you take the boys and wait in the truck so your teacher and I can talk."

Rachel did as she was told, though she dragged her feet a little, pulling her younger brothers by the hand.

Julie tried not to sigh as she took a seat on the bench in front of the auditorium. "I know things are very hard right now, for all of you—"

Rachel's father sank down beside her. He seemed weary in every muscle and bone, much older than his years. "Yeah, it's been tough," he said, almost shyly, "without Miranda—that was my wife and the kids' mother—but we've managed."

Julie nodded, full of sympathy, but frustrated, too. "Rachel says you're thinking of leaving Blue River. Where would you go?"

Strivens shrugged. Shook his head.

"People mean well," Julie went on, when he didn't answer aloud. "The stuff they've donated, the food, the clothes—it's not charity in their view, Mr. Strivens. It's just their way of helping you get back on your feet after the fire—like you might do for them if the situation was reversed."

Strivens swallowed visibly, gazing out into the dark parking lot. His shoulders stooped and his hands dangled between the patched knees of his pants. "Folks say it's better to give than to receive," he reflected slowly, without looking at Julie, "and they must be right, though I couldn't say for sure. All my life, I've been on the receiving end." He paused to sigh. "All I want is to do right by my kids, believe it or not."

"I believe you," Julie said. And she did. Being a single parent herself, she knew how rough life could be at times, and how frightening, even with Libby and Paige helping out in every possible way. "It means so much to Rachel to stay in Blue River and graduate," she said. "And your boys—they've probably settled in pretty well, too, haven't they?"

Strivens smiled, but he still didn't look directly at Julie. "So what you're saying is, I ought to swallow my cussed pride?"

"That's *not* what I meant at all," Julie lied.

He laughed. Met her gaze. "Sure it is," he said. "But that's all right. I was thinking—those McKettricks got so much land and money, they can donate a fine single-wide for the use of the needy, maybe they'd have a job for a hardworkin' man, too."

"Maybe," Julie agreed, smiling.

"Reckon we both ought to be going," Strivens said, rising.

Julie did the same.

The man walked her to her car, waited politely until she was inside, with the engine running and the doors locked. Then he waved one hand and sprinted toward his old truck, where his children were waiting.

A few minutes later, Julie knocked on the door of Paige's apartment. Across the street, the cottage looked lonely and dark.

Paige greeted her with a bright smile, and Calvin, ensconced on the sofa in his pajamas, looked almost like his usual self. Apparently, his illness was only the twenty-four-hour stomach kind of thing.

Tears of love and relief and who knew what else filled Julie's eyes.

"You're staying for supper," Paige said, pulling her inside and shutting the door. "And that's all there is to it. No arguments, no excuses."

Paige's place was small, but it was part of a Victorian jewel of a house converted into apartments decades before, and it had charm aplenty—tall mullioned windows with built-in seats, wood floors and a working brick fireplace, among other things. Julie particularly envied the huge claw-foot tub in the bathroom.

Julie sniffled and wiped at her eyes with the back of one hand, hoping Calvin hadn't noticed that she was crying.

No such luck.

Even when he was sick, Calvin didn't miss much.

"What's the matter, Mom?" he asked, with great concern, when she bent to hug him and rest her chin on top of his head for a moment.

"It's nothing," she said. "I just had kind of a long day, that's all."

Calvin took her hand and tugged, and Julie dropped to sit close to him on the sofa. Harry, curled at his feet, eyed her balefully but didn't stir. "Guess what?" the little boy whispered.

Julie smiled. "What?" she whispered back.

"I drank a supersize ginger ale today—every last drop!"

"Did not," Julie teased.

"Did, too," Calvin insisted. "Aunt Paige bundled me up and put me in her car and we went to the drive-through. Harry went with us. He had part of a cheeseburger."

"Wow," Julie said, exchanging glances with Paige.

Paige, clad in jeans and a long-sleeved sweatshirt, made a face at Julie and went into the kitchenette, where she began ladling something savory-smelling into a bowl.

"Beef stew," she said, returning to set the food on the table in the small dining area. "Have some."

"Don't mind if I do," Julie answered. She washed

her hands in Paige's spotless bathroom, admiring the magnificent bathtub, then joined her sister at the table.

The stew was delicious, and she felt better after the first bite.

"I didn't throw up even *once* today," Calvin called from the sofa.

Julie chuckled and shook her head, while Paige, seated across from her, smiled over the rim of her tea-cup.

"Calvin," Julie said, "I'm eating."

"Oops," Calvin replied. "Sorry. I guess you're not supposed to talk about throw-up when people are try-ing to eat."

"Guess not," Paige sang out. Her dark eyes were gentle as she watched Julie raise and lower her spoon. "You're working too hard," she added, very quietly, for Julie's ears alone.

"Can you suggest an alternative?" Julie asked.

There were so many things she wasn't letting her-self think about. Like how soon she needed to have her and Calvin's belongings out of the cottage, so the new owners could move in, for instance.

Like Garrett McKettrick, and how she'd let herself get in deep with him, knowing better all the while.

"You have your share of the money Marva gave us," Paige said, referring to the tidy sum their mother had divided between the three of them before leaving Blue River a few months before. "Why don't you take some time off from teaching, reconsider your options?"

"Options?" Julie whispered back. Calvin was off the couch, gathering his stuff to go home.

Paige propped her forearms on the table's edge and leaned in a little. "Garrett?" she mouthed.

Julie sighed. "Get real," she said. "He's not an option."

"Whatever you say, sis." Paige smiled. "He looked good on TV this afternoon. Nasty shiner, though."

Julie had seen the press conference, along with the entire student body of Blue River High, since Mr. Dulles had called a special assembly for the purpose. Flags all over the state were flying at half mast, too.

Her heart pinched, remembering. Although disillusioned by Senator Cox's recent fall from grace, as he surely was, Garrett had spoken with quiet dignity of his political mentor's years of dedicated service to the people of Texas.

Time tripped back a few notches.

I'll be leaving in a few days, she heard Garrett say. She'd been holding the ice bag to his eye, and he'd pulled her onto his lap...

"He won't be sticking around long," she said aloud, without thinking first.

"Garrett is going someplace?" Calvin demanded, appearing at her elbow, with his jacket on over his pajamas and his glasses crooked. "Where?"

Julie smiled and moved to straighten Calvin's glasses, but he wouldn't let her fuss. He stepped back out of her reach and blurted out, "Garrett can't go away. He promised he'd teach me how to ride!"

"Calvin—"

"He can't go!" Calvin almost shrieked.

Paige didn't say anything, but her eyes were sad as she looked at her nephew.

"Your dad is coming back for a visit this weekend," Julie reminded the boy calmly. "And you're going to meet your grandparents. Won't that be nice?"

Calvin began to wheeze, and then to gasp.

Before Julie could respond at all, Paige had his inhaler out of his backpack and up to his mouth. The familiar puffing sound the device made seemed to echo through the room like a series of small explosions.

"Easy," Paige said, one hand resting on Calvin's small back as he struggled to breathe. "Take it real easy, big guy. You're going to be all right."

Slowly, the little boy's breath began to even out. As soon as he'd had his medicine, Julie hoisted him onto her lap and held him, murmuring, "Shhh," and then, "Shhh" again.

"Garrett can't go away," he whimpered. "It isn't fair if he goes away."

"Hush, now," Julie said, meeting Paige's gaze. She was still standing nearby, still holding the inhaler. "We can talk about this when you're feeling better."

Calvin began to cry then. Since he rarely wept, the sound was especially heartbreaking to hear.

Paige's eyes glistened.

Julie's own vision was a little blurred.

She held Calvin until he began to settle down. Even when the tears had subsided, though, tremors went through his small body, and Julie was afraid he'd have another asthma attack—a worse one, perhaps—one that wouldn't stop when he used his inhaler.

"I want to go back to the ranch," he said, his voice muffled. "I want to see Garrett."

"Honey," Julie told her son quietly, "Garrett might not be on the ranch. He had to go to Austin, remember? To hold the press conference you and Aunt Paige watched on TV this afternoon? I'm sure he has a lot of things to do there—"

Calvin drew back, looked up at Julie. "Don't you

want to see Garrett, too?" he asked, with his heart in his eyes. And in his voice.

"Sure, I do," Julie answered, very gently. "It's just that I'm pretty sure he's working, that's all."

Calvin studied her for a long time.

"Maybe you should both spend the night here," Paige said. "It's late and Calvin isn't feeling well. I'll sleep right here on the couch, and you two can share my bed."

It seemed an odd conversation to be having, when the cottage, Julie and Calvin's home for so long, was just across the road.

But the cottage wasn't home anymore.

She and Calvin didn't *have* a home.

Paige was waiting for an answer, so Julie finally shook her head. "You've done enough," she told her sister, giving her a hug. "We're not throwing you out of your bed."

Twenty minutes later, Julie, Calvin and the dog stepped into the warmth and brightness of the ranch-house kitchen, and Julie's drooping spirits were instantly lifted.

CHAPTER EIGHTEEN

GARRETT LAUGHED AND caught Calvin easily when he ran across the big room and launched himself into the man's arms.

Julie's heart stumbled at the sight.

"I saw you on TV!" Calvin shouted exuberantly. "Aunt Paige said you looked good even with a shiner!"

Garrett, wearing jeans, a long-sleeved black pullover shirt and boots, laughed again and stood the boy on the bench that ran along one side of the long kitchen table, so they were eye to eye.

"Is that right?" he asked, finally. He slanted a mischievous glance at Julie. "Your aunt Paige said that?"

Calvin nodded. Then he took a closer look at the shiner in question and frowned. "It's turning green and yellow," he said.

"They do that," Garrett explained easily. "I'll be good as new in a few days."

"That's better, then," Calvin decided, clearly relieved.

Garrett had been resting a hand on either side of the boy's waist, so he wouldn't fall off the bench. Now he raised one to ruffle Calvin's decidedly messy hair. "I heard you were under the weather, cowboy," he said. Over Calvin's head, Garrett fixed that McKettrick-blue gaze on Julie and didn't look away for a long moment.

When he spoke to Calvin again, his voice was gruff with masculine concern. "You feeling better now?"

"I *was* feeling better," Calvin replied, "until Mom told me you were going away and you probably wouldn't even *be* here when we got back from town tonight." The child turned his head, gave Julie a triumphant I-told-you-so look before focusing all his attention on Garrett again. "I stayed with my aunt Paige *all day* because I had a fever and I kept *barfing*—"

"Calvin," Julie interrupted. "That will be enough detail, thank you."

Calvin rolled his eyes, and Garrett chuckled.

"I had to use my inhaler, too," Calvin threw in.

Garrett's expression was fond as he looked at Calvin, but there was a certain respect in it, too. "You'll be all right, little pardner," he said, without a speck of condescension. Except for the "little pardner" part, he might have been talking to a grown man. "Sturdy fella like you? 'Course you will."

Calvin all but blossomed under Garrett's quiet certainty that he was All Right. "Sure, I will," the child agreed manfully.

Now that Calvin's worth as a human being had been declared, for all time and eternity, the subject took a new turn.

Julie, standing there in the kitchen, still wearing her coat and holding her purse, had to do some emotional scrambling to catch up.

"Esperanza's in Blue River, playing bingo," Garrett told his pint-size sidekick. "But she cooked before she left, so there's corned beef and cabbage in the Crock-Pot upstairs in my kitchen." He grinned at Calvin before lifting him down off the bench to stand on the floor again.

"We've eaten," Julie said, still dazed. Her remark seemed incredibly mundane, considering the thing she had just realized.

She didn't just *like* Garrett McKettrick.

She didn't just enjoy having sex with him.

She was deeply, profoundly, hopelessly and permanently *in love with him.*

Furthermore, she thought, even more shaken than before, loving Garrett was nothing new. She'd probably fallen for him a long time ago, as far back as high school even. Because they were so different—Garrett the popular rich kid, the high school rodeo star, Julie the drama queen/rebel—she'd repressed the attraction, kept it buried.

That had been so much easier when Garrett was someone she saw around town occasionally, or at weddings and funerals and other events where the entire community tended to gather.

Living under the same roof, it hadn't taken long to find him irresistible.

A few days.

Calvin gave her a look that was part reproof and part loving tolerance. "Mom?" he said. "Earth to Mom. Come in, please."

Calvin was into retro-TV, so *that* line must have come from *Lost in Space* or *Star Trek.* Julie chuckled, got busy taking off her coat, putting it away, along with her purse and tote bag.

In the guest-suite bathroom, she splashed her face with cool water. Since the small amount of mascara she'd applied that morning had long since worn off, it didn't loop under her eyes, raccoon-style.

Julie straightened, dried her face with a hand towel

and remained in front of the sink, squinting into the mirror above it.

Now *what are we going to do, Smarty-pants?* she asked herself silently.

When there was no answer immediately forthcoming, Julie marched herself back to the kitchen. She would help Calvin wash up, tuck him into bed for the night and—and what?

Lie in her bed and stare at the ceiling for hours, probably.

The prospect was dismal, especially after the day she'd put in.

"Maybe you could just keep Austin and me company while *we* eat," Garrett was saying as she rejoined him and Calvin and Harry.

Julie glanced at her watch. Started to decline the invitation.

Spending time in close proximity to Garrett McKettrick, however appealing the idea might be, would only make bad matters worse. That long-ago Julie, the one with the white lipstick and the black clothes, hadn't been wrong about *everything*, after all.

She and Garrett not only hadn't traveled in the same circles back then, they hadn't occupied the same *universe.*

They were older now, and undeniably, they were sexually compatible.

But she and *Gordon* had been, too, though not quite to the same soul-shattering degree.

Still.

Seeing a pattern here, Remington? taunted the voice in her head. *You're two-for-two—you and Gordon wanted different things, and so do you and Garrett, and you might as well face it.*

Cut your losses and run.

Garrett was watching her a little too perceptively. "Please?" he said.

"Please?" Calvin echoed.

It took Julie a moment to recall what they were talking about, her son and the man she wished had been his father.

Oh, yes. Garrett wanted them to come upstairs, sit with him and Austin while they ate their supper.

Julie might have been able to refuse Garrett, out of principle and because she needed to draw up lesson plans for the next day and go over her notes from the *Kiss Me Kate* tryouts, but she didn't have the heart to quash the hope shining in Calvin's little face.

"All right," she conceded, "but we can't stay very long."

Calvin punched the air with one fist and whooped, *"Yes!"*

Harry barked, doing a three-legged spin, caught in a backwash of boy-joy, and in spite of everything, Julie laughed.

It was Garrett who carried Calvin up the stairs to his second-floor apartment. Austin showed up just in time to lug Harry.

Julie followed, smiling to herself. Feeling less exhausted, less confused.

Wiser, but a whole lot sadder, too.

"Tough day?" Garrett asked, in his kitchen, when Julie repeated that she'd already eaten at Paige's, and Calvin was okay, too.

He lifted the lid off Esperanza's Crock-Pot and the savory aroma of corned beef and cabbage filled the room.

Calvin and Harry were in the living room, with Austin, with the TV blaring and the fireplace crackling cheerily away in welcome.

"Yes," Julie said. "I did have a tough day, as a matter of fact. But it wasn't nearly as tough as yours, I'll bet."

He gave a crooked grin, carried a plate to the table. "I wish you could stay," he said, very quietly.

Julie sighed and looked away. She wanted the same thing, but it wasn't possible, with Calvin not only at home, but recovering from his illness. And it also wouldn't be smart.

"So what happens now?" she finally asked Garrett, barely resisting the urge to lay a hand on his arm.

She'd asked herself that same question earlier, and she was still waiting for the answer. Maybe Garrett had one.

He didn't.

Garrett looked down at the plate of food in front of him, motionless for the moment. "The governor and some of the state legislators have already been in touch, according to Nan. It looks as though she'll be appointed to finish out her husband's term in the U.S. Senate. She's always worked closely with Morgan— well, until recently, anyway—so she knows the issues inside and out."

Julie nodded. There it was, the handwriting on the wall. "And she'll need your help and advice, of course."

"At first," Garrett said, avoiding her eyes. He wouldn't meet her gaze.

"'At first'?" Julie echoed, surprised.

Inwardly, she braked hard when hope sprang up in front of her like a deer on a dark and icy road.

"Something's happening between you and me," Garrett said quietly. "I'd like to find out what."

Julie thought about Calvin, decided he wasn't listening, because he and Austin were laughing about something they'd seen on TV, and even Harry contributed a few barks of comment.

"Maybe we should just agree that it's been fun and part ways," Julie heard herself say. *Maybe?* jibed the voice in her head.

He set down his fork. Watched her for a long moment before replying. "Why do you say that?"

"Because we're different," Julie said. "You're a McKettrick," she went on, with a slight smile of self-deprecation, "and *I'm* a high school English teacher with a child to raise."

Garrett arched an eyebrow. Dear God, he was good-looking, Julie thought, even with a black-and-purple-and-green eye, streaked with yellow. "All of which means?" he asked, his voice gruff.

"We don't have a whole lot in common," Julie said slowly, and with emphasis.

Garrett grinned at that. "Sometimes that's good," he said. "And there's one thing we *do* have in common."

Julie blushed, looked away.

"Sex," Garrett whispered, close to her ear. His breath was a warm, tingling rush against her skin. "We both like sex."

"Everybody likes sex," Julie said.

Garrett chortled at that. "You *are* naive," he said.

Julie leaned in close. "I'll bet *you've* never had a complaint," she challenged.

This time, Garrett laughed outright. "Thanks for the vote of confidence," he said. "And I have to ask this. Have *you* ever had a complaint?"

Julie blushed. Hard.

"Well, *no*," she said. "But—"

In the living room, Austin and Calvin hooted in unison. Whatever was playing on TV, they were enjoying it to the max.

Garrett chuckled, but his eyes were solemn. Searching hers, probing deep.

Julie felt as though her very soul had been laid bare to the man.

"There are some things I have to do," he said, after a long time. "I'll be gone for a week, maybe two. Will you be here, Julie—on the Silver Spur—when I get back?"

"Wh-what are you really saying?" she asked.

"That there's something going on between us," Garrett reiterated quietly. "And I need to know what it is before I make any major decisions."

Julie opened her mouth, closed it again.

She had never been at such a loss for words.

It simply wasn't like her.

Garrett raised himself far enough out of his chair to lean over and kiss her lightly on the mouth.

He tasted of Esperanza's delicious cooking.

"Will you wait for me?" he asked, drawing back just a fraction of an inch.

Everything inside Julie was responding to his mouth, to the need for another kiss, for a lot *more* than another kiss. Even Smarty-pants didn't have anything to say.

"Wait for you? I don't understand."

Garrett grinned and *damn* it was sexy. Definitely an unfair advantage. "I have some things to do in Austin and in Washington," he answered. "Loose ends to tie up. When I get back here, the first thing I'm going to do is take you to bed. The second thing is—well—I'll probably take you to bed all over again. Assuming we ever get *out* of bed in the first place."

"So," Julie said, in a whisper that was barely more than a breath, "you want to have sex again."

"And again," Garrett confirmed. "And again."

Julie raised an eyebrow. And then she asked, only partly in jest, "What's in it for me?"

"Multiple orgasms?" he said, so quietly and so close that his lips were actually touching hers now.

She laughed, wishing she could collect on *that* promise sooner rather than later. "You are *too* cocky, Garrett McKettrick," she murmured, drawing back just slightly. "How do you know I wasn't faking before?"

"You weren't faking," he said, with damnable confidence. "I have the scratches on my back to prove it."

"That could be part of the act," Julie said.

He laughed. "Okay," he replied. "Were you faking?"

"Hell, no," Julie answered, and tasted his mouth, because she couldn't resist.

It was against her better judgment, all of it.

She was merely putting off the inevitable. And there didn't seem to be a damn thing she could do about it, that night at least.

"They're kissing!" Calvin yelled.

That pretty much tanked the moment.

Julie turned and saw her son standing in the doorway between Garrett's kitchen and living room, making quite a picture in his pajamas and Austin's cowboy hat. Since the hat didn't fit, he had his head tilted back a little, so he could see under the brim.

"What?" Austin called back.

"I said Mom and Garrett are *kissing!*"

Garrett rolled his eyes and chuckled; otherwise, he seemed unruffled.

Julie, on the other hand, was mortified. On top of that, her nipples had gone so hard that they ached, and she was damp, too.

She'd already made the mental shift: This thing happening between her and Garrett wasn't going anywhere.

Her body was slower to buy in.

Austin stepped into the doorway behind Calvin and took the boy lightly by the shoulders, turning him around, heading him into the living room again. He glanced back over one shoulder, grinned the grin Paige probably still couldn't get out of her mind.

"Go right on kissing," he said. "Don't let Cal and me bother you."

Garrett had taken up his fork again. He seemed to be enjoying the corned beef and cabbage, since he went on eating, but his gaze was on Julie and it shone with tenderness and comedy and desire and a whole mix of other things that weren't so easily identified.

"Will you wait for me?" he asked again, when he'd finished his supper, carried his plate and silverware to the sink, rinsed them before dropping them into the dishwasher.

"I'll wait," Julie heard herself say. It really wasn't such a noble sacrifice, after all. Unless she wanted to crowd poor Paige out of her bed, forcing her to sleep on the couch, there weren't a lot of choices.

Until the house she and Paige and Libby owned together was habitable, and that might be weeks, she really didn't have anywhere to go.

"When will you leave?" she asked, when Garrett

stood behind her chair, instead of sitting down again, and began to massage her shoulders.

"Probably tomorrow," he answered. "The funeral will be held in a few days, and Nan has meetings scheduled with the governor and various state legislators."

Julie frowned. "Meetings? The same week as her husband's funeral?"

"She's a strong woman," Garrett said.

Or a cold one, Julie thought, though she immediately decided she was being unfair. Morgan Cox had, after all, been embroiled in an embarrassing and steamy scandal when he died.

She glanced toward the doorway where Calvin had appeared earlier and lowered her voice, just in case he was eavesdropping again. Or still.

"Well, she's certainly a better woman than I am," she said. "If that had happened to me, about the last thing in the world I'd be doing would be jumping in to fill the man's seat in the Senate."

Garrett took her hand, rubbed his thumb lightly, musingly, over her knuckles. "Nobody," he said gravely, "is a better woman than you are, Julie Remington."

"Now," she said, struggling against an insane need to break down and cry, preferably sitting on Garrett's lap, with her face buried in his neck, "you're just flattering me."

He held on to her hand, raised it to his mouth, retraced with his lips the path he'd taken earlier with his thumb.

Hot, shivery shards of wanting poked and prodded Julie from within.

"Don't," she pleaded.

He didn't release her immediately.

She made no effort to pull away.

Austin made a great deal of noise to let them know he was approaching the kitchen; appeared with his plate and silverware and his usual heartrending grin. Coupled with the sadness lurking behind the sparkle in his eyes, the effect was powerful.

"Cal's asleep on the couch," he confided, crossing the room to set the plate and silverware in the sink.

"I'd better get him to bed," Julie said, unable to keep from sighing softly as she rose from her chair. "He has a tendency to get overexcited anyway, and when he's sick…"

A look passed between him and Austin, who lingered at the sink, though he didn't rinse his dishes. He just leaned against the counter, his arms folded, and watched his brother thoughtfully.

"If you need any help while Garrett's gone," Austin said presently, when his brother had disappeared into the living room to fetch Calvin, "just let me know. I'll be glad to lend a hand."

It was a brotherly offer, nothing more.

Julie couldn't help visualizing Paige and Austin standing side by side.

They'd be wonderful together, she thought whimsically. He had pale brown hair, while Paige's was dark. His eyes were the standard McKettrick blue, hers a deep and vibrant brown.

They would have the most beautiful children.

"Do I have something on my face?" Austin asked, with a grin.

Embarrassed, Julie laughed and shook her head. "Sorry," she said. "I didn't mean to stare. I was just thinking—"

Would she have told him what she was thinking—
that he and Paige would have made a great couple—if
Garrett hadn't come back just then, with a sleepy Calvin in his arms and Harry at his heels?

Probably not.

"Want me to carry the dog downstairs?" Austin
asked his brother.

Garrett looked from Austin to Julie and back again.
And he frowned, not in an angry way, but in a thoughtful one.

"I'd appreciate it," he said.

Julie, suddenly in a hurry to be on the move, led the
way out of Garrett's apartment and down the stairs to
the main kitchen.

Garrett followed, carrying Calvin, and Austin came
as far as the foot of the staircase, where he set Harry
down and immediately retreated again.

She watched from the doorway of Calvin's room as
Garrett took his glasses off, put him into bed and gently
tucked the covers in around him.

The boy stirred. "'Night, Garrett," he said.

"'Night, buddy," Garrett replied, his voice throaty.

"You going away?" Calvin asked, in a sleepy murmur.

"For a few days," Garrett answered, "but I'll be back."
He glanced at Julie, still hovering on the threshold.

"For sure?" Calvin mumbled, as Harry leaped onto
the bed to curl up behind his knees.

"You have my word," Garrett said.

Calvin opened his eyes just long enough to look at
Garrett and smile. "Good," he said. "That's good."

Garrett lingered a moment, stroking Calvin's hair
back from his face with a light pass of one hand. Then,

just when Julie was beginning to think she couldn't bear the sheer wonder of the sight of the two of them together for another moment, Garrett stood, crossed to her, steered her out into the hallway.

Very quietly, he closed the door.

When Julie started for the sitting room, though, he stopped her.

Pulled her against him.

His hands rested on her backside, deliciously possessive.

Julie whimpered, full of sweet despair, but she didn't try to pull away. She was pretty sure she didn't have the strength—or the willpower—to do that.

And Garrett kissed her.

His lips touched hers, gently at first, then with unmistakable hunger.

Julie still didn't pull away. No, indeed, she slipped her arms around Garrett's neck and rose onto the balls of her feet to kiss him back.

"I'm staying," he told her, when they both had to breathe.

"Calvin—" Julie whispered back.

"We'll be quiet," Garrett said. And he pulled her straight into the other bedroom, the one where she'd expected to spend a miserable and lonely night.

Life was full of surprises.

Garrett was full of surprises.

Julie's heart was thudding away in her throat. "But—"

He closed the door, turned the lock.

"What if we *can't* be quiet?" she asked.

Garrett hauled her shirt off over her head and tossed it aside. Took a moment to trace the round tops of her breasts, rising above her bra, with the tip of one finger.

"We can be quiet," he assured her.

"Speak for yourself," Julie argued, remembering the primitive, gasping *desperation* of the climaxes she'd had the last time she and Garrett made love. He knew just where to touch her, just *how* to touch her.

Garrett chuckled. Then he removed her bra. Weighed her bare breasts in his hands, chafing the nipples to tingling hardness with the sides of his thumbs.

Julie moaned, but very softly, because Garrett muffled her cry with another bone-melting kiss.

She felt a lot of things in the next few moments—confusion and hope and, of course, the fierce and rising need for completion.

Garrett kissed her for a long time, using plenty of tongue, a harbinger of things to come, and then he bent his head and boldly took one of her nipples into his mouth to suckle.

Julie gasped with pleasure, but softly, and leaned back, supported by the steely strength of the arm he'd curved around her waist, giving herself up to him. The more vulnerable she was to Garrett's lips and his tongue, the better it felt.

He turned to her other breast, taking his sweet time to enjoy her pleasure as well as his own, but when he eased her down onto the bed, sideways, Julie knew what was going to happen, knew she wouldn't stop him.

Knew she would soar.

"Shhh," he said, getting her naked. Arranging her on the edge of the mattress, parting her legs, nibbling the insides of her thighs.

She trembled, murmured his name, groped for him with her hands.

"Shhh," Garrett said again. He nipped at her, the way

he had that other time, but this time, there were no jeans to serve as a buffer, and no underpants, either.

"Oh, God," Julie whimpered.

He parted her.

"Garrett—"

He slid his left hand up her body, pausing to squeeze gently at one breast and then the other, fondling them.

"Hold on," he said. "The ride is just about to start."

That was when he put his mouth on her, and drew her in, and the pleasure was so great that her hips flew upward, seeking him, wanting more. She covered her mouth with both hands, to hold in cries of frantic welcome, and surrendered.

Garrett put his hands under her, lifted her to his mouth, held her there.

She needed him more and then still more, but she didn't dare move her hands, even to beg, because she knew she'd yell fit to raise the roof.

The build was excruciating—Garrett knew when she reached the edge and he eased up, whispering against her most tender flesh. Then he would tease her a little, with the tip of his tongue, and then—

When, at long last, Garrett let her have the orgasm he'd been taunting her with, Julie's entire body buckled in the grip of it. Grasping at Garrett, tangling her fingers in his hair, she gave a long, low, keening wail of satisfaction.

The climax was protracted, a series of ferocious spasms, and Garrett granted Julie no quarter. He devoured her, drove her to peak after peak, even when she was sure she couldn't endure the climb again.

The lovemaking that followed was alternately fevered and sacred.

It was very late—or very early—when Garrett awakened Julie from a deep, sated sleep to kiss her goodbye.

She cried, not only because he was going away, because even then she knew that everything would change after this night.

Probably forever.

Three Days Later

THE FUNERAL WAS relatively dignified, Garrett thought, considering the national media attention surrounding Senator Morgan Cox's short, spectacular fall from grace, followed so soon by his dramatic death.

There were plenty of mourners—Mandy Chante being notably absent—and although the press was in attendance, they had the decency to keep their distance, at least until the services were over.

Following the solemn church ceremony, the gleaming, flower-draped casket was lifted into a hearse and taken to the private side of the Austin airport, then loaded into the cargo hold of a private jet. The plane was provided by certain powerful political interests Garrett preferred not to think about.

He was putting one foot in front of the other, that was all.

Showing up and suiting up, as his high school athletic coach used to put it.

Since leaving the ranch, he'd had several job offers, all of which were high profile, but none were more promising than Nan's. She would serve out the remaining two years of the senator's term as an appointee, but all the while, she and the bosses would be grooming *him*, Garrett, to run in the next election.

Young as he was, Nan had reasoned, Garrett was well known in the state, thanks to his time on Morgan's staff. Plus, he was from an influential Texas family.

Garrett McKettrick, United States senator.

It had a ring to it.

And yet he couldn't stop thinking about Julie Remington, her little boy and the Silver Spur.

Some women, he knew, would have been impressed by his shining future in government.

Julie was not one of those.

Then there was the Silver Spur. Austin still didn't want to believe that Tate was serious about either turning the ranch back into the family enterprise it had been since Clay McKettrick founded it in the early 1900s or just calling it quits, but Garrett knew that was a fact.

Tate was as much a McKettrick as any of them, and he loved the Silver Spur.

He just loved Libby and the twins more, that was all.

Garrett couldn't blame him for that.

Nan, buckling in beside him aboard the borrowed jet, elbowed him lightly in the ribs. The kids were all present, the older ones talking quietly among themselves or just thinking their own thoughts, the smaller ones overseen by attentive nannies.

"All this will be over soon," the widow said.

Her eyes were clear, though red-rimmed from private weeping, and Garrett couldn't help thinking what a class act she was. She was, in fact, downright noble.

Garrett managed a smile, patted her hand. He was a good talker, but right then, he couldn't think of one damn thing to say.

"You'll want to find a place in the Washington area," Nan told him quietly. She paused, looking out the window as the jet taxied along the runway, building up speed for take-off. "I plan to spend a lot more time on the job than Morgan ever did."

Garrett closed his eyes for a moment. The woman had just been to her husband's funeral. Her *philandering* husband's funeral. Now, she was on her way to a city where she had many friends, yes, but even more enemies.

"What?" Nan prompted, with gentle humor, and when Garrett looked at her again, he saw that she was smiling.

"We're having some problems on the ranch," he said. "Rustlers, mainly. Tate's getting married at New Year's and he has full custody of his daughters, for all intents and purposes. He's talking about selling out, doing something else with the rest of his life besides running that ranch."

"Maybe that would be a good idea," Nan mused, surprising him a little. "As you know, I kept my father's ranch after he and Mom were both gone. Oh, it's nowhere near the size of the Silver Spur, but I've worried about that place plenty over the years. Sometimes, I think my life—with Morgan, I mean—might have turned out differently if I hadn't been so stubborn about holding on, keeping that land in the family…"

Her voice fell away.

Garrett sighed. He didn't follow her logic, but that didn't mean she wasn't right. "There's not much point in speculating," he said quietly. "Is there?"

She shook her head. "No," she said. "There's nothing to do now but go on. Make the best of a truly tragic situation."

Garrett waited a beat or two before he spoke again,

making sure they wouldn't be overheard. "Did you know about Mandy Chante?" he asked.

Her answer took him off guard. "Of course I knew," she said. "Didn't you?"

He bit back a swear word. *"No,"* he said.

Nan broke the news gently. "Miss Chante was only the latest of many, Garrett."

"You seemed so shaken up when he made his little announcement at that fundraiser—"

"I *was* shaken up," Nan told him. "But it wasn't because the news came as any big surprise. It was the *public announcement* that had *me* worried." She craned her neck, scanned the immediate area to make sure none of the children or nannies were listening in. "That was when I knew he was losing it."

Garrett frowned. "Losing it?"

"Maybe it was only a midlife crisis," she said, her eyes luminous with sorrow. "Or stress, or a breakdown, or the beginnings of some neurological disease. Morgan wasn't himself, that's all I meant."

Garrett wondered why Nan or the state politicos thought he was *smart* enough to be a senator. Yes, Morgan had seemed distracted in the days and weeks immediately preceding the Mandy Announcement, but hell, the man held high office. He was up to his ass in alligators most of the time, so why *wouldn't* he be distracted?

"I think," Nan said sweetly, "that that cowboy-idealism of yours clouds your vision sometimes, Garrett. You see what *should* be there, not necessarily what is."

His first impulse was to deny Nan's observation, but he remembered Tate saying much the same thing about his blind loyalty to the senator, only in slightly cruder terms.

He closed his eyes, hoping Nan would think he wanted to catch some sleep.

In his mind, he heard Tate's voice. *Things change. People change.*

Damn if he hadn't changed, too, Garrett thought.

The question was—how *much* had he changed?

CHAPTER NINETEEN

HECTIC.

That was the word Julie would have chosen to describe the last week of her life. Between ferrying Calvin to and from Paige's apartment every day, a full schedule of classes, and the tryouts for *Kiss Me Kate*, she'd barely had a chance to draw a deep breath.

She missed Garrett, and fiercely, but if pressed, she would have admitted there was an upside to his being gone. This way, she didn't have to resist having sex with the man—a tall order, considering that he could arouse her merely by running that earth-from-space blue gaze of his over her. If he touched her, kissed her—well, she was completely lost then.

All common sense deserted her. Instantly.

With Garrett gone, she'd expected to gain some perspective, find the strength to put the brakes on before both she *and* Calvin got their hearts broken.

Seated at a large table in the restaurant at the Amble On Inn that Saturday morning, waiting for Gordon and Dixie and the elder Pruetts to show up for the scheduled visit with Calvin, Julie took a sip from her coffee cup. The little boy sat quietly beside her, coloring the place mat provided, using stubby wax crayons in an odd combination of hues.

Calvin was still a bit too pale for her liking, and he

seemed thinner than before, but he was over the stomach flu. Since Garrett's departure, though, he'd been especially quiet.

"Maybe they're not going to show up," he said, lifting his eyes from the printed place mat.

The words punctured Julie's heart, but she smiled. She was very good at smiling whether she felt like it or not. A questionable skill, to be sure, but one that had stood her in good stead since she was a little girl, huddled shoulder-to-shoulder with her sisters on the front porch of the old house, watching their mother drive away with her lover.

"Smile," Libby had whispered to her all those years ago, trying so hard to help. "It won't hurt so much if you smile."

Paige, the little one, had let out a wail of despair and run toward the front gate, sobbing hysterically and calling, "Mommy! Mommy, come back!"

Libby and Julie had rushed to stop Paige from chasing behind the car, both of them trying to smile.

Both of them with tears streaking their cheeks.

It still hurts, Lib, Julie told her sister silently. *Even when you smile.*

"I'm sure they're just late," Julie said to Calvin, checking her watch. "Maybe they had car trouble or some other kind of delay."

Calvin rolled his sky-blue eyes. The lenses of his glasses gleamed with cleanliness that sunny morning, because he hadn't been up long enough to smear them. "They have your cell number," he said.

A lightbulb went on in Julie's beleaguered mind. "Which reminds me," she said. "Your dad told me you called him a couple of times. Is that true?"

Calvin squirmed a little, but there was defiance in his expression, too. "Yes," he said. "It's true."

The door of the restaurant swung open and both of them looked in that direction, expecting Gordon and his wife and his parents.

Instead, Brent Brogan nodded in greeting and strolled over to the counter to order take-out coffee.

"Did you think I wouldn't let you call your dad, if you asked me about it first?"

Calvin considered his mother's question with the concentration of a Supreme Court justice. He was stalling, of course. Hoping Brent would stop by the table to pass the time of day, or the others would arrive, giving him time to frame an answer.

No luck.

Julie waited patiently, her hands folded in her lap.

Calvin sighed, and his small shoulders drooped under his clean T-shirt and lined windbreaker. His hair was slicked down and his face was clean and if Gordon dared to disappoint him—well—Julie didn't know *what* she'd do.

"The other kids at school, they can all call their dad pretty much whenever they want to," Calvin confessed. "I wondered what it was like. So I used Aunt Libby's cell phone when she was babysitting me—she left it on the counter in the kitchen—and I called my dad."

Julie blinked a couple of times, wanting to cry and refusing to give in to the urge. Calvin was going through some big transitions for such a little boy, and the last thing he needed was a weeping mother.

Brent, having collected and paid for his coffee, waved to Julie as he turned to leave. She waved back.

"Was that a bad thing to do?" Calvin asked earnestly, pushing his glasses up the bridge of his nose.

"Borrowing your aunt's cell phone without asking? Definitely not a good thing to do. But calling your dad? That's normal, buddy." She paused, resisting a urge to smooth his hair or pat his shoulder or fuss in some other way. "What was it like?"

He looked genuinely puzzled. "What was what like?"

"Calling your dad, like any other kid."

Calvin raised one eyebrow. "Do you really want to know?"

She leaned in. "Of course I want to know, Calvin," she told him. "That's why I *asked* you."

"It was weird," Calvin replied, frowning at the mystery of it all. "He's my dad, but he's *not* my dad." He blinked at her, confounded. "I know it's hard to understand—"

Julie sighed, smiled. It wasn't an effort this time. "I think I follow," she said.

Calvin opened his mouth, about to reply, but Julie's cell phone rang at just that moment. Gordon's name flashed on the screen.

"Hello?" Julie said.

"Julie? It's Gordon." He sounded happily apologetic. "We got a late start out of Dallas this morning, and then we ran into some traffic, but we're almost there."

Julie smiled, happy for Calvin. Although he tried to act blasé, she knew the little guy would have been crushed if Gordon and the others had been no-shows.

"We'll wait," she said.

"Good," Gordon said. "Mom and Dad are so excited about meeting their grandson. They'll probably want a million pictures."

The voice of an older person sounded in the background on Gordon's end. "A million won't be half enough!"

Julie's heart warmed. "See you soon," she told Gordon.

Barely ten minutes later, the Pruetts arrived.

Gordon's parents were sweet people, delighted with Calvin and cordial to Julie. They'd brought him a pile of presents, all cheerfully wrapped, and Dixie got out her digital camera, the way she'd done on the first visit, and started right in on getting those million pictures snapped.

GARRETT WANTED TO get home, that was all, and the sooner the better.

Even flying seemed too slow.

A flash of something caught his attention, though, and he went to investigate, swinging the Cessna toward the dry riverbed, where he and Tate had taken a look around the other day.

There were at least two rigs parked down there, between the Quonset huts, one of them the property of the Silver Spur. He didn't recognize the other, a sleek white extended-cab pickup, but that wasn't strange. There were a lot of trucks in the county, let alone the state.

It was something else that bothered Garrett, something visceral, almost subliminal. A clenching sensation in the pit of his stomach.

Frowning, Garrett pulled his cell phone from the pocket of his denim jacket, and speed-dialed his brother.

The answer was brisk and businesslike, as usual. "Tate McKettrick."

"I'm over the old camp," Garrett said. "Did you send a crew out there to do repairs or something?"

"No," Tate said slowly. "I thought you were still in Austin—or even Washington."

"Well," Garrett replied, swooping low over the camp, "you thought wrong. I'm back."

"For how long?"

"That depends. I don't like the looks of this, Tate. Something is definitely going on down there. You'd better call Brent, or even the state police, and get them out here quick—"

"Garrett," Tate interrupted, "meet me at the airstrip. Don't try to handle this by yourself."

Garrett didn't get a chance to answer.

Two men came running out of the Quonset huts, and they both had rifles.

He was in too low and too close to escape; the bullets ripped through the right wing, and the Cessna pitched wildly to one side.

"Garrett!" Tate yelled. "What the hell?"

Garrett's voice was dead calm as he uttered what he was pretty sure would be the last words he ever spoke. "I'm going down," he said. "Don't sell the ranch."

"Garrett!" Tate repeated, sounding panicked.

Garrett didn't reply. He was too busy struggling with the controls.

He was in one hell of a fix. If he managed to set the plane down without the fuel tank exploding, the men with the rifles would finish him off for sure. If he botched the landing or fate didn't cooperate, he and the Cessna would be blown, as the saying went, sky high.

He tilted the nose slightly downward, lined up with

the riverbed, muttered a quick prayer and bellied out the plane.

The metal shrieked as it tore away, and cracks snaked across the windshield.

The machine ground to a deafening stop, and then there was silence.

Garrett waited, holding his breath, for the blast.

It didn't happen.

One heartbeat, another.

A cold sweat broke out all over his body.

His head was bleeding, but nothing was broken, as far as he could tell.

Of course the riflemen were still out there, and they would come after him any second now. No doubt Tate was on his way by now, Austin with him, and Brent Brogan must have been called as well.

The figurative cavalry was coming, bugles blaring, but his brothers and the police weren't going to get there in time, no matter how fast they were traveling.

He leaned down, felt under his seat until he found the trusty .357 Magnum he'd never had to use before.

Always a first time, he thought.

A face loomed in front of the shattered windshield.

Garrett gripped the .357, hoping it was out of sight. Let his head loll to one side and waited.

"I think he's dead or knocked out," Charlie Bates told his partner. "Open the door, though. We've got to make sure."

CHAPTER TWENTY

CHARLIE BATES? Garrett thought, playing possum while he waited for the door of the plane to be wrenched open. His palm sweated around the handle of the .357, but he had a good grip and the safety was off, so all he had to do was pull the trigger.

But, Charlie—a rustler? Maybe even the head of a whole *outfit* of cattle thieves?

Shooting a plane out of the sky definitely qualified as a desperate act; the rest was supposition on Garrett's part.

Time seemed to grind by on sticky gears, halting and then restarting again.

Easy, Garrett told himself. *All you need to think about right now is staying alive.*

You have so many good reasons to stay alive.

Julie.

Calvin.

Tate and Austin, Libby and the twins, and the Silver Spur Ranch.

Reasons aplenty, Garrett figured.

Listing them helped him to calm down and to stay focused.

Charlie was no longer looming in front of the plane's shattered windshield—no, he was on the ground now, with his buddy, the two of them cussing and pulling to get the door of the plane open. It must have been dented in good, that door, because they didn't seem to be making a whole lot of progress.

They were creative cussers, though.

In the distance, Garrett thought he heard the faintest sound of sirens, but when the door finally started to give way, the scream of bent metal drowned out every other sound except that of the blood pounding in his ears.

Then Charlie stuck his ugly mug into the cockpit, and Garrett stuck his .357 under the man's chin.

"Don't move," Garrett told him.

The scrambling noise of somebody getting the hell out of Dodge indicated that Bates's partner was already on the run. Of course, there could be more of the sons of bitches out there—he'd only seen two, but that didn't mean the tally was right.

With Tate and Austin, the cops, and half the hands working the Silver Spur on their way, whoever it was wouldn't get far.

And Charlie Bates wasn't going anywhere at all.

Not with the business end of a .357 under his chin.

"You wouldn't shoot me," Charlie said. His Adam's apple bobbed up to the end of the pistol barrel and then back down, and he put on a sickly grin. "Why, I've known you since you were knee-high—"

"You know, Charlie," Garrett said, with rueful ease, "up until a few minutes ago, I would have said pretty much the same thing about you. That you wouldn't shoot me, I mean. But damn if you or your buddy didn't blow my airplane out of the sky with a deer gun."

Charlie gulped again.

"How long have you been stealing our cattle, Charlie?" Garrett asked, to pass the time of day.

He could hear a rig tearing toward the road—it was probably the white extended-cab he hadn't recognized—and there were definitely sirens, coming closer.

Charlie considered denying the charge, Garrett saw that in his face. Or maybe he was just stalling. Either way, he took so long answering the question that Garrett dug the pistol barrel in a little deeper to inspire confession.

"It started out, we'd just take a cow here and a cow there," the older man finally said. "Sell 'em for cheap and pocket the cash."

Garrett nodded. "Go on."

Charlie's gaze shifted nervously to one side; the sirens were almost on top of them now, but someone else had gotten there ahead of the law and the paramedics.

Garrett heard Tate yell his name.

"I'm all right," Garrett yelled back. His gaze was locked on Charlie's. The old rustler stood on what was left of the wing, and his foothold might have been a little shaky. "Watch out for Charlie here, though. I've got a pistol all but jammed down his worthless, thieving gullet, but he might be armed."

"I ain't armed," Charlie whined, sweating now. "I had a rifle, but I set that down when I climbed up onto the nose to see if you were gonna give us any trouble or not."

"Guess you know the answer to that one," Garrett said. There was no pain, but he was starting to feel a little light-headed, as if he'd been riding horseback under a hot Texas sun without a hat.

Tate must have dragged Charlie down off the bent wing, but it was Austin who climbed up and stood in Bates's place.

Eyes scanning the length of Garrett's body before

landing on his face, Austin carefully relieved him of the .357. There were other voices outside the plane now— all around—cops, cowboys and God knew who else.

It was over.

"You hurting anywhere in particular, brother?" Austin asked.

"No," Garrett answered honestly, "but I'm sure as hell *numb* in a few places."

"Maybe you ought to sit tight 'til the paramedics can check you out."

Garrett shook his head. He smelled gas and engine oil. "The fuel tank could still go up," he said. "Let's get clear."

Austin nodded, waited a beat, then moved aside.

Garrett made it out onto the wing, but he would have fallen into the stony bottom of the riverbed if Austin hadn't grabbed hold of his arm just as his knees buckled underneath him.

Tate hurried over to help, and each of them got under one of Garrett's shoulders to hold him upright.

Garrett felt it coming.

Either Tate or Austin yelled for everybody to get as far from the plane as they could.

The three of them hadn't covered more than fifty yards when the explosion back-blasted them, sent them sprawling in the dirt.

Garrett swore, turned his head to look back. Heat scalded his eyeballs dry, and he had to avert his gaze again, blink to make them stop burning.

Flaming debris rained down from the sky.

"Shit," Austin said, clearly impressed by the experience. "We damn near bought the farm that time."

Tate was already getting up off the ground. He'd lost

his hat, and his clothes were dirty and torn. He put a hand out for Garrett, and Garrett took it, let his brother haul him to his feet. This time, he was able to stand on his own, though he swayed a bit before he steadied himself.

"Yeah," Garrett agreed. "We damn near did."

Brogan approached, shaking his head. He watched the plane burn for a few moments before he spoke. "Either somebody up there likes you," he told Garrett, "or you're one lucky son of a gun."

Garrett laughed. "I figure it's both," he said. "There was another guy with Charlie—in a white pickup?"

"We've got him," Brogan replied, with a smile. He gave the burning plane another glance, shook his head again. *"Damn,"* he said. "That is a sight to see."

Garrett rubbed his chin. He beard was coming in again. "I guess my career as a crimefighter has probably peaked," he quipped.

The chief grinned. "I reckon we can take it from here," he said. "Though there will be plenty of questions for you to answer down the road a ways, after the paramedics check you over and your brothers take you home so Esperanza can fuss over you and all."

The sky tipped, landed at a crazy angle.

Garrett passed out.

When he came around again, he was lying on his back on a stretcher in the back of an ambulance with an oxygen mask on his face.

One of the ambulance attendants—Garrett didn't recognize him, so he must have been new in Blue River—was beside him.

Austin was at his other side and the rig was moving, eating up road at a good clip.

Garrett tried to take off the mask, but the paramedic—
Al, according to the name stitched on his shirt—stopped
him.

Austin knuckled Garrett lightly in the shoulder.
"Relax, cowboy," he said. "We're just taking you to the
clinic, so the docs can look you over. Maybe take an
X-ray or two."

Garrett nodded and closed his eyes.

THE VISIT WITH Gordon and his parents lasted for a couple of hours, and by the time it was over, Calvin's bat-
teries were starting to run down. Julie explained that
he had just recovered from a stomach flu and they all
left the restaurant at the Amble On Inn together, Gordon carrying a now-sleepy Calvin, his father lugging
all the presents they'd brought.

Since it was a fairly long drive back to Dallas, Gordon and Dixie, along with the elder Pruetts, of course,
planned to spend the night in Blue River. It was agreed
that they would all get together again for breakfast in
the morning, this time at the Silver Dollar Saloon, provided Calvin was well enough.

Julie had planned to leave her son in Paige's care
again and spend the rest of the afternoon packing over
at the cottage.

The county ambulance, not the local one, streaked
past as she was waiting to pull out of the motel/restau-
rant parking lot, and at the same moment, Julie's cell
phone jangled in the depths of her purse.

Julie didn't dig for it.

Tate was behind the ambulance, in his truck, and
Libby was with him.

Every instinct Julie had kicked in. Instead of making

a right, toward the cottage and Paige's apartment across the street from it, she took a left, and followed Tate and Libby and, ahead of them, the ambulance.

Calvin, buckled into his car seat in back, had already nodded off. He must have been pooped, Julie thought distractedly, not to be awakened by the shrill screech of that siren.

Two nurses and a doctor were waiting at the entrance to the clinic with a gurney.

Tate parked nearby and leaped out of the truck, and Julie pulled up alongside. Libby, seeing her, rolled down the window.

"It's Garrett," she said. "He's all right, really, but—"

Garrett.

Julie's heart seized like a clenched fist. It was actually painful, like being grabbed from the inside.

She turned, saw the paramedics unloading Garrett from the back of the ambulance. Austin jumped out after him.

Julie tried to get a good look at Garrett, but he had something over his face and there were too many people in the way.

She shoved open the door of her car. "Will you look after Calvin?" she asked Libby, breathless.

Libby smiled faintly and nodded.

Julie followed Garrett and the others into the clinic.

"What happened?" she asked, snagging hold of Austin's shirtsleeve when he would have gone right into the examining room with the rest of them.

"Some rustlers shot his plane down, that's all," Austin said.

And then he was gone.

Some rustlers shot his plane down.

That's all?

Julie swayed.

Libby came in with Calvin, who was baffled, blinking away sleep. "I'm not sick," he said. "Why are we at the clinic?"

Libby squeezed her nephew against her side. "Stay calm," she told Julie, in her cheeriest big-sister voice. Then, after a beat or two, she asked, "Do you want me to call Paige? See if she can come and pick Calvin up?"

"That would be good," Julie said. Anxiety swelled inside her. What was happening to Garrett at that moment?

Was he dying?

Surely he would have been airlifted to Austin or even Houston or Dallas if he'd been so seriously injured, wouldn't he?

On the other hand, the man had been in a *plane crash,* according to Austin. He could be *so badly* injured that there wasn't time to take him to a city hospital. Maybe he needed immediate medical care just to survive.

Maybe it was touch and go.

Life and death.

"I still don't understand why we're at the clinic," Calvin said, looking up at his fretful mother.

Julie didn't want to tell her little boy that Garrett, one of his all-time favorite people in the world, had been brought here—he was sure to freak out and besides, she didn't have enough information to explain what was happening.

"Your mom is visiting somebody," Libby said, as she and Julie exchanged glances. "That's all. Just visiting."

"Oh," Calvin said. "Like when Gramma had to spend the night here at the clinic in a hospital bed after she drove your car through the front wall of the Perk Up Coffee Shop and put you out of business for good, Aunt Libby?"

"Like that," Libby said, giving him a tender smile. Then she bit her lower lip. "Sort of."

Tate came out of the back, and he was so focused on Libby that he might or might not have noticed Julie and Calvin standing there.

"We'll be here for a while," he said to Libby. "They're taking X-rays."

Libby nodded.

"Who?" Calvin demanded. "Who is getting X-rayed?"

Tate looked down at the child, registered his identity, then rustled up a faint smile. "One of my cowboys took a spill," he replied. He was perceptive, for a man, it seemed to Julie, dazed as she was, but then, he was also a father. A good one.

He knew bad news about Garrett might be more than a little guy could process.

She felt a rush of appreciation for her future brother-in-law.

And tears of worry scalded her eyes.

Libby got out her cell phone and went to the other side of the lobby to call Paige.

"This—cowboy," Julie choked out, staring up into Tate's blazingly-blue eyes, "is he going to be all right?"

"We think so," Tate assured her, and he even grinned, though there wasn't much wattage behind it. He was pale beneath his tan and his five o'clock shadow.

Julie nodded, dashed at her eyes with the back of one hand.

"Paige is on her way," Libby said, returning.

Julie just nodded again.

Libby took her by the arm, led her to a chair and sat her down.

Tate disappeared into the back again.

Paige came, spoke in whispers with Libby, took Calvin and left again.

Julie felt as though she were underwater, inside one of those old-fashioned diving bells with the heavy brass helmet and only a little face-wide window to look through.

Blood hummed in her ears.

Libby sat down beside Julie, rested a comforting hand on her back. "So," she said gently, "Paige and I were right. You *are* in love with Garrett."

There didn't seem to be much point in denying the fact, especially to one of the two women who had always been able to see right through her.

Julie nodded miserably, knotted her fingers together so tightly that the knuckles ached. A tear trickled down her cheek and dropped onto her right thumb.

Libby hugged her. "It's okay," she murmured. "We can talk about it later."

The wait seemed endless.

Finally, though, Tate and Austin came out of the examination area together. Both of them looked done-in, but they were grinning, too.

"Garrett wants to see you," Austin told Julie, when she and Libby stood to wait for news. "Hell, he hasn't *shut up* about wanting to see you since I told you she were out here."

Julie almost laughed, but it was a purely hysterical reaction. "He's all right, then?"

"Garrett's fine," Tate said, but he moved into Libby's arms, and closed his eyes as he rested his chin on the top of her head. "Just roughed up a little, that's all."

"Come on," Austin told Julie. "I'll take you to him."

Garrett was sitting on the edge of an exam table, pulling on his boots. His clothes were filthy, and so was his hair, but that grin of his was bright enough to knock Julie Remington right back on her heels.

His shiner had lightened considerably.

"Hey," he said hoarsely, drinking her in with his eyes.

"Hey," she replied.

"See you around, Austin," he told his brother, without looking away from Julie's face.

Austin laughed and left the room.

"I love you," Julie blurted out, the moment she and Garrett were alone in the room.

And then she blushed crimson.

"I was about to tell you the same thing," he said. "Nothing like almost getting killed to straighten out a man's priorities. Which is not to say that I hadn't already decided to come back here and ask you if you're totally sure you wouldn't want to be involved with a political animal like me."

Julie went to him. Her eyes were wet and she couldn't seem to speak.

Garrett slid off the exam table to stand, put his arms loosely around her waist.

She lowered her head, but Garrett made her tip it back by tilting his own to one side and catching her mouth in a light kiss.

"I love you, Julie Remington," he told her.

She looked up at Garrett, almost unable to believe she'd heard him correctly. "Really?"

He laughed. It was a throaty sound, all man. "Really," he said. "Will you marry me, Julie?"

She blinked. "Marry you?"

He nodded. "I was thinking we could maybe muscle in on Tate and Libby's wedding, come New Year's, tell the preacher to make it a double."

Julie's eyes went so wide they hurt around the edges. "Yes," she said. Amazed at herself. Amazed at *him*. "Even if it means living in Washington or Austin, instead of Blue River, I'll marry you, Garrett McKettrick."

"Washington or Austin?" He seemed puzzled. His arms were still around her, and he pressed her close, and the contact practically struck sparks.

"Isn't that where you 'political animals' like to hang out?"

"This particular animal," he said, nuzzling her mouth again, getting ready to kiss her in earnest, "wants to live on the Silver Spur with his wife and his stepson and tend to business."

He murmured the part about tending to business, just as his lips touched hers.

Julie's knees went weak.

He kissed her as if he meant it.

"THIS IS GOING to be my room?" Calvin asked, a few days later, upstairs in the ranch house, in Garrett's apartment. "Really?"

Garrett winked at Julie, then put his hands on Calvin's back and gave him a little push over the threshold. "If it suits you," he said, "it's all yours."

Julie looked on, smiling. After giving the matter a lot of thought, she'd agreed to share Garrett's room, and Calvin seemed to be okay with that.

Calvin stepped inside, looked around. Garrett and Austin had moved the old furniture out, and replaced it with Calvin's things from the cottage. There was a flat-screen TV mounted on one wall, and he would have his own bathroom, too.

"Can Harry sleep here, too?" Calvin asked, looking up at Garrett.

Garrett crouched, so he could meet the child's gaze directly.

Julie ached with love for both of them.

"Sure, he can, pardner," Garrett answered gravely, ruffling Calvin's hair. "Harry's a member of the family."

Calvin beamed. "He can even get up and down the stairs by himself now," he crowed, as the dog strolled in to join them, having spent the morning lounging in front of Garrett's fireplace.

"He's pretty handy for a three-legged dog," Garrett agreed, rising to his full height and turning to Julie with mischief dancing in his eyes.

"Ready to go out to the airstrip and check out the new plane?" he asked. Calvin had been promised a flight later on; for now, he'd be staying at the ranch house with Esperanza.

Julie nodded, feeling all shy and warm, and very much in love.

She felt a tingle at the prospect of being alone with Garrett, even in the narrow confines of his Porsche.

He'd be trading that in for a truck soon, he'd told her.

He was just a rancher at heart, and not a politician at all.

Go figure.

They were both content to be silent during the short drive to the airstrip. There, the jet gleamed in the sun, considerably larger than the Cessna destroyed in the crash.

"This is yours?" Julie marveled. They hadn't gotten out of the Porsche.

"Tate and Austin and I bought it together," Garrett answered, looking at her instead of the sleek private jet. "Technically, it's the property of the Silver Spur."

"Pretty fancy for counting cattle from the sky," Julie remarked. Charlie Bates and his accomplice were in police custody, but the case was far from closed. The rustling operation was a big one, and some of the thieves were still at large.

Garrett chuckled. "We'll use a helicopter for that," he told her, squeezing her hand. "Or do it the old-fashioned way—on horseback."

Julie swallowed hard. "Are you sure, Garrett? That this is what you really want? Living on the ranch, I mean, and getting married? Giving up your crack at being a senator?"

He leaned across the console and tasted her mouth. "I'm sure," he told her. Then he inclined his head toward the jet again. "Come on," he said. "Let's go take the tour."

Julie felt a sweet shiver of excitement. The jet's door stood open, and the steps had been lowered.

Garrett got out of the Porsche, sprinted around to Julie's side and opened the car door for her.

He took her hand, pulled her toward the plane.

At the base of the steps, Garrett swept Julie up into his arms, carried her easily up the incline, both of them laughing.

The inside of the plane was as elegantly simple as the outside. There were eight seats, upholstered in buttery leather.

A silver wine cooler stood on the marble-topped counter separating the small galley from the main cabin, holding a bottle of champagne. Two crystal glasses had been set out as well.

Garrett drew up the stairs, then shut and secured the door.

A delicious little thrill skittered up Julie's spine. "Are we going somewhere?" she asked, almost breathless.

He took her into his arms. "Oh, we'll be going *lots* of places," he drawled, bending his head to nibble at the side of her neck. "Starting with Paris."

"Paris? You mean, right now?"

"No," he said, "I was planning to *make love* right now."

She blushed, but she didn't pull back out of his arms. "Good," she told him, "because I've got Calvin to look after and my classes to teach and a musical to put on, and I don't have the faintest idea where my passport is or even if it's still valid."

Garrett kissed her, thoroughly and for a long time, before he replied. "Calvin will be fine with Libby and Tate for a few days," he said. "Paige found your passport, and it hasn't expired."

Julie opened her mouth, closed it again. So much had happened recently that she could barely keep up.

Tate had hired Ron Strivens, for instance, and he and the kids would be moving to the ranch soon. With a lot of help from Libby and Paige, Julie had managed to pack up the contents of the cottage, most of which were in storage for the time being.

"That still leaves my job," Julie pointed out. "And the rehearsals for the musical."

"You're on vacation, as of today," Garrett told her, "and several of the parents are going to cover the rehearsals."

Julie slid her arms around Garrett's neck, tilted her head to one side. "Well, Garrett McKettrick," she said, "do you *always* get what you want?"

His grin was wicked. "Most of the time, yeah."

"And we're going to Paris? Just like that?"

"We're going to bed first," he said. "*Then* we're going to Paris." Garrett held her a little closer, flicked at her earlobe with the very tip of his tongue. "In the meantime, you might want to fasten your seat belt..."

* * * * *

The Texas McKettricks aren't done yet.
When an injury ends Austin's world-class
rodeo career, he returns to Blue River
as a last resort. But instead of peace and quiet,
he finds nurse Paige Remington, who is determined
to help him heal in body and heart.

Look for The McKettricks Of Texas: Austin
by #1 New York Times *bestselling author*
Linda Lael Miller!

Please turn the page for a sneak peek at
Where the Creek Bends,
a brand-new book from
#1 New York Times *bestselling author*
Linda Lael Miller.

After a disastrous attempt at marriage, Madison
Bettencourt returns home to Painted Pony Creek
to care for her ailing grandmother and winds up
confronting the mystery of what happened to her
childhood best friend and unexpectedly finding
love.

Enjoy this excerpt from Where the Creek Bends,
available late fall 2024!

CHAPTER ONE

SHE BURST—NO, *ERUPTED*—through a shimmering splash of sunshine, like a human bullet, or an angel stepping in from a neighboring realm where magic was the rule rather than the rare exception.

Half blinded by the glare—it was mid-July, the Montana sky was sugar-bowl blue, and he was sweating in his town-marshal getup—Liam McKettrick squinted hard, sure he was seeing things.

Too much stress, too little sleep.

But she was real.

A bride, in full regalia, veil billowing, lacy skirts and snow-white train trailing in the dry dust of Bitter Gulch's Main Street, was heading straight for the Hard Luck Saloon.

Liam, standing on the balcony outside the make-believe brothel above the very authentic—and currently empty—establishment below, bolted for the back stairs.

Whatever was going on here, he damn well wasn't about to miss it.

He'd just entered the saloon and established himself behind the long bar, idly wiping out a glass with a piece of cloth, when she arrived.

She struck the classic swinging doors with both palms and enough force to send them crashing against the inside wall, then stomped across the sawdust floor to the bar.

After hoisting her slender self onto a stool, she threw back her veil, blew a strand of brown-gold hair off her forehead with one determined breath, and slapped one hand down onto the polished surface between them.

"Set 'em up, bartender," she said.

Liam was doing his damnedest not to grin.

The whole thing was bizarre.

And way more fun than he'd ever expected to have on an ordinary day in the "town" of Bitter Gulch—an oasis of fantasy, a place where men, women and children came to escape the modern world for a while and experience the Old West.

Standing at the southern edge of Painted Pony Creek, Montana, Bitter Gulch was Liam's brainchild; he'd designed it. Hired his younger brother, Jesse, to oversee the construction phase.

Liam swallowed, unable to look away from the bride, especially now that she was up close and very personal. Just across the bar.

She smelled of dust, subtle perfume, and something sugary.

"What'll it be?" he asked, his voice slightly hoarse. He didn't use it much, his voice, as a general rule, and it was only eleven o'clock in the morning, according to the huge antique clock on the opposite wall.

So his social skills were still resurfacing.

She paused to ponder the question, looking solemn. She had wide hazel eyes, heavily lashed, and full of—something. Indignation, clearly, and confusion.

Pain, too, though she was doing a fairly good job of hiding that.

Liam's heart, usually heavily defended—like an isolated cavalry fort in those thrilling days of yesteryear, besieged by furious warriors riding painted ponies—hitched, and hitched hard.

"Whiskey," the woman decided.

"What kind?" Whiskey was whiskey, and he could have poured a shot without asking another question, but he wanted to extend this encounter.

It was amazing.

She was amazing, with those expressive eyes. Her skin was flawless, her lips full, and her shining brown hair now slightly out of kilter under the exquisitely made veil, a lacy affair that might have been assembled from starlight and spiderwebs in some strange and secret place beyond the tattered edges of the ordinary world.

"Any kind," she responded.

Liam nodded, put his hand out and introduced himself. "Liam McKettrick," he said.

They shook. Her hand felt dainty, but strong, too.

"Madison Bettencourt," she replied, straightening her spine and lifting her chin a little. Tears rose along her lower lashes and smudged her mascara when she brushed them away with the back of one hand. "By now, I would have been Madison *Sterne*," she told him. "But I bolted."

Liam poured two fingers of Maker's Mark into a clean glass, listening not just with his ears, but with the whole of his being.

It was an unusual thing, the way his senses seemed to be revving up, as if he were a race car instead of a man.

He'd never felt anything quite like this before.

"Ice?" he asked. He pushed the glass toward her, slid it, more like. He wasn't planning on making any sudden moves, lest she dissolve into sparkling particles and disappear. "Maybe some cola?"

Madison glanced back at the double doors, looking a little uneasy. "Ice," she said resolutely. "Otherwise, I'll take it straight."

Again, Liam wanted to laugh, but he knew that would be a mistake.

He filled a paper cup at the ice machine, brought it to Madison without another word.

"Is this place real?" she asked, after dumping the ice unceremoniously into her glass, causing some of it to splash over the rim and stand melting on the scarred wooden surface of the bar.

"What do you mean, is it real?" Liam asked, amused, and not completely able to hide it, try though he did.

"It's like going back in time or something," Madison responded after a long sip of whiskey and an almost comical sigh of satisfaction. "One minute, I was at *my wedding*, across the road, finding out I'd just said 'I do' to a total pushover of a mama's boy, and the next—" She paused, raised and lowered her shoulders in a semi-shrug, and gazed sadly down into her drink.

A moment later, the lovely shoulders slumped slightly, and the sight gave Liam a twinge deep in his chest. If he'd known her for more than five minutes, he would have put his arms around her right then and there, held her close. Reassured her somehow.

Yet another bad idea.

A few seconds of silence stumbled by. Then she looked up, met his eyes, and finished with "The next minute, I was here, in the Old West. In a real saloon." Another sigh. "You know what I wish, Liam McKettrick the bartender? I wish I really could go back in time. Be somebody else. Live a different life—an entirely different life."

Madison took another swig of her whiskey. At this rate, she was going to be disastrously drunk, and soon.

Liam moved the bottle out of sight and leaned against the bar, bracing himself with his forearms.

She looked him over, taking in his collarless white cotton shirt, the black waistcoat he always wore when he spent time in Bitter Gulch. Along with his tall scuffed boots, suspenders, and itchy woolen trousers—not to mention the shiny silver star pinned to his coat—the outfit added to the ambience.

And Bitter Gulch was all *about* ambience.

That was the point of the exercise.

Tourists came from all over the world to don costumes, live the Old West experience. Movies were filmed there on occasion, along with TV series for all the major players in the streaming game.

Liam knew most of the visitors wouldn't have lasted a day in the *real* Old West, but then, that didn't matter. They were paying to pretend, not to teleport themselves back to a previous century, when most of the amenities they were used to had yet to exist. Hot and cold running water had been a rarity in communities like Painted Pony Creek, electricity a fledgling science, and Wi-Fi—well, nonexistent, of course.

He pictured his kids, Keely, nine, and Cavan, seven, riding in wagons or on horseback everywhere they went, stripped of their cell phones, their tablets, the huge flat-screen TV in their grandparents' family room, and smiled.

God, he missed them.

"You wouldn't like it," he responded at some length.

He'd gotten lost in those lovely eyes of hers, along with his own thoughts.

"I wouldn't like what?" she asked, still putting on a brave front.

"Life in the past," he replied. "There are reasons why we're advised to live in the present, you know."

She let the remark pass.

"Are you really a lawman?" Madison inquired, having drained her glass while Liam was pondering the situation and, as always, wishing Keely and Cavan were with him instead of far away, staying with their grandparents in Seattle.

Liam allowed himself a minimal grin, really just an uptick at one corner of his mouth, hardly noticeable to the casual observer. "No," he replied. "I'm an architect."

Madison frowned, musing again. She was getting tipsy, and Liam wondered how much champagne she'd had before deciding to ditch the mama's boy.

What a numbskull that guy must be.

"You don't look like an architect," she responded solemnly.

"What does an architect look like?" he asked.

"I don't know," Madison answered, still as serious as the proverbial heart attack. "But I'd have pegged you for an actor, with your dark hair and those indigo-blue eyes and—well." She paused, gestured with both hands, indicating their surroundings. "When I picture an architect, I guess I see someone more—ordinary. Like an accountant."

"An accountant," Liam echoed, hiding another grin.

"Whatever," Madison said, and now she sounded cheerier, although the word got tangled up in her tongue before she turned it loose.

Resolutely, she slapped the bar again. "More whiskey."

"Look," Liam reasoned. "Maybe it isn't the best idea—"

"Are you cutting me off?" she interrupted, though calmly. Her beautifully shaped eyebrows drew together for a moment.

"No," Liam replied. "I'm just suggesting that, after what happened today, you might want to pace yourself a bit. That's all."

"Do you want to know, Liam McKettrick, architect and barkeep, just what *did* happen? I mean, bartenders are supposed to be good listeners, right?"

"I'd say I'm a pretty fair listener," Liam allowed. Then, knowing he'd already lost the argument, unspoken though it was, he picked up the bottle he'd set aside moments before, twisted off the cap, and poured her a double.

"I could use one of those right about now," Madison replied after another healthy swig of liquor. "A good listener, I mean."

"Okay, shoot," Liam said. He'd done a lot of listening in his life, largely because he was, as the saying goes, a man of few words. So many people were uncomfortable with silence, felt a need to speak into it. "What happened?"

Madison mirrored his earlier posture, leaning on her forearms, all but hidden by puffy sleeves, and said in a confidential tone, "You won't believe it."

"Try me," Liam urged. Standing back a little, to give the runaway bride some space. No sense crowding her.

She seemed solid, but magical, too, which meant she could be a figment of his imagination, not a regular woman.

"I really thought Jeffrey was the man for me," she

began, shaking her head, apparently reflecting upon her previous choices. "I mean, he was so different from my first husband. Tom was a lying, cheating dirtbag."

Liam raised one eyebrow, though he was pretty sure she didn't notice that. She was too involved in the story she was telling.

"Your first husband?" he prompted casually, picking up the cloth, wiping down the spotless surface of the bar, glancing at the clock again. In less than an hour, Bitter Gulch would be open for business, bustling with appropriately costumed employees and the usual horde of families on summer vacation.

This delightful interlude would be over.

And how many times could something like this happen in one man's life?

"Yes," she began. "His name was—is—Tom Wainwright. He's an airline pilot, very good-looking and very macho. We were married for three years."

Liam thought of his own marital history. Reminded himself he was in no position to judge, given that he'd gone into that crap show of a marriage with both eyes wide-open.

His late wife, Waverly, a model and sometime actress, had been beautiful, with her fit, slender body, her gleaming dark hair, her stunning green eyes.

She'd also been a walking red flag, vindictive when she was angry, which was often, jealous of just about everybody, and prone to straying, although Liam hadn't known that until he was in way over his head, with two children to think about.

Inwardly, he sighed. "Go on," he said.

Madison's fascinating chameleon eyes seemed to be fixed on another place and time. "He promised," she said.

Liam waited.

"Tom knew I wanted children more than anything, and he promised we would start a family as soon as he got promoted, after we moved, that kind of thing. And, like a fool, I believed him." Madison paused, looked down at her drink. Her left hand, shimmering with a doorknob of a diamond and an impressive wedding band to match, trembled slightly. "Turns out, he never wanted children. He was just stringing me along, waiting for my grandmother to die, so he could raid my inheritance. And if all that wasn't bad enough, he got another woman pregnant. I divorced him."

"Understandable," Liam said, not wanting to break the flow. He felt honored, somehow, receiving her confidences in that quiet and otherwise empty saloon.

And very sympathetic. After all, he could identify. He would have divorced Waverly, for similar reasons, if she hadn't gotten sick. She'd died only six months after she'd been diagnosed with a virulent strain of leukemia.

Everything he'd felt for her had dried up and blown away like so much dust once he'd finally admitted to himself that she'd been unfaithful, not just once or twice, but dozens of times.

But she'd been so desperately ill.

And she *was* the mother of his children.

He'd had to stand by her, whether he wanted to or not.

And stand by her he had, until the end, though even as she was dying, Waverly had been distant with him, cold.

If it weren't for you and these kids, she'd said once, lying skeletal in her hospital bed, breathless and bitter, while machines beeped and wheezed around her, *I would have been famous. I would have been somebody special.*

The memory, brief as it was, caused Liam to shut his eyes for a moment.

When he opened them again, Madison was throwing back more whiskey.

She teetered a little on the stool in the process, and Liam reached for her, caught himself just short of grabbing her forearm to keep her from falling right into the sawdust.

"So that was that, with Tom at least," she went on, sounding resigned. "I met Jeffrey a year later—I think I mentioned that he's an accountant—and he really fits the stereotype of the nerdy guy who's more interested in numbers than people...and—"

She fell silent again. Staring down at her drink, probably fighting back tears.

Liam had never longed to put his arms around a woman the way he did then, but that was a risk he didn't want to take.

She might vanish.

Anyway, somebody was bound to come looking for her soon—the nerd groom, for example, or her mother. It was a wonder no one had tracked her down yet, in fact, since Brynne Garrett's fancy wedding venue was just on the other side of the road.

He'd noticed the crowd gathered around the flower-draped gazebo earlier, though it wasn't an unusual sight, since Brynne and her business partner, David Fielding, did a land-office business throwing lavish weddings, many of them complete with fireworks, strange costumes, and paid extras.

Now he imagined the drama and chaos that must have started when the bride turned her "I do" into an "I don't" and fled the scene in a fist-clenching fury.

Again, he allowed himself the faintest of grins, savoring the memory of her spectacular arrival, a creature of light and flame and sweet, sweet frenzy.

"And today, you married Jeffrey," he ventured to get the conversation moving again.

"Sort of," she said, with another sigh and another swirl and another swig.

More like a gulp.

"How do you 'sort of' get married?"

"I went through with the ceremony," she recalled. "We exchanged vows in front of that lovely gazebo, and the minister pronounced us husband and wife. We went into the lodge then, since it was time for the reception to start. Jeffrey's mother sidled up to me, all smiles, and said she was so thrilled to be going on the honeymoon with us. Turned out, Jeffrey had bought her an airline ticket, behind my back, and even reserved a room for her at our hotel."

"Uh-oh," Liam muttered with conviction. In any other circumstances, he would have added a whistle for emphasis.

"I'm such a fool!" Madison lamented. "Jeffrey actually invited *his mother* to join us *on our honeymoon*, and I didn't see it coming. I should have, because there were plenty of warning signs, but I didn't!"

Liam was sympathetic—and fascinated. "What happened then?"

"I confronted Jeffrey and he admitted it was true. His mommy needed a vacation, and she'd always wanted to visit Costa Rica. Can you believe it?"

Liam was stuck for an answer, so he didn't offer one.

"I told Jeffrey we were through, this time for good, and I refused to sign the license, which meant we weren't legally married. We'd been through the motions, but none of it was binding.

"He got really upset and said I was just being self-ish and overdramatic. I told him he and his mother both needed therapy, and turned to leave. He grabbed my arm, trying to stop me, I guess, and when he did that, I completely lost it. I whirled on him, ready to pop him one, right in the mug. I didn't, but he stumbled backward anyway, lost his footing and fell into the cake."

Liam was really enjoying the scenes unrolling in his head. It was like something out of a movie.

Madison seemed almost cheerful now, even smiling a little as she recalled the encounter. "His mother—*Yolanda*—tried to help him up. She slipped in the frosting and scattered cake on the floor and fell on top of him. They were both squirming around in the goop, trying to get back on their feet, when I left."

"I take it this wasn't the first time Jeffrey's mother had been a problem?"

Madison drew a deep breath, causing her perfect breasts to rise beneath the silk and lace of her bodice, and exhaled loudly, in obvious frustration.

Remembering, she shook her head. "That woman—Yolanda, I mean—was always interfering. She was awful, actually. Always passive-aggressive—with *me*, that is. Clingy and possessive, too, forever fawning over Jeffrey, calling him her baby boy." She paused, shook her head. "I'm such a ninny."

"You don't strike me as a ninny," Liam observed moderately, wondering how long it had been since he'd heard that old-fashioned term. "Maybe you're being a little too hard on yourself?"

"Kind of you to say so," Madison said, softly and

sadly. "But I have to take full responsibility. I wanted an ordinary man—somebody solid and dependable—not an overgrown jock like Tom. I thought Jeffrey was that man, and he said he wanted children, so I guess I was willing to overlook some of his faults—after all, I'm not exactly perfect myself."

Liam figured that was debatable, but he didn't say so. That would have been flattery, and he didn't deal in that.

"The signs were there all along," Madison continued quietly, reflectively. "Yolanda was around way too much. She went to movies with us, for heaven's sake, and crashed more than one otherwise romantic dinner. We took a day trip to the beach once, and she followed us there."

"Wow," Liam said, because speaking his thoughts about Jeffrey's relationship with his mother would have been rude. Plus, it was none of his business.

Madison fixed her gaze on him in the next moment, eyes slightly narrowed, brows raised. "What's *your* mother like?" she asked forthrightly.

The question took Liam aback, unexpected as it was. "Different," he said after a few long moments. "From Yolanda, that is."

"She doesn't interfere in your life? Invite herself along on your dates?"

"God, no," Liam said, trying to picture his independent mother behaving the way this Yolanda person apparently did. Cassie McKettrick loved her children, for sure, and she had been an active, attentive parent when they were young, making sure they led happy lives and behaved themselves. For all that, she had always been more than a mother, more than a wife.

She was an artist, a businesswoman, a thriving entity in her own right.

Now that all three of them were grown men, he, Jesse and Rhett, the youngest, Cassie was too busy sculpting museum-quality pieces, helping run the family's sizable ranch near San Diego, and serving on various charity boards to be overly concerned with what might be happening in the lives of her sons.

The faintest blush pinkened Madison's cheeks. "I'm sorry. I shouldn't have asked such personal questions."

"Don't be sorry," Liam said. He could hear car doors slamming now, female voices rising and falling, drawing nearer.

It was over this odd encounter, and Liam wanted it to last longer. A *lot* longer.

"That will be my friends," Madison said, draining the last drops of whiskey and melted ice with an obvious swallow.

She was right, of course.

There were footsteps on the wooden sidewalk out front, and some of the chatter was discernible now.

"I'm sure she's here somewhere," a woman said.

"I saw her heading this way," said another.

"I wouldn't blame her for taking to drink," offered still another.

And then the saloon doors opened again, and four women in voluminous gowns of pale pastels—pink, blue, green, and yellow—surged inside all at once, good-naturedly colliding with each other as they came.

"There you are, Mads!" cried the blonde in pink.

"We were worried about you," chided the brunette in blue.

"Big-time," confirmed the redhead in green.

The last of the company, dressed in yellow, wore a turban, and apparently had nothing to add to the conversation.

"Is he gone?" Madison asked, turning slightly to look back at the gaggle of probable bridesmaids, given the way they were dressed.

She was just as beautiful in profile.

"Gone?" the blonde echoed, pink skirts swishing as she crossed the sawdust floor to touch Madison's shoulder gently. "For now, yes. He left the venue right after the cake incident, with Mommy tripping solicitously along behind him, tsk-tsking all the way." She laughed, and Liam decided he liked her. "I suppose they're probably at the hotel by now, recovering from the humiliation."

The brunette giggled and did a little dance. "Mads," she said, "this was absolutely *the best* wedding I've ever been to!"

"It was a disaster," Madison reminded them, somewhat dryly.

"Social media gold," objected the redhead. "By now, videos of Jeffrey and his mother squirming around in all that cake goop are bouncing off satellites and landing on phone screens all over the world!"

"Who's this?" purred the one in the yellow turban, giving Liam the once-over.

"This," Madison said with an exaggerated gesture of one hand, "is Liam McKettrick, the listening bartender/architect/town marshal."

He inclined his head slightly, in an unspoken "hello."

"Liam," Madison went on expansively, "meet my best friends—"

She reeled off their names, rapid-fire. Not one of them stuck in Liam's brain.

"I think it's time we got you home," the blonde—Alisa, Ariel, Annette?—said, turning her attention back to her friend, the runaway bride. "You need to get out of that dress, have something to eat—"

"And sober up," put in the redhead.

"Home?" Madison ruminated. She was definitely drunk. "And where is that, exactly?"

The blonde poked an arm through Madison's and helped her off the bar stool.

The almost bride hesitated, frowned. "Wait. I didn't pay for my drink!"

"On the house," Liam said.

"Thanks," said the blonde with a brief glance his way.

With that, having surrounded her, the group maneuvered Madison toward the doors.

Liam followed, at a little distance, amused by the colorful birdlike bevy of women, all of them talking at once.

It took some doing to get through the swinging doors, since walking single file evidently hadn't occurred to them.

They navigated the wide sidewalk, still in a cluster, then made their communal way around the hitching rail and water trough directly in front of the saloon.

Liam leaned against one of the poles supporting the narrow roof above the entrance, watching them all, trundling toward a white compact car waiting in the road.

Nothing would ever top the sight of Madison Bettencourt storming into the saloon in that grand gown of hers, bellying up to the bar, and demanding whiskey, but the present spectacle was bound to run a close second.

It was like watching the old clown-car routine at the rodeo, only in reverse.

Instead of clowns streaming endlessly out of some run-down rig in the middle of a dusty arena, there were these beautiful women, all of them in impossibly full skirts, trying to squeeze a beleaguered bride into the front passenger seat.

The enterprise took at least five minutes of stuffing volumes of fabric inside, and Liam enjoyed every comical moment.

He had the decency not to laugh out loud, but only just.

Once Madison was contained—somewhat—the blonde managed to get behind the wheel with a little less fuss, but still considerable effort, and watching the remaining trio wedge themselves into the back was like something out of a Monty Python movie.

Finally, Ms. Bettencourt and her retinue were inside, except for the parts of their colorful gowns filling the car and spilling out the open windows, and the blonde executed a wide U-turn, narrowly missing the empty stagecoach standing in front of the livery stable as she did so.

Thank God the horses hadn't been hitched up yet.

Liam watched the vehicle—most likely a rental, given its nondescript design—until it zipped beneath the archway at the end of the street and finally disappeared.

Then he went back inside the saloon.

Costumed barmaids and dance hall girls were arriving, having entered through the back way, tying apron strings and adjusting feathery headpieces as they came.

"Wait till you hear about that wedding over there at the lodge, boss," chuckled Sylvia Red Bird, the piano player and sometime torch singer. "Craziest one yet."

Liam pretended to be clueless. "You were there?"

"No," Sylvia replied, grinning. She was eccentric, to say the least, dressing herself in trousers, a pointy-collared shirt, a striped vest and a top hat for her shift at the Hard Luck. Sometimes, when she helped out in the gift shop across the street, next to the old-time photography place, she wore authentic medicine-woman garb, which she created with her own hands. "Didn't need to be there. It's all over town what happened. The ceremony went off without a hitch, according to Miranda, from over at Bailey's restaurant, but when it came time for the reception, all hell broke loose. The bride shoved the groom right into the wedding cake, and his mother tumbled after him!"

Liam hid a grin. "Is that so?"

"It's so," verified Molly Steel, who was paying her way through community college over in neighboring Silver Hills by dancing with, and for, saloon patrons. "I saw the videos. They're all over YouTube and Instagram and probably TikTok, too. I laughed till I thought I'd die."

"You better show me those videos," Sylvia told Molly, "soon as we go on break."

Slowly, the saloon filled, first with staff, then with customers. Several of these, it soon became apparent, had been guests at the thwarted wedding.

There were a lot of toasts, followed by laughter and anecdotes told from just about every perspective: the young and the old and everybody in between. The caterers. Even the groomsmen, who were all in a jocular mood, despite the groom—ostensibly their buddy—being dumped at his own wedding reception. They were knocking back liquor like there was no tomorrow, laughing a lot, shaking their heads at their friend Jeffrey's unnatural attachment to his mother.

Sheriff Eli Garrett showed up at eight o'clock or so, as he always did whenever there was a big shindig in or around Painted Pony Creek, accompanied by his good friend the chief of police, Melba Summer.

"Quite a day," Eli sighed, taking a place at the end of the bar.

"So I hear," Liam acknowledged. "Whiskey? Maybe a gin and tonic?"

Eli sighed. "I wish," he said. "I'm still on duty, so it's coffee for me, I'm afraid."

Melba, truly beautiful and tough as logging chain, stood beside Eli, smiling. "Sheriff's just trying to preserve his stellar reputation," she remarked. "Afraid I'll muscle in one of these election years and push him out of office."

Liam laughed, and so did Eli.

Both officers were served coffee—like always.

"The groom's mother, Yolanda somebody, turned up at my office a few hours ago, still coated in cake and frosting," Melba said. "She wanted the bride arrested for assault."

Eli nearly spat out his coffee. *"Assault?"*

"Well," Melba reminded him, "she *did* cause Mr. Sterne to topple backward into that mess. Do you have any idea what a cake like that *costs*, Eli Garrett?"

Eli sighed again, shoved a hand through his light brown hair. "Actually, Chief, I do. My wife orchestrates most of these events and it's downright scary the price of goods and services these days. It's not uncommon for the bridal gown alone to run in the thousands. And all for *one day*. I sure hope the star of *this* show got her money's worth, given the way the event turned out."

Melba sipped her coffee. "The bride," she said, "is a Bettencourt. You know, *those* Bettencourts, the ones who struck silver back in the day? The ones who built that big old house out at the end of Sparrow Bend Road? She's not hurting for money, I can tell you."

"I thought all the Bettencourts had died off, except for Coralee, of course," Eli said, in due time, having finished his coffee and shoved the cup away with a hint of reluctance. "And she's holding on by a thread, from what I've heard."

"Nope," Melba said, sounding pleased to set the sheriff straight on the matter. "She's got a granddaughter, Madison. The woman who was supposed to get married today. In my opinion, she came to her senses just in time to avoid tying herself down to a total waste of human bone and muscle."

Eli shook his head. "Small towns," he muttered. Then he thanked Liam and turned to leave.

At the Hard Luck Saloon, officers of the law got their sandwiches, sodas and coffee free. So did firefighters, paramedics and half a dozen old-timers who knew how to spin a damn good yarn.

From the sound of things, Madison Bettencourt was going to be starring in more than her fair share of tall tales for a long time to come.

And Liam wanted to hear every last one of them.

Don't miss Where the Creek Bends,
available late fall 2024!